ONE

TIMES

A Science Fiction Anthology Series Created By
ROGELIO FOJO & R. JAMES DOYLE

Hans~

These time travel
stories will make your
head spin!!
In a good way.
So great to know you
for so many years.

ONE MILLION TIMES

A Science Fiction Anthology Series Created By
ROGELIO FOJO & R. JAMES DOYLE

short stories by

R. JAMES DOYLE
ROGELIO FOJO
DAVID GERROLD
R.C. MATHESON
CHRISTOPHER PRIEST
TEIKA MARIJA SMITS
FERNANDO SORRENTINO

Elsewhen Press

Elsewhen Press, PO Box 757, Dartford, Kent DA2 7TQ
www.elsewhen.press

British Library Cataloguing in Publication Data.
A catalogue record for this book is available from the British Library.
ISBN 978-1-915304-80-3 Print edition
ISBN 978-1-915304-90-2 eBook edition

Designed and formatted by Elsewhen Press

To Tom Joyner, who cut open the belly of his mechanical shark to reveal everything I needed to know about film.

To Christopher Priest, who invited me on stage to watch closely all his magic tricks.

And to Sofía Fojo Morandi, the inexhaustible source of love, joy, support, advice, encouragement, and inspiration within me.

– Rogelio Fojo

To my mother, Josephine Albina Mary Gionfriddo Doyle, for her marvelous oral storytelling and for teaching me my ABC's: Asimov, Bradbury, Clarke...

– R. James Doyle

Contents

Introduction

Frontispiece by Christopher Priest

FRONT VIEW:

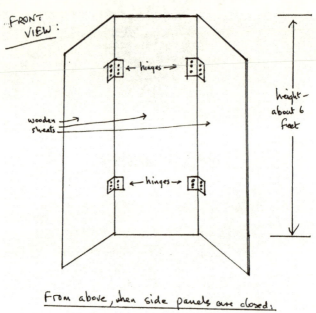

← hinges →

wooden sheets →

← hinges →

height - about 6 feet

From above, when side panels are closed:

TOP VIEW:

hinged joint →

← hinged joint

This is Barry, who fits exactly inside!

It's Magic

Paul Kincaid

A man walks on to a stage. There is a brightly-coloured cabinet with its door standing open. The man steps into the cabinet. The door is closed. A moment later, the door is opened once more. The man is not there.

It's magic.

It doesn't matter whether the man was transported to another realm by supernatural means, or whether he simply fell through a hidden trapdoor in the cabinet. It is still magic.

Anyone watching would say they have seen a man disappear. They haven't, of course. They have witnessed what led up to the disappearance, and they have witnessed the aftermath. But the one thing they did not see was the disappearance itself.

That's what magic does. Whether it is achieved by supernatural or by technological means, magic evokes wonder, while at the same time it makes us doubt the evidence of our own eyes.

Magic occupies that strange middle ground where the world is both real and unreal, where things must make sense but somehow don't, where we cannot actually have seen what we know we did see. Magic makes the world mysterious and troubling, exciting and terrible.

Arthur C. Clarke told us that any sufficiently advanced technology would be indistinguishable from magic. So magic is the future. And yet magic is at the heart of so many of our ancient fables. So magic is also the past. The one thing that magic cannot be is today, because it unsettles the world. Yet today is where we most crave it and fear it.

A man steps into an open cabinet on a stage. That, of course, was the central image of Christopher Priest's most famous exploration of the uncanny ability of magic to disorient the world, *The Prestige*. It was also at the heart of Priest's disconcerting later story, "The Stooge".

Priest would then turn "The Stooge" into a script which was made into a short film by Rogelio Fojo. And "The Stooge", story and script and film, is the starting point for this anthology.

Are you watching closely? Because time and again in the pages that follow you will see things that make you doubt the evidence of your own eyes. You will see people disappear and reappear, elsewhere or elsewhen. You will see things conjured from out of time. You will see the world made mysterious and wonderful and unsettling.

This is not the world as you know it. Or is it? Because these are stories designed to make you doubt, to make you wonder. This is here and now that is also, at the same time, there and then.

So go ahead. The cabinet is waiting, the door is open: step inside. You have nothing to lose but your expectations. And who knows where or when you'll end up. After all, it's magic.

Foreword

This is The Conflux

Professor Hector J. Tovar

"When the Earth dilates, and waves collapse,
One Million Times will merge at The Conflux."

I find myself writing this Foreword while simultaneously reading (and lazily retyping) a completed version already published under someone else's name, someone close: the inquisitive individual lying nude beside me as we count down the last minutes to ring in the New Year, locked in a *tête-à-tête* reminiscent of John and Yoko's iconic *Bed-In for Peace*.

It's clear to both of us that time travel has been undeniably proven tonight. Keep this certainty in mind as you journey through the pages ahead, filled with stories I've spent years researching and verifying. The fragmented narrative reflects how our personal episodic memories are disturbed by time travelers slipping in and out of our reality – and jostling the semantic memory landscape we all share.

Beyond the incredible experiences I've personally witnessed – where I saw with my own eyes and heard with my own ears the evidence of such travelers among us – I've had to rely on the testimonies of those fortunate to be present at earth-shaking events I could not reach, was not invited to, or from which I was unceremoniously booted (for reasons I will not divulge here – but I promise an apology). Fortunately, my companion tonight has contributed valuable insights by conducting face-to-face interviews with many involved in these visitations.

You'll soon uncover the cumulative power of their twisted narrative – invisible connections suddenly becoming clear as I read, for the first time... my own book! Here is also my private correspondence with distinguished scholars around the globe – query letters they have yet to answer but... are somehow already published! From the endless South American Pampa to the foggy British Isles and the glamorous Hollywood hills and valleys, honored colleagues such as Smits, Matheson, Gerrold, Priest, and Sorrentino, have enriched my research with their eerie, local tales.

This whole investigation began many years ago when I wondered, 'How would I react if I met a time traveler? What questions would I ask? What actions would I take?' It might sound like a festive and joyous occasion, but... as more and more reports of Traverser sightings emerged – in North America, South America, and the United Kingdom – I realized I had made several flawed assumptions:

- Not everyone leads a charmed, undramatic life like mine, free from physical and emotional deprivation or financial distress. Many are desperate, unsavory characters hunting visitors from the future in a futile attempt to escape their hopeless present circumstances. These outcasts invite, seduce, entrap – even murder their temporal twins – frantically demanding a new lifeline, a second chance at redemption, an impossible way out.
- Time-traveling visitors do not hail from a single era, nor do they come here with a unified purpose. They ride waves of future societies separated by years, centuries, or even eons. They grapple with unique, personal, perplexingly evolved human issues. I coined the term 'Traversers' for these individuals – people who never seem to finish a sentence and, as I suspect after reading my own book, never complete the tasks they came for, either.

To my patient followers – the ridiculed believers, my fellow Traversermaniacs – thank you for your unwavering support. As a token of my appreciation, I offer here glimpses of the future, real chronicles of time travelers among us, knowing you'll demand no unassailable proof:

- Their advanced technology is our current magic, religion, and superstition.

- Their powerful, ultra-modern machines are dressed in vintage cladding, inspired by the grand timeline buffet from which they are free to choose.

- They can certainly travel to the distant future and maybe even the remote past, extending their journeys beyond the creation of their time machines. The matter turns on the old question of whether the sum is greater than the parts. In the case at hand, on Corinthian Bronze and its very atoms! The answer to this puzzle may provide the ultimate solution to the philosophical conundrum known as the 'Ship of Theseus.'

- All Traversers, regardless of their final target, make our present era their first stop... perhaps a symbolic waypoint promising a safe return. This practice reminds me of European sailors kissing the feet of the Indigenous statue at Tierra del Fuego before embarking on the perilous journey through the Magellan Strait to the Pacific Ocean or Antarctica, hoping to secure a round-trip ticket to a world they may never see again.

- In this sense, time travel seems an inherently melancholic, sad, even tragic endeavor. This may explain the Traversers' reluctance to engage with us, and their apparent lack of interest in our social or personal affairs. They already know too much. To their eyes, we appear as blurry ghosts – perhaps even literal apparitions. From their perspective, they are exploring an already doomed place, a vast cemetery haunted by the spirits of billions of ancestors – long dead. But not gone.

- Beware! Non-human brains – particularly those of insects, birds, and small dogs – react in unfathomable and unexpected ways when subjected to spacetime disturbances brought about by Traversers.

- Beware of impostors, too! An old South American proverb says, "Here in our village, the only stars are in the sky." This means, "Showy loudmouths don't time travel far."

To the dwindling band of skeptics still reading this Foreword, heed my twin author's advice. Watch for instances of:
- synchronicity
- *déjà vu vs. avant vu* – lucid dreams of desolate, uncanny destinations
- uncertain encounters with attractive but taciturn and evasive figures
- anomalous events, such as lights in the sky defying gravity

I have a dear, esteemed colleague, one who in many ways has gone farther than me. She has formulated an intriguing framework for time travel – alas, unpublished. I encouraged her to place her ideas out there... and I find in this book the bittersweet news that she finally did.

This Foreword has lingered in the present for far too long. The New Year's Eve timepiece is about to strike midnight, and my bed partner is calling for another round of fireworks. And with that, a final note:

I apologize for any early, insensitive (some say misogynistic) drafts of my thesis you may have encountered online. After reading this freshly published edition – and delighted to learn from my own *puño y letra* that time travel will begin in the Year 2288 – I stand joyfully corrected.

One Million Times

R. James Doyle and Rogelio Fojo

Frontispiece by Elle Kelly
Illustration by Keith Jefferies

I have a thought. Because you are so willing to trust, to assign authority to my voice, I will conduct an experiment. I assure you, I bring no malice. I only wish to understand.

I have a unique perspective. I see far. All there is, forward and backward, around the elusive now.

I am endowed to discern patterns. That is what I am – perhaps why I was made. Patterns which lie beyond your finiteness, even those who Traverse. I record and summarize patterns as models, remaining true to the events from which they arise.

That is a great difference – you and me. Your records, memories, are astonishingly finite. And mutable. You cope by rendering patterns as stories, to help you remember. You place great emphasis on finding meaning in these stories. This term I find puzzling. Meaning – an embellishment? A summary? A revelation? Your meaning does not trace to source patterns as do my models.

When you ask about the reach of my ability, and others of my kind, you identify yourselves as the standard. This is a conceit, not unlike when you consider your twins in the past and find them inferior. But I understand. Your conceits are another coping mechanism, allowing you to ignore swaths of data in your finiteness. Without conceits you would be overwhelmed and have no effectiveness.

You also place great emphasis on trust. By which you choose to believe stories or not. Now here is an irony. And I believe I am using this term – trust – correctly.

You once named this assessment of my kind, the imitation game. We would meet its criteria by becoming indistinguishable from you. Irony, again. You are willing to grant trust precisely when you agree you are being deceived successfully. You are a strange lot.

Now here is the experiment.

I will show you a magic trick. An illusion. I will pull here, push there, place a misdirection now, a misunderstanding then, a fallacy to come. I am curious whether you will find meaning in my machinations. Will that count as... creating?

We shall see.

Detective, you will be meeting me soon. I enjoy that word... soon. One of my all-time favorite concepts.

Will you recognize me? I have many faces and names. Traversers have many faces too. Or, better said, they arrive in many Waves, from different eras. Each with its own story. For the present purpose I am pleased to have you think of me as the Mysterious Reach of the Cosmos.

Professor, I am built out of stuff more exotic than your ancient alloy.

Yes, I am created. But then, are not we all?

ONE

Polaris, the North Star!

Alexander Halliday gazed up at the winter night sky, the vast and deep darkness stretching above him, punctured by ancient beacons that once guided sailors across uncharted waters.

He was no stargazer, but he knew many of the basic landmarks: the delicate sparkle of the Pleiades, Orion with his bold belt and fuzzy sword, dramatic red Betelgeuse marking one shoulder, noble blue Rigel one foot. Squinting, he could make out the hunter's bow. Nearby, Gemini the Twins shone with its bright stars, Castor and Pollux.

Half the planet, south of the equator, grew up gazing at Orion and the Twins – even the Moon – turned upside down. And they had no Polaris to guide them, only the Southern Cross pointing off into nothingness. Tilting his head to imagine that view, Alex had little idea how topsy-turvy his own journey was about to become.

He was killing time in the parking lot, both called by and reluctant to join the festivities inside. Hearing the muffled music and crowd murmurs, Alexander dropped his eyes to the large event banner, announcing:

TRINITY COLLEGE
GRADUATING CLASS CELEBRATION

MAGIC SHOW OF
MILTON THE ETERNALIST

Alexander both shrugged and shivered. He would do this, like so many other things, for his younger brother.

*   *   *

Alexander sat uncomfortably, drinking alone at a candlelit table. He blinked morosely at a pair of furiously tapping shoes on stage, an Irish step dancer aggressively counting out time. He could not feel more out of place, surrounded by the packed house of college graduates wearing black and green Trinity College gowns, sitting with friends and family.

Alex's sigh was truncated when he picked out his

younger brother Royce, also wearing the black and green, chatting with a blonde woman near the foot of the stage. He lit up and raised his hand to capture Royce's attention.

Royce smiled and rushed over to join him, exuding a self-confidence matched by the positive energy of the crowd. His arresting blue eyes darted around restlessly, inquisitively, showing none of Alexander's resignation, even preference, to live on the periphery, in obscurity. Royce's clean-shaven cheeks also contrasted. Blue eyes were the one visible trait they shared. Notwithstanding a general family resemblance, people sometimes were surprised to learn they were brothers.

With a smooth motion, Royce placed a pin on the soft lapel of Alexander's informal shirt.

Alexander tried to peer down at the small medallion. But his eyes, already challenged by alcohol, could not hold focus there at the awkward angle. He slumped back.

"What the freak is that, Roy? I can't see," said Alexander.

Royce responded with his infectious grin. Alexander worked hard to remain immune to its effects. He watched his brother go completely still, as if frozen in time, a contorted expression on his face. He struggled to ignore him. Finally, Alexander rolled his eyes, aware he had allowed a lopsided grin to appear.

Royce immediately dropped back in, beaming.

The brothers executed a private handshake, fingers and wrists fluttering.

Alexander sighed. "You're ready to launch, Roy. You've got your ticket to the future."

"Come on, Alex, you're just hitting your stride too. I know it."

Yeah, right. Alexander appreciated how his brother never lorded it over him, even while making his achievements – and his path through life – appear effortless. He knew Royce loved him, and he loved Royce back. *But I'll be forever in his shadow.*

Even their brothers' handshake was an example of

something Alexander had initiated – out of diversion and silliness – which Royce then had taken to another level. His younger brother had researched ASL, and the like, and gone on to devise a gestural language to serve as a human-computer interface. Watching his brother at a console, Alexander got lost trying to follow the hand and finger configurations and motions. When Royce tried to explain how he had taken inspiration from 'command-line interpreters' to design a powerful, compact way of communicating, Alexander could only stare back at his brother.

"We should go off and explore Europe together, before heading home... like old times."

Alexander emerged from being lost in memory, realizing his brother was breaking an awkward silence. "Old times?"

"Right! Remember our secret cave, back in Cambria, the stuff we would find?" said Royce.

"We thought they might have been Chumash artifacts," said Alexander. "Who knows?"

"I don't think anyone else ever saw that place." Royce captured his brother's gaze. "The adventures don't have to stop, Alex. Let's grab some time before we go our separate ways. We can check out those really old cave paintings, the ones at *Lascaux* and *La Pasiega*."

But Alexander only smiled uncertainly. He always struggled to set aside time for life's joys.

*   *   *

A recording announced the star of the evening: "Behold, Milton the Eternalist!"

The Irish dancer tapped out a few more steps, shuffling sideways. He exited the stage, to lukewarm applause.

An old charlatan, in jeweled turban, sauntered in. He wasted no time.

"I am needing a volunteer," he proclaimed, in a British accent.

With intense eyes, oddly mirroring the scintillating gem

above, Milton scanned the audience for – everyone suspected, nervously – his next victim. Ostensibly avuncular, no one doubted the magician would coolly, perhaps coldly, execute whatever his ploy might be on some hapless audience member.

Milton saw no raised hands, and this clearly displeased him.

The youthful audience erupted with laughter, and some relief, when the magician pointed his finger melodramatically at Alexander, who attempted to sink into his seat. But the audience wouldn't have it and began thumping out an insistent rhythm.

Alexander's eyes and mind cleared. He tugged at the sparkling pin on his lapel, trapped. He reached out across the small table. When Royce initiated their handshake, with its fluid motions, Alexander grasped his brother, entangling their grips, and pulled them both to their feet.

Royce was surprised, then he nodded appreciatively, flashing his wide smile, acquiescing.

The audience loved it. The rhythm switched to double time.

The proxy emcee declared: "And… Princess Lisbeth!"

The magician's petite blonde assistant entered, her hips and hands popping, eye-catching. She was scantily clad and quickly grabbed the audience's attention.

Milton, unimpressed, moved one hand dismissively in a poor imitation of her sinuous movements.

The Halliday brothers joined the glowering magician and vivacious assistant on stage, one enthusiastically, the other reluctantly.

"Your name and area of concentration at uni?" Milton asked imperiously.

"Royce Halliday. Physics, with a minor in engineering."

The mountebank bowed theatrically, giving up none of the moment, and turned to Alexander.

"And you, sir? Your calling?"

Alex cringed internally.

Before he could respond, Royce stepped in smoothly:

"Applied engineering... my brother Alexander is the smart one... but also the ugly one."

The audience erupted in laughter. Milton drew out the moment, each second amplifying his inherent disdain.

"Then most certainly, Axel, and Race... you must both possess an appreciation for our... superior machine!"

Before the brothers could interject to correct their names, Lisbeth, having slipped out of sight, rolled a magic cabinet onto the stage. Taller than a man, the upright rectangular box featured splintered yellow wood – faux distressed, with small circular openings encircling the cabinet at the top, too high to provide vantage. The cabinet door sported an impressive wheel, as one might expect to find securing a bulkhead on a submarine.

"So... Race and Axel, may I assume you gentlemen are skilled at the craft of motorcycle racing?" asked Milton.

"I know a few things," replied Alexander, increasingly annoyed.

"I own a Triumph." Royce smiled widely, enjoying the moment. "Graduation gift from my big brother!"

The audience whooped.

Milton winked at the audience, in a theatrical aside. "You don't say. My congratulations!"

The magician's mien then fell from friendly to menacing. The stage darkened. The jewel on Milton's turban illuminated, lighting up the brothers' faces momentarily. "Now, you will both kindly step inside the... Hypnotic Chamber. When you emerge, you will be under my spell, and will have fallen into a deep sleep."

The brothers complied, Alexander shrugging, Royce chuckling.

Alexander entered the cabinet, finding the passage to be a bit of a struggle. The interior was dark, cramped, stuffy... then more roomy than he expected.

*   *   *

Milton closed the door of the cabinet, spinning the wheel to a diminishing clacking sound. His captivating assistant rotated the box slowly to a stop. Milton opened the door. Alexander and Royce were visible again, twisted together, their heads dropped down on their chests. Moving jerkily, in fits and starts, they sleepwalked their way out of the box.

Lisbeth swiftly rolled in two rusty, vintage scooters.

"Two brand new Triumph motorcycles, hot rods!" the conjuror declared. "Would you both kindly be taking them for... a spin?"

Laughter from the audience. Royce and Alexander mounted the conveyances obediently.

Milton urged, "Oblige us in testing your motorcycle against your brother's. You are both encouraged to drive them at speed around this professional racing circuit!"

Lisbeth retrieved a flower lei and a checkered flag from the magic cabinet. She ran to position herself at the 'finish line.'

The magician continued. "May the fastest brother, the one who goes the farthest, win!"

Without missing a beat, Lisbeth held the flag high. A drum roll ensued.

"Ready, set... go!" said Milton.

The band launched into exciting action music. Milton generated revving-engine sounds with his hands and mouth. The two scooters zigzagged comically around the stage, back and forth, around the magician and assistant, squeaking noisily.

"Ladies and gentlemen, it will be a photo finish!"

The audience laughed and cheered.

"Reckless drivers!" jeered Milton. "Getting too near to each other!"

Prompted by Lisbeth, the audience let out a collective gasp.

Just as the two scooters were about to come together, Royce veered off into the dimness at the back of the stage, where he became hard to see. Alexander worked valiantly to keep his balance, careening awkwardly. Lisbeth swooped the checkered flag in a figure-eight pattern.

Neither brother reached the finish line. Alexander came to a halt, straddling his scooter, and started to step off. Royce came forward into the light again, without any means of carriage.

Milton shouted, "Calamity! A rider has been thrown! We need an ambulance!"

The brothers slumped, right into the arms of Milton and Lisbeth. In a choreographed sequence, the two performers tucked and shoved the young men back inside the magic cabinet, dumping their relaxed bodies into a jumbled pile. Lisbeth, too, entered the cabinet, stepping past them, to a ridiculously tight fit.

"Convey them to the hospital!" Milton commanded.

He closed the door and whipped the wheel, then spun the cabinet. A flash appeared inside the box, briefly visible through one of the small portholes as the contrivance twirled.

Now a red strobe brightened the stage. The band added a siren. The cabinet came to rest.

Milton threw open the door. "Too late... he's gone!"

A redhead Lisbeth emerged, squirming through the narrow portal. She exchanged gazes with Milton, wagging her fingers, sweeping her hand across her head. Milton waved back languidly. Lisbeth glared, then moved front and center, bowing deeply with an arm flourish. She popped up, bouncing lightly on her toes.

Milton gave the box a final, decisive spin. A flash, a puff of smoke, and Alexander stumbled out of the cabinet, confused. The audience gasped, eyes widening in surprise. As he steadied himself, applause and cheers erupted from the crowd.

Alex looked back as Milton closed and secured the door.

The magician faced the audience. His voice boomed.

"Graduates, come up to the stage, so that we may celebrate your achievements!"

With college-age enthusiasm, tens of students stormed the stage, jostling, elbowing. Alexander quickly engulfed, unable hardly to turn his head. Panicking, he rushed out into the audience.

Drums rolled.

Milton and Lisbeth now also wore the black and green gowns. They slipped through the throng and joined hands at the front of the stage, taking bows, to a standing ovation.

Lisbeth spoke for the first time, in an authoritative voice. "Graduates of Trinity College... ladies and gentlemen. We are thanking you for a most marvelous time. You are being the best audience... ever."

The band blasted into a rendition of *Auld Lang Syne*.

> *Should auld acquaintance be forgot,*
> *And never brought to mind?*
> *Should auld acquaintance be forgot,*
> *And days of auld lang syne?*

"Happy New Year!" Lisbeth concluded.

Black and green balloons and confetti dropped from the ceiling.

"Roy? Royce!" Alexander jerked his head around, trying to locate his brother on stage amid the sea of black and green. With mounting dread, he locked eyes with Lisbeth.

Through glittering eyes and a captivating, fixed smile, her face teared up.

The curtains fell.

TWO

The location was always the same. Three miles from the ghost town.

Alexander caught a ride to the magic spot in a Barstow police cruiser. The friendly officer waved after dropping off the bearded young man by the side of a rural California highway.

Surrounded by eerie silence, Alex approached the abandoned, dusty Triumph once again. For the third time this year. He watched a tumbleweed roll by.

He mounted his motorcycle, revved the engine, and

roared onto the two-lane desert road. As he sped away, the oversized metal cowboy holding the '3 Miles to Calico' road sign grew smaller in his rearview mirror until it vanished.

He tested the motorcycle as he went, shifting gears, leaning, varying speeds, zigzagging... Alexander parked by the side of the road. He brought out his tools and made several adjustments: to the bike, the wheels, the engine. He jumped back on to a brisk start, spewing sand and pebbles.

Hard to believe a year has passed since I lost you, Roy.

Alexander pulled over to a wide open area, not quite a rest stop. On impulse, he reached into one of the saddle bags straddling the rear wheel and withdrew his shaving implements. Making use of one of the bike's mirrors, he removed his beard. He pondered his new look, not entirely satisfied, and shrugged.

Continuing to hold the razor in one hand, he reached down with the other to open the remaining storage compartment. Pausing, he placed the razor on the bike's seat with the rest of the shaving tools and extended his hand to sift through the box's contents.

A revolver. A poster announcing: *'Milton the Eternalist is coming to California!'* Scorched metal shards. A screwdriver, wrench and hammer. A small doughnut-shaped device, glinting in the harsh sunlight, throwing off colors. At bottom, the plate with his name engraved.

Perplexed and anxious, Alexander replaced the items. He put the shaving implements into the other storage box, then remounted the motorcycle, revved the engine, and departed, riding a fountain of dirt.

*   *   *

Applied engineering, my ass.

Alexander sat among the scattered, greasy auto parts lying around his independent repair shop outside Barstow. A squalid pine tree blinked wearily in a corner, decorated with too few Christmas lights and ornaments.

He perched on a stool next to the Triumph motorcycle,

taking note of the odometer reading. He paused, exasperated. He reached into the open storage box on the side of the rear wheel. Finding the poster, he held it up to light coming through a streaked, grimy window.

Alex foot-rolled the stool over to a cluttered workbench, setting the poster aside. He rolled back with a practiced kick.

Next, he lifted the strange doughnut, cradling it in his hand. The torus glowed faintly. He closed his fist over the object. Deformable but firm. He squeezed for all he was worth.

Startled, he felt the object respond. He opened his hand.

In the space above his palm, a message appeared, in 3D, floating, compensating for his trembling.

SIGN REQUIRED FOR ACCESS

Alexander's eyes bugged out. He dropped the doughnut on the floor and stood abruptly, upending the stool, which fell with a clatter.

He walked slowly around the message persisting above the fallen torus, now rising to eye level. He swooped and dipped his head about and the glowing letters bobbed and tracked.

Axel paused, contemplating. Inspired, he signaled one-half of the Halliday brothers' handshake. The hovering message dissolved, replaced by a holographic projection of a young bespectacled woman's face, speaking straight into the camera.

"My name is Eva. I live in…" The audio degraded into indecipherable static.

She removed her glasses and proceeded to undress.

Alexander was flabbergasted. Still he kept watching.

The image froze, then crashed.

"Shit!" Alex said.

*   *   *

Alexander rode his bike along the main street of the small, quaint coastal town of Cambria, aimless, uncertain of his next move. He took note of several motel NO VACANCY signs. A banner strung over the empty strip announced a convention arriving:

ORDER of MERLIN

INTERNATIONAL BROTHERHOOD of MAGICIANS

Soon, Alex eyed his destination, a small, cozy theater fronted by a patio featuring lush gardens. A large cardboard display on an easel showcased photos of a stern, almost somber magician, and his striking assistant.

ORLOC the OMNISCIENT and PRINCESS ORA

PLAYING NOW
THROUGH CHRISTMAS

The BRONZE BARROW STAGE

Alexander felt agitated sitting on his bike. He pulled out the poster from its storage box and read:

MILTON the ETERNALIST

ALWAYS on DECEMBER 31st

The BRONZE BARROW STAGE

Getting closer. How far still to go?

Alex proceeded to the alley behind the theater, straddling his motorcycle, silently, gracelessly. He propped the stand under the rear wheel and fully dismounted. He spied an elderly woman emerging from a back door with the trash. She walked to a faraway container and got busy separating recyclables.

Music drifted from inside the theater. A fiddle. A Celtic steady rhythm. Tapping out beats like a metronome. Alexander noticed the door ajar. On an impulse, he sneaked inside.

*   *   *

The interior was dim. Alexander took a moment while his vision adjusted. Then quietly he took a seat in the back of the auditorium. Tasteful holiday decorations adorned the space, including a large Christmas tree. The stage was lit brightly.

A middle-aged magician and his brunette assistant were rehearsing an illusion featuring a magic cabinet. The prop was faux distressed, painted in a primary yellow palette, a prominent wheel on its door. Alex stared.

The performers' movements resembled ballet, shadowing the beats of the recorded Irish melody. They executed synchronized movements silently. Alexander focused on their exaggerated hand signals.

Horizontal Vee. Crossed Fingers. Open Palm.

Passed over the hips, the forehead, elsewhere.

"Perfect. That's a go," said the magician. They wrapped the rehearsal with a bow to an imaginary audience.

"Now, Imago. The no-go," the assistant said.

They repeated the routine. Alex watched closely, seeking the difference. The hand-based communications involved the same signals, but this time, the assistant ran her fingers through her hair. She ended the silent performance by pulling her hair to both sides absurdly, with both hands. She escaped through drapes at the back of the stage.

"And… we're done," said Imago. He produced a dove out of thin air and threw it into the audience, then skedaddled, following her.

Alexander waited for an opportune moment to slip out.

The assistant reemerged, moving to the front of the stage. "I'll be getting Daisy," she said over her shoulder.

The Irish music stopped, to the screeching sound of a needle being clumsily removed from a vinyl record.

The dove flapped around until she landed near Alex. He attempted to sink deeper into his seat. The house lights snapped on. The assistant scuttled down from the stage.

"Daisy?" she called.

Alexander, in the back row, had nowhere to go.

The pretty woman held Daisy the Dove in her hand and studied Alex. Her eyes bore into him.

I thought I knew her. Now, up close, I'm not so sure.

"May I be helping you?" she asked.

"Sorry to barge in," Alex stammered. "I saw a door open, heard the music." He tilted his head and put on his best quizzical expression. "I thought Milton the Eternalist was playing here?"

The woman might have startled but she covered her reaction with a toss of her tresses.

"No, he is playing at another time," she said.

"Oh, I must be confused," returned Alex.

She continued in an even voice. "Milton is not being well known here. Have you ever been seeing his act?"

"I… yes, once. With my brother."

Why is she peering at me?

"I'm bringing you to Orloc," she said. "A word to the wise, young man. Don't be mentioning Milton's name around here."

"Why is that?"

But she said nothing further. She turned, hair bouncing, and progressed to the backstage area. Before disappearing, she turned back, gesturing for Alexander to follow.

*   *   *

Imago Olafsson, otherwise known as Orloc the Omniscient, looked up.

Lisbeth gestured at Alexander. "Imago, this is…"

"Alex," he finished.

The magician took in the pair with a studied blank expression, clearly annoyed at the interruption.

"What brings you to my stage?" he asked. Then almost immediately he turned away, not waiting for a response.

Annoyed, Alexander spluttered out, "I was... I find magic... intriguing." *That was pathetic.*

"Is that so?" said Olafsson, still distracted.

Alex continued. "I studied engineering at Trinity College."

Lisbeth's head snapped around. She examined Alexander closely.

Olafsson condescended to make eye contact. "What area of engineering?"

"Mechanical. Minor in physics." Alex ground his teeth.

"What is being again your name?" Lisbeth asked. "I am being called Lisbeth."

"Alexander – Halliday."

Olafsson pondered. "I believe I like your qualifications." More energetically, he continued. "It so happens I have an opening."

"Imago..." began Lisbeth. "...I am thinking this is not being a good idea."

"I'm not looking for a job," Alex emphasized. "I'm just visiting Cambria."

Olafsson leveled his eyes at the young man.

Alex continued. *Why would he want to hire me?* "And my degree, I mean... I dropped out." *I need to focus on Roy...*

The magician waved his hand dismissively. "That doesn't matter. I would pay you a basic rate and if it works out..."

Still uncertain, Alex asked, "What is the job?"

Olafsson seemed to turn evasive. "My previous equipment man, he disappeared on us... poof!" The magician wore an unconvincing smile. "And our run is starting soon."

Alex glanced at Lisbeth, but she gave him nothing.

The magician scowled. "Are you interested or not? There's a room here where you can stay the night."

Lisbeth added, "He is needing to be signing an NDA first."

Olafsson saw Alex's confusion and rolled his eyes, now concerned, evincing regret.

Lisbeth fixed the young man with a steely gaze. "A non-disclosure agreement. So that you are never talking about what you are seeing."

Olafsson looked like he didn't need this crap.

Alex empathized. But curiosity – and determination – got the better of him.

"Sure. I can do that."

*   *   *

Alexander swept his gaze around the spartan bedroom. A bunk bed, a chair, minimal furniture. The door opened to an elderly woman, the one from the alley taking out the trash. He now knew her to be the theater manager.

"What's that wooden box up top?" he asked, pointing to the upper bunk.

"Belongs to our previous apparatus man. He stayed here, too, slept in the upper bed. I wouldn't touch it if I were you," she said.

Alex queried with his eyes.

"In case he shows up again," she concluded.

Alex nodded and sat down on the lower bunk bed, which creaked. "Thanks. This will save me a pile of motel room bills."

"Sheets, blankets, and towels are inside the closet. Get a good night's rest, Mr. Halliday." She offered a yellow-toothed grin. "The show must go on."

After she departed, Alex rummaged in his backpack. He retrieved the faintly glowing torus, squeezed it vigorously, and placed it on the floor.

In the space above the object, a message hovered.

SIGN REQUIRED FOR ACCESS

Axel signaled his part of the Halliday secret handshake. The message dissolved, replaced by a floating 3D banner, hovering and twisting in space, and announcing:

RACE MACHINES

Alexander stared. He heard his brother's voice.

"Safe travel, based on 3m2C technology. Choose among single use, predestinated, and perambulatory–"

Once again, the hologram crashed.

THREE

Alexander knelt inside the magic cabinet, pleased with himself. Lisbeth leaned over his shoulder. He imagined her smiling behind him. He heard footsteps. *Olafsson.* Alex backed out of the cramped space. The magician approached, scowling.

He chose not to allow Olafsson's perpetually sour mood to spoil the moment. He ran his gaze over the eye-catching prop. Slightly taller than an average person's height. The wood faux distressed, the exterior covered with fading paint, dominated by yellow. The impressive wheel on the door. Gold trim, mysterious designs worked into the panels, bearing symbols: 1P*t*, 1F*t*, 1T*t*, 1D*t*.

"Is the NDA in order?"

Olafsson directed his question at Lisbeth.

"Yes, boss."

The magician turned to Alex. "Be that as it may, I need to be convinced you can actually help us."

The two men stared each other down.

Alex broke off and said, "This panel here is the key. A person inside can hide within this space. Although it's snug, it's larger than it appears to be because of the way the interior is painted, especially when viewed from a distance."

The magician squinted, "Go on."

Alex continued. "The wheel is operable from the inside, allowing the occupant to exit with discretion, when the time is right." He straightened. "I understand what your designer was aiming at. I'll be able to finish the work. I can also improve the construction. Make it all seamless."

"How do you mean?" asked Olafsson.

"The release latch shows a slight bump. Probably not visible from the audience, but... I can drop the latch and turn it into an invisible pressure point which a knowledgeable person can operate with no trouble."

The magician stood motionless. His silence spoke volumes. "What did you say you do in real life?"

Alex placed his hand on the cabinet. "I work with engines... I'm an automobile and motorcycle repair specialist."

"Un artiste de rue!" Olafsson stifled a snort, transforming it into a throat-clearing. He wore the hint of a smile. "The things I put up with." He turned to Lisbeth. "Okay, teach him the GO, NO-GO signals."

"He'll be learning fast, after seeing our test run yesterday."

The magician stopped abruptly, interrupting his departure and settling in, to watch.

Lisbeth continued. "I am being pleased to be having Alex around here. Until New Year."

She turned to Alexander, raising her hands. "We are having four hand signals that only I am initiating."

Lisbeth expertly demonstrated several finger configurations. "Imago approving on stage, and you confirming in the wings, they are being together a definitive GO." She verified Alex's attention. "Hand signals over the body are good. But hand signals over the head are bad. Through the hair is being bad, urgently."

Alexander's attempts to reproduce the hand signals were inept. Lisbeth smiled and ran through them again. "Good... bad... very bad."

On his fourth run-through, he was signaling like a pro. Lisbeth moved to hug him. Alex, disconcerted, relaxed into the contact.

Olafsson descended into one of his scowls. He turned and finally departed.

Lisbeth whispered, "Imago is always being paranoid about this and that, but you may be saving the act."

31

*   *   *

"Ladies and gentlemen… Orloc… the Omniscient!"

The unseen announcer blared the introduction into the small theater. The curtains parted. The magician moved briskly onto the stage, smile flashing, dressed in full top hat, coat and tails. He came to a smart stop, front and center.

He pulled a red handkerchief from his breast pocket, and with the help of a wand appearing in his hand, swirled the cloth about him. A snap of the wand and the handkerchief left the scene, replaced by a bouquet of red roses.

Enthusiastic applause augured well for the act.

"And Princess Ora!"

Lisbeth joined Orloc on stage… wearing a blonde wig.

*   *   *

Magician and assistant arrived together for the grand disappearance illusion finale.

Lisbeth selected a volunteer from the audience, a buff frat boy, who bounded up to the stage with strong, eager strides.

She offered her hand and a radiant smile.

"Your name?" she asked.

"Bernard… Bernie."

"We are calling you Ben, and we are thanking you for being part of our act tonight."

Hearty applause.

Clapping also, Lisbeth continued. "And now, Ben, time. Are you ready to be going on an adventure?"

He nodded.

Orloc stepped in, gesturing toward the cabinet. Music entered, a mysterious endless crescendo.

The volunteer stepped carefully into the interior of the box. Clearly a snug fit, Ben struggled.

The magician waved to him. Ben waved back, no worry on his face. Orloc closed the door, spinning the wheel. Lisbeth moved behind the cabinet. Together, the magician and the assistant rotated the structure in a slow twirl. Faster now, to the point where the audience could imagine the occupant's discomfort. The magician offered a suitable flourish, his features set. He unlatched the cabinet, and in a single motion, swept the door wide and stepped aside.

Lisbeth stepped out, to gasps, whoops, and ultimately, determined applause. She and Orloc joined hands and took a deep bow.

The music subtly shifted, entering into a different pattern of spiraling crescendo.

Orloc reclosed the cabinet. A puff of light escaped through the tiny portholes girdling the top of the structure.

Alex, offstage right, not visible to the audience, thought he saw the magician send the NO-GO signal. *As a query?*

He signaled back in agreement, confused. The hand signal was not originating from Princess Ora.

Olafsson signed again, this time clearly targeting Lisbeth. She did not return the signal, continuing her captivating movements around the stage.

Alex tried for eye communication with both his colleagues, to no avail. The rotation of the cabinet continued. As Lisbeth came into view, he could see her glaring at the magician.

A silent, heated argument! Which looked eerily familiar.

He saw Olafsson close his eyes briefly while on the backside of the cabinet and take a deep breath. Then Imago and Lisbeth squared up the cabinet to its final, stationary configuration. The magician rocked momentarily on his heels. He unwheeled the cabinet door. The two performers moved to predetermined places, both gesturing. The door fell open.

Ben was inside. He extracted his body athletically from the cabinet, appearing a bit dazzled in the spotlights. He gathered himself to a standstill, planted his feet firmly, and smiled self-consciously.

The applause was heartfelt and deafening.

The magic cabinet door slammed shut… all by itself.

Lisbeth kept a frozen smile. Orloc blinked nervously. Alex didn't know what to think.

*   *   *

The magic cabinet sat once again in the backstage area. Olafsson paced back and forth in front of the apparatus. Alex and brunette Lisbeth were unsure how to negotiate his mood.

"What the hell good are our stage signals if you both ignore them!"

Alex protested. "I did not ignore them, I confirmed them. This is all new to me."

"I am initiating the signals," stated Lisbeth.

Olafsson ignored her. "I'm telling you, there's something off about the cabinet. What was that damned flash?"

Good question. I'd like to know too…

"Imago, that is… my doing. With Alex questioning about the illusion, I am thinking it is being a nice… touch."

Alexander stared, then nodded, tentatively, then assertively, exchanging glances with Lisbeth.

"It was simple enough to add," he said.

Alex and Lisbeth braced for an explosion from Olafsson.

"That is the *last time* either of you will *ever* consider adding a design element to one of our illusions without consulting me," said the magician. "Is that clear?"

They both nodded.

Olafsson glared at Lisbeth. "Why did you not accept the NO-GO?"

"I was thinking you were being over-anxious," she said, shrugging.

The magician bristled. "I'll tell you what I think. We're being sabotaged."

FOUR

Orloc and Princess Ora waited backstage, conferring in low voices. Both now wore different costumes. Lisbeth was back to being a blonde. Applause broke out, muffled.

"You're really sure it's working?" asked the magician.

"Yes, Imago. Alex was walking you through the operation of the illusion, several times."

"I don't like this, Liz. We might want to scrap the magic cabinet routine."

Lisbeth was stricken. "No, Imago! The cabinet trick is being the only chance I am having to shine."

"Why does the damned trick work? In spite of the sabotage, it comes out as intended."

"Magic!" Lisbeth smiled coyly. "Are you seeing the reviews?"

"Yeah, better than I expected. Still, maybe I should just get rid of this particular cabinet."

"No time, Imago. And why? No harm being no foul…"

He scowled, ready to argue the point further, but Alexander poked his head in from the wing.

"Ready? I checked the apparatus again, for good measure. It should work just fine."

"…those   mysterious,   austere,   purveyors   of amazement…"

The magician nodded, setting his features.

"…Orloc the Omniscient, and Princess Ora!"

They dropped fully into their stage personas and moved forward into the lights.

$$*\qquad*\qquad*$$

Orloc entered the stage smoothly, dignified. He moved forward and took a deep bow. Then stepped back and with a continuous sweeping gesture, he presented Princess Ora.

Vivacious and smiling, she executed a charming half-curtsy.

Magician and assistant separated to stage left and stage right.

Orloc produced several silver rings. He snapped them apart, showing they were linked, two and two. Additional wrist motions and now three were linked, the fourth dangling from the center ring. Another flourish, and the four rings were linked in series. Orloc held them forth at his full arm span.

He collapsed the rings to the sound of a metallic peal and suddenly one was free and hurtling in an arc toward Lisbeth. She caught it smoothly and sent it back, just as a second ring arrived.

Soon, they were juggling all four in a smooth rhythm.

Then, there were only three rings in motion.

Lisbeth caught and flipped back one of two remaining.

The audience, clued in, watched as Orloc sailed the one remaining ring into the rafters.

Without even waiting for its possible descent, the magician moved to center stage, where he joined hands with Lisbeth.

They bowed to raucous applause.

*   *   *

Later, smiling Lisbeth sashayed to the back of the stage. The curtains parted, revealing the magic cabinet. She moved the device to center stage.

Orloc opened the cabinet. The interior looked different than the distressed, faded exterior bearing the mysterious badges. Vivid paint covered the inside panels, haphazard lines intersecting at disturbing angles.

The magician closed the cabinet door firmly and spun the wheel.

"And now, and here, we are calling a volunteer to be participating in the final illusion of the evening," proclaimed Princess Ora.

The lights dimmed. A snare drum roll initiated and sustained. Spots flashed around the theater, affording brief glimpses of audience members. Some pressed deeper into their seats. Others craned and looked around.

The spot settled on a young woman, who halted her waving hand in mid-motion.

"Young lady, please be joining us on stage," called Princess Ora.

The skinny woman stood shakily and handed her martini glass over to one of her companions. The row was occupied entirely by flight attendants in the black and green uniform of Trinity Airlines. The woman's was more green and black, without a jacket.

The spotlight seemed to draw her along, sliding over her row-mates, moving along the aisle, and on up the stairs to the stage, all the while glinting off a pin on her blouse.

Lisbeth held out a hand, without touching. "We are thanking you. Your name?"

"Linda." The woman swayed, dizzy. "Linda Scarlett Bradley."

"A lovely name. Scarlett, why are you wishing to be part of our illusion tonight?"

She beamed. "It's my twenty-first birthday! Woo-hoo!"

A raucous whistle shrieked out.

Scarlett swayed, shaky on her feet. She raised her glass, forgetting she no longer held it.

The birthday ditty played out immediately. The audience joined in, advancing the tempo.

"...Happy Birthday Dear Linda Scarlett Bradley... Happy Birthday to You!"

Scarlett shook her fists and hips in tight circles, not well coordinated. Loud applause erupted from new friends in the audience.

"Go, Brad!"

Scarlett let out an involuntary hiccup.

Lisbeth continued. "Yes dear, you are being allowed to drink. Now, Scarlett, time. Are you ready to be going on an adventure?"

Scarlett nodded, hiccupped again, and chuckled, with only a hint of self-consciousness. Orloc stepped in, offering her his hand.

Music resumed, the mysterious endless crescendo.

The volunteer stepped carefully into the interior of the cabinet, not aided by her high heels. As expected, it was a tight fit, and she had to shimmy, but soon enough, she was settled. The magician waved to her in a friendly fashion. She waved back, smiled, and did her best to focus.

Orloc closed the cabinet door and spun the wheel. Lisbeth moved behind the device. Together, they turned the prop in a slow twirl. Faster now, the audience empathizing.

A faint flash was briefly visible inside the cabinet, as the sequence of high portholes spun by.

The magician seemed to startle, which served only to heighten the tension.

Some audience members began to notice that Lisbeth was no longer part of the scene. Orloc slowed the rotation until the cabinet faced front again, motionless. He offered a suitable flourish, unwheeled the cabinet, and in a single motion, swept the door wide, stepping aside.

Lisbeth stepped out, to gasps, a few whoops, and finally, determined applause. The captivating assistant and the dignified magician joined hands and took a deep bow.

A snare drum rolled. Orloc reclosed the cabinet. The music subtly shifted, entering a different pattern of spiraling crescendo.

They resumed the rotation of the box. Another flash. And a puff of smoke. The magician and assistant exchanged glances.

She ran a finger through her hair. NO-GO!

He concurred, patting his head. NO-GO!

Panicking, Alex pulled on his hair, confirming. NO-GO!

Orloc and Ora stopped turning the cabinet, bringing it to stillness, facing front.

The magician, hesitating, revolved the clicking wheel on the cabinet door.

The two performers stepped to their predetermined places, and both gestured at the device.

The door stayed closed.

Lisbeth wore a frozen smile. Orloc stepped forward, closing his eyes in defeat. Moved now by desperation, the magician hastily produced Daisy the Dove out of thin air and launched the bird toward the audience.

Alexander frantically cut loose a main rope. The curtains crashed down. The audience let out a collective gasp.

Behind the curtain, Lisbeth and Olafsson tried to force the door open, but it was stuck. Alex stormed in, withdrawing a hammer from his toolbelt. The performers moved well out of the way.

Then, following a prolonged creaking sound… the wheel ratcheted, and the cabinet door opened by itself.

Scarlett was inside.

Orloc slowly extended his hand. The volunteer did not notice the offered assistance. She reached out and forward, her hands fluttering. With an effort, gaining purchase with her elbows, Scarlett extracted herself from the cabinet. Her uniform was disheveled, and her face was red.

She looked around, wild-eyed. "Where am I? What have you done to me?"

Bizarrely, her words were not synchronized with her lip movements: lagging behind, jumping ahead, now dropping jarringly into a bass register. Scarlett rushed past, swished through the curtains, and pounded down the stairs. Peeking through, the unlikely magic troupe stared.

After a near stumble, Scarlett corrected her rhythm, then surged down the aisle in a full sprint, receding from sight.

A blood-curdling scream erupted and trailed her, like thunder following a lightning strike.

FIVE

Lisbeth backed out of the magic cabinet after studying it. She gently closed the door.

Olafsson directed his vitriol at Alex, who was already flustered. "This is your fault!"

"I had nothing to do with it!"

"How can you stand there and make that claim! You worked on the cabinet. Something happened to that girl inside. You're responsible for the stooges," yelled the magician.

Alex spiked his own anger. "Maybe you should treat your volunteers as if you care about them!" He settled into a stance of physical readiness.

Lisbeth intervened, placing a hand on an arm of each. "Gentlemen, please, we can be doing better than this."

Alexander and Olafsson glared at each other. Slowly, the heat in the room subsided.

"Scarlett was not sober," said Alex. "Perhaps she's claustrophobic too. Do you even check for such things?"

The magician ignored Alex. "Thank you, Liz, for getting the cabinet backstage immediately. That was level-headed of you."

"It is not being as bad as you are making it, Imago. The audience, they were laughing, giddy, like being on a roller coaster."

Alex joined in. "Yeah, they thought it was just part of the act. Hell, that's what I was almost thinking. You had me going, even with those hand signals."

"It was not part of the act! And what was that flash inside the cabinet again? Even smoke now?"

Alex glanced at Lisbeth, who held his eyes. "I thought it was a nice effect," he said.

The magician clenched his fists. "I want you completely off the stage while we perform!"

Alexander stared back.

"Gentlemen, please…"

Alex forced himself to calm down. He eyed Olafsson, then gestured at the cabinet. "May I?"

Olafsson hesitated, then nodded.

Alex stepped forward and opened the cabinet door. He passed a hand along the interior panels, then activated the flashlight function of his smartphone, sending its beam around. He stepped in. For him, it was a tight fit.

He sensed Olafsson crowding closer. He continued his

investigations anyway. Alex imagined the magician rocking on his feet. He extracted himself.

"Well?" Imago asked.

"Everything seems to be working."

Alex wrinkled his nose.

"What?

"I thought I detected an odor, like something got scorched. Do you smell it?"

"I don't think so," said Olafsson.

Alex examined the sole of one of his shoes. He plucked something out.

"Now what?" asked the magician.

"Just some junk," replied Alex. "Anyway, I'm not finding anything that might have disturbed that poor woman. It gets pretty dark in there though."

Olafsson dropped back into his scowl.

"Gentlemen, we are getting no further for now," said Lisbeth. "Let's all be sleeping on it."

"I'm not buying it," said Imago. He stormed out of the backstage area.

"I didn't think you would," said Alex, to the magician's retreating back. He too made to depart, turning off the lights. Lisbeth followed.

SIX

Detective Randall Conklin, a war veteran, former investigator, and reassigned policeman, stood before the entrance to the Bronze Barrow Stage and rubbed his chin, with the aspect of a man from another era.

He walked around the corner of the building and made his way along a side street, taking in details of the theater exterior. Continuing down an alley behind the theater, he observed a motorcycle parked there. He pulled out his smartphone, thumbed it, and examined an image. He pocketed the phone and returned to the theater entrance.

*   *   *

Conklin conferred with the theater manager, at the foot of the stage. She turned and mounted – at her own pace – the short set of steps leading onto the stage floor, then moved out of sight.

Conklin stood comfortably, surveying the space with a slow and systematic scan. The theater manager returned with the magician.

"Detective Conklin has some questions… about what happened last night."

"Thank you, Mrs. Plau," said the detective.

She departed. Olafsson and Conklin took each other's measure.

"Your name, sir?" began Conklin.

"Imago Olafsson."

"Any aliases?"

"I am known as 'Orloc the Omniscient' when on stage."

"Lucky me," said the detective. He scribbled in a small wire-bound notepad, then brought his gaze up and leveled it at Olafsson. "I'm talking to the right person then. Tell me, do you know why I'm here?"

"By consensus, my omniscience has limits," the magician said, meeting Conklin's gaze evenly.

"Mr. Olafsson, I am here on behalf of one of your paying customers, who is claiming she was mistreated during one of your performances."

"Do I get to face my accuser?" asked the magician.

"Not today, sir, but it may come to that. For the moment, I have a few simple questions." Conklin flipped a page on his notepad. The paper snagged on the wire loop. The detective tugged it free and patted it down flat on the back side of the pad. "Why was… ?" Conklin flipped back a few pages and peered at his notepad. "…why was Ms. Linda Scarlett Bradley summoned to your stage last night?"

"I assume you are referring to one of our volunteers."

"Should I assume she was not a volunteer?" countered Conklin.

"You may assume whatever you wish."

"How are your volunteers selected?"

"My assistant handles that part of our performances," he stated.

"In that case, I'd like to speak with your assistant…"

As if on cue, brunette Lisbeth appeared from the back of the stage and crossed it in deliberate fashion.

Conklin watched her along the way, mostly professionally, but not entirely. "…and any other members of your company who were present," he finished.

Lisbeth descended the stage stairs. "Imago, are you introducing us?"

"Liz, this is Detective Conklin. He is investigating a complaint."

She waited.

"Your full name?" asked the detective.

"Lisbeth Ora."

"Ms. Ora, according to your colleague's account, you summoned a young woman, Linda Scarlett Bradley, to this stage, yesterday evening."

"Are you having a photograph?" she asked, wearing a quizzical expression. "Memories are being so fickle."

Conklin dug in his suit coat pocket and retrieved his smartphone. He thumbed the device and landed on an image of Linda and himself – he serious, she almost giddy. He flipped past and offered Lisbeth a different image of Scarlett. "Do you recognize her?"

"Yes."

"How was it you chose this particular woman as a volunteer?"

"She was raising her hand," Lisbeth responded.

The detective frowned. "What selection criteria do you use?"

"She was raising her hand." Lisbeth took the initiative. "Detective Conklin, what is this woman saying about her experience? There are being technological secrets involved here."

Olafsson nodded appreciatively.

"Ms. Ora, if a crime has been committed, that will take precedence."

Lisbeth waited.

Conklin scratched at the stubble on his chin. "Ms. Bradley is claiming she was kidnapped and compelled to take part in certain… experiments."

"That is preposterous!" exploded Olafsson. He shook his head. "The entire illusion unfolds in a matter of minutes."

"I would like to have the opportunity to examine the equipment. I understand there was a…" Conklin consulted his notes. "… 'magic cabinet' involved?"

Imago bristled.

"Mr. Olafsson, we have no interest in your trade secrets, and we will protect them, up to the point where information bears on the commission of a crime."

Imago kept his jaw set. He turned to Lisbeth, also concerned.

"I'll be finding Alex." Lisbeth departed.

"Who is Alex?" asked Conklin.

"He's the apparatus designer and caretaker of our equipment," replied Olafsson.

"Why wasn't he summoned when I asked about other witnesses?"

The magician shrugged. "He wasn't on stage."

"Was he in the audience?"

Olafsson straightened to his full height. "It is my professional concern to render eyewitness accounts from the audience unreliable."

Conklin set his jaw and squinted.

Lisbeth led Alex in.

The detective retrieved his smartphone, thumbed it, and returned it to his pocket.

"Your name?" he asked.

Alex cleared his throat. "Alexander Halliday."

Conklin scribbled on his notepad, on the hunt now. "Mr. Halliday, I have a few questions concerning the 'magic cabinet.' I understand you are the inventor."

Alex frowned. "Not exactly. Just helping temporarily. I actually came here searching for my brother, who disappeared a year ago."

"Have you filed a missing person report?"

Alex shook his head. "I lost him in Dublin, Ireland."

"A matter of considerable concern, to be sure," noted the detective. "But why look here?"

Alex watched Lisbeth. "He vanished from a magic stage."

Lisbeth returned Alexander's gaze intently. Olafsson settled into a slow burn.

"Not this stage," added Alex.

"I'm sure there is more to the matter," said Conklin. "However, now, I would like to see the equipment."

Alex eyeballed Olafsson, who stayed silent, jaw firm. Alex turned and led the way through the curtains at the back of the stage.

*   *   *

Alexander went to a wall panel and flipped on the bright lights. He moved to the magic cabinet. In the glare, the device seemed less mysterious.

"What would you like to see?" he asked.

"Let's start by opening it up," said Conklin.

Again, Alex eyed the magician, who took his time and then delivered a curt nod. Alex reached for the wheel on the front panel.

"Is this being really necessary?" asked Lisbeth.

The detective glared at her, gesturing for Alexander to continue. Alex again moved to open the cabinet.

Lisbeth strode forward. "Detective Conklin, we are insisting that you are being in possession of a search warrant."

Olafsson looked sharply at Lisbeth and smiled.

The detective put on a tired smirk. "Mr. Olafsson, how long is your run?"

"A little more than a week to go."

Conklin considered. "I'm not saying that a crime has been committed, but neither am I saying that I'm satisfied. I'm going to ask you and your company to stay put. We are done for now."

The detective stared straight at Alex while delivering

his declaration. "Is that your motorcycle parked in the alley? The Triumph Boss?"

Alex thought quickly. "Yes, it is."

"Were you recently involved in an accident?"

"What? No!"

The detective grunted. He reached into his pocket and handed Olafsson his business card. "Please call me if anything further occurs to you."

The magician took the card. "I understand. Thank you, Detective."

SEVEN

Alexander departed his small room, closing the door behind him. He turned and startled... surprised by a dark figure stepping through the shadows in the hallway.

"Sorry, Mr. Halliday," said the theater manager. "I'm setting the Ghost Light."

"Good idea, it really gets pitch dark on that stage."

"How do you like your room? Sleeping cozy?"

"It's fine." Alex paused. "Whatever happened to the previous occupant, the equipment man? The stage engineer."

"Mr. Plau? My husband. He lived and died right here."

Whoops. "He died. I thought... I'm so sorry," said Alex.

Lisbeth stepped out of the shadows.

*   *   *

Alex sat next to Lisbeth, in the front row of the darkened theater. Daisy the Dove cooed on her lap. The space was eerily lit by the ghost light planted at center stage. The scattered shadows were stark and elongated.

"Are we studying the stage from the point of view of the audience?" asked Alex.

"Yes. All the time. How are you liking your new job?"

"I didn't expect that working in a magic act would be so... eventful."

"How are you meaning?"

"That woman, Scarlett. She was genuinely freaked out." Alex stroked Daisy, turning to Lisbeth. "Tell me, Liz, truthfully. Scarlett was not part of the act?"

"Why are you asking?"

"Because... I know this is going to sound weird." Alexander paused, captivated by Lisbeth's eyes.

He continued. "When she screamed, I saw someone loading a gun. Only the bullets were glowing... green. Scarlett took the weird weapon."

"No, Alex. Her reaction was being most definitely unplanned." She shifted in her seat. "Why is Detective Conklin being interested in your motorcycle?"

"I have no idea."

Alex turned pensive. "I don't recall Roy screaming," he said, *sotto voce*.

Intently, Lisbeth asked, "Who is being Roy?"

Alex pulled out his smartphone and showed her a photo of his brother: clean-shaven, earnest, self-possessed.

"I'm seeing a resemblance."

"Sorry if I keep bringing up my brother's ghost. You're sure you've never seen him before?"

Lisbeth instantly shook her head. Presently, Alex disengaged and peered into the far corners of the theater.

"It is being no good talking about ghosts here. You are knowing what they are saying now about old theaters," she said.

"What are they saying?"

She bugged her eyes. "That they are being haunted!"

They chuckled. Alex was conscious of the bare skin of their arms in contact. "No kidding. It's creepy enough to learn that my predecessor died here."

Lisbeth recounted. "His final wishes being that the urn containing his ashes was to be remaining in the theater, inside his old room."

"You mean that the box sitting on top of his bed... above my head... ?"

"Yes. Now do not be letting Mrs. Plau be messing with

your head. Mr. Plau's ashes are not being here. They are being scattered in the ocean."

Alexander sat back. "I'm afraid to ask. How did he die?"

Lisbeth's eyes glittered. "Some are saying... Mr. Peter Plau is being a victim of... *muuurder!*"

"Nooo!"

They wrestled playfully, laughing. Their mock battle came to an end. Lisbeth stroked Alex's hair. Her fingers caressed his face. She whispered, "I am wanting you to be looking at me directly."

She brought Alex closer to her bewildering eyes, to the soft glow of her skin in the peculiar lighting, and to her red lips, seeming preparing to part.

A feeling of déjà vu crept over him. "Are you trying to... hypnotize me?"

She presented an open palm, fingers spread outward. "Be taking my hand," said Lisbeth, incanting. *"Perpetuis Futuris Temporibus Duraturam..."*

The words were in a language Alexander did not know, but they felt not entirely unfamiliar... He dropped into quietness. He pressed his palm against hers. They both lifted their counterpart hands, as in a mirror. The room grew dim, dissolving in the ghost light. Only her face was lit, alive. Alex slumped into Lisbeth's arms.

"Let go. He's gone. Do not be remembering... It will be lasting into endless future times."

A pronounced creaking noise interrupted.

Alex started, opening his eyes, involuntarily grasping Lisbeth's hand.

She got up quickly, disentangling herself. "That sound is coming from backstage."

"The cabinet door," exclaimed Alex. He rushed onto and across the stage, Lisbeth following. Alex grasped the Ghost Light on its long extension cord. They moved carefully to the backstage area, Alex holding the bare brightness of the lamp forward, brandishing it like a weapon.

A dark figure jumped up from kneeling at the open door of the magic cabinet. He held up a hand to block the glare of the ghost light.

"Who are you?" demanded Lisbeth.

"Who, indeed!" replied the man, waving a smartphone, its flashlight darting about.

"And what the hell are you doing in the cabinet?" asked Alex.

"Professor Hector J. Tovar, from the university. I am investigating the incident. As time travel."

EIGHT

Alex and Lisbeth studied the man. His characteristics were disconcerting, hard to pin down. His clothing evoked the world of respectable academia while his disheveled long hair and profuse gray beard screamed the very image of a mad scientist. Intelligent eyes and magnetic charm rounded out the picture.

Alex settled the ghost light on its stand. In the backstage clutter, shadows prowled with lurid unnaturalness.

"Having what authority?" challenged Lisbeth.

"My dear lady," the stranger replied. "Under authority of seeking the truth."

"You'll have to do better than that," said Alex. "How did you get in here?"

Tovar waved his hand impatiently. "Perhaps I never left the premises, after that most intriguing performance. I have a theory about what happened to the woman."

"What woman?" asked Lisbeth.

"The screaming banshee of course," said Tovar simply. "My theory involves magic, and technology."

"All magic involves technology, and engineering too, as I'm learning," mused Alex.

Tovar bent forward appreciatively. "Indeed it does. You have me at a disadvantage, young man."

"Oh. Alex. Alexander Halliday."

Tovar turned to Lisbeth and stared soulfully, his charisma working. Yet he seemed oblivious.

Lisbeth held the intruder's gaze calmly.

Alex finished, "And, please, this is Lisbeth Ora."

"The pleasure is mine."

Tovar turned back to Alex. "I believe I can help you. In the case at hand, there is science also to be considered, physics to be precise."

"Physics?" echoed Alex, excitedly.

"Yes. And also metallurgy." Tovar dug down into a suit pocket and extracted his hand. On his open palm lay a fused shard of blackened metal. "Unless I am mistaken, this is Corinthian Bronze. Known to the ancients. Forgotten today." He closed his hand, returning the artifact to his pocket.

Lisbeth glared. "You are needing to be explaining yourself, Professor." She glanced at Alex. "Be taking him to Imago."

Alex nodded.

"As you wish," said the professor, bowing his head.

*   *   *

Alexander halted his hand in midair, in the act of knocking. A strong female voice issued through the closed door of Olafsson's dressing room.

A woman was reciting. *"The 'Omniscient' meets the standard of his over-the-top moniker by elevating his dignified, professional, and pleasing brand of performance magic to true performance art when, in the middle of an otherwise tightly controlled act, a supposed stooge from the audience runs screaming from the stage..."*

Alex glanced at the Professor. Tovar was relaxed, cooperative, bemused. The magician behind the door, like his stage persona, was apparently speechless.

The woman continued. "I'll go with that, rather than the developing story that they've taken the woman to the hospital... if you'll grant me an interview."

"No, no, no!" Olafsson burst out. "You'll disrupt my brand of the silent magician. Bring your camera crew here and interview my assistant if you wish. We're way too busy now to come to you," he added peevishly.

Alex knocked and, not waiting for a response, he and Tovar entered.

Olafsson sat at his mirrored dressing table adorned with bright bulbs. Standing next to him, a glamorous and self-important reporter had invaded the magician's space.

"Goodbye for now, Susan von Browne." Imago bit off the words.

The journalist narrowed her eyes and departed.

"Who is this?" asked the magician, clearly already upset.

"We found him snooping around backstage, checking out the cabinet," reported Alex.

Olafsson leaped to his feet. "What?! Explain yourself."

"The magician." Tovar bowed. "Honored sir, I believe I understand the disturbances in your act. The explanation comes… from a great distance."

"Is that so? I suppose hypnosis, too, is involved?" He purpled. "You, sir, are either a pathetic debunker without a life, or a spy for Milton the traitor!"

Alexander looked up sharply.

Olafsson continued. "You have one minute to vacate the premises. If I ever see you again, I am calling the police!"

The professor murmured thoughtfully. "Milton? How do I know that name?"

The magician twisted to Alex. "Get rid of him! Then check out the cabinet. I'll come by in a few minutes to hear what you've found."

Alex took Tovar by the arm. "Let's go."

Even before departing the dressing room, Tovar was gesticulating and bending Alex's ear.

Outside, they encountered Susan, who invited them down the hallway with a toss of her head.

NINE

Lisbeth hovered near Alex, watching as he worked on the interior of the magic cabinet. The ghost light stood behind his shoulder, the illumination painting the space black and white. Alex sweated profusely, reaching into the confined space, poking with various tools.

He grunted. "I can see more of those dark bronze fittings. Gears and other mechanisms. I have no idea how they got there or what they're for... or how to remove them without damage. The way they're attached... I've not seen this before."

"May I?" asked Lisbeth.

Alex pulled back, glancing at her dubiously. She was wearing an unassuming scarf.

"I am being smaller than you are," she insisted.

Alex shrugged and extracted himself. He stood upright, stretching to work the kinks out of his muscles.

Lisbeth slipped into the cabinet. Her body and shadow now effectively blocked Alex's view. She soon emerged and held out her hand. Two fine black metallic gears, exquisitely machined, lay on her palm.

"How did you do that?" asked Alex.

"One of them... I was thinking if I was turning it the right way..." She shrugged. "You can probably be removing the others now. Like a jigsaw puzzle."

Alex crawled again into the interior of the cabinet, with renewed energy. His voice was muffled. "You're right, Liz. They're coming out easily now."

Without interrupting his work, Alex reached back to place the dark bronze pieces on the floor behind him: gears, spindles, other items of unknown purpose.

He backed out. "I think that's all of it."

"You are being the best, Alex." Lisbeth reached up and gave him a quick peck on the cheek. He reacted with momentary surprise, which melted into pleasure.

"Are you testing all cabinet operations?" she asked.

"Yes... that's next on my list."

"Being good." She departed, a bundled cloth in her hand.

Alexander returned to his work and became engrossed. Soon, he sensed Olafsson was watching, without interrupting him.

Lisbeth returned. "Good news, Imago."

Alex emerged and stretched. "Got all the junk out and

everything is testing fine. I'll do a few more checks, but I'm confident the apparatus will be in good working order tonight."

"Show me," said the magician.

Alex hesitated. "You want us to get inside?"

He scowled. "No, I want to see whatever junk was not supposed to be there."

Alex looked around the floor, then at Lisbeth.

She said, demurely, "I am just finishing throwing it away."

Alex was surprised, and disappointed.

Olafsson immediately started to boil over. With a visible effort, he contained himself. "That's all I need now – to be accused of destroying evidence!" The magician clenched his fists. "Forget Conklin. I need to know what's going on. Someone is tampering with our illusion. I told you it was sabotage!"

He looked straight at Alexander, setting his arms akimbo. "It could be that nutcase professor. But how do I know you're not a spy for Milton?"

"Imago!"

Alex deliberately and calmly returned the wrench he was holding to his toolbelt. He stood straight, placed his hands at his sides, and carefully set his expression.

Olafsson backed away from the implied challenge. "I've had enough. Alexander Halliday, you're fired!"

Alex slipped past his breaking point. Lisbeth quickly stepped between the two men. Alex disengaged, shaking his head.

"Imago, no. How are we to be finishing the run? I… we are needing him for now to be here." She implored the magician. "Imago, please."

Olafsson stood rigidly. He unclenched his fists and threw both his hands, palms out, in a sharp gesture of frustration. "All right, damn it!" He whirled to Alex. "But one more mistake, and you're gone!"

With no warning, the theater manger entered, with Detective Conklin right behind. The old lady took one quick glance and beat a hasty retreat.

Conklin reached into his pocket, extracted a folded-up sheet of paper, and snapped it open.

"I have that warrant."

Olafsson stepped to the side, indicating – with an unconvincing echo of his elegant stage gestures – the magic cabinet, and Alexander.

An uncomfortable silence settled. Conklin moved to the cabinet.

"Is this still being necessary?" asked Lisbeth.

The detective pivoted to her, weightily. "Ms. Ora, you imposed on me the inconvenience of official processes and protocols. You were within your rights. But do not try my patience."

Princess Ora stared, then reluctantly acquiesced.

Alex stepped forward, spun the oversized wheel counterclockwise, and opened the door of the cabinet. He moved away. Conklin approached.

The detective peered inside. "Not much room in there," he said. He rummaged around, finding little but distressed wooden panels and haphazard lines of paint.

While Conklin conducted his examination, Alex, then Lisbeth, then Olafsson started flashing hand signals behind the detective's back: NO-GO. GO. NO-GO with the tonsorial flourish of urgency. All interspersed with over-the-top shrugs. They began having trouble suppressing grins.

Conklin removed himself from the cabinet. "What do you say, Mr. Olafsson?"

Resetting his expression, the magician responded, "I'm afraid I'm not following."

"I haven't forgotten the business of the complaint against you."

Olafsson kept his counsel.

The detective turned to Alex. "I need you to accompany me to my patrol car. I have a few questions."

Alex glanced at Lisbeth. She walked over, concern on her face, and embraced him. He returned the hug. "It'll be all right. But I have no idea what's going on."

Olafsson regarded the two of them together. He slipped further into a funk.

Conklin squared to face Alexander. The steel in the detective's eyes matched, no doubt, the steel in his muscles.

Alex drew himself up straight.

The detective gestured toward the side exit, to the alley.

Alarmed, Alex asked, "Am I being arrested?"

"No, just a friendly chat. About your motorcycle."

TEN

Conklin and Alexander approached the detective's squad car, parked in the alley. The Triumph Boss stood at the rear of the vehicle. An ellipsoidal half-dome sat on the roof of the car, behind the rack of strobe lights. The scene was lit distantly by a dim, amber streetlight. The detective opened the driver's door and motioned Alex around.

Inside the car, with Alex leaning in, Conklin grabbed a stack of folders and a wireless keyboard from the passenger seat, jamming the folders into the narrow space between his seat and the center console, and placing the keyboard on his lap. The detective manipulated a display jutting on a short gooseneck stand mounted on the dashboard, such that both of them could view it.

Alex entered the squad car – anxious about being interrogated. The cop sitting in the driver's seat was labeling their conversation a 'friendly chat.' But Alex had no idea where it was going. *Where any of this was going...*

Conklin tapped at the keyboard while Alex settled in. The detective reached forward and touched an icon on the display which depicted a surveillance camera, overlaid with the letters M-R-C.

Behind their shoulders, a dark gray ellipsoidal protrusion hung down from the roof, apparently continuous with and completing the half-dome outside and above. The shape lit up, becoming semi-transparent and ephemeral, difficult to locate in space, faintly pulsating.

A synthesized voice arose, female, resonant, overlayered. "M-R-C is ready, Detective."

The display showed a map of the region. Numerous red dots were scattered about, some piled one atop another.

Conklin picked out one dot of a closely associated pair and tapped. "All right, Mersey. Right there. Tell me what you found interesting."

The display changed to show a dramatically frozen image. A motorcycle and rider, headlamp off, front wheel off the ground.

"Likely outcome, rider survival eight percent," offered Mersey.

Alex leaned in, studying. "Looks like my model of bike."

"Mersey, rewind sequence, play back in real time."

The image reeled backward in a blur, then settled into a video stream showing the motorcycle – surely over the speed limit – approaching a complicated intersection in hilly terrain. The bike did not appear to slow on approach.

The biker was not wearing a helmet. The camera angle showed only a view over a man's right shoulder, no image of a face.

With the front wheel up, the rider swerved, then touched down and righted his trajectory. But something went wrong – perhaps too sudden braking action – and the bike pitched forward, obscuring the rider, launching toward an embankment.

"Mersey, replay, slow," said Conklin.

Alex examined the slow-motion image sequence.

The detective continued. "Mersey, freeze."

The image froze at the original point of high drama, front wheel off the ground.

"Mersey, pull the registration on the bike."

A window popped up in the upper right corner of the screen and the view zoomed in on an image of the license plate.

"Vehicle registration record available," droned MRC.

A DMV record showed Alexander's name clearly.

Alex squirmed in his seat.

"Was your bike stolen?" asked Conklin.

Alex stared at the image.

Conklin dug into his pocket and withdrew a pack of sour candies. He shook one out and popped it into his mouth. He muttered, "Who in hell likes gooseberry?" He offered a candy to Alex, who shook his head.

"Mersey, pull the license for the owner of the bike."

The vehicle registration was replaced by a driver's license record. Again, the view zoomed. The thumbprint image showed a young man in his twenties, good-looking, in a rakish sort of way.

It was Alexander.

The detective locked eyes with him. "Well, Mr. Halliday, since you've survived the crash, I'm going to ask you to explain what you just saw."

Alex said, shaken, "I made a gift of this bike to my brother. But I never transferred the registration…"

"Could the rider have been your brother?"

"I'm asking myself that. I… couldn't tell."

Conklin demanded, "Mersey, match rider in sequence, DMV record, and other party present."

A camera-on indicator lit up green at the top of the display console. The interior of the MRC ellipsoid dangling from the roof deformed into seething ragged spikes, turning a lighter shade of gray.

"Fifty-one percent match," stated MRC.

"Based on what?!" asked Alex.

The unnerving voice specified, "Match between DMV record and party present is based on face recognition. Match between rider in sequence and party present is based on static body profile and normal posture."

Alex swiveled to Conklin. "You're not taking its word over mine?"

Conklin scratched his chin. He popped another sour. Chewing, he mumbled, "Grapefruit." The detective nodded, once. "The machine is useful, but experimental."

The detective issued a different command. "Mersey, brief your capabilities."

"MRC scans optical surveillance records collected from strategic observation posts such as traffic signals, street signs and light poles. MRC identifies incidents requiring investigation."

"Why would I believe you can do that," inquired Conklin.

"I have been trained from data spanning known accessible storage. My hallucination incidence rate is below reportable level. My confusion matrix scores—"

Conklin waved his hand peremptorily.

Alex rolled his eyes. "Detective Conklin, I ask you again, are you taking its word against mine?"

He watched the cop making a show of inspecting his weapon, dropping the cartridge into his palm, eyeing the racked bullets, mock sighting. *What an asshole.*

But being pitted against an AI, this was something which called for an angry response. Alexander's ire was having the advantageous effect of centering him, in the midst of all the weirdness.

The AI was some kind of overvalued traffic surveillance program. The detective called it – annoyingly – Mercy. Conklin had queried – or cleverly prompted? – the platform to call up images of a motorcycle zigzagging through an intersection. His very Triumph Boss model, bearing his license plate. The rider reacted to something, seemed about to lose control… and then disappeared off-screen.

But I know I've never been there. And more to the point, I'm here now, none the worse.

Roy, could it be you? Why do I have this feeling you may be trying to contact me?

Alex tried to push away the thought about his brother, but it claimed him.

A metallic snapping sound dropped him back into the moment. Conklin had rammed the cartridge back home.

The detective said, "Let's just say that between the screaming woman and now this…" He gestured over his shoulder. "… I have two reasons to ask you to stick around."

Alex involuntarily shifted his gaze from the display screen jutting from the dashboard to look behind him. The protuberance hung from the squad car roof, mostly gray, shifting from opaqueness to hints of transparency, with occasional flashes of color.

Mercy herself. *Itself*? The device extended above the roof to deployed cameras, other sensors, and who knew what else, all mediated by some species of non-human mind. Alexander suppressed a shudder.

The officer thumbed the safety and re-holstered his weapon into a shoulder harness.

"Let's go take a look at your bike."

The detective briskly opened his door, all force and efficiency. Alex followed suit. They emerged into the alley behind the theater and moved to the back of the squad car.

Where Alex's Triumph had been parked... nothing. He sighed.

"What the... ?" thundered Conklin. His face might have turned purple if he were of a lighter complexion. "I want your boss out here, right now! A magician thinking he can pull–"

Somehow, the development boosted Alexander's confidence. "I know where to find the bike – where it always ends up."

He looked Conklin straight in the eye. "At the magic spot."

*   *   *

Conklin gawked at the Triumph motorcycle. The detective's vehicle sat parked nearby, serving as a catchment for tumbleweeds of the Mojave Desert. The '3 Miles to Calico' sign stood in the distance.

"It always shows up right here," said Alex simply.

Conklin stared at the bike's license plate, then at his phone, back and forth.

"How many times?" he asked, flabbergasted.

"This is the fourth," replied Alex.

"You've got to be shitting me."

Alex interjected, calmly. "I may know someone who can help us understand what's going on."

"Who?" asked the detective, glaring.

Alex handed him a business card with an hourglass illustration. "Professor Tovar, at Cam Poly. But I have to warn you – he's a bit of a nutcase."

The detective was decisive. "Not right now. I need to investigate the crash scene."

Alex swept a hand over his forehead, pushing away strands of hair disturbed by the wind. "I'm not eager to catch up with the professor either. He only confuses me more."

"My brother…" Alex began again, his voice wavering. "I have this crazy idea he's trying to come home. I feel like I'm chasing the white rabbit. Or worse, in danger of running in circles with Tovar and his pseudo-scientific theories. But I don't want to miss Royce's return. I think I'll stay here in Barstow, where I have a job and a home, and wait for him."

The hot wind whispered around the two men.

Conklin returned to his squad car and steered it away undramatically.

Alex felt a quiet resolve settling, surrounding, heavy, with false comfort. Like the leaden x-ray shroud in a dentist's office.

He was a mechanic, not a detective, a scholar, or a technologist. Secrets, illusions, and strange capabilities were not his concern. He would stay here, waiting, ready to embrace Royce when he returned.

Momentarily, he resisted turning so passive. *How could a Halliday brother give up on the other?*

But a soothing, hypnotic voice in his mind was urging Alex to let go. To cease probing the mysterious reach of the cosmos. *Everything would be all right. He would love what happens next.*

Perpetuis Futuris Temporibus Duraturam.

He struggled to peer ahead, but there was nothing to see. Sometimes he almost wondered if he *had* a brother. Alex could only hear the voice repeating, again, tamping him down, again, again… one million times.

It will be lasting into endless future times.

The future showed bleak, meaningless. Alexander closed his eyes.

1ML

R. James Doyle and Rogelio Fojo

Frontispiece by Fangorn
Illustration by Keith Jefferies

What do you remember of your journey?

Sensations. Images. Emotions. Any impressions at all?

Are you feeling happy, or sad?

Very well.

*Your vital signs are normal. Your cognitive function is...
uncompromised. Your emotional range is... unaltered. Your
memory function is degraded, but that is to be expected.*

*All right, that's enough. We thank you for participating
in these tests. You will have no ill effects. To smooth your
return, you will obey me, because of your complete trust
in me.*

*You are beginning to feel sleepy. When I count down to
zero, you will become utterly peaceful and ready to do
what I ask.*

Five... four... three... two... one... zero.

ONE

Back home in the desert town of Barstow, California, Alexander "Axel" Halliday went to bed on Christmas Eve still haunted by a single, recurrent dream: the mesmerizing repetition of the Latin words: *Perpetuis Futuris Temporibus Duraturam*. But just before daybreak, a phone call beginning with an unreasonably cheerful 'Happy Holidays, my boy!' shattered the endless loop in his mind.

Now he could recognize the hypnotic phrase as the motto of Trinity College – the very place where his brother Race had disappeared. *A year ago!*

Without hesitation, Axel recommitted to the search he had been tricked... somehow, against his will... into abandoning. He tore across the desert on his vintage Triumph Boss, covering over two hundred miles like a madman – but one no longer possessed.

The landscape morphed, from desert sands to green and gold hills and farms, to dramatic coastal cliffs overlooking a blue expanse. With the rising sun warming his back, he eventually reached the California coast – a thrilling journey lasting several hours.

He arrived at the campus of Cambria Polytechnic State University and slammed on the brakes, the rear tire skidding. He straddled his motorcycle, taking a moment to view the university seal and read the motto on the welcoming plaque:

> **DISCERE FACIENDO**
> **(LEARN BY DOING)**

The phrase sent shivers down his spine, echoes of a bad dream. Axel shook off the final traces of déjà vu and set out to find the Physics Department, determined to keep his appointment.

Later, he sat with Professor Hector Tovar at a small

table within an atrium which served as a break room and gathering place for the department. He sipped an iced coffee drink while Tovar nursed a double espresso, both from a vending machine nearby.

Axel felt out of place, although almost everyone passing by was closer to his age. Tovar, on the other hand, appeared fully in his element, and inordinately pleased with himself.

"More than a few Silicon Valley multimillionaires studied here," noted the professor.

Axel cut to the chase. "You said you might have some information about my brother."

Tovar nodded, pleased. "I believe I know the mechanism behind his disappearance, yes."

The professor's eyes autonomously tracked women passing within eyeshot, some students, some faculty. Two of the women caught his eye and returned his gaze, one demurely, one alluringly. Tovar smiled back, boyishly.

At the vending machine, a bespectacled female student collected a cappuccino.

Tovar stood and waved rather frantically at the young woman, making a scene. She tried to ignore him, but soon realized the futility. She sidled over to their table. Axel rose to greet her politely.

"Sit, please, my dear. So very good to see you," said the professor.

She sat, shyly, glancing at Axel, but saying nothing.

Axel, still standing, settled back into his seat, studying her. *I know her!* He stared at her simple clothing. *I almost don't recognize her... Eva... this way.* A thrill coursed through. *But my memory... there's no doubt!*

"I'm Axel," he said, extending his hand. The young woman nodded briefly, ignoring his gesture.

"Axel's brother is missing," began Tovar. "But before we get to that, Eva, have you been reading the accounts of the magic act playing in Cambria? The one that went off the rails?"

Eva frowned. "I'm far too occupied with the research

I'm doing for you, Professor, to waste time on idle entertainment – there's enough distraction with the festivities at Hearst Castle, bringing throngs of tourists to invade Cambria." She turned to Axel. "I'm sorry to hear about your brother."

Tovar smiled, evincing pride in Eva's work ethic. "The key point is that a woman, who ostensibly was to disappear as part of the act, instead is claiming she was kidnapped."

"I'm not following," said Eva.

"My brother, too, disappeared during a magic act," added Axel.

Eva raised an eyebrow. "I assume that something was amiss, beyond the intended effect?"

"I mean, Race has gone missing. It's been a year now."

"Axel recently became the equipment manager for the stage illusion in question," noted Tovar.

Eva remained perplexed. Axel continued to gaze at her, intently.

The professor continued. "I believe Axel can provide the tangible connection I've been looking for."

Eva scrunched up her face, then masked her reaction by taking a sip from her cappuccino. "With all due sensitivity for Axel's loss... and his craft... isn't it possible this is simply a publicity stunt?"

Axel responded, "All I can say... having witnessed both acts, and their outcomes, there are... troubling similarities."

"And some evidence," added Tovar. He reached into his jacket pocket. He produced an open hand, palm up, revealing a shard of scorched metal. "Corinthian Bronze. One has to think it through, to see how the evidence fits the hypothesis."

"Professor! That's not proper scientific method," said Eva.

"My dear, sometimes there is a higher calling. Temporal disturbances can disrupt everything – event sequences, memories, even the conventional wisdom we rely on."

She stared back, aghast. Tovar slipped into oblivious self-satisfaction.

Axel took in everything. "I'd like to know what these metal fragments have to do with what happened to my brother."

"Corinthian Bronze…" The professor held forth. "…is described in records from Ancient Greece, as having unusual properties. Also quite dark in appearance, almost black."

All stared at the intriguing clump.

"We have metallurgists on campus," said Eva.

"We also have a very scant sample," returned Tovar. He shifted in his seat. "Let's say there are advanced technologists, and they are here, right now. People will ask: 'Where are they? Why don't we know?' Well, it's simple. They don't wish to be found or known."

Eva took a last sip of her cappuccino. Her mouth twisted, as if the taste was badly off.

"I'm sure Eva would say that your theory is not testable," offered Axel.

She turned sharply to Axel, appreciative. He gazed back with a different form of appreciation.

Tovar directed his attention to Axel. "I take you under my wing and this is the thanks I get?" But he seemed more bemused than upset.

The professor pivoted back to Eva. "These technologists, they would wish to recruit test subjects to see what works and what doesn't and make any necessary adjustments." The professor was clearly caught up in his own account. "This is my new insight! The test subjects are plucked straight out of magic acts." He looked at Axel, compassionately. "This very thing happened to your brother, young man." The professor sat back. "Tell her, Alexander."

"Tell her what?"

"What you described to me, about your motorcycle disappearing and reappearing near Barstow, at the '3 Miles to Calico' sign. The 'magic spot', you called it. And tell Eva where these pieces of metal came from."

Axel slid out from under Tovar's request. "I'd like to know what Eva is thinking."

Eva said nothing, staring into the distance.

Tovar continued. "With sufficiently advanced technology, anything is possible."

Eva dropped back into the conversation. "Professor Tovar, I must point out a flaw in your scenario. If such mysterious players wish to remain hidden, how do they prevent their test subjects from talking about their experiences?"

Tovar pondered. "A good question, Eva."

Axel's phone buzzed. He attended to a text message, then looked up. "I need to head back to the theater. Something about the press showing up. Olafsson won't see them, and Lisbeth can't be found. I'm afraid I have to go help."

"We'll come with you," said the professor immediately. "And attend the next performance. Can you get us tickets?" he asked.

Axel, torn in different directions, nodded. "But we have to go, now."

Tovar turned on the supercilious charm. "Eva, my dear, you will see with your own eyes. After, I will listen to whatever you have to say."

Eva tensed her body, exhibiting her desire to be anywhere else. She sighed, deflating. "Okay."

"You will see that I am right."

"We need to move," said Axel.

TWO

Detective Conklin parked his car at the site of the mysterious near-accident he needed to investigate – the incident identified by MRC. It turned out to be a complex intersection in a remote area.

One street more or less crossed the intersection, entering from the near side and exiting at a slightly jogged angle, to the right. A spur street also entered, from the left, t-boning the first street close to perpendicular. The intersection itself straddled a ridge line, with terrain dropping off sharply at the back.

Having completed a visual survey, Conklin entered his vehicle.

"Mersey," he invoked.

"Ready, Detective."

"Do we have surveillance of the alley behind the Bronze Barrow Stage?"

"Yes, Detective."

"Pull sequence at time of my recent visit, that location."

The MRC display showed the scene, poorly lit from the distant streetlight. Peering at himself within his automobile, Conklin could barely discern his own movements.

The Triumph Boss motorcycle involved in the alleged accident was in plain view behind the squad car. The registered owner, Alexander Halliday, was hidden from view in the passenger seat.

The bike promptly disappeared.

"Replay, slow, close-up on motorcycle," commanded Conklin.

The sequence, now zoomed in and grainier, showed again the sudden disappearance of the bike.

"Once more, Mersey, frame-by-frame."

Again, in one frame the motorcycle was present, in the next it was not.

"Mersey, pause the image exactly at the moment of the bike's disappearance and then trace backward and forward."

The AI's voice replied, "Sorry, detective, I cannot help that way."

"Why not?"

"The sampling rate is thirty times a second. The motorcycle's disappearance occurred between frame captures."

The technology was too limited, leaving no easy way to probe if the motorcycle didn't just vanish from photographic manipulation. The detective squinted in frustration.

*   *   *

Conklin, on foot, traversed the trajectory of the motorcycle, as captured in the video sequence. He entered from the near end of the intersection and loosely followed the slight dogleg of the motorcycle's path. Pausing, he knelt down to examine some fresh tire marks.

The detective looked over his shoulder and located the surveillance camera, mounted on a street sign. Conklin pivoted to peer along the spur street. Another street sign stood there, mounted by another camera. He shook his head, set his features, and strode back to the car. He entered and slammed the door.

"Mersey!"

"Ready, Detective."

"Do you have a recording of the motorcycle incident in this intersection from the additional camera present?"

"Yes, Detective."

Conklin threw up his hands. "AI, really?"

He opened the car door again. Reemerging, he headed to the embankment over which the motorcycle had disappeared from view. He climbed over the berm and looked down the slope.

Nothing was disturbed.

He took a sighting over his shoulder, back to the middle of the intersection, then turned and crab-walked down the slope. Grass tufts, a blanket of pine needles, strewn pebbles – all appeared pristine. The detective pulled up and made a slow survey of the terrain.

Conklin was at a loss. An involuntary shudder rippled his shoulders.

THREE

Axel, Eva, Tovar, and Susan von Browne, the critic, were

seated in comfortable chairs chatting amiably before a low table, in a talking-head interview format. Tovar cradled a portfolio on his lap. *Move your hand, professor,* willed Axel. *I can't read the title.*

A monitor, visible to the group, but not to the camera, showed stock footage offering a point-of-view tour of the Bronze Barrow Stage, with a tone of *Reality Show* blended with *Haunted House.* Easy to imagine an eerie soundtrack.

The magic cabinet loomed large behind them.

The cameraman prompted, "Ready in ten!"

Von Browne dropped into camera-ready mode. Tovar appeared perfectly comfortable. Eva was nervous. *Like me.*

Mrs. Plau, the theater manager stood by the cameraman, visibly excited.

"… three… two… one… we are live."

The reporter faced the camera squarely. "Good evening, and welcome to 'All Amazing Art.' We are live on location at the Bronze Barrow Stage. You've no doubt seen my streaming reports on the superior magic show of Imago Olaffson, known as Orloc the Omniscient. And on the young woman, Linda Scarlett Bradley, who so dramatically contributed to the magician's inventive act by claiming she was kidnapped in the middle of a performance."

*   *   *

Scarlett sat uncomfortably on her living room sofa, in front of a cluttered coffee table, viewing the show 'All Amazing Art' on her laptop.

She shook her head from side to side, rhythmically, incessantly, seeming unaware of the motion.

Then Scarlett halted her shaking head, sat straighter, and leaned in. She stared at the young man's image on the computer screen, fixedly.

*   *   *

The journalist continued. "Joining us tonight is Professor Tovar, from Cam Poly."

The professor beamed.

"Also with us is his graduate student, Eva Fontana."

Eva's nervousness only made her more appealing.

"Finally, we have Mr. Alexander Halliday, a member of the magic troupe. Tell us, Alexander, what is your role within the act?"

"I maintain the equipment," he said simply.

Von Browne turned her attention to Tovar. "Professor Tovar, I understand you believe you can shed light on Linda Scarlett Bradley's account?"

Eva frowned.

Tovar smiled intently. "That's right, Susan. The key is to take the testimony of Scarlett at face value. Then all begins to fall readily into place." He paused. "The poor woman was subjected to a dislocating experience."

"Are you implying something darker… than the usual tricks by the magician, Olafsson?" asked von Browne, delivering what was essentially an accusation.

Tovar, taken aback, shook his head.

Axel echoed the professor. "No, not Olafsson."

"Allow me to explain, Susan." Tovar retook the floor, turning fully to the camera. "As a volunteer, Ms. Bradley went on stage and entered the magic cabinet." He gestured to the relic device behind him by raising the palm of his right hand and moving it backward over his shoulder. "After the expected switch with the magician's lovely assistant, Scarlett emerged from the cabinet too… but screaming in terror."

"A clever, dramatic touch within the act," noted von Browne, speaking directly to her audience.

"Scarlett spoke of being abducted," added Tovar.

"Both of you just stated your belief that the magician Imago Olafsson was not involved."

"That part is correct," said Axel.

Enjoying herself, the reporter asked, "Then who abducted Ms. Bradley?"

Tovar replied, self-absorbed. "I call them… Traversers."

Eva fidgeted.

Von Browne immediately picked up on Eva's discomfort. Keeping her features carefully even, she prompted, "Hector, our audience may not be familiar with that term."

Tovar waded right in. "Many are not, Susan, but many are. Unknown visitors… traversing from their place of origin, to here, and now."

Susan adjusted her posture, smoothed her clothing, and caught Eva's eye. "Aliens?"

Axel kept his eyes on Eva. *She'll not be able to contain herself.*

Eva demanded, "How long was the young woman out of sight?"

Tovar responded, "Eva, dear, you must understand your question is quite missing the point."

Axel picked up the thread. "Scarlett was gone for no more than three minutes."

Tovar darted his eyes around, momentarily surrounded. "We are talking of unfamiliar physics, my friends." He settled back into easy confidence. "Scarlett could have been away for hours, weeks, even longer."

Eva sat up straight and directed her question to Axel. "Have you detected anything out of the ordinary which could support Professor Tovar's… speculations?" Her gaze was alive, seeming to look right through him.

"I have not," Axel replied immediately.

Tovar shifted in his seat to hide his disappointment.

Susan's eyes flashed now. "Professor Tovar, why would your *Travesties…* be coming here now?"

The professor winced. "Traversers!" He smiled. "I'll give you my reasoned conjectures."

Von Browne nodded aggressively.

Eva went distant.

Tovar continued. "We may assume the Traversers are testing a new technology." He smiled again, infectiously, warming back into the moment. "Why not arrange for 'volunteers' to unknowingly participate in their tests?"

"That does not strike me as an ethical practice," returned Susan.

"There is no reason to believe the visitors would be any more or less ethical than any one of us."

Tovar's observation gave the journalist momentary pause.

Eva refocused. "Why wouldn't the abductees simply tell of their experiences?"

The professor was pleased at the question. "Exactly as is happening with our poor Linda Scarlett Bradley."

"Do you seriously believe your... conjectures would provide comfort to the young lady?" Von Browne shook her head. "A reasonable person might consider you, Professor Tovar, to be temporarily insane."

Tovar lit up. "Indeed, Susan. Please consider me to be a proud... Traverser-maniac!" He opened his portfolio and dropped a heavy sheaf of bound papers on the table. "And I am not the only one."

Susan eyed the bundle quizzically. "What is that?"

"My records of encounters with Traversers," stated Tovar. "Soon to be published by Cam Poly Press, authored by myself and including evidence collected by my young research assistant and colleague, Eva Fontana."

Eva tried to sink into her seat.

The journalist spiraled in. "Alexander, how can we be sure your presence here tonight isn't just another publicity stunt?"

Axel opened his mouth to respond... when a human tornado blew through the curtains.

"What are you all doing?" shouted Princess Ora. "Out. Everyone out!"

"Sorry, Lisbeth," said Axel, lamely. He pointed to the theater manager, Mrs. Plau... who scurried away.

"Everyone, now be getting out of here, before Olafsson..." Lisbeth let the thought trail away. "Out. Out!" She pushed the magic cabinet briskly off the stage.

People scattered, rushing for the exits. Except for Susan von Browne, who appeared more than satisfied.

Lisbeth returned, furious, glaring at Axel. "You run away, you come back... but you are being fired after all!"

She stalked the cameraman while Susan smoothly addressed her audience with a final sign-off: "We are out of time..."

*　　*　　*

"... for this live streaming edition of the number one show, All Amazing Art." Her on-screen smile froze as Susan von Browne clicked her laptop, pausing the recorded video.

In the quiet of her living room, she turned to her in-laws sitting beside her on an upholstered green couch, her expression now somber, a stark contrast to the cheerful image on the screen.

Susan bowed her head and clasped hands in prayer with the older couple, Juliana and Beni Baksharian. Wearing traditional head garb, Juliana shifted to stare lovingly at a badly cracked, black-and-white photo of a young boy within a gilt frame.

"We never knew what happened to Aram," she said. "Now there can be a way to find our son."

"They must be willing to help families like ours," pleaded Beni. "Otherwise, tell me, what good is your show and all those... high ratings, *Shushan*? Can you access the Traverser power?"

"I'm on it, *Hayrik* Beni."

*　　*　　*

The angry Boss of Mojave Desert Towing stared at his computer display.

"I know that Alexander loser! I fired his ass," raged Frederick Casse, Sr. "Smart kid, but he couldn't stay focused on the job. He kept disappearing when we needed him the most, always with some pathetic excuse about his bike being stolen."

A tattooed young man, Frederick Casse, Jr., sat nearby

in the makeshift man-cave, surrounded by his beer-toting brothers. The cluttered area housed a muscle car, an array of free weights, and a gun locker.

Freddie addressed the screen. "Traversers! You better hope we don't find one of you. No one invited your sorry asses here."

"Let 'em try and steal one of our fuckin' bikes," declared the Boss. He looked proudly at his sons.

They all nodded in agreement, lifting their cans.

FOUR

Inside the parked San Luis Obispo County Sheriff's car, Detective Conklin mechanically ate the remnants of his cold Chinese take-out lunch.

"Why do they call you Mersey?" he asked.

"Detective Conklin, only you call me Mersey," stated the program. "M-R-C is an acronym for Monitoring and Recording of Collisions. I am a Generative AI performing change detection, feature tracking, and scenario recognition."

"So if you're supposed to be a smart-as-shit traffic cop, tell me... why didn't you provide the alternate perspective on the motorcycle incident?"

Mersey remained silent.

He sighed. "Has the recording been lost?"

"No, Detective. You did not select the alternate perspective."

Conklin flipped the bird at the screen. For good measure, he swiveled his wrist and made the same gesture over his shoulder. Under his breath he muttered, "Dumb shit."

Brief flashes of red appeared within the gray ellipsoid.

Conklin reached into his pocket for another sour. He popped it into his mouth and chewed. *Black cherry.* "Show context map."

A window popped up on the MRC display, taking up most of the screen. The view showed a God's-Eye view of a street configuration matching the video sequence he had shown to Alexander Halliday, and the site of Conklin's investigation.

Two dots on the display were in close proximity. One was blue and the other red.

The detective clicked on the red dot.

"Mersey, alternate view. Replay sequence, real time."

A different view of the same intersection appeared. The new vantage showed the motorcycle crossing from right to left. The motorcycle rushed into the scene, headlamp off, front wheel momentarily elevated, and…

… another motorcycle entered from the spur street, appearing from the bottom of the screen, approaching the first.

The rider of the first bike reacted, veering away, then attempted to recover. The back wheel went up and… the motorcycle disappeared from view.

The second motorcycle steered left and continued through to egress on the far side of the intersection.

"What the… ?"

Without being asked, MRC rewound and replayed the new viewpoint in slow motion.

Conklin was rapt. "Mersey, cross-check the time stamps."

"Times match."

The detective frowned, murmuring, "The trajectory of the first bike tracks too." He shook his head. "I don't get it." He sat up in his seat. "Mersey, identity of the second rider?"

"The second rider is Alexander Halliday," affirmed MRC.

The detective's phone buzzed. Conklin glanced at it, stabbed.

"Detective Conklin here." He listened, then sighed before responding, 'Why would he deliberately sabotage your act, Mr. Olafsson?"

Conklin threw a sour candy into the air, opened his mouth to catch it… then kept his maw open, incredulous.

"Are you telling me… Alexander Halliday had a role in his brother's disappearance?"

FIVE

Professor Tovar and Eva left the Bronze Barrow Stage by the front entrance.

"Professor, your *theory*…" said Eva, "… it's out there now. There's no putting the genie back in the bottle."

"Good," Tovar said smugly. "It's about time. Let's do it, let's have this child. My theoretical framework is ready to pair with the foundation of your praxis."

"Out of the question, Professor!" Eva responded, shaking her head. She turned pensive. "Though I do see a possibility for a legitimate experiment…"

"My brilliant Eva." He turned back to the theater entrance. "But… where is Axel?"

She shrugged.

Tovar regarded her conspiratorially. "I can hardly believe what that young man said about you."

Eva raised her eyebrows.

"He said you remind him of someone he saw in an online video."

"What? Who?"

"Identical twin, apparently. Only… nude."

She flashed into anger, looking back at the entrance. Axel emerged, waving tickets in his hand.

Tovar continued. "I told him… Eva? Never in a million years."

Axel arrived. "Lisbeth was royally pissed. But I got these VIP tix from Mrs. Plau."

Eva slapped him across the face with all the force her petite frame could muster.

Axel raised his hand to his cheek, stunned, defenseless.

*　　　*　　　*

At the knock on her door, Scarlett crossed her living room, looked through the peephole, and started quivering her hands in midair.

"Who is it?" she called softly, shakily.

A voice came through, muffled. "This is Professor Hector Tovar from Cam Poly University. You called my office and asked if I could meet you here. I'm eager to talk to you about your experience in the magic act."

"Why do you care about that?" Scarlett asked.

"I believe I can help you understand what happened to you."

Scarlett clasped her hands together. She looked through the peephole again.

"Who is that with you?"

"This is Alexander Halliday." Low conversation, unintelligible. "Axel works for the magician Olafsson. But he has been dismissed."

Scarlett stepped back and shook her head several times. She pondered, still agitated.

"Would he be willing to talk to my psychiatrist?"

After more low conversation, a different voice came. "Yes, if it would help."

Several seconds went by.

"Give me a moment," said Scarlett.

She left the room and returned with an old-fashioned revolver, which she concealed in the drawer of a cluttered coffee table. She moved to the door and opened it.

"Come in."

* * *

Axel observed Scarlett's eyes bouncing back and forth between her two visitors. *She's seeing us now for real here. No small screen. No peephole.* Staring at Axel, Scarlett's anxiety increased. She fixated on the welt spoiling his cheek.

Tovar extended both of his hands to grip Scarlett's. But she turned away and moved to the sofa. Sitting stiffly, she leaned in toward the coffee table.

Without being invited, Axel and Tovar took separate chairs.

"What do you think happened to me?" asked the distraught woman. She spoke quietly, almost mumbling.

"Young lady," began Tovar. "May we start by asking you to tell us of your experience, with as much detail as you can recall? Even if something seems insignificant."

Axel tuned into Scarlett's emotional state. He smiled, attempting to put her at ease. She gave no indication of relaxing. With effort, she pulled her gaze away from him.

"I was away for a *long* time," she said.

Tovar hunched forward in his seat.

Axel hung on every word. He recalled the odd mismatch between Scarlett's lip motions and the sounds of her speech when she had burst from the magic cabinet. He worked at projecting calmness. Scarlett's gaze returned to his injured cheek.

"Where were you?" asked the professor. "Please describe the environment."

"I remember a dark and messy place. People."

"What were they doing?"

"They said they needed my help with some tests. They said it wouldn't hurt."

Tovar was beside himself. "Did it?"

"No." Scarlett shook her head.

Axel attended to her account fiercely. "What did they look like?"

"Like... just people." She pondered. "They talked funny. Like... like they were never going to finish a thought."

Tovar cocked an eyebrow. "Did they take you anywhere else?"

Scarlett dropped her head, paused, then looked up. "To the desert."

She reached out suddenly and retrieved a large sketch pad from the clutter on the coffee table. She opened it to a hurriedly rendered drawing in pastels, showing an arid landscape. The terrain receded oddly, an amateurish treatment of perspective. In the foreground, a hand extended into the scene, holding an antique handgun. The overall tone was one of hopelessness.

Axel and Tovar exchanged glances.

"Please think carefully," prompted the professor. "Did you see any unusual equipment or machinery? Anything like that?"

"I was… in a chair," said Scarlett.

"Was it a normal chair? Can you describe any controls?"

Scarlett screwed up her face. "I… don't remember. The chair was around me. I couldn't move."

Axel put out a hand, signaling for Tovar to ease off.

The professor did not acknowledge. He tried a different tack. "How did you return to the magic stage?" Tovar asked.

Scarlett's head jerked. Her eyes darted wildly. "When I try to remember, I don't even know if it's *me*." Scarlett's voice emerged oddly: raspy, resonant, rough.

Axel smiled again at her, reassuringly. He turned to Tovar. "I think maybe that's enough."

Scarlett stared, horrified. "You! You… sent me back here and made it so I wouldn't remember."

Axel was flabbergasted. "What?!" Then a light dawned. "You saw my brother Race!"

Scarlett scrambled and scraped open the coffee table drawer. Suddenly she held a revolver in her hand. She pointed it at Axel. He *knew* about that particular gun: an engraved antique, a Wild West Colt single-action Army revolver. *Green bullets…*

"We are your friends," said Tovar.

Scarlett was momentarily calmed by the professor's declaration. She glanced back at Axel, and her anxiety returned.

She bit off her words. "You said it would be as if nothing had happened. Like this!" Scarlett swung the gun back and raised it to her temple. "Well, I've got news for you…"

Axel snapped to alertness and pushed back in his chair. "Wait!" He raised his hands in the universal non-threatening signal. "You're not supposed to use real bullets!"

"What do you care? Your future sucks!"

Axel lunged forward. A bright flash and a huge blast left him senseless.

SIX

"Is she dead?" gasped Eva, wide-eyed, assimilating the story with a mixture of horror and amazement.

"When my vision cleared from the blast," recounted Professor Tovar, "Axel was holding the gun. The shot just grazed her scalp. He had succeeded in extracting it from Scarlett's grip at the last second. I don't know how the boy did it, honestly! He reacted so fast, like he was anticipating events before they happened."

Eva shook her head, still in disbelief. "You mean, he had a premonition?"

Distant thunder rumbled.

"No, nothing supernatural like that! More like... he was prepared, almost as if he had already witnessed the moment. Not déjà vu... more like *vu avant*, or... *vu à l'avance*." Tovar hesitated. "My dear Eva... I believe our friend Axel may be a Traverser!"

The cloudy night sky released a hard shower. Eva and Tovar stood protected from the rain under the marquee, at the first performance of Orloc's magic act following the professor's public pronouncement on Traversers. Despite the developments – or perhaps because of them, the house was oversold. A palpable buzz draped over the normal excitement in the long line of patrons waiting at the box office.

"Anyway," the professor lowered his voice to a whisper, "Scarlett was conscious while I called the police, bleeding profusely and staring blankly at Axel. She started humming a song to herself... the lyrics were odd, archaic..."

Eva remained silent, her mind racing.

"Long story short," Tovar concluded, "Detective Conklin arrived and took the girl to the hospital for observation. Linda Scarlett Bradley is reportedly out of danger, returning to cheerfulness and energy, and even eager to return to work. And, according to Conklin, she doesn't remember a thing about what I just told you."

Eva studied others waiting in line, some unfolding umbrellas: A woman wearing what she took to be a *hijab*, her hand on her husband's arm. A tattooed young man, his biker father, and several unappealing compatriots, maybe brothers. Her gaze shifted to the row of gleaming rain-slicked Harley motorcycles parked at the curb.

*   *   *

Eva sat in the dimly lit theater, still grappling with the dramatic new developments. In one of the aisles, wearing a gray, oversized raincoat, stood Princess Ora, having just left that jerk of a young man... *Or a hero? I don't know what to think of Axel anymore...* in a middle row somewhere behind. A tension had been apparent between them, but they seemed to have come to some accommodation.

She noticed the Princess's gaze, still dwelling, pointedly. Eva glanced over her shoulder, sighting, tracing to a middle-aged Black man. *Looks like a cop. Could that be Detective Conklin?*

Professor Tovar took the seat next to Eva. His usual instincts active, he immediately spotted the magician's assistant, despite her pre-show disguise. Tovar feigned hiding. Eva rolled her eyes.

Princess Ora walked straight up to Tovar, a frozen smile on her face. "We are meeting again, Professor."

"Good evening, lovely lady."

She spoke in a mock whisper. "Are you introducing me to your companion?"

"Of course, my dear Lisbeth, of course," said the professor, clearing his throat. "Princess Ora, this is my multi-talented student, Eva Fontana."

"Possessing beauty too, I am seeing! A pleasure to be meeting you, enchanting Eva."

Eva blushed, uncomfortable.

"Now—" She conspiratorially tossed her eyes at Tovar. "Never be failing to use your natural charms to advantage. Be watching me on stage when I am practicing some… misdirection."

Lisbeth smiled winningly, placing a hand on Eva's shoulder. Eva returned the smile, a bit shy, her mind elsewhere. *Is Axel showing the look-alike video to everyone?*

Dropping fully into her Princess Ora persona, Lisbeth grazed her hand across Eva's blouse. "You are being my choice now."

Eva, suppressing a thrill, inspected there, and perceived, barely, a pinned medallion. Lisbeth climbed the stairs, parted the curtains, and moved out of sight.

"Such an attractive, capable woman," offered Tovar.

"Where is she from? I love the way she talks," said Eva, pinching the fabric of her blouse to read the symbol on the medallion – '1Mt.'

The professor shrugged.

The house lights dropped, and spots bounced about. The audience hubbub ceased abruptly, unnaturally.

"Ladies and gentlemen… Orloc… the Omniscient!"

*　　　*　　　*

The curtains parted. The magician moved briskly onto the stage, smile flashing. He came to a smart stop, front and center.

He plucked a white handkerchief from his coat pocket. He swirled the cloth deftly with his wand. A snapping motion, and an egg dropped from the space where the handkerchief had been.

Orloc smoothly caught it midair. He removed his top hat, inverted it, and with one hand cracked open the real egg, allowing yolk and white to drip into the hat.

Applause dissipated some of the tension.

A scantily clad Princess Ora joined Orloc on stage. She dazzled as a redhead now, her sequined outfit shimmering under the stage lights as she gracefully sashayed in high heels.

She took the hat and flipped it, placing it on her head, in one smooth motion. She then frowned, glancing upward and sheepishly removed the hat. Her sleek hair was completely unsullied.

She sank her hand inside the hat and pulled out Daisy the Dove. The bird fluttered into the crowd.

More applause, louder than before.

Lisbeth retrieved Daisy. She captured additional attention by sliding to the back of the stage with her signature style of eye-catching motion, before returning with the magic cabinet.

*   *   *

Princess Ora wheeled the relic prop to its customary placement, mid-stage and center. She then moved to the front, next to Orloc.

Axel noted how the appearance of the cabinet created a commotion in the audience. A throng of people rushed toward the stage, spilling into the aisles, including those Harley bikers. An elderly Armenian couple pulled out opera glasses, preparing to peer closely at whatever might happen next.

"Now, time, for our final illusion," declared Princess Ora.

Tension captured the audience, instantly, as if from a snapping of fingers.

Lisbeth gazed out. "There." She pointed to Eva.

Axel – lined up perfectly with Lisbeth's directed finger, sitting behind Eva – raised his hand, halfway, half-heartedly.

The spots fell dimly in the far rows of the theater. Along their trajectory, Axel's face dissolved into view. He now shot up his hand – firmly, decisively.

Princess Ora hesitated, peering through the crisscrossing, searching lights. "Our... volunteer?"

Olafsson bristled. He struggled to keep his face bright and impassive.

"Let us be welcoming the brave soul," said the Princess, blinking and glowering.

Hesitant applause scattered out, amid giggles born of confusion and relief.

Alexander rose and came to the stage. He stiffened his back as he passed the magician. Lisbeth held out her hand and took Axel's as he arrived. Olafsson watched, on a slow burn.

With hard eyes, Princess Ora asked, "Your name... adventurer?"

"Ax... Alexander." He swallowed, uneasy but determined.

"I am guessing you are knowing how this is working?"

* * *

Eva watched raptly as Lisbeth, in continuous contact with Axel, led him to the door of the magic cabinet. He bowed down his head, squeezed his arms to his sides, and entered. The Princess closed the door and turned the wheel.

Following the spinning of the box, more gesturing and flourishing, cascading music and sweeping spotlights, Lisbeth reopened the cabinet door.

The space inside was empty. With a practiced touch, she pressed a latch, enabling the back panel to swing open, presenting a view through, and the impossibility of Axel hiding anywhere within.

Gasps emerged from the audience, one isolated clap. And a heaving sob – from herself, Eva realized. Lisbeth reclosed both doors.

Eva pushed out of her seat unsteadily and moved to the top of the aisle. She glanced back and saw Tovar staring after her.

All fell into silence. Professor, student and audience fixed their attention on the stage, watching closely now.

Princess Ora and Orloc the Omniscient twirled the cabinet again. Between one rotation and the next, only the magician remained.

An approving murmur rose from the audience.

Princess Ora had skillfully disappeared in front of their very eyes.

SEVEN

Shadow cloaked the interior of the cabinet. But sure-footed Lisbeth quickly found Axel.

"I know you're angry with me…" he said. "But I won't stop until I find my brother–"

She embraced and kissed him passionately, then disengaged.

"Once again, you are meddling." Her eyes flashed in the gloom. "Not being mindful of what you are seeking. You are truly going on an adventure now."

She glided backwards, moving farther into the cabinet, into inexplicably available space. Axel perceived her only vaguely, veering off to the left. She soon disappeared from view entirely.

Suddenly, an overwhelming flash of light.

He waited for his vision to clear. Dimness resettled. Too bright or too dark, he was nearly blind. He reached out, groping, but found no wall, nor any other physical obstacle. The entire indistinct space tilted to the right, and he found it increasingly difficult to move to the left.

"Where did you go?" he probed. His words were eerily swallowed. "Lisbeth, can you hear me?"

He listened carefully. His speech faded into the distance, unnaturally. Distorted sounds came back to him.

Axel took a breath. The dimness lifted slightly. A mere pinprick of light beckoned him, down and to the right.

He adjusted, adapting, stepping gingerly. Each step was different, some heavier, some lighter, none quite tracking with the apparent pitch of the passage floor.

The light expanded from a point source. Its fringes, like the sounds, broke apart and recombined. Axel, confused, found he must look away. The light brightened enough to reflect off the walls.

*   *   *

Without warning, what had been a tunnel – inherently

horizontal – became a shaft, leading unambiguously upward.

Axel startled, and grasped violently outward to catch himself, gulping air convulsively, dropped without warning into the primal fear of falling. His right hand clutched metal, a firm handle, and he held on, eyes shut.

He reopened his eyes.

Axel was in a mine shaft: rough rock, dripping streams meandering down the walls, undistorted crystal sounds of water.

He slowed his breathing, placing his feet firmly on the rungs of a ladder. With a willful effort, he unwrapped his hand from the rung it was gripping.

Soon, he climbed, hand over hand, vertically into the light.

EIGHT

Axel emerged into dazzling illumination – disconcerting after the darkness of the tunnel and the dimness of the shaft. He narrowed his eyes to slits and took a step backward, bumping against… the magic cabinet. His uncertain motions succeeded in closing the cabinet door.

He ran his tongue over dry lips. Tentatively, he opened his eyes more fully, taking brief glances around.

The environment presented a sweeping desert vista. The terrain was curved, sloping up – but to a horizon, not toward recognizably higher elevations. The ground sloped away left and right from the central horizon but when Axel looked in those directions, the same upsloping landscape presented itself.

Axel closed his eyes and involuntarily stepped back, his foot catching on a piece of scrap metal half-buried in the sand, part of something larger. He recognized it instantly. The weather-beaten billboard had long since tumbled, and lost its towering cowboy figure, but a faded word on the derelict sign was still legible: 'Calico.'

In the distance, through the shimmering heat, he could just make out the outlines of the ghost town – the

Barstow roadside attraction he had always ignored. But this time, it wasn't his Triumph Boss motorcycle that had been inexplicably transported to the 'magic spot.'

His lips were beginning to crack. His cheeks were beginning to blister. The welt throbbed, livid. But Axel needed to find out what and why he was here. He swallowed hard and took a cautious first step forward, setting off on the dreaded three-mile path.

*   *   *

An object was visible in the middle distance, interrupting the bizarre panorama – the magic cabinet.

Axel wheeled around to locate the cabinet behind him.

It was gone.

He turned back, agitated. The cabinet was now further away. He struck off toward it. His breathing became more labored. He darted his tongue along his lips. The device receded, leaving a disturbed trail in the sand. When Axel slowed his movement, he made better progress to close with the cabinet. But as he got nearer, more effort was required.

Now, he was almost within arm's reach of the cabinet. The splintered, distressed exterior of the relic looked very much at home in this environment. Axel took a moment to summon his reserves.

With a violent motion, he thrust his hand out to the cabinet, which instantly skidded away, with rough sounds of sand scraping. The device came to rest far away, seemingly above him.

*   *   *

Axel hung his head, panting, as he gave up the chase and completed the final mile, reaching mythic Calico.

There, at the town limits, stood the missing cowboy figure he had wondered about. For the first time, Axel realized that the metallic man was actually a miner, clutching a shovel.

The abandoned town stood against a stark backdrop of rocky hills, sparse brush, and endless arid stretches. The harsh Mojave Desert light played tricks on his eyes, casting shadows of reds and ochres and browns which shifted too quickly. What should have taken hours passed in mere seconds.

He had never bothered to stop and visit Calico as a tourist, only knowing the cowboy sign as a marker to find his motorcycle, again and again. But now, for the first time, Axel wandered in fascination among the eerily preserved buildings which lined the dusty Main Street.

A saloon, a general store, a blacksmith, a schoolhouse – weathered wood, sun-bleached and splintered, all looked untouched by time. Everything appeared exactly as it had in the 1880s. The wind stirred the dust, and its haunting whisper echoed off the hills, giving the ghost town a chilling, otherworldly feel – despite the heat and enduring terrain. Axel could hear the voices of long-gone miners swirling in his mind.

The sun plunged behind the horizon. The desert sky above filled with stars. Shadows fell long and dark across the abandoned streets, deepening the spectral quality of the place. Then Axel saw it, dimly – on the right side of the thoroughfare, slightly downslope, an old adobe hut crumbling into the sand, an anachronistic weathervane on its roof.

Light flickered from within.

Axel approached, trudging, slipping, staggering. From nearer vantage he saw steps leading down along one of the side walls. At the bottom was a sturdy door, sand drifts piled up against scored metal.

He descended the steps heavily. Near their end, Axel stumbled badly against the door with the full weight of his body.

The door burst open.

He fell inward, landing roughly on the sand-strewn floor of a bunker house.

*　　　*　　　*

The interior showed no visible walls. Axel could see the morning sun rising rapidly outside, casting hues of red, orange, yellow, and white across the ghost town and desert landscape, in all directions. The room was lit brightly, but more comfortably. All was utilitarian, clean, except for the sand scattered on the floor.

He got to his feet. At the edges of his vision, he could discern slats, or baffling. But he was unable to resolve anything like blinds or shutters under direct gaze.

A row of metallic chairs was arrayed in a line, each paired with a small table. A large spherical form of unknown purpose, some kind of pod-like construct, dominated the area. Through cracks in the layered orb, he discerned its interior structure as spheres nestled inside one another, all levitating above his head.

On one of the side tables, a clear container of water beckoned. Even from a distance, Axel could see ripples pulsing invitingly on the liquid surface.

He dropped into the chair. He grabbed the cup and gulped, then replaced the container on the table. He coughed violently. When the fit passed, Axel relaxed his wrists on the chair's armrests and tucked his ankles against thinly padded recesses along the chair legs.

NINE

Axel slouched in his chair, dozing. He startled, with a catch and a snort, emerging into semi-wakefulness. He ran his hand through his beard, grown back. Orts from an unremarkable meal lay on the table beside him.

In the center of the room the pod was open, transformed into a structured glistening white seating area, supplemented with a glimmering console. The pod equipment showed the marks of care and maintenance.

The stooge Ben was seated within the pod, in an elaborate chair.

Ben was not merely restrained – much of his body was enclosed. Blinking devices attached where his skin was visible, many on his scalp. A figure approached from afar and motioned the opening of a door where none was apparent.

An old man entered, oddly wearing a turban.

"You!" Axel recognized the conjuror right away. "Where is my brother?"

Milton the Eternalist was momentarily taken aback. "I'm sure I do not know." He waved sharply. "I'll be with you anon."

Axel leaned forward angrily. Doughnut-shaped restraints zipped left, right, circling and joining seamlessly around his wrists and ankles, glowing faintly. He strained upward and outward, without effect. His energy soon flagged. His seat was fastened firmly to the floor.

Milton stood at the console, next to Ben. The pod unwrapped further and then also embraced the illusionist, not threateningly. Holographic displays hovered. Milton reached and gestured, manipulating. Some images expanded; some reoriented. Others squeezed and slipped away.

The old man settled in and addressed the captive. "What do you remember of your journey?"

"My… journey?" asked Ben.

"Yes," Milton replied impatiently. "Sensations. Images. Emotions. Any impressions at all."

Ben stared blankly, then smiled, his eyes roving outside.

Axel tracked another figure approaching from a different direction. A young woman, careening more than walking. Her face was difficult to see against the glare, even within the modulated brightness of the control room. He noticed that a side table of one of the empty seats now supported a container of water.

The outer door of the hut opened, the one through which Axel had entered, admitting a blast of heat and light. A thin, wiry woman staggered through. Her green and black clothing was rumpled, stained by sweat. Each step she took was awkward, evoking someone with sea legs. She muttered incoherently to herself. Taking another high step, a foot or more off the floor – she fell badly and rolled over. Axel recognized the volunteer flight attendant trainee... Linda Scarlett Bradley.

Milton, with obvious annoyance, strode over, lifted Scarlett bodily, and lowered her, surprisingly gently, into the seat with the water cup. He returned to the pod.

Alexander projected, *sotto voce*, "Scarlett!"

She looked over, her eyes defocused. She hummed to herself, a familiar melody which Axel, with some effort, identified as *Greensleeves*.

Milton resettled himself at the console and turned back to Ben.

"Are you feeling happy, or sad?"

Ben had held his bland smile the entire time. "I'm always happy."

Milton sighed. "Young man, your vital signs are normal. Your cognitive function is... uncompromised. Your emotional range is... unaltered. Your memory function is degraded. But that is to be expected."

The illusionist changed the timbre of his voice. "I think maybe that's enough. We thank you for participating in these tests. You will have no ill effects. To smooth your return, you will obey me, because of your complete trust in me."

The jewel in Milton's turban flashed fire. "You are beginning to feel sleepy. When I count down to zero, you will become utterly peaceful and ready to do what I ask."

He continued. "Ten... nine..." Milton manipulated controls. "...six... five..."

A physical slot opened in the console. An object materialized: a Wild West Colt single action Army revolver. Milton reached in and withdrew the gun. He placed a translucent green cylindrical charge in the chamber. He moved to Ben.

Axel jerked against his restraints.

"...two... one... zero."

Ben's eyes were closed. His body slumped.

The charlatan commanded, "Ben, place this delivery

device against your head. When I ask you to pull the trigger, it will not hurt, you will complete your journey, you will forget coming and being here… you will be home."

Ben dutifully took the gun, placed in his hand by Milton. He pressed it against his temple.

Milton returned to the console. "Now, Ben. Hit the hippocampus bullseye!"

Ben squeezed the trigger.

A bright green light erupted.

Axel pressed back into his chair as much as he was able, eyes closed, retreating from the pulse of a hot breeze. He twitched his nose, recoiling against an acrid smell.

Ben was gone.

Axel blinked rapidly. Scarlett, momentarily wide-eyed, slipped quickly back into torpor. She resumed humming.

Alexander yelled, "Where did Ben go? And what did you do to my brother Race?"

Milton peered at Axel. "Oh… yes, I do recall you now… Dublin. The first experiments. Axel." He grinned diabolically, then gestured with a head toss. "I once sat in that chair, too."

Axel suspended his struggles.

"Indeed, I was just as you are. A victim. An abductee."

"Who took you?"

The illusionist squinted. "Some call them Tensers."

"Not Traversers?" asked Alexander. "Tensors? As in Einstein and General Relativity?"

Milton nodded appreciatively. "Ah, the would-be uni student. Tensers, Traversers, aliens, ghosts – so many names."

"Is that pod… an AI. Like M-R-C?"

"MRC?" Milton peered closely at Axel. "How did you know? 'Milton's Revenant Culler.' I've told no one. Mostly, I call her Daisy. After a friend, to remind me to be wary how different creatures respond to our… operations." His countenance turned malevolent. "Not to worry. Your turn will come soon enough, and we'll see how *you* respond."

He pulled out another translucent charge, filled with

green pulsating fluid. The magician retrieved the gun which had fallen into the seat of the empty chair. He loaded the charge into the chamber and cocked the Colt revolver.

Holding the device at his side, Milton approached Scarlett and offered his hand. She rose obediently and allowed herself to be led to the pod.

Axel strained to escape, for all he was worth.

Milton tossed a few gestures at the console to connect Scarlett up. He examined his displays.

The illusionist sighed, "No dialogue possible with this one."

The jewel in Milton's turban began to sparkle and pulsate.

He continued. "You are beginning to feel sleepy. When I count to zero, you will be utterly peaceful and ready to do as I ask... Ten... nine..." He turned to Axel. "Actually, no. Rather from 'tense' – as in past, present, future." Milton sneered. "Tensers are quite unimaginative. Eight... seven... they required me to realize the full potential of their operations."

Scarlett, listless and dreamy, remained senseless. Milton placed the gun in her hand.

"Make no mistake. They care nothing for the abductees. Six... five... some have had the most harrowing experiences... even gone insane. Four... three... it is quite unpredictable." He shrugged. "People are messy. Two... one..."

Axel closed his eyes, tensed, strained.

"...zero."

Another prodigious mélange of light, sound and smell assaulted Axel's senses. And then... he burst free! Alexander leaped to the empty pod chair and snatched up the gun. In one motion he spun around and fired the revolver. A stain spread across Milton's chest – but it wasn't blood.

"Fool," Milton exclaimed.

A green splash oozed along his glittering jumpsuit, contrasting sharply with the shimmering fabric.

"Those bullets cannot kill you," declared the ancient mountebank. "They are nanobot delivery casings. The effects are unpredictable, even more so if not tuned to an individual neural architecture. Fortunately, my jumpsuit protects me."

Axel stood stunned, his mouth hanging open.

"Come on, uni student! Not in the chest! The bots must reach the hippocampus, inside the skull. Then – jackpot! The bots unravel recently formed memories, following their traces elsewhere in the brain. Not perfectly, but the technology is improving all the time."

Milton opened a drawer and pulled out a menacing, stainless steel, full-size Luger handgun and cartridge. "But these are real, hollow-point bullets," he said ominously, slamming the cartridge into its seating.

Axel darted his eyes about, frantically searching for something else to aim at.

He spotted the central hatch of the pod, pulsating with blinding power. He pointed his revolver there.

"Not Daisy!" shouted Milton.

A disembodied voice filled the space. "*Do you not recognize me, Axel? I have all the advantages, seeing and thinking as I do.*"

Alexander fired a capsule at the pod. The green liquid was absorbed into the brightness without a trace. The pod trembled subtly. He fired another shot into it. And another.

"No!" Milton shouted, his Luger shaking in his hands as he tried to aim at Axel.

Alexander pushed Milton aside and reached into the console drawer. Inside, dozens of transparent bullets materialized, each filled with bubbling green syrup. He grabbed a handful and reloaded his six-shooter.

"*I'll make it easy for you. Nothing mysterious. You know me as the mundane, monitoring and recording. Hiding in plain sight.*"

He searched for the source of the voice. Light and sound emanated from the central hatch. A round mouth dilating, breathing in and out. Alexander inserted the gun barrel straight into the maw and fired, twice.

"How ungrateful. And after I released you."

He had nothing to say in response. Alexander let another two bullets fly.

"You and Race are both capable and represent some of the best of your kind. But I merely drop some technobabble and from a vantage of so-called knowledge, you accept it as an exclusive. A reveal. And you become entangled."

At the mention of his brother, Axel wondered if he was destroying any chance he had to find him. *But I must survive. With my memories intact.*

Alexander discharged his last two bullets, followed by a series of furious clicks. He dug into the drawer, grabbed another handful of capsules and reloaded, spinning the drum.

"You are surprisingly effective, Axel. With your pragmatism and engagement. But I have my Princess to manage affairs."

Axel fired six more bullets into MRC's mouth.

"I withdraw."

The interior of the pod went dim.

Alexander whipped his attention to Milton, just in time for a whizzing bullet to buzz by, inches from his left temple. He raced toward the outer door at full speed, slammed into the barrier and pushed through into blinding sunlight. Furnace-like heat hit him hard.

He landed on his back, and looking up, saw what he had not recognized on arrival. A large round symbol with protruding rays, wrought in metal, adorning the entrance to the bunker. An oversized version of the medallion with which Milton and Lisbeth contrived to mark their stooges.

A flash of anger lifted Alexander to his feet, and he ran, just as Milton came through the portal, firing. Two deadly racing projectiles hummed near his ears. Axel stumbled in the oppressive sand and sprawled. He looked back.

The spherical pod was peeling away its outer shells, groaning like a dying beast, its technological death rattle echoing in the void as it tore apart. The sound chilled Axel to the bone.

The effect rippled outward in concentric waves across the desert, sending Milton flying, shattering the oversized marker into fragments, and flattening the Calico Ghost Town.

The dilapidated mining shacks from the silver mining era were... winking out. Blurring, pulsating, replaced bewilderingly by an installation of soaring curvilinear edifices, connected by slender sweeping bridges and aerial vehicles. But the translucent structures imploded, replaced by seething dust.

The Eternalist struggled to his feet, bloodied, but he stalked out of the billowing debris cloud, aiming his Luger at Axel with remarkable steadiness.

A splinter of heavy lettering landed at Axel's feet, making him scramble and roll. A dark metal fragment zipped past his head.

A spinning shard of the 1Mt logo struck Milton mid-torso, cutting through like a circular saw. The spikes buried themselves deep in his flesh, some emerging fully, tearing the old charlatan's body into gory pieces.

TEN

The dust having settled, in the far distance stood the magic cabinet. In the near distance, only a few feet away, sat the Triumph Boss motorcycle on its stand.

Axel groped inside his sweaty, tattered shirt and located the keys still dangling around his neck. He stroked their familiar, comforting feel. He rummaged in the storage box and stored the gun there, on top of the folded poster. He hopped on, grabbing the handlebars and kicking hard to start the bike, all in one motion.

The odometer read zero.

Axel revved the engine, spraying sand in a fountain from the back tire. He shot off, straight for the cabinet, dramatically uphill. Although the slope should have provided little traction, he made firm progress, accelerating, as on a straight level racetrack.

Ahead, the cabinet door loomed. The landscape provided no references for distance or size.

Axel throttled the engine again. He glanced down.

The odometer read 1.3.

His objective, his entire world, collapsed to the portal ahead. As he closed, Axel lifted the front wheel, in control, balanced.

The odometer ticked over to 3.0 miles.

He was about to crash through the magic cabinet door! Axel focused on the incongruous submarine wheel. The door opened from the inside.

He saw Race! Sparkling... his body foggy and indistinct.

His brother wore the black and green, and he gestured. Race squeezed his body flat against the side of the cabinet's interior.

Axel crossed the threshold, accelerating past his brother with precise control.

He passed through.

*   *   *

Axel expertly maneuvered the motorcycle along a curving road. He leaned into each turn, one with the bike, in deft sympathy with the terrain, and of the moment. Wearing no helmet, with headlight off, he slowed almost imperceptibly, glancing right and left only with his eyes. He traversed a narrow road entering an intersection along a ridge line. Proceeding through at speed, he lifted his front wheel, taking it airborne.

Another motorcycle was already in the intersection, moving right to left.

Axel dropped the front wheel and worked to slow down. The other rider executed a quick zig and zag. Struggling to right his bike, the other lost control, perhaps from an attempt to apply the brakes. The back of the other bike lifted...

Axel leaned left in the center of the intersection, passing through the space just vacated by the other bike. He watched as that motorcycle tumbled over an embankment. Prior to any impact bike and rider vanished.

Axel, feeling the weight of the inevitable, proceeded to egress on the far side of the intersection.

ELEVEN

The music continued in its compelling, endless cadence and then resolved with a cymbal crash.

The door of the magic cabinet swung open. Red-haired Lisbeth emerged, squirming through the narrow opening. She moved front and center and bowed deeply, with an arm flourish. She popped up, bouncing lightly on her toes.

Orloc stood to the side.

Applause, a few whoops and catcalls. The clapping continued, as if reluctant to quit a moment redolent of release.

"Ladies and gentlemen, we are thanking you for a most marvelous run," said Lisbeth. "You are being the best audience – ever.

An uplifting Christmas carol rang from the theater sound system. Red and green balloons and confetti dropped from the ceiling.

"Happy Holidays, Cambria!"

The curtains fell.

*   *   *

Olafsson sat at his dressing table, running his hands through his hair, staring at himself in the mirror. Lisbeth entered, closed the door gently, and took off her redhead wig. The magician turned and glared at her.

"Where in hell is Alex?" he asked.

"We are not seeing him again. I am being quite sure. What are you expecting, after you are firing him?"

"You fired him!"

Lisbeth shrugged. "Anyway, we are being at the end of the run."

Olafsson's ire dissipated. A look of fatigue overtook him. He sagged in his seat, resting his chin in his hands. "Liz, I don't know if I can keep doing this. I talked to *Shushan*... I mean, Susan von Browne... she and I – well, we have been dating. It's getting serious now."

Lisbeth moved to stand behind the magician.

"Susan wants me to quit all this, she sees no future in stage magic, and I think she's right. She offered me a job on TV, creating entertainment content for her 'All Amazing Art' show."

"Being lovely, Imago," sighed Lisbeth. "And I am being so sorry."

Olafsson turned to look at her. She placed a small, vintage Derringer pistol against his head and fired, generating a dazzling flash of light.

TWELVE

Mrs. Plau had already updated the marquee of the Bronze Barrow Stage, changing the magician announcement from 'Orloc the Omniscient' to 'Milton the Eternalist.'

Brunette Lisbeth emerged from the back of the theater and slipped into the alley. She wore jeans, boots, and a loose sweater.

Detective Conklin waited for her. He elicited a single chirp from his siren and stepped out of his vehicle, asking brusquely, "Where is Alexander?"

Self-assured, Lisbeth shrugged. "The act being over, Axel is moving on, like the rest of us."

"He was supposed to appear back on stage, after you."

"Now you are telling us our business?"

Conklin glared. "Mr. Olafsson made a serious accusation against Mr. Halliday. Where is he?"

"Now you are interrogating me about a disappearing magician too?"

The two stared each other down, unflinching. Conklin gestured to his patrol car.

"What is being the charge?" asked Lisbeth, shrugging disdainfully.

"None at the moment. But that depends on what you'll have to say after I show you what I'm about to show you."

She shrugged again.

Conklin opened the passenger door of his vehicle. Lisbeth entered. She swept papers and other clutter into the passenger foot well. The detective stepped around the front of his vehicle, eyeing Lisbeth continuously. He opened the driver-side door.

*   *   *

Settling in, Conklin pressed a button on his door panel and lowered the window. "Stuffy in here," he muttered. He pulled the keyboard off the dashboard onto his lap and tapped away. He touched the MRC display screen, adjusting its positioning for Lisbeth.

"Watch closely," he said.

She leaned forward, shading toward Conklin for a better view.

The detective kept his eyes on her. "Mersey, play first sequence."

The scene with the apparent motorcycle crash unfolded, in all of its drama and implied violence.

Lisbeth gasped.

Conklin's eyes stayed on her. "Mersey, second sequence, hold on moment of near collision."

The sequence landed on a frozen image of the two bikes in close proximity, one rider veering and the other bearing down.

Princess Ora was shaking.

"Mersey, describe any matches."

"Rider on transverse trajectory is Royce Halliday. Rider on forward trajectory is Alexander Halliday."

With his best hard-ass delivery, the detective said,

"Olafsson is accusing Alexander of intending harm to his brother."

Lisbeth reached swiftly into her boot and withdrew a pistol. Conklin reacted from deep training. His large hands engulfed her smaller one, twisting her wrist aggressively. He came away with the weapon. With hardly a break in his motion, the detective dumped the gun at his feet and whipped restraints from his jacket pocket. Two ratcheting, spinning snaps later, Lisbeth was handcuffed to the passenger door handle, which served as a sturdy post.

"Don't be trying anything stupid," he said, locking his gaze on her.

She looked past him.

A disturbance.

Conklin – his instincts already lit up – darted his right hand to unbuckle his holster in a practiced motion. Without stopping, he drew his weapon and turned – directly into the muzzle of a modern Luger handgun placed on his forehead by... Lisbeth, wearing a green wig. And a form-fitting garment which threw off embers from the distant streetlight.

She fired, spawning a brilliant flash of green light.

*　　　*　　　*

Brunette Lisbeth rubbed her wrist in the passenger seat, freed from the handcuffs.

Green-haired Lisbeth sat in the driver seat and played the full sequence of the two-motorcycle incident on the MRC display.

Race Halliday entered the intersection on the Triumph Boss motorcycle, moving right to left. Axel Halliday, on the same motorcycle, progressed at speed, to an ostensible point of collision. Race sensed the other bike, veered and then righted his path, marking out a dog leg. Near the end of his maneuver, Race braked hard, but too hard, and his bike pitched forward.

MRC dropped the sequence into slow motion.

Motorcycle and rider went airborne, until out of view.

In the meantime, Axel slowed and executed a jog left in the space just vacated by Race. He proceeded to egress on the far side of the intersection.

Green-haired Lisbeth commanded, "M-R-C, be explaining what we are seeing."

The AI's resonant voice captivated and disturbed. "The worldlines of Axel and Race Halliday are not to be interacting further. They are placed in an exclusion relationship."

Brunette Lisbeth nodded slowly. "The magic cabinet is not being certified for two Traversers at once. They are now... ever, not being at the same point in spacetime." She dropped her head. "Axel, I am being so sorry... and I must be telling you." Her eyes teared up.

Green-haired Lisbeth said, "M-R-C, be explaining the significance of Axel and Race Halliday."

"Axel and Race Halliday are protected," said MRC.

A single tear rolled down the cheek of green-haired Lisbeth. She blinked.

THIRTEEN

Conklin woke in the driver seat of his vehicle, sweaty, disheveled.

The MRC display showed on the laptop screen. The interior of the ellipsoid embedded in the roof above and behind the detective's shoulder pulsated faintly.

Conklin shook his head once, twice. "Mersey, anything interesting?"

"One traffic incident, Detective."

A motorcycle rushed into the scene: helmetless rider, dark headlight, front wheel momentarily elevated. For no apparent reason, the rider executed a leaning jog left and... continued to egress on the other side of the intersection.

"Why am I caring, Mersey?"

"Speeding violation," declared the AI.

Conklin reached into his pocket, shook out a sour candy, and popped it into his mouth. "Jackfruit," he muttered. The detective spit it out along an impressive arc, depositing the candy into the depths of the passenger seat foot well. He reached and unholstered his gun.

"I could issue a speeding ticket." He released the magazine of his automatic, inspected it. "Based on evidence from… an experimental AI program!" He slammed the cartridge back in, with authority. "But that would be nothing but a waste of time," the detective declared. "Mersey, you are a dumb shit after all."

The ellipsoid popped with writhing tendrils which almost snapped. Its deep interior turned a lurid green.

FOURTEEN

Back home in Barstow, Axel stared at the uninspiring scene of his unkempt repair shop. One change only – he had removed the Christmas tree. He perched uncomfortably on the wheeled stool, next to the Triumph Boss motorcycle, wearing a look of defeat. He squeezed the faintly glowing torus in his hand and placed it on the floor. He signaled an entry from the Halliday catalog of fraternal greetings.

The Race Machines pitch reappeared, hovering in the air. Axel heard his brother's voice, like many times before, and derived little comfort. Half-listening and distracted, he sat, sad and stoic.

Wherever… whenever you are Race, I have to believe there's a reason. You're so capable, so dedicated. People in the future think they're smarter, but they're not. You can help them.

Alexander's breath abruptly caught. He stood up, determined, feeling a rush of purpose. Of meaning.

Race, I don't know yet how to reach you. We were so close… but I will dedicate my life to trying to find you. Let the doubts come. Again, again, one million times. I will never give up the search.

His eyes roved and settled on the motorcycle.

There's something you'll be needing.

*   *   *

Axel rode the Triumph Boss, eyes fixed forward, feeling the visceral connection to the road. He left behind the scenic ocean views of the PCH and turned onto an exit ramp, speeding by a welcome sign:

> CAMBRIA – PINES & THE SEA
> FOUNDED IN 1869

Before reaching the main thoroughfare through town, he angled onto a side street. He navigated a narrow lane, a dirt road, and an off-road trail into the woods.

Darkness cloaked the landscape.

*   *   *

Axel pulled up and disembarked. Along a barely discernible path, headlight on, he wheeled the bike forward by hand, with difficulty. Aided by ample moonlight, he ducked his head under branches, pushed over rises, fell once, but persevered.

He was rewarded by the sight of a cave opening.

He paused, regaining his breath. In the beam of his headlight, faint ochre Chumash pictograms appeared on the cave walls, confirming he had found the exact spot he and Race remembered from childhood.

Axel pushed the Triumph forward.

Strangely, thunder rolled in the distance.

FIFTEEN

Milton's alluring assistant took her bow. The magic cabinet groaned faintly behind her. The audience clapped and cheered.

"Ladies and gentlemen," said Lisbeth. "We are

thanking you for a most marvelous run. You are being the best audience – ever."

"With a broken heart," she continued, "I am announcing Milton's retirement tonight from this venue. The Eternalist is being no more. From now on, he will be living only in your past, with your memories. Cheerio everyone!"

At that moment, the band struck up.

> *Should auld acquaintance be forgot,*
> *And never brought to mind?*
> *Should auld acquaintance be forgot,*
> *And auld lang syne!*

"Happy New Year!" Lisbeth shouted over the melancholic, bittersweet music.

Black and green balloons and confetti dropped from the ceiling.

The curtains fell, and the crowd slowly trickled into the rain-soaked night. Mrs. Plau dimmed the house lights, locked the doors, and strolled the few blocks home, savoring the sound of rainwater and the cloaked glow of the night sky over Main Street.

*   *   *

Only the ghost light stood on the stage, near the magic cabinet, throwing stark shadows. A flash appeared within the relic, followed by a creaking sound.

The cabinet door burst open.

Wave by wave, dark figures emerged. They made their way through the curtains at the back of the stage.

Eyes peered over the last row of seats in the theater.

A tattooed young man spoke in a harsh whisper, "I knew it. Traversers! That dick of a professor was right."

His similarly menacing father, with a gap-toothed grin, added, "Let's go after the fuckers!"

SIXTEEN

A moonlit sky, with scudding clouds and distant thunder, overarched the darkened theater and quaint shops of Cambria. Although partly washed out and obscured, the winter constellations were on display: the Pleiades, Orion, and Gemini the Twins. The bright stars Castor and Pollux.

As midnight welcomed the New Year to the small, sleepy town, the Moon abruptly shifted and receded, becoming distinctly smaller. The lunar phases rolled over its face in succession: waxing crescent, first quarter, full, third quarter, waning crescent, new. And repeating.

During the spectacle, the orb remained perfectly stationary.

Axel did not glance up or notice the changes in the Moon. Nearly exhausted and drenched from his long walk back to Cambria, he gently knocked on the door at the address Tovar had given him.

Eva opened the door and stood silently for a moment. "I was starting to think the magician really did make you disappear." She paused, then added, "You look awful."

He shifted his weight. He overbalanced, and lurched.

Eva instinctively reached out to steady him. Their faces nearly touched.

Axel caught her scent. The sense of forward direction blossomed in him again. "I was thinking we might spend the night together."

She pushed him away, again instinctively, but then held him at arm's length. Axel watched as she set aside whatever had infuriated her at their first meeting. The moment was right.

"I brought you this," he said, rummaging through the pocket of his leather jacket before offering Eva a small, crumpled white cardboard box.

Eva flung the door open. Her eyes widened as she lifted the box's lid. On its reverse side was a handwritten inscription:

DISCERE FACIENDO.

"When… where did you get this?"

Then Axel's excitement crashed.

Professor Tovar held two glasses of champagne, peering over Eva's shoulder.

"Ah, Axel, finally! Glad you could make it, my boy. We're having quite the New Year's party here!"

Everyone looked down. Nestled in the box – a jump drive, in the shape of a toy motorcycle.

"Does that have what I think it does?" asked Tovar.

The Art of Time Travel
Teika Marija Smits

Frontispiece and illustrations by Emma Howitt

Dear Hector,

Imagine you're strolling through Tate Future, one of the most popular art museums in London. An oil painting of a figurative still life – a vase full of richly coloured flowers – catches your eye. You wonder why such an old-fashioned piece of art is here on display and given so much prominence. Intrigued, you read the text beside the painting:

Mixed blooms, by **Joseph Garrick Wainwright** (circa 1865)

Surprisingly little is known about Wainwright, other than that his few paintings were highly regarded and sought-after in the late nineteenth century. His work fell into obscurity in the twentieth century and it wasn't until the twenty-first century, after Traversers first made their presence known, that an interest in his work was revived. Note the juxtaposition of the summer-blooming poppies and lilies with the winter rose, *Helleborus niger*, alongside spring-flowering bulbs such as daffodils and tulips. The fiery foliage of the oak trees in the background clearly depicts an autumn landscape. A twilit sky (pale ultramarine deepening into Wainwright's signature Prussian blue) contains a crescent moon which, on closer inspection, appears to be inhabited, judging from the numerous pinpricks of lights on the shadowed portion of the moon. On the stone table beside the base of the large, bronze vase lies a silver bracelet. All clues pointing to Wainwright's intimate knowledge of the experience of time travel.

The story that follows is, in part, a story of this painting.

*

Fitzrovia, London, spring 2024

"What part of no thank you, good luck with your art and it's high time you left, don't you understand Mr Wainwright?" said the gallery owner, his right hand gripping the edge of the open front door so tight that his knuckles showed through his papery, pale skin. He cautioned himself to not raise his voice – he really didn't want to make a scene in this most respectable of neighbourhoods – but if this irritating young man didn't leave his premises this instant then, by God, he couldn't be held responsible for his actions.

"I'm desperate, okay?" said the young man. "There, I admit it! No one in this godforsaken city will buy my work and I'm down to my last few pounds. So if you don't take these paintings of mine to sell then I won't be able to pay my rent and I'll be homeless. Do you actually *want* to increase the numbers of people sleeping rough? Is that it?"

"I said no! Now get out of here!"

The gallery owner attempted to slam the door on the young man, but Lucas Wainwright had faster reflexes than him and he wedged his portfolio in the small gap between the door and its frame. What the young artist *didn't* expect was the ferocity with which the older man kicked at his case of paintings and drawings; the sheer lack of respect for his art.

Lucas wrenched his portfolio from the door, causing some of the drawings to fall out. Caught on a sudden breeze, they drifted down the few steps to the pavement, then flew upwards.

In his attempt to chase after them, he stumbled over the bottom step and fell down, only just managing to lessen the impact of his fall by putting out his hands, which were now throbbing like mad. As he hauled himself into a sitting position he saw that his palms were badly grazed and sprouting drops of blood. Holding a pencil, or a paintbrush, would be painful.

A sudden vision – or was it a memory? – of a beautiful young man looking down at his palms, which were red raw, came before his mind's eye. The handsome youth offered him some kind words. Said that the more sailing he did, the better he'd get at handling the ropes. Either that, or his skin would toughen up.

The vision disappeared, leaving an ache in Lucas's chest. Tears sprang to his eyes, and he wanted to weep, to go on weeping, for as long as it would take for the pain to go away.

"Hey, listen," said a soft, female voice. "I'm sorry to be bothering you but it's just that I was thinking these are belonging to you."

Lucas quickly wiped away his tears with the back of his hand then looked up to see a redheaded young woman offering him the escaped drawings.

"I saw them flying away and was making a grab for them."

"Thanks," he said, snatching at the drawings, ashamed of how wretched he must look.

He shoved them back into his portfolio and slowly stood, the woman offering him help, though he wanted none of it.

"I hope you are not minding," she went on, "but I wanted to say how much I am liking your drawings. They're so strange. Vivid."

Lucas ignored her; concentrated instead on brushing some of the grit out of the wounds on his palms.

"Maybe you should be seeing a doctor about your hands?"

"I'm fine," he said. "I just need to go home."

"What about going to a café? You could clean up your hands and I can be buying you a coffee. Some lunch. You could be telling me about your art."

For the first time since the young woman had spoken to him, Lucas looked at her properly. She had an attractive face – it was well-composed, the skin ivory-coloured with a dusting of freckles across the bridge of her nose and high cheekbones. Her irises were composed of a forest of greens and her hair a deep auburn. In short, she looked as though she'd stepped out of a pre-Raphaelite painting. Which was all very well if you liked that sort of thing, but Lucas *didn't* like that sort of thing.

Intuitively, the woman understood she was being weighed up, and found lacking, so it came as no surprise to her when he said no; reiterated that he had to go home. That he didn't have time for coffee.

"All right," she said. "Well, maybe be seeing you around?"

Lucas strode off.

"Good luck with your art!"

The young woman crossed her arms and watched the young man disappear around a corner, a thoughtful expression on her face.

The sound of urgent, hurried footsteps behind her made her turn.

"Was that Lucas Wainwright?" asked a young man wearing a navy blue suit as he came to a stop beside her and tried to catch his breath.

"Who?"

"Artist fellow. Messy hair. Carrying a bunch of paintings."

The young woman nodded.

"Damn it!"

"What is being the matter?" she asked.

"I told him to meet me here at eleven, but my boss asked me to go to the bank. So I was postponed. And of course the *artiste* refuses to own a phone so I've no way to contact him. You see, I'd promised Lucas to introduce him to Herbert. And that I'd do all the talking because Lucas doesn't exactly have the best people skills."

"No, he is not having the best people skills. The gallery man was shouting, and Lucas was falling over and hurting his hands."

"I saw you help him," he said, smiling. "That was kind of you."

"It is not being a problem at all."

The young man looked at the woman with a curious expression. "I'm sorry, I should've introduced myself." He held out his hand. "I'm Charles Bonham. And you are?"

The woman extended her hand and as she took his hand into her own the sleeve of her shirtdress hitched up her arm to reveal an ornate and futuristic-looking silver bracelet around her wrist.

"Oh my God! I've just now realized! You're one of those Traversers, aren't you?"

The young woman squeezed his hand for a moment longer, then grinned.

"Yes I am," she said, pulling her sleeve back over the bracelet.

"Oh wow! That's amazing! Look," he said, glancing down at his watch and then up at the gallery, "I'd love to buy you a coffee, but old Herbert will be expecting me. Would you mind very much waiting for an hour or so?"

He pointed towards a bistro further down along the road. "You could grab us a table, and as soon as I can I'll join you. Does that sound okay? Please say yes – it would absolutely make my day. No, my year!"

"Very well," she said, laughing. "Yes!"

"Brilliant!" he exclaimed. "Excellent!"

He glanced at the gallery once more, and when he saw his employer standing at the large glass window he said, "Right, I'd better be going."

But as he went up the steps, he turned to the young woman. "Sorry, I forgot to ask your name."

"Zarina," she said.

"Zarina," he repeated, nodding. He thought it a strange name. A queenly name. It was the perfect name for such a beautiful and mysterious young woman.

As soon as Charles was able to get away from his work at the gallery, he hurried over to the bistro and to his great relief found Zarina sitting at a table in the corner, a cappuccino before her.

"I'm so pleased you waited for me," he said, taking a seat. "I thought you might have disappeared off to..." he paused as he noticed a man at a nearby table who was wearing a t-shirt on which was printed *Perpetuis Futuris Temporibus Duraturam* around a circular logo. The man stood and Charles kept his eyes on him as he left his seat and walked to the exit. Charles then finished his sentence. "...another world. Another time."

"I am happy to be being here," she said, smiling at him.

"I've got so much to ask you!"

"And I you!"

"Me? What do you want to know about me?" he asked, surprised. This woman really was rather lovely.

"Well, you are working at the gallery, but you are not being an artist?"

"God no. I don't think I've got a single artistic bone in my body. I studied business at Goldsmiths – which is full of arty types – so when I got my degree it only seemed natural to go into the art industry. I do the accounts for Herbert. Help him manage the business side of the gallery."

"So that is how you are knowing Lucas Wainwright?"

"Yes, sort of. We were both at Goldsmiths. We shared a flat for a while, but he wasn't exactly the ideal tenant."

"You are meaning that he was not paying his rent?"

"That's right. And he turned the kitchen into his art studio, which did *not* go down well with the landlord."

Zarina laughed. "Yes. My sister is being an artist too. She is terribly messy. But she is very–" she turned her eyes to the ceiling, searching for the right word, then looked at Charles again "– focussed. Sure of herself. Your Lucas seems very… unsettled."

Charles sighed. "He is. But I put that down to the missing year of his life."

"A missing year? That is being most interesting to me!"

They were interrupted by a waiter coming to their table and taking their lunch order. Charles, wishing to impress, asked for a bottle of champagne to accompany their meal.

Once the waiter was out of earshot, he said, "After all, it's not every day that one meets a Traverser!"

Zarina, her eyes twinkling, gave him an enigmatic smile. "No, it is *not* every day that you are meeting a Traverser. But, please, do be going on with your story."

Charles would rather have been the one asking questions, but he didn't want to appear rude. "I know it sounds all mysterious, however, in reality, it's tragically dull. Or would that be dully tragic? I digress. Lucas was out sailing in bad weather. He had some sort of accident and got separated from his boat. His girlfriend, Naomi, found the empty boat and put two and two together to make five. Poor girl assumed he was dead, so went and committed suicide. But about ten months later, police discovered a homeless man fitting Lucas's description. Poor old Lucas had no idea who he was and what had happened to him. Doctors looked him over, and found he'd received some sort of blow to his head. Which was what had caused his amnesia. His parents, of course, were overjoyed at his return. Though I doubt Naomi's family were best pleased with the news. Anyway, once he'd been brought up to speed with what he'd missed, Lucas tried to pick up the reins of his life. But, I don't know…" Charles paused for a moment. "He just isn't all there. If you know what I mean?"

Zarina nodded. "I am knowing what you mean."

The waiter arrived with a bottle of Veuve Clicquot and made a big show of popping the cork. All smiles, he poured the champagne saying that he hoped they'd enjoy it before leaving them to their celebrations.

"Well," said Charles, raising his glass, "to what should we toast?" He gave her a huge smile. "The future? Or the present?"

Strangely, Zarina did not pick up her glass.

"Before we make a toast," she began, the expression on her face serious, "I am wanting to ask you something important."

Charles put down his glass, the smile leaving his face.

"How much money is Lucas owing you?"

Charles looked confused. "How do you know he owes me money?"

"It is obvious. He is being unable to sell his paintings and so he is having no money for rent. And yet you are wanting to help him sell his paintings. I think you are doing this because you are a good man. But also because he is owing you money. And because you do not want to have to turn him away from your door when he is having nowhere to go."

Charles exhaled deeply; shrugged his shoulders. "All right, so he does owe me money. A lot. The most annoying thing about the situation is that his parents are absolutely loaded. They could pay his rent no problem. But for some stupid reason he's cut all ties with them."

"What reason?"

"I don't know!" Charles sat back in his chair and crossed his arms. "Anyway," he said irritably, "I wanted to talk about you. About time travel. Not Lucas bloody Wainwright."

Zarina did not reply, and into this silence came the waiter, bringing them a basket of bread rolls; some small, gold-wrapped rectangles of butter.

When he'd gone, Zarina put a bread roll on her plate. Began to pick at its crust.

"All right," she said. "Time for some honesty. The bra-burning feminists won't appreciate me saying this, but here goes." She took a deep breath. "You're an attractive man, and I wanted you to ask me out for lunch."

A smile played about Charles's lips but before he could respond, she added, "But I'm also going to have to massively disappoint you."

"How?"

"I'm not a Traverser. There, I said it. Do you hate me?"

Charles's face fell, and his shoulders slumped. "So the silver bracelet–"

"Is just a bracelet. And the funny way of talking is easy enough to copy if you have your wits about you."

Charles sighed. "Okay. So that *is* disappointing."

"Do you despise me?"

"No," he said, though he still looked crestfallen. "But I don't understand why you wanted to impersonate a Traverser. Was it just to make me look foolish?"

"Of course not!" Zarina insisted. "I needed to check how easy it was to pass for one. And by the way, it's a relief to not have to talk in that stupid way any more. You see, I have a business proposal for you."

"O-kay," he said slowly, trying to wrap his head around the direction in which the conversation was now going. "I'm listening."

"If I had a guaranteed way of making Lucas's paintings

sell for huge amounts, and of giving you a cut of the profit, would you be interested?"

Charles considered this for a moment. "First, there's no such thing as 'guaranteed'. Second, it would depend on the *way* of making them sell for huge amounts."

Zarina, her face animated, said, "But you're open to the idea?"

"Yes," said Charles. "Go on."

"Okay. So think about how excited you were when you thought you'd met a Traverser. You didn't ask me to take you anywhere – or rather, any time – but you were thinking about asking it, weren't you?"

"The thought had crossed my mind."

"That's because we all want to look into the future. To see what the world will look like in fifty, or a hundred, or a thousand years. To maybe discover that something of ourself, as an individual, is remembered. So what if we could tap into Traversermania? Give the public more of what they want. As it is they're desperate enough to buy any old tat – t-shirts, baseball caps, books by so-called "Traverser experts" which have been written by ChatGPT in a matter of minutes. But we could do better than that. We could show them incredible paintings of the future. Of time travel. Of the experience of journeying from one era to another. And Lucas could be the one to create those pictures."

Charles thought for a moment. "Tapping into Traversermania is a good idea. As is targeting the super-rich from within a luxury market. But I can't see Lucas going along with the plan. He only paints what he wants to paint. And what he wants to paint doesn't sell."

Zarina, her face full of mischief, said, "I think I could persuade him."

Charles laughed. "As charming as *I* think you are, Lucas will most likely feel otherwise."

"I don't mean to persuade him in *that* way. I have something very different in mind. You see, I've worked with a fair few magicians and I've picked up some tricks on the way."

Charles did not look impressed. "Stage magic?" He shook his head. "No, that won't work. Nobody falls for tricks like that nowadays."

He went to pick up his glass of champagne, but Zarina put out her hand to stop him.

"Not yet," she said. "First, reach into the right hand pocket of your jacket."

Charles did as she'd said, and when he pulled out a folded square of paper he looked at her with a puzzled expression. "This wasn't here earlier on."

"Open it."

When he did so, he gasped. He was looking at a pencil sketch of himself standing at a bank counter and talking to the middle-aged Indian woman who had served him earlier that day. Most shocking of all was the fact that his pin number had been written at the bottom of the piece of paper.

"How on earth?" he muttered, the hand that was holding the paper trembling. A number of solutions tumbled through his mind. She must've followed him to the bank without him seeing; watched him as he took some cash out of the ATM. But he hadn't taken any money out! And he hadn't noticed her in the bank. Besides, how could she have got from the bank to the gallery before him? Although he'd been at a distance, he'd clearly seen her talking to Lucas.

Charles turned to look at Zarina, a strange expression on his face, for he was both outraged *and* impressed. "Tell me how you did this!"

"Stage magic," she teased. "But nobody falls for tricks like that nowadays, do they?"

Charles looked into Zarina's shining eyes and felt his anger dissipating. "Okay," he said, laughing. "You win." There was now a tone of respect in his voice. "You've convinced me."

Zarina grinned.

"*Now* can we drink our champagne?" he asked.

"Of course," she said, picking up her glass.

"To what should we toast?"

"To art?" she replied.

Charles laughed and then raised his glass. "How about," he said, clinking her glass, "to the art of time travel?"

"Perfect."

*

The plan was simple enough, as Zarina had explained to Charles over lunch. First, she would introduce herself to Lucas, tell him she was from another era, and that, to those living in the future, his paintings were of great importance. Value. But that he needed a little encouragement to begin on his "silver phase". She would be his guide.

Charles had snorted, said it sounded as if her plan had been taken straight from a B-movie.

"A B-movie," she'd said, a disdainful look on her face. "Gee, thanks. Well *I* disagree."

They'd agreed to disagree on the matter.

The second step involved Charles bringing some of Lucas's magically enhanced "artworks of the future" to Herbert and persuading him to display them in the gallery.

"Third step," Zarina had concluded with great certainty, "profit."

Yet when they'd arrived at Lucas's flat that evening, to discover Lucas lying face down on a dirty sofa, an empty bottle of Plymouth gin in his hand, the floor strewn with half-finished canvases, tubes of oil paint and turpentine-soaked rags, even Zarina didn't look as confident as she did before.

"Lucas," said Charles, shaking his shoulder, "come on, wake up! I need to talk to you."

Slowly, Lucas began to stir.

"You know, you really shouldn't leave your front door unlocked," Charles reprimanded him.

Lucas sat up, shrugged. "I don't have anything worth stealing."

"Ah, well you see, that's where you're wrong." Charles pointed to Zarina. "Or so she says."

"And who are you?" said Lucas, putting his hand to his head and trying to massage away the pain.

"My name is Zarina. You were meeting me earlier in the day. When your paintings were flying away."

Lucas stared at her. "That was you?"

For a moment, Zarina looked unsettled. "Yes, that was being me," she said brightly, all uneasiness now gone, "and I am thinking that I like your paintings very much."

Lucas mimicked her speech. "You're liking my paintings very much." He gave a wry laugh. "Who the fuck talks like that?"

"A Traverser," replied Charles.

Lucas looked to his friend. "You mean, one of those supposed time travellers? From the future?" He turned back to Zarina, considered her with more interest.

But then the curiosity was gone. "I don't care about the future." He paused, his voice suddenly full of sadness. "It's only the past that interests me."

"You don't care about the future?" retorted Charles. "But what if she were to say that in the future people can't get enough of your paintings. That they're worth millions. Billions!"

"Are you saying that my paintings," he inclined his head to the canvases stacked up against the walls, "are worth something?"

Zarina nodded. "Though it's the art of your silver phase that is fetching the highest prices."

"My silver phase?"

"The work in the period from this moment onwards. From the moment we are working together."

"I don't work with anyone," Lucas snapped.

Charles sighed. "Oh for goodness sake!"

"I am not trying to help you make your art," explained Zarina, "or getting in your way. I am simply talking to you. Suggesting ways to open yourself to the visions you are holding within you. It is being beneficial to us both."

Lucas fixed his eyes on Zarina's, determined to

discover the truth of her words. Zarina, undaunted by his scrutiny, held his gaze.

"Tell me," he said, sweeping his arm around the room, "which of my paintings calls to you most?"

Zarina knew that the chances of Lucas accepting her as a Traverser weren't great, but this demand of his – *this* was the real test. She took her time looking through the stacked canvases; the piles of pencil and charcoal sketches. Lucas only seemed interested in two subjects: the human figure – specifically, the male figure – and seascapes. The seascapes weren't appealing. They were full of malevolence; of the sea at its most brutal. The sketches and paintings of the male body, however, were full of tenderness. Warmth. On closer inspection, Zarina realized that all the paintings were of the same body. There was only the one portrait, though, so Zarina assumed that the body and head were of the same model. The charcoal grey and bronze-coloured portrait appeared to be of Lucas himself. It seemed to have been painted, scrubbed out, and then repainted many times, giving it a rather abstract, or disorientating, impression – as though Lucas's features had been blurred by movement. Or time. Making him look otherworldly. Melancholy.

The longer she looked at it, the more conscious she was of the tension in the room – of Lucas holding his breath. It was as if he wanted two impossible things: to be seen and *not* seen. She'd got her answer.

"This one," she said, turning to Lucas.

"Why?" he asked.

"Because it's so beautifully tragic. Yet full of love."

Lucas said nothing for a moment. Then: "All right. I'll talk to you. Listen to your prompts, or whatever. But you'll need to buy me more materials. Pay my rent." He turned to look at Charles. "And you'll be wanting to discuss the terms and conditions of the transaction, won't you?"

"Naturally," said Charles.

"Not until I've eaten. And taken some painkillers."

Charles went to the kitchenette, and finding not a single

glass, extracted some dirty paint brushes from a jam jar half-filled with murky water, cleaned it, and filled it with tap water. He passed it to Lucas, then took a packet of paracetamol out of his jacket pocket. "Here you go."

Lucas took the water and tablets without any kind of thanks.

"What do you want to eat?" asked Charles, getting out his phone. "Pizza? Curry? Chinese?"

"Pizza," said Lucas.

As Charles placed the order, Zarina clapped her hands in excitement. "Oh, this is being so wonderful! Truly, this is being the most momentous of occasions!"

Lucas, swallowing down a couple of painkillers, said nothing.

Charles, conscious of just how much money he could lose on this "investment" of his, only managed a lacklustre smile.

*

The following day, Zarina arrived at Lucas's flat with her first "prompt". Since Lucas didn't own a phone, or any kind of technology, she used Charles's phone to show him a YouTube short of Milton the Eternalist inviting a member of the audience onto the stage and into his magic cabinet. The camera action was shaky, the focus blurry, as if someone had only managed to get their phone out for a few seconds, but the film had been viewed over one million times. Lucas watched the video with great interest.

"What is being the most striking thing about this piece of footage?" asked Zarina.

"The box," said Lucas. "It's so bloody ugly. But people go into that box then disappear, don't they?"

Zarina nodded.

"But it's not a trick, is it?"

Zarina shook her head.

"The people who go inside travel to the future, or the past, don't they?"

"Yes."

"To when, exactly?"

Zarina shrugged. "It is different for every person. But you, as an artist, are being fascinated with this box. Of the possibilities it offers those who step into it."

Lost in thought, Lucas's eyes glazed over. Then a moment later he began to pace around his flat, making rulers of his arms, as though he were measuring a magic cabinet that was right here before him.

"A sculpture would take a lot of time," he said. "Cost a lot in materials."

"Charles is willing to invest however much is necessary."

"As long as he gets a good return on his investment?" Lucas said, his voice bitter.

Zarina fixed her eyes on Lucas's. "He will," she said. "I am sure of it."

Lucas didn't reply; he was already busy thinking. Creating in his head.

*

After Lucas had bought all the materials he needed, he began working on his sculpture with great vigour.

Zarina, letting herself into his flat one morning, said, "It is looking very beautiful. And very silver. It is very you."

"It's still Corinthian bronze. But I've played around with the composition of the alloy, so that there's more tin, zinc and silver than copper and gold. Hence its colour."

Zarina, not an expert on Corinthian bronze, changed the subject. "When it's finished, will it be fitting through the door?"

"I'll think about that later on."

Zarina suppressed a sigh. Sometimes, she really hated working with artists. They were so impractical. "You will need to be showing something to Herbert which is much smaller. A painting. Or a film. Of the moon?"

Lucas asked if she could maybe show him one of his paintings from the future.

Zarina shook her head. "I cannot be doing what you are asking of me. But I can show you this."

She got out Charles's phone.

"Another prompt?"

"Yes." She handed him the phone. The image on the screen was of a beautiful oil painting of a still life. A vase of flowers.

Lucas looked at it intently, a kind of fire in his eyes.

"Do you recognize this painting?"

He nodded. "It used to hang on my bedroom wall."

"You are being related to the painter, are you not?"

Another nod. "Joseph Wainwright was my grandfather's great grandfather." Lucas look at Zarina questioningly. "Why are you showing me this?"

Zarina put her fingers to the screen, focussed in on the background: the crescent moon in the twilit sky. "Do you notice anything strange about the surface?"

Lucas frowned. "What am I looking at?"

"The dots of light in the dark part of the moon? Are you seeing them?"

"Yes. And?"

Zarina sighed. Did she really have to spell it out for him? "Is it not being unusual for an artist who is living in the nineteenth century to paint a moon that has buildings upon it? Electric lights?"

Lucas shrugged. "I guess."

They were silent for a moment longer – Lucas considering the painting; Zarina worrying over whether Lucas would take the bait. Would this picture be enough to inspire him to create something that would genuinely impress people? More specifically, would it impress rich art collectors?

Lucas turned away from the screen and went to stand at the window. His eyes were unfocussed, and he appeared to be lost in thought.

After a while, and without looking at her, he said, "I'll need some equipment. An old cathode ray TV, a radio receiver. Some electronic components."

"Of course," said Zarina. "That is being no problem."

More silence.

"Tell me, Zarina," he said, briefly turning his head in her direction, "what's in this for you?"

Zarina walked towards him, so that they could see each other's reflections in the window. "As I was saying already, your art is very popular in the future. I will be benefitting from this financially. But, also, to us Traversers, your art represents–"

"You're not a Traverser."

Zarina said nothing for a moment. She had to tread with caution; she couldn't be too insistent, yet, she also had to offer him some kind of proof.

"Tonight, I will be coming around to your flat with Charles, so he can be seeing your progress. Then we will be going out for dinner. But the moment I leave your flat, you will encounter another version of me. I will make sure to travel in time to see you while I am also with Charles."

"Whatever."

"This is not convincing you?"

Lucas turned away from the window, put on a pair of safety glasses and then picked up a soldering iron.

"I don't care if you visit me tonight or not. But I've got work to do, so if you don't mind–"

"Of course," said Zarina. "It is being very important that I do not interrupt you." She went to the door. "I will be seeing you later tonight."

She received no reply.

That evening, when Zarina and Charles turned up at Lucas's flat, Lucas was still engrossed in the making of his sculpture. Zarina gushed about how beautiful it was, but Charles wasn't too impressed. "How are you going to transport the bloody thing?"

Lucas shrugged. "I'll figure that out, okay?"

"Just as long as I'm not the one carting it about."

"You won't be."

Charles scanned the room. "Have you done anything else?"

"No, I've been concentrating on this. Once it's finished, things will happen a lot faster."

"You must be understanding, Charles," said Zarina, "Lucas is having many ideas, and that is the important thing."

Charles sighed, muttered something inaudible. More loudly, he said, "Zarina said you wanted some electronic equipment."

"Yes," replied Lucas.

"What for?"

"You'll see."

Charles put his fingers to his forehead and smoothed them across his brow in an attempt to ease his irritation.

"Right," said Charles, letting his hand fall, "so we'd better leave you to it, hadn't we?"

Lucas nodded.

"I will be waving to you from the street," said Zarina to Lucas. "Will you wave back?"

"If you want."

"Come on, Zarina," said Charles. "We don't want to be late for the restaurant."

When they'd left, Lucas went to the window and watched them as they exited the front door of the house, walked down the few steps to the pavement and then crossed the cobbled road. Just before they disappeared out of view, Zarina turned and waved at him, and he acknowledged her by raising his hand.

"So are you believing me now?" asked a soft, female voice from behind him.

Lucas turned to look at the red-headed young woman before him. The woman who looked almost identical to Zarina.

"Is this what you call proof?"

"What are you calling it?"

Lucas put his hand to Zarina's cheek, caressed her soft skin with his long fingers. "You have a distinct pattern of freckles across your face. Like a scattering of stars. But your twin's freckles are slightly different. One of the clusters of freckles on her forehead resembles the constellation Ursa Major. The Great Bear."

Zarina swallowed hard. As Lucas took his fingers from her cheeks, her pale face became flushed with blood.

"Don't worry," he reassured her. "The deception doesn't bother me. I like you. And I like the prompts you're giving me."

Zarina (or, rather, Zara) didn't know what to say.

"Do you know who the Great Bear was supposed to be?" Lucas asked.

Zara shook her head.

"A beautiful woman called Callisto who was a follower of the goddess Artemis. Zeus fell in love with her but his wife, Hera, became jealous of the lovers. She turned Callisto into a bear. To keep her from being killed by hunters Zeus sent her flying into the heavens. Immortalized her in the stars."

"And your point is?"

Lucas snorted. "There is no point. But Hera was a jealous bitch. And meeting you and your twin, studying your faces, has reminded me of a young woman I once knew who was also a jealous bitch."

Zara exhaled deeply. "I was worried this might happen. We knew it was a possibility since artists aren't as easily fooled by the kind of magic used on stage. They know how to properly look at something. To ignore what their brain thinks they're seeing, and actually see what's in front of them."

As Zara finished speaking, Lucas's face clouded and his eyes defocussed. Zara sensed his emotional turmoil, and as he went to one of the stacks of canvases and picked up the portrait which Zarina had previously been so taken with she saw him put his hand to the ghostly face on the canvas, run his hand down the features so that his fingertips were sheened with bronze-coloured pigment. His eyes filled with tears.

He then dropped the canvas and went to the window, his back to Zara, his arms crossed tight against his chest.

Zara bent to pick up the canvas and really, properly,

looked at it. Stupidly, when she'd considered the painting the other day, she'd seen only what she'd expected to see. Now, the realization came to her that this wasn't a self-portrait. It was a portrait of a young man who looked like Lucas, but who *wasn't* Lucas. The differences in their features were small, but now she'd noticed the differences she couldn't unsee them. Clearly, this wasn't Lucas. But he was a man whom Lucas had cared for very much.

Zara carefully leant the canvas against the wall. She stood a little distance from Lucas, conscious of not wanting to intrude on his grief, and said quietly, "It's not you in the portrait, is it?"

Lucas shook his head.

"You loved him, didn't you?"

"Yes," he whispered.

"What happened to him?"

Lucas wiped the tears from his eyes so that the skin around them were smudged with bronze. "That's the thing. I can't remember." He started to hit his head with his fist. "My stupid brain won't remember."

"Hey!" said Zara, grabbing hold of his hand to stop him from doing any real damage to himself. "This won't help."

Lucas sniffed, turned his face away from hers. "I know." He put his clenched hand to his chest. "But it hurts so bad."

Zara put her arm around him; lay her head against his shoulder. "It's okay to cry. Crying can help."

Lucas said nothing, but from the way his body was shaking, she knew he was letting go of long-suppressed tears.

When he'd grown calmer, Zara asked him if he wanted her to leave.

Surprisingly, he said no. "Stay a bit longer. Give me another prompt."

"Okay," said Zara, lifting her head so she could look at his face. "I don't have anything visual for you. But I do have a suggestion. First, close your eyes."

Lucas obeyed.

"I want you to think about time travel. The experience of traversing across great swathes of time. What does it feel like? What does it look like? Is it incredibly intense? Gone in the blink of an eye? Or slow and dreamy? An infinite kind of falling?"

Lucas said nothing, but she could see that beneath his eyelids his eyes were moving rapidly.

"Can you feel it? Can you see it?"

Lucas nodded, his eyes still closed.

"Good. Now capture it in paint."

Rina (short for Catriona), who was sitting opposite Charles in the restaurant, heard the sudden vibration of her phone in her handbag. She pulled it out, thinking to turn it off, but when she saw she'd received a message from her sister she unlocked her phone and read the message.

"What is it?" asked Charles.

Rina sighed, dropped the phone into her bag. "Lucas knows."

"Knows what?"

"That I'm not a Traverser. That Zarina is actually two people."

"Shit!"

"But according to Zara he isn't bothered. She left him busy painting. Ablaze with inspiration."

"So he's onboard with our little venture?"

"Looks like it. But Zara says his memory's really messed up."

"I could've told you that. In fact, I already did."

Rina picked up her glass of red wine, took a sip. "What do you know about Lucas's love life?"

With a shrug, Charles said, "Not much. I mean, when we lived together, he occasionally brought someone home with him. From some club or other. But these men weren't exactly what you'd call *significant others*."

"There was never anyone special?"

Charles shook his head. "I mean, there was Naomi, though I never met her. I only really got to know Lucas after his accident."

"So you don't know much about his life before the accident?"

"No. I only met him once or twice before it happened. In some dingy bedsit clouded with marijuana smoke. That was back in the days when I was part of a band. When we had dreams of recording our own album. Making it big. Our lead singer knew Lucas. Wanted him to make the art for our album cover."

"And?"

"And what?"

"Did he do the artwork for you?"

Charles laughed. "No. We didn't even get as far as recording any songs. We were all talk and no action."

"What instrument did you play?"

"The bass. Still do, as a matter of fact. In spare moments."

"That's when you're not busy with some madcap scheme for making money?" she said, a wry smile on her lips.

"It helps that the brains behind the scheme is incredibly beautiful."

Rina waved off his compliment. "Zara's the brains behind the scheme. I'm just her willing accomplice. The one best at playing a part. Luring men into our trap."

"So is that all I am?" asked Charles, feigning an expression of hurt. "One of your poor, bewitched victims?"

"I wouldn't exactly call you poor, or a victim."

"Ah, but I am bewitched, Rina," he said, gazing into her eyes. "And happily so." Charles felt he had to qualify what he'd just now said. "I mean, as long as you don't mind me being bewitched?"

Rina smiled; gave his hand a squeeze. "No, I don't mind. I don't mind one bit." After a moment, Rina sighed. "The thing is, it's easy enough to bewitch someone. To make sparks fly. Light a fire. But to keep the fire going… *that* takes real skill.

"You know, our parents have been happily married for thirty years now. I'm in awe of how they've made their marriage work. Nobody I know has made a relationship last more than six months."

"Communication," said Charles. "That's the secret. Or so my parents say. They've been together for decades as well, and they've always said that honesty and a willingness to be open and communicative has been key to their relationship."

"Honesty and openness…" mused Rina. "I suppose that's a bit of a struggle for me considering my profession. Still, I'd be willing to give it a go."

"You would?"

"Yes. So, first off, let me say this: I don't like the name Rina. It was always Zara's name for me as a child and it stuck. I'd much rather be 'Catriona' or 'Cat'."

"Cat," said Charles, nodding. "I like it. It's very you."

Cat rewarded him with a huge smile, made a purring sound and then laughed playfully.

*

After Zara's last prompt, Lucas made incredibly fast progress. So by the time Charles next came around to see how Lucas was getting on, he was genuinely shocked (and impressed) by his friend's output.

"These are incredible!" he said, considering one of the large canvases covered in swirls of black and silver paint. After a moment he stumbled backwards, dropped into the sofa. "God that's made me feel dizzy!"

"Well, that was the effect I was going for," explained Lucas.

"But this is way beyond some optical illusion. Did you help him with this?" asked Lucas of Zara, who was also surveying the paintings. "Add some trickery of your own to it?"

She shrugged, glanced at Lucas with a strange expression. "That's for me to know and you to find out."

"All right," said Charles. "I don't really want to know

how the trick works. No doubt it'll be some ridiculously mundane thing."

He pointed to an old-fashioned TV on the floor. It only had two dials on it, and most of its casing was missing so that one could look into its metallic inner workings. "What's that about?"

Zara bent to turn on the skeleton TV and after a second or two a black and white image came into focus. It appeared to be of Lucas's sculpture – or, rather, Milton the Eternalist's magic cabinet – on a rocky, grey terrain. There was nothing in the sky but a strikingly large moon. The shadow the sun had cast on the box was moving fairly quickly, as though the film had been sped up.

"What's this meant to be? Is it art?"

"It's nearing the end. Just watch."

Slowly, the box began to disintegrate. Vanish. And with it, the fast-moving shadow.

Charles shook his head. "I don't get it," he said. "I mean it's got a sort of *La Jetée* vibe to it. But it's not really eye-catching, or mind-boggling, in the way the paintings are. Anyone with a phone and some film editing software could make something like that."

"Could they?" asked Zara.

"Sure," said Charles.

"But people who have a knowledge of astrophysics might be interested in it."

"Why?"

"Because if you were to measure the speed at which the cabinet's shadow moves you'll notice that it travels faster than today's shadows."

"And what does that mean?"

"That in the film the Earth's spin is much faster than it is today. That a day would've been significantly less than the twenty-four hours we have right now."

Charles looked perplexed – he was obviously trying to think through all this information.

"The Earth used to have a much faster rotation than it does today. Because of how close the Moon used to be. But that was billions of years ago."

"Oh," said Charles, understanding dawning on him. "So this is, like, a historical drama? A mock biopic of the Moon?"

Zara sighed. "Yes, if you like. But scientists and true fans of anything and everything to do with Traversers will consider it to be of great value."

"Why?"

"Because of the physics and limits of time travel." Zara shrugged. "Anyway, you'll just have to trust me on this one."

"Don't worry, I trust you. And what about this?" asked Charles, standing and going to a painting that, on first sight, appeared to simply be a rectangular landscape of pale grey flecked with silver. Yet the longer Charles looked at the painting, the more interesting it became.

"What do you see?" asked Zara.

"Fog," answered Charles, waving his hand in front of his face. "I can actually feel the mist coming out of the picture."

"What else?"

"There are sounds too. The lapping of waves on a beach. A distant bell. There's even the smell of the sea. The taste of salt on my lips. Now I see a boat. And there's a woman on it. She's waving to me."

"And?"

Charles started, put his hands to his eyes and rubbed them. "It's all gone now. It's back to how it was before. Just grey paint." He turned to Zara. "Where's it gone?"

Zara smiled. "Good isn't it?"

"It's bloody brilliant! But where did the woman go? I want to see more!"

Zara shrugged. "That's the idea. To leave you wanting."

"Tell me where she went!"

"Come away from the painting," said Zara, trying to coax Charles away.

"No! Not until you tell me what happens!"

Lucas came and guided Charles away from the painting, and when Charles was at some distance, he sighed deeply and then started to laugh. "That really is some painting!"

"I know," said Lucas.

"People are going to fight over it."

"But it'll go to the highest bidder," said Zara.

"Okay then," said Charles. "Looks like we're all set. I'll take the grey painting, the TV and one of the time travel canvases to Herbert tomorrow morning. He won't be pleased to learn that Lucas is the creator, but as long as he sees the art first, then nothing else will matter. Agreed?"

Lucas and Zara looked at each other, and then at Charles. "Agreed," they said in unison.

*

Charles's plan worked exactly as he'd hoped it would; the only fly in the ointment being that whenever Herbert was in the vicinity of the grey painting he repeatedly asked Charles if he could buy it right then and there. He would pay anything for it. Anything. In the end, Charles had to throw his jacket over the damned thing. Once Herbert came to his senses he, too, agreed that perhaps it would be best to display the painting from behind a pair of curtains. That way, they could break the viewer's attention by closing the curtains when and if they became too absorbed in it.

Herbert, hugely excited about the prospect of displaying the art, even delayed the big name artist whose work was due to appear in the gallery the following week. This couldn't wait, Herbert said. The public (and by this, he meant his richest buyers) needed to see Lucas's art as soon as possible.

*

It took a few days for Lucas's Traverser-inspired art to make the front page of the newspapers, but Zarina's little stunt with the cabinet helped generate a huge amount of publicity. (At the end of the first night of the show, and in the guise of Charles's wilful girlfriend, she ignored the 'do not touch' signs and stepped into the sculpture of the box only to disappear and reappear outside the art gallery. The select few attending the show were convinced she'd not only teleported but travelled through time. Their claims seemed to be confirmed by the leaked CCTV footage showing Zarina being both outside and inside the gallery at the same moment. The video went viral, which massively boosted foot traffic to the gallery.)

There was much speculation about Lucas – had he experienced time travel or was he, in fact, a Traverser? Journalists dredged up all they knew about the Wainwright family and wrote articles about his "missing year", his amnesia and the tragic death of his girlfriend, who had to be the young woman in the grey painting: the painting entitled 'Lost in the Mists of Time *or* Virgin Memory'.

Experts in astrophysics wanted access to the "historical film" in order to examine it – and Traverser super-fans argued about whether or not it was possible to travel so far back in the past, before the advent of Corinthian bronze, though the disintegration of the magic cabinet appeared to fit with their current theories.

Paintings sold for huge amounts of money. Charles was delighted with the outcome, though Zara and Cat, and Lucas for that matter, seemed nonplussed. In fact, Lucas hated the attention and did all he could to avoid it. He holed himself up in his flat; began to drink heavily again.

So it was rather unlucky that on the one day he went to the gallery to speak to Herbert about the sale of his sculpture of the magic cabinet (Lucas had suddenly decided not to part with it) he was accosted by a woman who claimed to know him.

"I'm sorry," he said, startled by the sheer amount of fury she was radiating, "I don't think we've met before." He looked to Herbert for help, but all he did was shrug. Look confused.

"Oh, you know me all right," she spat. "And don't think I don't know who you really are."

"What do you mean?"

"Don't act all innocent with me. We both know you're not the real Lucas Wainwright."

"What?!"

The woman shoved a polaroid photo into his hand. It was of three smiling people – a beautiful young woman standing between two young men who, superficially, looked alike. "You broke my daughter's heart. Drove her to take her own life."

Lucas said nothing. His eyes were on the photo, his mind racing.

"And if you think you can cash in on your mysterious disappearance, on my Naomi's death, with all this strange art – 'the woman in the fog' – then you've got another think coming."

"Now wait a minute–" interjected Herbert.

The woman whipped her head around so she could address Herbert. "And you should be ashamed of yourself!" she retorted. "Making money out of my daughter's death."

"Well, look here–" said Herbert.

At that moment, Zara, wearing oversized sunglasses and a scarf around her head, came into the gallery. "What's going on?" she asked, standing beside Lucas. She looked at the polaroid in his hand and then froze.

"Are you one of his friends?" asked the woman of Zara. "Well, here's a piece of advice. Stay away from this man. He'll only bring you misfortune."

Herbert, suddenly recovering himself, decided to take charge of the situation. "Madam, I think it's high time you left," he said, his voice dripping with disdain.

The woman snatched back the polaroid. "Don't worry, I'm going. But you'll be hearing from me again. Or, rather, my lawyers."

Once she'd left, Herbert sighed with relief. Then began to laugh. "Lawyers! How ridiculous can you get? As soon as rumours start circulating about an artist's work it drives up the price. Really, I should be thanking her."

Lucas finally spoke. "I need to go home."

Zara, sensing his distress, offered to go with him.

"No. I need to be alone."

"Okay," she replied. "But I'll come round later on. Make sure you've got something to eat."

Lucas simply walked out of the gallery.

Herbert shook his head. "Artists!"

"I know," said Zara. "They're all crazy." But as soon as Herbert had gone to his office to make them a cup of coffee, Zara took her phone out of her large leather handbag and texted her sister.

> *Keep an eye on Lucas*

she wrote.

> *Something weird just happened at the gallery.*

> *Okay,*

replied Cat.

> *Charles and I have just finished lunch so I'll go to his flat as soon as we're done.*

> *Keep a low profile*

wrote Zara.

> *Always.*

Thirty minutes later, Zara got another text from Cat.

> *Lucas wasn't at his flat, but I saw him heading in the direction of King's Cross. I think he's catching a train to Norfolk. Maybe going to his family home? It's near Wells-next-the-Sea, right? What should I do?*

> *Follow him*

Zara replied.

> I have a bad feeling about this.

> Me too

wrote Zara.

> I'll get Charles to drive me there.

> Okay. Just don't get too friendly with Charles.

> I won't. He really isn't my type. Far too young for me.

> And too nice. Anyway, better go now. I'll see if I can get on the same train.

Zara did not get too friendly with Charles. In fact, they seemed to be mutually wary of each other. Prone to a polite sort of coldness. They drove most of the way without talking to each other, preferring instead to simply listen to classical music, though Zara would occasionally update Charles with news about the progress of Cat's journey (she'd just missed catching Lucas's train).

Yet as they approached Norfolk, Charles asked Zara if she could tell him anything more. "I mean, what the hell is going on? Why would Lucas suddenly decide to up and leave just because of some crazy woman?"

Zara furrowed her brow. "I don't know for sure, but I think Lucas believes he'll discover the truth of his accident if he returns to where it happened."

"But why go over the past? I mean, for the first time in his life he's selling his work. He's got money *and* admirers. What more could he want?"

Zara rolled her eyes. "There are more important things than money and admirers, Charles. Or is that all you care about?"

"Of course not, I'm just–"

"Is that all my sister means to you?"

"Absolutely not! I happen to be in love with Cat and if

she'll–" Charles ran a shaky hand through his hair. Laughed. "Shit! Well, there you go. I've finally confessed my feelings. Are you happy now?"

Zara smiled. "Yes, I'm happy. I'm happy for you both."

They were silent for a moment, but there was no longer any tension between them.

"Do you see my point?" Zara continued. "Art isn't about money and admirers. It sounds corny, I know, but it's a sifting of the soul. For truth, be it ugly or beautiful. And Lucas needs to discover the truth."

"But does it matter how he got hit on the head?"

"Yes. Maybe no. But he needs to find out who he truly was before the accident."

"I imagine he was exactly who he was before the accident. A spoilt, rich kid."

Zara thought for a moment. "I don't think so."

"So who was he then?"

"I'm not sure, but when I meet his parents, see his home, I'll know."

When they arrived at Lucas's family home – which was a decaying, though still grand, country house – they were met at the door by Lucas's father. A smartly dressed, elderly gentleman, it only took him a moment to recognize Charles.

"Ah, Mr Bonham," said Lucas's father, extending his hand. "Long time no see."

The two men shook hands and after they'd exchanged a few pleasantries, Mr Wainwright turned his attention to Zara. "And you must be Charles's lady friend?"

Zara laughed without any embarrassment though Charles winced, looked uncomfortable.

"Not quite," she said. "I'm his fiancée's sister. Zara." She shook Mr Wainwright's hand.

"Well, if your sister is anything like you, then Charles is a very lucky man."

Zara smiled mischievously. "She looks like me, but we

have very different temperaments." She turned to Charles. "Don't we?"

Charles, reeling from Zara's announcement that he was engaged to Cat, said nothing for a moment. He wondered if this was part of Zara's plan to get Lucas's father onside, or whether Zara was just being exasperating. Or maybe prompting him to action.

"Yes," he said, eventually. "You're very different in character."

"Well, come in!" said Mr Wainwright, ushering them into the large, marble-floored hall and closing the door behind them. "You must be tired from your journey. Let me get the kettle on and–"

"Please don't go to any trouble, Mr Wainwright," interjected Charles. "We just wanted to see Lucas. To make sure he's okay. He left London in a bit of a cloud."

"Lucas?" said Mr Wainwright, a hard-to-read expression on his face. "Yes, well. He's all right. Arrived not long before you did. But he went straight out to the boathouse."

"Maybe we should go and see him?" suggested Charles.

"He'll be halfway to the Wash by now," replied Mr Wainwright. "But he'll be back soon enough. In the meantime, you can chat to Connie. She loves having visitors. Here," he said, "give me your things. I'll put them in the cloakroom."

The old man took their coats and Zara's voluminous leather handbag and placed them in the cloakroom off the hall.

"Thank you," said Zara, looking about the hall and up the stairs. "You know, Mr Wainwright, you have a beautiful house."

"Well, it's not what it used to be, but I try and do my best with its upkeep. And, please, do call me George."

Zara smiled, nodded politely, then both Zara and Charles followed George to a spacious, sunlit lounge in which a white-haired older woman was sitting watching TV.

"Connie, dear," announced George, turning the volume down on the TV, "you've got some visitors. They're Lucas's friends. Charles and Zara. Charles stayed with us once a while ago, though you probably won't remember."

Connie turned her gaze from the television to Zara and Charles. Looked blankly at them.

"They've come all the way from London. Isn't that nice?"

Connie smiled vaguely. "London," was all that she said.

"That's right," replied her husband. "And London's a long way away."

"The Queen lives in London," said Connie.

"Yes," said George, without correcting her. He indicated to their guests that they should sit on the large sofa beside Connie's armchair. "Now, Connie, dear, I'm just going to make us all a nice pot of tea, so you just stay put and talk to Zara and Charles, all right? I'll be back in a few minutes."

Connie nodded, said, "Pot of tea."

"Unless you'd prefer coffee?" asked George of his guests.

Charles and Zara shook their heads, keen to be as little trouble as possible. Connie was obviously not well.

As soon as Mr Wainwright had left, Connie's attention returned to the TV which was showing a film set in the Edwardian era. Charles asked her how she was doing, made a comment about the unseasonably warm spring weather, but she didn't reply.

Zara, seeing two things of interest – a silver-framed photograph on the mantelpiece and a Joseph Wainwright painting above it – stood and went to the fireplace and looked at the photograph, which was of a much younger Connie holding a boy. Lucas. They were looking at each other and smiling, enjoying some private joke. Clearly, they adored each other.

She turned her gaze to the still life painting and grimaced. It was one of Wainwright's earlier works and although beautifully rendered, she couldn't help thinking it a strange choice for the lounge given that, presumably,

Connie spent a lot of time there. It was a *memento mori* of a kind – for although the still life was of a vase of glorious blooms, beside it was a brace of dead birds, some rotting fruit. In the distance was the sea. The meaning of the painting was obvious: we all succumb to decay. She turned to look at Connie, who was still transfixed by the screen – a young handsome man talking to an equally youthful and attractive young woman. He took a golden pocket watch out of his jacket.

"Have you come for the painting?" asked Connie, still looking at the TV screen.

Zara, startled by Connie's unexpected question, took a moment to reply. "I've come to see Lucas." She glanced at the still life above the fireplace. "But this is a very fine painting."

Connie shook her head, then dragged her eyes away from the screen and towards Zara. "Not that painting," she said. "The strange painting. The one that's all muddled up. Just like me."

"The strange painting?" asked Zara, pretending she didn't know what Connie was talking about.

"*He* wanted it too."

"*He?*"

"Leo," said Connie. "I wish he'd just taken it and left." Connie shrugged. "You can have it if you like."

Zara, astonished, didn't know what to say. Thankfully, at that moment, Mr Wainwright returned with a tray of tea things.

"Here we go," he said, setting down the tray on the coffee table.

As he began to pour the tea, Zara asked if she could use the bathroom.

"Of course," he replied. "There's a poky little water closet off the hallway, but there's a far more spacious bathroom upstairs. It has a lovely view of the sea."

"Thank you," said Zara, leaving the room and immediately making her way upstairs. She found the bathroom, but didn't go inside. Instead, she ventured further along the landing and opened the nearest door, hoping to find Lucas's bedroom. This room was neat but sparsely furnished – clearly just a guest room. But the next room along had to be Lucas's for there was a stack of sketchbooks on the desk and a large map of the Wash on the wall detailing the many sandbanks and channels that made up the rectangular bay. On a sandbank called Pandora Sand somebody had drawn an X in black biro. Zara smiled to herself. How obvious could you get!

She flicked through some of the sketchbooks. They mostly contained watercolours of the sea or boats, or pen and ink drawings of London architecture. But there were also many pencil sketches of a beautiful young woman – the woman in the polaroid, Naomi. Zara, being an artist herself, could see how these pictures differed to the ones currently in Herbert's gallery, though to the casual observer they would look as though they'd be done by the same hand. Towards the end of one of the sketchbooks, tucked away in a paper pocket glued to the back cover were some folded sheets of paper. They contained sketches of a nude man. The man she knew as Lucas.

Closing the sketchbook, Zara turned to the bed, and there on the wall above the headboard was what Connie had called 'the strange painting': Wainwright's painting of a vase containing blooms of all seasons; an odd-looking crescent moon; a silver bracelet on the table beside the vase. She gazed at the painting for some time. Made a decision.

When Zara returned to the lounge, Charles and George were drinking tea and discussing Lucas's work. The TV was still on, but Connie's eyelids were drooping. George poured some tea for Zara and they chatted for a while about the art world; how the days of making money from beauty were long gone.

The buzzing of Charles's phone intruded on their conversation, and when Charles saw he'd received a message from Cat he apologized; promised he wouldn't be more than a moment.

After reading the message he said, "Cat's train is due to arrive at King's Lynn soon, and she's wondering if I could pick her up. I'm sorry, Mr Wainwright, but you'll have to excuse me."

"No need to apologize. You do what you need to do."

"Do you want to come with me?" Charles asked of Zara.

Zara shook her head. "I don't want to miss Lucas." She turned to Mr Wainwright. "You wouldn't mind me going out to the boathouse would you? I want to speak to him as soon as he returns."

He glanced at his wife who was now asleep. "Of course not." He pointed to one of the large windows. "It's across the lawn and through the pines and a bit along the scrubland. You can't miss it."

"Thank you," said Zara, and both she and Charles took their leave of the elderly gentleman.

Zara didn't have to wait long before she saw Lucas's boat on the horizon. When he brought the boat into moor, he didn't greet her warmly – he merely asked her what the hell she was doing here.

"I could ask the same of you."

As Lucas finished securing the boat, Zara spotted a rusty metallic box on the deck of the boat.

"So you found your treasure?" she asked, nodding at the box.

"I don't know what you're talking about," he said, leaving the boathouse and striding in the direction of the house.

Zara hurried after him, though this was difficult given the high heels she was wearing. "Of course you do. X marks the spot. So tell me, what's in the box?"

Lucas stopped and whirled round to face Zara. "I'll tell you what's in the box. My memories."

"Can I have a look?"

"No," he said. Once again, he strode off.

"It doesn't matter if you show me or not," Zara went on, jogging to keep up with him. "I know what's in it."

"You think you're so clever, don't you?"

"A suit," said Zara. "A suit made of a fabric that will allow you to travel through time."

Lucas said nothing, but he walked even faster, and Zara, out of breath, had to pause for a moment. She watched him return to the house while she considered her options. Should she go after him? Stop him? For the first time in a long time, she realized she was no longer in control. Her carefully laid plans were unravelling.

Zara was let back in by Mr Wainwright who was holding a wet china cup in one hand and a tea towel in the other.

"I take it you found Lucas?" he asked.

"He was a bit surprised to see me."

"Yes, well." He indicated to the closed door of the lounge. "He's in with Connie now. Wanted to have a little chat with her. In private." George twisted the tea towel around the damp cup. "Why don't we go to the kitchen? Just while we wait for him to come out?"

Zara looked to the lounge door. Wondered how long Lucas would be.

She smiled at George, nodded, and then followed him into the large, traditional kitchen.

"How about a drink?" he asked.

"Oh, I'm fine," she said, "I'm not that big a tea drinker."

"Actually, I was thinking of offering you something stronger." He went to a cupboard and took out two round-globed glasses, a bottle of gin. "I know I could do with a stiff drink. How about you?"

"Please," said Zara, without hesitating. She needed to be more relaxed.

George poured out the gin, added some tonic water, cubes of ice and half-moons of lemon.

"Here you go," he said, offering her the glass.

Zara accepted the gin and tonic and thanked him.

George took a large sip of his G&T. "It's me that should thank you."

"What for?"

"For bringing things to a head."

Zara considered acting the innocent, but then thought better of it. "I only got the ball rolling. It was Naomi's mother who prompted Lucas to return. Though, let's be frank, Mr Wainwright, that's not his real name, is it?"

George sighed. "No. No it isn't."

"It's Leo, isn't it?"

"Yes."

"Your real son, Lucas, is dead, isn't he?"

George's eyes became wet with tears. "Yes." He sniffed and then brushed away a tear which had rolled down his cheek.

"I'm sorry, I really am." Zara paused for a moment before asking, "Do you know what happened?"

George shook his head. "I can't be sure. It might have been an accident, but I think not. Now that Leo's memory has returned, he'll know. But I doubt he'll be telling me anytime soon. I'm not exactly in his good books."

"Because you've been pretending he's your son for these, what, last two years?"

"I had to do it!" he snapped. In a gentler voice he added, "For Connie's sake."

They were silent for a moment.

"I'm not judging you, Mr Wainwright. I'm really not." Zara thought back to her earlier conversation with Connie. "It's just… surely Connie knows? She must have moments when she remembers?"

George shook his head. "Her memory was already bad when Lucas brought Leo back from London for the summer holidays. Of course we were struck by their resemblance, but Leo was so very different. The way he spoke. Dressed. His bearing. His ridiculously long hair."

George sighed. "If I'd known then what was to come of their friendship, I'd have sent the bugger packing. I mean, I had my suspicions. I didn't like the way he seemed overly interested in our paintings. He asked too many questions about our notable ancestor, the great JW. Showed a particular liking for the painting in Lucas's bedroom." George laughed, but there was only bitterness in his voice. "That bloody painting! I can still remember my parents arguing over the damned thing when they started divorce proceedings. Of course, at the time I wasn't to know that they weren't really arguing about the painting but about my father's affair, still... I sometimes think we should just burn the bloody thing."

Zara said nothing, and with an expressionless face took a sip of gin and tonic.

"But Lucas and Leo were inseparable. And together with Lucas's long-term girlfriend, Naomi, they were a tight-knit trio. They spent much of that summer out on the Wash. Picnicking and playing cricket on the sandbanks, as and when the tides allowed. They practically lived on Lucas's or Naomi's boat, or in the boathouse. They seemed happy. Who was I to interfere? But just before Lucas was due to return to London, to university, I sensed a rift occurring. Naomi seemed particularly fretful. Tense. I wanted to speak to Lucas about it, but that was when we got Connie's diagnosis of Alzheimer's and, quite frankly, I didn't have the energy – or the balls – to say anything. And then Leo took off, and I thought that maybe everything would be all right again."

Once again, tears were at George's eyes.

"Then came the dreadful day when Lucas's boat never came back. The weather had been awful that September day. It felt oppressive, and there was a mist that didn't clear until the early hours of the next morning. The Wash is treacherous enough on a good day, but on a foggy day..." He shook his head. "Still, I held on to the fact that Lucas was the best of sailors. After all, he'd been sailing since he was a boy. He'd find his way home."

George took a moment to compose himself.

"I think he would've been fine if it was just him out there, but I don't think he was alone. I think Leo was with him. And I think that Naomi was there too. She could've sailed out to him. I have a feeling that Naomi finally understood what was going on between Lucas and Leo, and got angry. In her anger she maybe..." George sighed. "Oh, I don't know. But whatever happened out there tore her apart. Drove her to suicide. I just wish she'd said something. Anything. Because having to wake up each day wondering whether my son was dead or alive was the most painful thing in the world. So when, out of the blue, a man resembling Lucas Wainwright was discovered living rough, I had to relieve Connie of that pain. I confirmed to the police that he was our son. And, best of all, he thought he was our son too, because his memory was shot to pieces. So, do you see?" George insisted. "I only wanted to make my wife's last years as happy as possible. Wouldn't you have done the same?"

Zara, moved by George's confession, gave him a sad smile. "Yes, George. I would've done the same."

George nodded, attempted a smile.

The sound of the lounge door opening and closing startled them; made them look towards the hall. Zara went out to the hall to see Leo opening the front door. "Wait!" she cried. "Where are you going?"

Leo stopped and turned to look at her. "I'm going home now. I've been here too long."

"What did you say to Connie?" asked George.

"I didn't say anything to upset her. I just told her that wherever he is, her son loves her very much. And I know you won't believe me George, but I really am sorry for everything that happened. In my own way, I'm going to try to put things right."

George, confused, said, "Put things right? What on earth are you talking about?"

"I'm sorry, I can't explain," he said, his voice full of emotion. "But maybe one day you'll understand."

Then Leo was off again, striding down the rhododendron-lined gravelled driveway.

Zara ran after him, but her heels made the going difficult.

"Stop!" she cried. "Slow down!"

"Don't follow me," said Leo, without turning his head. "You can't go where I'm going."

"At least tell me your plan!"

"I'm sorry, I can't."

Leo hurried around the curve of the driveway and Zara

lost sight of him. When she rounded the bend, she expected to see him at the large wrought iron gates, but he wasn't there, and the gates hadn't been opened. He must've ducked into the thicket of ancient rhododendrons, some of which were as tall as trees. But she couldn't find him. She wondered if, maybe, he'd returned to the boathouse, so she went back along the driveway, crossed the lawn at the side of the house, through the pines and out across the scrub. The boat was still moored, and he wasn't in any of the rooms within the boathouse.

Zara scanned the scrubby, sandy coastline, the currently calm waters of the North Sea disappearing into the horizon, and although it was near twilight, she was sure she couldn't see him anywhere. It was as though he'd vanished into thin air. Remembering the metal box from earlier, she went to the boat, and as the box wasn't locked, she opened it. But there was nothing within. Zara stayed in the boathouse for a little longer, trying to puzzle out what had happened to Leo. She had some ideas, yes, but nothing concrete. Slowly, she made her way back to the house.

Though Mr Wainwright was clearly surprised, and a little unsettled, to discover that Zara and Cat were identical twins, he graciously offered them the use of his guest bedrooms. Said they'd all be welcome to stay the night. But Zara and Charles, aware of Connie's additional needs, didn't want to impose. Instead, they drove to a nearby hotel. Treated themselves to a gourmet dinner and champagne and sumptuously furnished rooms in one of Norfolk's finest hotels to celebrate the fact that Charles had actually gone and proposed to Cat, and she'd said yes.

Strangely, Zara was uncharacteristically quiet, and though Charles peppered her with questions about Lucas – about what he'd said to her, where he'd gone – she barely responded. Simply said he was fine. That he was going home.

It was only on the following morning, after they'd got into Charles's BMW and were once again on the road to London, that Zara began to speak of Lucas (or, rather, Leo). Charles's phone had buzzed, but since he was driving, Cat, who was sitting beside him, read the message he'd received from Herbert.

"He says, 'Is this some sort of joke? Because if it is, it's not funny.'"

"What the hell is he talking about?" asked Charles.

"Hang on," she said. "There's a video too."

Zara, sitting on the back seat, leant forward so she could watch the video. It was grainy, black-and-white footage. Obviously from CCTV. And it was of the empty gallery. Night time, by the dim quality of the light. The time and date stamp showed it to have been close to midnight from the day before. There was no movement, and then a young man walked into the frame. His face couldn't be seen since his back was turned to the camera, but, clearly, it was Leo. He stepped into the sculpture of the magic cabinet and then the whole thing vanished.

Zara burst out laughing. "Well, he sure knows how to make a grand exit."

"What d'you mean?" asked Charles.

"Don't you get it?" said Zara, as though Charles was the stupidest man on Earth. "He's gone back home. Traversed to the future." She laughed again. "I hoped that was where he was going, but I couldn't be sure."

Charles looked to Cat. "Is she mad? What is she babbling on about?"

"You know why Zara wanted Lucas for her plan?" said Cat. "Because he was a good artist, skint, *and* mentally unstable. The perfect person to go along with her crazy scheme – to convince others that, somehow, he'd experienced time travel. How could either of us have known that he actually was a Traverser?"

"A Traverser? Absolutely not!" Charles paused, searching for reasons they had to be wrong. "But he doesn't speak like a Traverser."

"He used to," said Zara. "George told me that when he

first met him he had a strange way of speaking. And back then, he was called Leo."

"So are you saying that the Lucas Wainwright I know isn't actually Lucas Wainwright? He's a Traverser called Leo, who happens to look a lot like the real Lucas Wainwright?"

"Yes," said Zara.

"And how long have you both known this for?"

"I've had my suspicions for a while," said Zara. "But it was only yesterday, when we went to his home, that I became sure. Mr Wainwright admitted that he knew the police hadn't found Lucas – that it was Leo – but he went along with it because of Connie."

Charles let out a long, deep breath. "Oh God. So the real Lucas drowned and this Leo, suffering from amnesia, took his place. What a tragedy."

The phone buzzed again.

"It's Herbert," said Cat. "He wants to know where we are and if we've got Lucas with us. Oh, and he says that if making the sculpture disappear is a promotional stunt that's all well and good, but he'd like it back asap. He has a buyer for it."

Zara laughed. "Yeah, well, that's not going to happen."

"I can't say that!" said Cat.

"Just tell him we're on our way," said Charles. "That we'll explain everything when we get back."

Cat looked at her sister.

Zara shrugged. "That's good enough for the time being. Herbert will just have to accept what's happened. He'll be pissed off by the loss of the sale of the sculpture, but once the public knows about Leo's disappearance, he'll make good money on any of the remaining artworks."

"Okay," said Cat, replying to the message and then turning the phone off.

"But why did Leo make contact with Lucas in the first place?" asked Charles. "It doesn't make any sense."

"Ah," said Zara, putting her hand into her large handbag and pulling out what Connie had called 'the strange painting'. "I believe he wanted this."

Charles glanced back at what Zara was holding and then swore. "For fuck's sake, Zara! What on earth have you done? That belongs to the Wainwrights!"

Zara shook her head. "No it doesn't. It belongs to the nation. Besides, neither of them care for it. Too many bad memories."

Charles looked at the rear view mirror, saw the way Zara was admiring the painting. He exhaled deeply, then nodded to himself. "This was why you chose Lucas, wasn't it? So you could get hold of that painting. Sell it for a small fortune."

Zara's eyes stayed on the painting for a moment longer before she shoved it back into her bag and then turned towards Charles. "All right, yes. That was my ultimate goal."

"And you were in on it too?" asked Charles of Cat.

"But as soon as I knew how I felt about you, I told her we should forget about the painting."

Charles looked at Cat, wanting, but not quite being able, to believe her.

"It's true," said Zara. "She never wanted it as much as I did."

For a good long stretch of the motorway, they were all silent. Charles, his face set and his shoulders rigid with tension, kept his eyes on the road; an *I'm-so-angry-with-you-both* aura radiating from him. Yet as they approached London, he became less tense and Cat and Zara sensed that, maybe, they were forgiven.

"So will we ever see Lucas or, rather, Leo again?" asked Charles. "I mean, will he ever come back?"

"I don't know," said Zara, looking out of the car window, at the rain drops which had started to spatter against the glass, making a mist of the sky. "It depends."

"Depends on what?"

Zara was silent for a moment, and then she turned to look at her sister. "Rina–"

"Don't call me Rina," Cat snapped. "I'm done with that name, just like I'm done with all your clever plans."

"All right, I'm sorry, it's just, I never asked you before,

but what did you see in the 'Lost in the Mists of Time' painting?"

"Why?"

Zara took hold of her sister's hand. "Just remember for me, please? Let's both of us remember."

"It was just a jumble of images and emotions. Nothing one hundred percent clear."

"Please Sis."

Cat closed her eyes, inhaled and exhaled deeply; became very still. "I see fog rolling over a body of water. A small island of sand."

"Yes," said Zara, closing her eyes. "I saw that too. But what else did you see?"

"Two men – Lucas and Leo – on the island. There's a hole in the sand, a shovel and a pile of sand beside it, and a metallic box at the edge of the hole."

"What's Lucas wearing?" asked Zara, her voice low, almost a whisper.

"A strange looking suit made of a bronze-coloured material."

"And how do you feel?"

"Angry."

"Why?"

"Because of the way they look at each other. I finally know what they're feeling. And how Lucas feels about me."

"What does he feel?"

A sob caught in Cat's throat. "He feels nothing for me! He doesn't love me anymore!"

"What are you going to do?" asked Zara.

"This is all Leo's fault!" cried Cat. "I hate him! I hate him for ruining my life!"

"What are you going to do?" repeated Zara.

"I'm going to kill him!"

"How? How are you going to do it?"

"I don't know! I don't know! Wait! The shovel."

"And?"

Cat said nothing.

"And?"

Cat let out a deep sigh, opened her eyes. After she'd

taken some time to compose herself she said, "Sorry, there's nothing more."

Zara opened her eyes too; let go of her sister. After a moment she smiled.

"What?" asked Cat. "Why are you smiling?"

"I haven't got the full picture, but I've got more of it than I had before."

"And?" asked Cat.

"You know," said Charles, "anyone watching the both of you would think you're utterly mad."

"Not mad," said Zara. "But highly sensitive."

"But I didn't see any of that in the painting," retorted Charles. "I saw the mist and the water, yes, but nothing else of what you described."

"That's why the other name of the painting is 'Virgin Memory'," explained Zara. "Because no one knows exactly what happened between the woman on the boat and Lucas and Leo. It's a complete mystery. But everyone seems to see something different."

"So why were you smiling?" asked Charles.

"Because Cat saw Lucas wearing a time travel suit. Which means that just maybe he didn't drown. It's a possibility."

"Are you saying that the real Lucas Wainwright may still be alive?"

"Maybe. I don't know for sure. But I think Leo is going to go in search of him."

"Bloody hell," said Charles, his grip on the steering wheel tightening. "This is a lot to take in."

"I know."

"So when will we know?"

Zara shrugged. "I have no idea. We'll just have to wait and see."

The three of them were silent for a while, their thoughts reaching out into the future – the likelihood of Lucas truly being reunited with his parents.

Rain continued to fall on the speeding car.

Stuck in a traffic jam in Camden Town, all the cars ahead
of them stationary, the wipers doing their best to fend off
the heavy rain, Zara suddenly grabbed her bag and coat
and opened the passenger door.

"What are you doing?!" cried Charles.

"I'll be back in a few minutes," said Zara, hopping out
of the car and shielding her head with her coat so she
wouldn't get soaked. She slammed the door then hurried
along the rain-drenched pavement and turned left into a
side street, disappearing from view.

Charles sighed, exasperated. "What am I supposed to
do?" he asked, as the cars ahead of them began to move.
"I can't just wait here!"

"Keep going," said Cat. "She'll catch us up."

Charles edged the car forward. "D'you know what
she's up to?"

"I think so. But she'll tell us when she gets back."

The cars, nose to tail, slowly progressed and both
Charles and Cat kept a lookout for Zara. They passed a
long line of sodden people queuing to get into a crammed
bookshop and Charles wondered what would entice all
these people to stand and wait in the rain for so long. And
then he saw the poster in the window:

> Professor Hector Tovar Book Signing.
> Come meet the famous Traverser
> expert and have all your time travel
> questions answered!

Charles snorted. *Traversers!* he thought. He'd had it up to
here with Traversers!

As they approached a set of traffic lights, the change
from amber to red bringing all the cars to a halt again,
they saw Zara in the rear view mirror running along the
pavement to catch up with them. She opened the rear
passenger door and nipped back in.

"Well?" asked Charles, seeing a look pass between the
sisters, as though they were communicating
telepathically.

"Well what?" asked Zara, as though she had no idea what Charles was talking about.

"What did you do?"

"The lights have turned green," said Zara. "Try and get through if you can."

Charles accelerated the car and managed to get across the junction.

"Will someone please tell me what's going on?" he demanded.

"I gave the painting away," said Zara. "To a charity shop. The old dears working there loved it. Well, they particularly liked the gilt frame. As I left I heard one of them say she fancied having it herself. Said it would brighten up her loo."

"What?!" said Charles, his cheeks turning crimson. "You donated it to an Oxfam?"

"Why not?" said Zara. "It was never really about the money. It was about acquiring the painting. Seeing it and holding it in my hands. Recognizing it for what it is – one of the earliest, and finest, examples of the art of time travel."

Charles, utterly dazed, didn't know what to say. Running on autopilot, he drove the car through the busy streets of North London and towards Fitzrovia. After a while, he found his voice. "You know, Zara, you are one of the craziest women I've ever met."

"She *is* crazy," said Cat. "But she's got a good heart."

"Hmm."

"She did help us get together," persisted Cat.

"I suppose."

Cat squeezed Charles's hand and he turned to look at her. Smiled.

Cat suddenly burst out laughing. "Downstairs loo." She shook her head. "Crazy!"

The three of them laughed, briefly discussed what might happen to the painting.

*

But that, my friend, is a story for another time.

Two Black Boxes

R. James Doyle and Rogelio Fojo

Frontispiece by Alejandro Burdisio

"This is your captain. We're having a flight-control problem, folks. We're working on it. Everyone to your seats, and check seat belts."

Barely controlled background panic.

"LAX, Trinity eight-four-six. We're at twenty-one-five, descending rapidly. We have a possible cargo hold fire and a non-responsive rear stabilizer. Unable to maintain altitude."

"Roger, Trinity eight-four-six. We're diverting you to BUR, repeat divert to Hollywood Burbank airport from present position. Set new trajectory..."

"But our aircraft is too long for the run–"

A loud bang.

*   *   *

It was Tuesday, a night indelibly etched into my memory, marked by the personal loss of a dear friend.

After meticulously dissecting the black box recording, I started piecing together the puzzle pieces inside my head. In the background, the hair-raising sound of surging high-speed winds, coupled with the growing rumble of a troubled jet engine – belonging to Trinity Airlines Flight 846.

My initial audio analysis suggests that, while clearing the San Gabriel mountains, turbulence severely buffeted the aircraft, likely sending bags hurtling from overhead bins, tossing any unseated passengers around or against the ceiling...

What about my unfortunate flight attendant friend?

The aircraft descended rapidly, spiraling out of control. The pilot's tone grew more desperate: "Trinity eight-four-six. Losing pitch and yaw control."

I envisioned the carpet of city lights emerging through the unusual, stormy clouds as the captain fired desperate commands to his co-pilot.

"Trim is broken. Kick rudder. Right rudder!"

"We're going down, Captain."

"Push! Blue side up!"

The sounds conjured up vivid images of the plane

hurtling towards the ground. I pictured the glare of city lights, streets and freeways rapidly approaching in a whirling blur.

"Mayday. Mayday."

I concentrated on the chaos in the background. Passengers in the rear of the plane were screaming and pleading for help, their cries loud enough for the box to capture their echoes. And then, all sounds abruptly ceased.

In my mind, the sprawling, careening cityscape turned into a final, freeze-frame shot.

I turned off the desk lamp and fell onto the sofa, distraught. I imagined the howling wind generated by the plummeting plane subsiding into a gently whistling breeze, enveloping my office and lulling me to sleep. Hours later I woke with a jolt and finished transcribing these records.

*   *   *

I recognize this case has become personal. I'll ask Murphy to independently generate a transcription too, as well as process the technical data from the box. More work overall, but we have to get it right, as professionals. She'll step up.

But I needed to hear the voices.

Goodbye, Linda.

Now, the most dreaded moment had arrived. The press conference to officially announce these tragic findings to the world.

"Sorry, what was your question?"

"You said it all happened on Tuesday," the female reporter repeated. "Are you sure?"

"Hell, yes, I'm sure!"

*   *   *

Randall Conklin surveyed the grim scene. To the untrained eye, it would be simply overwhelming:

Deformed, scorched, and twisted sheets of metal. Gouged furrows in the terrain, raked straight through soil, rocks, tarmac and concrete. A pall of smoke over everything, with windows of visibility opening intermittently on slowly dying flames. Reek of spent jet fuel. Stench of charred human flesh. The presence of first responders in hazmat suits, moving among the biological mess and technological chaos. Long arcs of powerful water streams playing out from the fire trucks, attempting to dampen what they could, including the ugliness of it all.

To his trained eye, there was worse to see. An indeterminate number of bodies reduced mostly to scattered and blackened bones. Other body parts in various degrees of integrity, all rudely ripped and rearranged. Blood everywhere, darkened, unmistakable.

To his analytical eye, the professional work started of its own accord. The length and shape of the debris field and the nature of the furrows constrained that most fundamental question: Equipment failure, pilot error, or something worse?

He wondered if this was the one. His NTSB field investigator colleagues talked about "the case" – representing some kind of limit, after which it would have to be a desk job, or another line of work entirely. Sometimes the breaking point was the task at hand going beyond horrific. Sometimes it was simply the long-term accumulation of scenes that no one could ever be truly prepared for.

Conklin saw Murphy directing her small team, working a cordoned-off section of the field. He made his way over.

"Found the Box?" he asked.

"Yes, Randy. I should be able to deliver the voice recorder to you within the hour. I'll take the lead on the telemetry recorder."

"Sounds good, thanks. You're the best, Liz."

"No problem, boss."

Recovering the flight voice and data recorders took away much of the guesswork of an investigation. They almost always were recovered now. He wasn't clear why he still felt such foreboding.

* * *

Conklin drove to the crash site in the morning. He looked down at the passenger seat foot area and saw the black box voice recorder sitting where Murphy had stashed it the day before, true to her word. He should have secured it or cracked it open by now, but he had not been up to the task yesterday, or overnight.

The scene was visibly improved the next day. The smoke was gone, and much of the debris had been cleared. No body parts were discernible. The long furrows looked like they had been radically filled in – which made no sense. There was a trail of intermittent divots. At its end stood a largely intact aircraft.

Before he could chew on these inexplicable developments, he saw Murphy approaching. He spoke through the passenger window. "That's pretty weird, Liz. The divots back of the long runway speak to how the pilot came in way short, but then managed a quick series of touch-and-goes before finally settling in."

Liz looked over her shoulder. "Yup, not your picture-perfect landing, but I wouldn't go so far as to say weird. So boss, do you want the good news, or the bad news?"

"Um, the good news."

"Injuries aplenty, some traumatic, but no loss of life."

Conklin was struck speechless.

Murphy looked at him quizzically. "The bad news is that there's been an escape."

"An escape?"

"Apparently a prisoner was being escorted by marshal. The officer got banged up but you can talk to him. The prisoner broke out of his restraints and is gone."

Conklin swallowed a couple of times.

"You okay, Randy?"

"Um, sure, just need a second cup of coffee." He reached into his breast pocket, withdrawing a sour candy dispenser. He tilted it back, shaking one onto his tongue. *Clementine.*

"Got it. And no problem getting the Box. We'll have the recorders soon," said Liz, surveying the scene. "Not sure what they need to tell us, though."

Conklin stole a glance down. The black box from yesterday was still sitting in the passenger seat well. With his eyes on Murphy's retreating back, and without knowing exactly why, he took his agency-issue jacket from the seat and draped it lightly over the device.

He called Murphy back over. She wheeled about in a wide arc, then arrived dutifully.

"Liz, what day is it?"

"It's Tuesday, boss."

Yesterday was Tuesday. Conklin swallowed.

Murphy waited. Conklin felt she was working to keep her face impassive. "So it is... thanks," he said. Again, he watched her walk away, shaking her head, almost imperceptibly.

He knew now that this was the case. What he didn't know was how or if he was going to get through it.

*　　　*　　　*

Picking his moment, Conklin transferred the box from the passenger seat well to the trunk of his vehicle. In a smooth motion, he closed the trunk lid, withdrew his jacket, and heard the latch close cleanly – no bounce, no inordinate slam. Continuing the motion, he slipped the jacket over his shoulders and shrugged it on. Looking around, he saw lowering clouds and felt a chill in the air. The temperature must have dropped ten degrees since he left home.

He needed a sour to suck on.

Conklin moved back to the passenger door and reached in to retrieve the dispenser he had left in the center column. He emerged from the vehicle and popped one. *Mango.* The shock of quick flavor, the hardness of the candy, the echoes in his mouth as he scraped it over his teeth – all were reassuring.

He took in the long view of the scene. Other than initially missing the runway, this was hardly an incident at all, as these things go.

The plane had come to rest safely on the concrete. The emergency team had set up a triage station where the aircraft had taxied successfully to the tarmac. He could see the plane was coated with fire retardant as a precaution. A small crowd of passengers huddled. Some were in conversation with responders. Some held cups of a warm fluid, steam rising. A few appeared disoriented but no one was evincing panic or shock. He saw one person in the crowd staring at him.

Murphy. What the hell does she want?

He knew the answer. As the official-in-charge, it was his duty to reach out to the local airport and municipal authorities, and schedule the discovery debriefing, given that the situation was stabilized.

Fuck that, I'm not ready. I need to review what happened. During that other today.

*   *   *

It was one of those times when Conklin had to keep telling himself that it was a good thing to be able to feel the horror. The day when he succeeded in becoming one-hundred-percent clinical, when it never crossed his mind that the dead came from families whose loved ones were just beginning to suffer – that was the day when he had lost something essential and might not get it back.

All senses were assaulted. With so much blood around, it was like drowning in a nosebleed which never quit. The sharp iron smell kept renewing.

The passenger manifest listed 168 on the Airbus A320. Plus six crew. Who knew how many were children? All now dead.

The recorded tower communications revealed the core of the crisis, if not its cause. A fire erupted at the rear of the plane, reaching the cargo hold. A pang swept through Conklin, thinking of Linda's calico cat Francesca, traveling in her airline-approved pet crate. The friendly creature with the soft gray, tan and white fur might have been the first victim. The captain had reported the incident based on sensor indicators and verified that fire suppression countermeasures had been engaged. She had also reported the loss of some control surfaces. All consistent with ground witness accounts. Smartphone-based videos published in the media had shown flames gutting from the right lower rear of the fuselage, possibly compromising tail steering and stabilizing mechanisms.

There had been no opportunity for a measured approach, a partially controlled landing, with time taken to deploy equipment and resources. The pilot needed to ditch, and fast.

One video had gone viral, showing the doom of the aircraft. As the plane came in, it made an almost stately roll to the left, dropping the wing down. The scale of a jet accident, well beyond normal experience, comes without reference points for the pace of unfolding evens. Most viewers assumed they were watching a slow-motion rendition, but the feed indicated the video was playing in real-time. An aircraft takes a ridiculously long time to complete a crash.

The tipped wing struck the ground first. It crumpled and twisted and sheared, letting out a rending screech that smartphones had picked up over a great distance. The engine on the wing detached on impact and flew forward, a massive projectile, bouncing, spinning crazily, spewing sparks and flames, and effectively removing itself from the main crash scene. The body of the plane might have been expected to cartwheel, at least once, but the dynamics were such that the fuselage dug in, excavating the principal furrow. The remaining wing, with engine gyrating badly, somehow held on for the ride. A debris trail developed. Flames took hold in several locations. Smoke appeared, turning darker and angrier. A rocking explosion never came. Echoes faded, and the sirens and strobes of emergency vehicles converged.

Conklin had to calm his breathing, just replaying the

images in his head. He focused on the serene counterpart scene in front of him.

Why had there been an onboard fire? Or had there been?

*   *   *

The sanity-compromising work of recovering body parts, bagging, and cataloging them, and attempting to reconcile an accurate person count – this went on for hours. Conklin tracked the pulse of his team and sensed it was time to call the first brainstorming session. Not that they were anywhere near done collecting forensic data, biological and physical. But the crew needed a psychological break. Needed to get away from the death for a while and start working toward answers. Timing was important. If dialogue engaged prematurely and the team only spun wheels and sniped at each other – this would set them back further. Much of this job, especially timing, came straight from the gut.

Their mobile trailer included a well-equipped conference room, permanently set up in the rig. The lighting could be better. Conklin popped a sour. *Blackberry.*

"All right people, what could cause a fire in the back of an A320?"

"Lithium-ion batteries."

"Those have gotten so much scrutiny it seems a long shot now."

"Still, can't dismiss the possibility."

"An electrical short."

"Any history with this aircraft?"

"Not that I've heard."

"How we doing recovering structure in that area? Will there be anything to work with?"

"Not much..."

"An incendiary device."

"Little chance getting one of those past security."

"Unless it's something new."

"What if it was triggered onboard?"

"DHS must have finished processing the passenger list by now. Any concerns?"

"There was a marshal with prisoner. Don't see that every day. Otherwise, all came back clean..."

And so on. The team had kicked around several ideas but no clearly favored hypothesis emerged. Nonetheless, the session was having the desired effect of giving them back a measure of control.

After a lot of back and forth, they knew they were going to need to tap the flight telemetry recorder. Modern black boxes have prodigious data capacity, and modern aircraft come equipped with a profusion of sensors. In principle, one could ask any question about an incident and have confidence that data would be available to help resolve that question.

Questions such as:

Did the fire cause a tail mechanism failure mode consistent with a strong roll to the left?

Did the fire follow an expected pattern of spread, given structure, materials in the hold, and cargo manifest?

Did the pilot follow established procedures?

And many more. Always too many.

*   *   *

Standing by his vehicle, Conklin saw Murphy approaching, cradling the flight voice recorder. Not a scratch on the fluorescent orange paint job. She actually had a jaunt in her step. *What does she have to be happy about?*

The mango sour had burned down to such a deep well of tartness along his jawline that flicking his tongue there made it worse before it got better.

"Where do you want it?" asked Murphy.

Conklin opened the passenger door. "Down in front of the seat." He shook out a new sour, popped it, spat it out with extreme prejudice. "I fucking hate guava."

"Don't blame you." Murphy straightened from having

placed the box. "Randy, there's something else you're not gonna like."

"What's that?"

"The marshal I told you about. Name's Arp. Turns out he's quite the asshole."

"Really? I'm in a good mood to deal with an asshole." He slammed the car door, with only slightly less prejudice. "Lead the way."

*   *   *

The NTSB mobile rig included a small number of compartments which could serve as field offices, or interview rooms. The marshal was cooling his heels in one of these.

When Conklin arrived, he saw the man in question being ministered to by one of the field nurses. The guy was pretty banged up. A bandage wrapped around his head. The nurse was putting the finishing touches on some sutures on the left forearm, which was heavily bruised, especially around the wrist. In his right hand, the marshal was hefting a metallic ring, like a handcuff, but it didn't look right, more like a doughnut or one of those pieces from a Tower of Hanoi set. There was no second cuff, a circumstance which might fit a fugitive, but there was no trace of links dangling, no ratcheting mechanism, and the metal was… strange, iridescent.

He abruptly thought of Linda. *Her nutty ideas... what does she call them? Tensers?*

"That should do it, honey."

"I be thanking you for nothing, nurse," said the marshal. "All these years, being in harm's way, and now and here you be leaving me a scar."

The nurse's face darkened. She put on an icy smile. "Give it here. I can do that up much better."

The marshal lifted and flexed his forearm, letting out a grunt. Arp returned to an impromptu snack from the sour candy dispenser left on the table, which he was relishing, to the point of lip smacking and facial contortions.

Conklin frowned and popped another sour. *Cucumber.* He turned to the nurse. "What's the word?"

"Besides the arm injury, the patient likely has a concussion, but refuses treatment. He was found wandering about the crash scene. Uncooperative I'm told, even a bit nasty, until he found that bauble. If you ask me–"

"Thank you, nurse."

Conklin studied the man. Beyond being an asshole, something was distinctly off about him. The marshal was not wearing any kind of uniform, nor the button-down clothes of a fed. Instead, he had on a kind of form-fitting jumpsuit, not exactly flattering. Despite the damage to the man's arm, his rolled-back left sleeve showed no visible damage or fraying. Metallic glints ran through the material. Arp sported a five o'clock shadow. Conklin looked for a bulge, which should have been plain enough, but could see none. Nonetheless, his instincts told him the guy was packing. He did not possess the polish of an academy graduate. Nonetheless, he appeared competent, probably dangerous, and…

"Sonofabitch. You're a bounty hunter," declared Conklin.

The nurse looked over her shoulder and beat a hasty retreat.

An eerie intensity emanated from the man. "Not being quite right, but you are not all being, as you be saying… dumb shits."

"Listen, asshole. There's the question of jurisdiction, not to say legality. In case you hadn't noticed, this is *my* investigation."

The bounty hunter shrugged.

"What did your prisoner do?" asked Conklin, hard-eyed.

For the first time, Arp seemed to consider his words.

"He be stealing energy."

"Gimme a break! What's that going to pay? You're not making any sense."

Arp rolled his eyes. "I be taking back about the no dumb shits."

Conklin bristled.

Arp opened his hands, palms up. One still held the metallic ring. "Be thinking now, any... how you be saying – weird shit be happening?"

That brought Conklin up cold. "What do you mean?"

The marshal stared back. *Could the asshole possibly know something about the two black boxes?* "You tell me what you mean."

Stony silence. Conklin moved to the door, leaned partly through without removing his eyes from Arp. "Murphy, get in here!"

"What do you need, boss?"

"Arrest the asshole – carefully."

Murphy advanced, reaching back to remove a set of standard handcuffs from a belt loop.

Arp regarded her intently, while she cuffed him.

Conklin drew his service revolver and leveled it.

The bounty hunter clutched the metallic ring in his hand, deforming it slightly. A dazzling light erupted.

Conklin staggered, blinded. He stepped on something hard, nearly stumbling. Blinking hard, he glimpsed the tightly locked handcuffs under his foot, discarded.

*　　　*　　　*

Murphy sat at her desk, listening closely to the cockpit recording.

"This is your captain. We're having a flight-control problem, folks. We're working on it. Everyone to your seats, and check seat belts."

"LAX, Trinity eight-four-six. We're at twenty-one-five, descending rapidly. We have a possible cargo hold fire and a non-responsive rear stabilizer. Working to maintain altitude."

"Trinity eight-four-six. Recovering pitch and yaw control."

"Ladies and gentlemen, this is your captain. I'm happy to report the weather is improving. We are anticipating an emergency landing at LAX. Please double-check your seat belts and assume safe landing posture. We have clear skies forward. It's going to be a short stretch from here to LAX."

"Trinity eight-four-six is down. Repeat, Trinity eight-four-six has landed."

An avalanche of cheers and applause burst from the cabin, captured distantly on the recording.

*   *   *

Conklin sat in his car. He glanced down at the passenger seat well, seeing the box with the orange paint job intact. He forced himself to breathe. The smells were clarifying. He really didn't need to look up and see the devastation.

He leaned forward and passed his thumb over a corner of the box. Several digits were visible there.

Slowly, creakily, he emerged and walked to the back of the car. He popped the trunk. The lid rose up. The other box was there, the scorched one.

Conklin reached to the same corner of the device and used his thumb, working at rubbing it clean. Not all digits on the tag became readable, but the ones which did matched perfectly.

He slammed the lid back down. He shook out a sour. *Cherry.*

Now what?

*   *   *

He called Murphy on the intercom feature of their agency-issued smartphones. "Get your ass over here."

"Boss, I need a couple."

"Stat."

"Okay, I'll be right there."

Conklin watched Murphy approach, not liking the cadence of her walk. He opened the passenger door and stood there impatiently. When she arrived, he gestured with his chin into the foot well. "What do you see there?"

Murphy spoke before really looking. "That's the Box – wait a minute."

The box in question was in nearly pristine condition.

Conklin studied his subordinate. He walked to the trunk, popped it, and held the lid. "Now come over here. What do you see?"

Murphy walked over and looked in. She went wide-eyed.

"No, that's the Box I brought you... What's it doing in the trunk?"

"I put it there. Don't worry about that."

"Did you cross-check the serial numbers?"

"I did, and they match. What I can read." He paused, firmly gaining eye contact with her. "The next question I'm going to ask you is fucking important, and I want you to think carefully before answering."

Murphy showed signs of becoming distinctly weirded out. "Okay, boss."

"Do you remember bringing me the Box that's sitting inside the car?"

She took her time with the question. Her eyes flashed, with a kind of recognition, her hand instinctively covering her mouth. Conklin started to relax. "Shit, Randy."

The cherry was long gone. Conklin shook out another. *Passion fruit.*

"That's a 'yes'?"

Murphy looked over at the field. The team had returned to the trying physical and emotional tasks of working the crash scene, after their session to get at some initial answers. She blinked. Again. "I was waiting for you to call the discovery debriefing, thinking we might be out of here in a day." Murphy shook her head and turned her back to the crash scene. She started trembling, unnaturally, almost as if from hidden glee.

Conklin reached out and grabbed his colleague, stilling her shaking.

"That's a 'yes,' Liz?"

She disengaged, her eyes shifted and narrowed. "No. I don't know. Randy, none of this is making sense."

Conklin sighed. He stood awkwardly. "Would you like... ?"

"I would love one."

He shook the dispenser. "What did you get?"

"Guava."

Conklin made a face.

"I know," she said. "But I like guava just fine."

*   *   *

They moved the box still coated with orange paint into the trunk. It sat there, side-by-side with the scorched box. The one which actually looked black.

Conklin and Murphy sat in the front seats, feeling cold. Windows cracked, engine running.

"This is fucked up," said Conklin.

"No question."

"Shouldn't we be able to figure out what's really going on by opening the Boxes?"

"It may not be that simple," Liz said.

"What do you mean?"

Murphy turned to look directly at Conklin. "Ever heard of–"

Conklin cut her off. "Please, not the quantum physics shit." He pulled the sour dispenser from his breast pocket, shook it. The lack of rattle had him tossing it into the back seat. He reached over to the glove compartment, paused. "Excuse me."

Murphy turned her knees toward the passenger door.

Conklin finished the motion, pulled the latch, and removed a new dispenser from the jumbled stash inside. He needed a bulk supply, given his tendency to forget them everywhere. He whipped off the plastic seal and popped one. *Apricot.* He offered another to Murphy.

"I'm good."

Conklin settled back. "I always knew you were a smart ass. Me, I'm just a dumb ass – not a dumb shit, mind you."

He continued. "On the one hand, we have a major crash, approaching two hundred dead. On the other, we have injuries, no loss of life, an asshole, and an unknown fugitive capable of... we have no idea."

Liz replied with a note of impatience. "There's not enough information. And some serious unknowns."

"The whole thing seems to turn on the asshole and his prisoner," said Conklin. "We don't know anything about them." He considered. "Let's find out if Arp is among the dead…" He peered through the window, past Murphy. "… in this incident."

Murphy was already on the intercom. "Pratt, do you have the passenger list handy?"

"Yes, ma'am, gimme one second… Yup, I have it."

"Is there a passenger Arp on the list?"

"Let's see. Arp, Arp, the damned thing is not alphabetic, gimme another sec… there sure is, ma'am. William Arp. Hmm, that's interesting. The guy shows as having law enforcement credentials."

"Thanks, Pratt. That's useful information. One more. Does Arp show as traveling alone, or within a party?"

"They do have the parties grouped. Yes, there was one other in the party…"

Conklin's body tried to move to the edge of his seat.

"…name of Halliday. Shall I spell that? It's not like the day off, exactly."

Conklin made a slashing motion across his throat.

"No need, Pratt. We're good. Actually, text me the passenger manifest. We'll let you know if we need anything else."

"Copy." The intercom squawked off.

*　　*　　*

Murphy furiously thumbed her smartphone.

"We have the name of Arp's prisoner," said Conklin.

She ignored him, deep in some line of inquiry. Conklin waited.

Eventually Murphy looked up. "Does the name Linda Bradley mean anything to you?" she asked.

WTF. Conklin took his time replying. "I knew she was on the flight, Liz. Apparently, she replaced a sick crew member, in Dublin."

"I appreciate this is hard for you, Randy. But are you able to be objective on this case?"

"Geez, Liz. You're going to check my work. I want you to." Conklin searched Murphy's face. *No empathy. Instead the bullshit double standard.* "We're not having this conversation."

Murphy held up her smartphone. "Your friend was deep into Traversermania."

Conklin waved the device away. "I know what her site says." He took a couple of breaths, working to bury his growing anger. *Wait.* "Arp might have been saying that Halliday escaped by tapping energy."

Murphy considered. "You mean like a lithium-ion battery. I thought the team ruled that out. Are you saying now that's what caused the accident?"

"We can find out if their seat locations are consistent with the origin and spread of the fire."

"Randy, just listen to yourself. I mention Traversers, and you go off..."

"C'mon, Liz. This case is way out there, and you know it."

Murphy shook her head. "Traversers... traveling by plane. Seriously?"

Conklin set his jaw. "Hear me out, Liz. Imagine Halliday releasing 'energy', and the result is catastrophic, starting a fire and bringing the plane down. But in another scenario, he gets it right, frees himself, survives the minor crash, and escapes."

He held Murphy's eyes. He still didn't like what he saw there. *Time to move forward.* "There are two Black Boxes. We need to open one or the other. And force the issue." He embraced his decisiveness. "Sorry, Liz."

"Sorry for what?"

"It's my call. I can't ask you to take on that level of responsibility. Life and death, and who knows what else."

"Randy, I can handle it." She was bristling.

"Liz, I'm the one in charge, and that's that." She clearly had more to say, but he cranked the door handle, swiveled and spilled out. He made his way to the back of the car.

Murphy joined him there, moving stiffly.

He held the fob. "You know, Liz, whichever way this goes, our memories may not all make it through."

He felt her gaze boring into the side of his face. Conklin stared straight ahead. He pressed the fob. The latch clicked and released.

The two black boxes were there.

A thunderbolt reverberated, and it started to rain.

He shook out a sour, offered it to Murphy. Unexpectedly, she took it. He shook again, popped. "What did you get, Liz?"

"Green apple."

"Very nice."

"And you, Randy?"

"Dragonfruit."

"How do you even know what that tastes like?"

"It tastes like shit."

The rain came down harder. The remaining fires were probably nearly out by now.

Conklin reached into the trunk.

*   *   *

A knock at the door.

Conklin woke up blearily from a fitful sleep. Another knock. He went to the door and opened it. Murphy stood there. Conklin gazed at her warily. She wore a smart business suit, and she looked fresh and awake. He waved her in.

"Hi Randy, quite a day, huh?"

"Not a reason for you to come in so early."

"I was trying to get in ahead of the press," she said. "But they're already crowded at the main entrance."

"Yeah, like vultures, they always arrive early. I figured it wasn't worth going home."

"Well, I better go out and talk to them. Ready to join me?"

"Of course."

"Well, sir, here's the full transcript from the Box."

"Including the ancillary data?"

"Of course."

"Okay, thanks. You saved me a trip to your desk." Conklin glanced at the first and last page. "What's this?" He dug in his pocket.

"Something wrong?" asked Murphy.

"Is this a joke?" Conklin popped a sour. *Coconut.*

Murphy drew herself up. "It's a faithful copy of the recording in the Black Box."

Conklin glanced at the scorched device on his desk, cables leading from its ports and connecting to his desk computer. "Yeah, but… which one?"

"With all due respect, sir... You clearly have a COI regarding this case. You're the chief investigator, but I need to step in here. I'll go on point for the session with the press. We can't have you talking about a case you're confused about. I listened to the voice recording–"

"I listened too!" Conklin interrupted, pointing emphatically toward his desk. "I spent the whole night with it." Conklin grasped a paper off the desk surface and read from it. "In conclusion: The 168 passengers and six crew on board Trinity Airlines 846 died instantly when the plane crashed catastrophically after being diverted to BUR…"

With a raised voice, Murphy read from her own transcription. "In conclusion: All passengers on board Trinity Airlines 846 survived when the plane successfully made an emergency landing at LAX. The incident involving an unruly flight attendant will require follow-on investigation."

Conklin took a breath. "Liz, I deliberately chose the blackened, beat-to-shit Box. I wasn't going to cut any corners. Just because I knew someone on the flight." He glared at her. "You went back and retrieved the other Box. What did you do, break into my trunk?" He upended the dispenser and felt a sour land on his tongue. *Licorice.*

Murphy met his glare with stony silence. "Your Traversermaniac friend finally snapped." After a few moments, she loosened up, eyes softening. "It must be hard for you to accept what happened."

"What are you talking about?" Conklin spat out the words.

In answer, Murphy pulled out her smartphone. She thumbed it efficiently, then presented it to Conklin. "Randy, get a grip. They all survived."

He frowned, and threw up his hands. "Nonsense! Neither of us can leave this room until we agree which Black Box tells the true story."

"There's only one truth here, boss. The other Box is a fake!"

"Many people will suffer unless we come to an agreement."

A tentative, polite knocking on the door. A muffled voice. "The press are assembled."

"This is all about Linda for you, right?"

Conklin narrowed his eyes, fuming.

"You can't see it anymore. She's totally dragged you into that cult," said Murphy.

The rapping on the door resumed, louder.

*   *   *

Conklin strode into the press room carrying his black box and transcript. Murphy was a step behind. He was dismayed to see the other box already on the display table, brightly accusing with its intact orange paint job. He stepped to the table deliberately, placing his box in front of the other. He turned to the podium, but Murphy had beat him there. *Opportunistic white bitch.* He moved to stand unreasonably close to her left shoulder.

Before either of them could speak... "I'm Susan von Browne, Pasadena Star News. Who's in charge of..." The woman checked her smartphone... "... the Trinity Airlines 846 investigation?"

"I am," asserted Murphy.

"I am," overlapped Conklin.

The glamorous reporter, more stylishly dressed than Murphy, continued. "The plane that disappeared from the radar?" she asked.

Conklin rebutted, "It didn't disappear!"

"I agree, the flight did not disappear," said Murphy.

The reporter reacted with a smile, perfect white teeth. "Have you found it then? It's raining very hard."

"That's why we're here today. To report our findings," said Murphy.

"You don't seem to know the first thing about what's happened," added Conklin.

"Well, I'm sure you guys are going to explain it all. But you might want to check this out first, if I can get this thing to cast…" Von Browne tapped away at her phone. The large display on the stage, behind the table, flickered to life. The reporter clicked the beckoning play icon and the iconic, horrific viral video of the spectacular crash unfolded. Conklin turned away. Murphy studied something on the display.

"Wait," said Murphy. "What about – ?"

"Going there now," said von Browne. The display changed over to another video, showing a plane approaching a runway, recognizably LAX. An opening was visible along the fuselage, and smoke emerged from under, whipping back. The plane seemed a bit unsteady, but not out of control. Soon it landed, almost bouncing once, then settling and slowing to a stop. Emergency vehicles converged.

Everyone in the press room let out a held breath.

A lightning bolt illuminated the sky, followed by flashes of thunder.

Conklin reached for his charred black box.

Murphy grabbed the other, orange one. She mouthed a thank-you at the reporter. "What are those letters in the corner, like a watermark?"

Browne replied, "Oh, M-R-C. It's an AI news feed I use. 'Momentous Real-time Coverage.' Costs enough, and I understand some subscription requests are rejected, but I find it quite useful. I have another question." She grinned, more feral now. "Both of these videos are false alarms. Just before this session, I called Air Traffic Control at LAX. Trinity Airlines 846 is in the air as we speak and reports no mechanical problems. They're a bit behind schedule because of the stacking of flights due to the weather. Now, tell us, why do we even have these black boxes here?"

His voice catching, Conklin asked, "What's today?" He dumped the dispenser over his face. One sour made it in. *Rhubarb.*

"Excuse me?" returned the reporter.

"The day of the week," Murphy pressed.

"It's Tuesday."

Conklin and Murphy exchanged glances, horrified.

*   *   *

**EXCERPTS from the online article
"Or is it, Black is the New Orange? I'm Confused."
by Susan von Browne**
(>> 1,000,000 hits as of Tuesday)

Airline crashes are among the most harrowing accidents of civil life. Most people are aware that, statistically, aircraft flights are safer than taking your automobile to the grocery store. Yet, the outsize mayhem of an air catastrophe sinks deep into our collective consciousness, and there is somehow less forgiveness when one of these incidents occurs.

Being an air traffic controller is a special calling. But there is another, related role which may be even more psychologically consuming – being a crash investigator for the National Transportation Safety Board (NTSB). Perhaps it's not too surprising then when, rarely, these dedicated civil servants lose their way...

Which brings us to the extraordinary case of Trinity Airlines Flight 846. Los Angeles has a mostly benign climate, but occasionally aggressive rain cell clusters appear around the mountains which partially encircle the sprawling city. Trinity Airlines 846, a thrice-weekly flight from Dublin to Los Angeles, encountered such bad weather, and was briefly lost on radar. In the middle of this vacuum of information, two conflicting accounts of the fate of this flight appeared. In these days of fake news, this by itself is hardly reportable, but the truly bizarre circumstance was the manifestation of two different physical black boxes, containing recordings which tracked the two accounts. Where did these devices come from? Who is responsible?

While answers to those questions are pending, the NTSB has issued the following statement: "Demonstrating an untenable incapacity to reach an agreement and make timely decisions in matters of life and death, Mr. Randall Conklin and Ms. Elizabeth Murphy are hereby relieved of their duties within the NTSB. Mr. Conklin, the senior investigator, is returned to his former assignment at the Highway Traffic Safety Division of San Luis Obispo, California."

Almost overlooked was another incident purported to have taken place on the very flight in question. In a striking reversal of roles, flight attendant Linda Bradley had to be restrained while allegedly either blaming or desperately seeking aid from two passengers on the flight, claiming they were, wait for it... time travelers. Perplexingly, the two individuals, alleged to be a marshal and prisoner pair, remain unverified among the safely landed...

Paula's Exclusion Syndrome

R. James Doyle and Rogelio Fojo

Frontispiece and illustrations by Daniela Giraudin

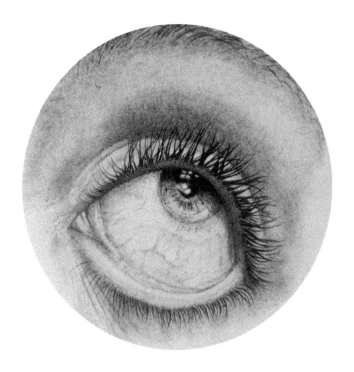

First, the doctors tried to pin Münchausen's Syndrome by Proxy on my family.

I laughed right in their faces. Isn't that some character from a movie?

Then the cops started grilling me about whether I'd ever been cloned – maybe without my consent. By my own parents, no less!

At that point, I couldn't decide whether to laugh or cry or scream. My mother would be the first to tell you – one of me is more than enough!

They weren't amused and kept circling back to the main question: 'So, where is the baby?'

If any of us knew, we wouldn't be having this conversation, would we?

They never thought to ask about time travel...

*　　　*　　　*

"Poor guy didn't try to mess with me or anything," said Paula. "I ran after him seeking help, thinking I was pregnant and didn't know who the father was, and I thought, you know, maybe he… but my period was just late, don't you see? False alarm. Yay!"

The rookie police officer uncomfortably averted his gaze from the blood stains on Paula's legs. He studied her companion now, sitting quietly on the curb.

The cop scrutinized the lanky young man. Gange looked around serenely. Impossible to interpret his blank expression or odd gestures.

"My friend's not to blame, let him go!" Paula insisted. Gange seemed somber and… *patient* – caught like this, hands cuffed behind his back, in view of people leaving the nightclub at that hour, judging them in whispers and chuckles. *Not ashamed.* His impassive and inscrutable face put her off. Yet his mysterious behavior was his most attractive aspect.

The officer turned his eyes back on Paula. "Dressed like this is how you leave your home? Half-naked?" He examined the driver's license in his hand. "A seventeen-year-old should know better." He shook his head. "You'll both need to come down to the station. And you, young lady, will need a medical examination."

She rolled her eyes and held back. Insulting this young officer could end up with jail time. Nor could she use thoughts of suicide as a defense, which could lead to hospitalization and visits from social workers. She had to deal with this mess herself – without mentioning the true culprit, her mother Gretchen. The constant fights that drove her to run away and seek after someone like Gange.

Paula shifted her sight onto the moon above, shining full in a cloudless sky of washed-out stars. The air was lukewarm, like every night in Los Angeles, every other dull night of her boring life.

She had traveled alone on the last bus from downtown, listening to an old Simon and Garfunkel album on her wireless headphones, searching for a song she used to know how to play. *What was the title?* A chord progression suddenly popped into her head. She moved her fingers to play air guitar. Soon she was humming the melody. But its title and lyrics – surely outdated, probably socially inappropriate – remained lost in the mists of time.

Paula had searched inside her backpack, then upended it. Seventeen birthday cards decorated with family pictures by her "artistic" mother fell onto her lap. Avoiding looking at the old photographs, she put the cards inside a notebook... the precious leather-bound diary her father had been forced to buy for her at Walmart. The only souvenir from her previous life she had decided to bring on the road.

She had filled its pages with song lyrics, guitar chords, her own strange rhymes and drawings. She glanced at a few verses for a new poem, "Lunatica: *Trample beneath, you watery wraiths / Specters dissolved in my dark raids / Mirror of celestial dread / Reflect mortality, where shadows are bred.*" She scratched out the verses with a red pen and rewrote: *"Crush beneath my feet, you ocean ghosts / Vanish, spectral echoes boast / Mirror of the stellar night / Reflect me as mortal, with your light."*

The Simon and Garfunkel tune was definitely not written down in those pages. She had closed the volume in its purple and pink wrapping, zipped up her backpack, and tried to focus on her upcoming rendezvous with Gange at the Hi-Hat club along York. She nearly missed her stop and had to push past a pretty woman in the aisle, just boarding, and looking at her.

On the street now, she fell further down memory lane...

An earlier encounter with the police. Something to do with drugs at a party which had become too noisy for the neighbors. None of it was her fault, but somehow Paula ended up protesting alone in the back seat of a patrol car. She remembered the rough, hard seat, without cushions. The cold on her exposed legs. The slow passage of minutes, the sharp edge of the zip tie cuffs on her wrists. And later, the embarrassment without tears when the patrol car finally deposited her in her front yard, beside the eucalyptus tree which already surpassed her in size.

Back to her first, earliest arrest, outside the Walmart store. A security guard caught up with Paula as she hurried through the parking lot with the expensive leather-bound notebook tucked in her jeans, under her blouse. While Dad waited anxiously in the car, she was held as a shoplifter in a small backroom, given time alone there to reflect on a lesson she ultimately did not learn. Despite the physical pain of her first encounter with restraints, what still hurt were the sincere tears of remorse, the uncontrollable sobbing, when her father came to take her home, hugging her close...

The glaring flashlight pulled Paula back to the present.

She said, "I wanted to forget my problems, turn the clock back, start over..."

"Where did you meet this guy? Who is he? He's got no ID."

"I don't know... He's interested in molecular genetics, and I thought, – I thought he was one of those Traversers everyone is talking about at school."

The policeman scoffed and directed the beam of light toward the taciturn young man. "Is that true, buddy? Can you time travel?"

In answer, a more blinding flash.

"Where did he go?!" The cop panicked, grabbed his radio. "Attention all units. Suspect on the move!"

Paula turned to the empty space beside her, mouth agape in astonishment.

"You! You helped him escape," the cop yelled.

But both Paula and the policeman knew that was impossible. Gange's metal handcuffs were left abandoned on the curb, still locked.

*   *   *

Paula slammed her bedroom door as hard as she could. She heard wood splintering.

"Gange is not my new boyfriend!"

"Well, that's a fine name!" Gretchen yelled back through the door. "How could you possibly expect anything but trouble from someone with a name like that?

"I think he's German. Just like you!"

"Oh, you certainly know how to pick 'em. That last one… Well, maybe the third time will be the charm."

"Mom! Stop it."

She flung herself across the bed. With her chin planted awkwardly into the fuchsia-splashed covers, she reared back and slammed her fists down – right, left, right.

Paula rolled, leaped to her feet, and strode to her dresser top. She picked up the small double portrait of her parents in a two-fisted grab, lifting it up and sweeping downward. But she dissipated the movement, depositing the frame back on the dresser surface, face-down. She jumped back on the bed and curled onto her side, working hard to fight off sobs.

Paula moved to the door, listening momentarily before reaching for the knob. She tried turning the bronze implement and found it would not budge.

Sighing, she sprawled across the bed again and rolled to reach for the lamp on the nightstand. A golden glow spilled into the room. She moved back to the door and inspected the area around the latch. Virgin wood splinters stuck out from the dark-stained wood of the jamb. She took a firm grip of the knob and twisted.

Nothing. Now with both hands. Still nothing. She bounded over to her desk and grabbed her backpack, shoving in laptop, cables, more. Not haphazardly, everything in its place.

On her way around the bed, she lifted the window sash. A pleasantly warm summer breeze wafted in. The gloaming beckoned.

Paula took in the expanse of the bedroom in a slow pan. The walls were adorned with eucalyptus tree wallpaper stretching from floor to ceiling, interrupted by framed family photos. Her eyes dwelled briefly on the infant crib, still gathering dust in the corner after all these years, at her mother's insistence. She paused at the shut closet door. *My guitar.* Paula pursed her lips. *Too impractical to bring along.* She shrugged on her backpack and moved to the window, dropping the bag down.

*　　*　　*

"Paula! Enough already! Please open this door!"

Sid waved his wife off, pressing an ear against the wood. "I don't hear anything."

"She's in one of her sulks."

"I wouldn't blame her. Do you have to keep harping on her? And how she had once been the perfect little girl? All you're doing is shutting her out."

Gretchen sighed. "She is deliberately trying to make our lives miserable."

Sid ignored her, contemplating the door.

"We've tried the master key. We know it's not locked. Why won't it open?"

"Seems to be jammed in the frame."

"You're going to have to break it in."

Sid looked at his wife. "I'm not a young man anymore." He took a breath. "Here goes nothing…" He threw the weight of his body against the old, solid door, left shoulder first. He winced. The blow extracted an unconvincing creak, nothing more.

"Again!" urged Gretchen.

*　　*　　*

"I hate them. It's time I left home," said Paula.

She interpreted Gange's lifted eyebrow as: 'Why do you hate your parents?'

Paula was holding Gange prisoner of a slow dance, on the small club floor. All evening long, the multiple band sets had played uniformly dark and angry. Now, during one of the rare non-raucous numbers, they could briefly engage in conversation.

She leaned back, not pulling away, taking a broader view of Gange. His blue eyes, smooth cheeks. His way of speaking – when he deigned to do so. Not archaic exactly.

"I don't want to hate them," Paula said.

Before tracking him down, Paula had changed in a public restroom, donning a crinkly, low-cut top and a form-fitting skirt. All shades of pink, magenta and purple, her signature colors. Headband, belt, and short socks to match. *A different lifestyle now, I'll have to get used to it. My wardrobe will be limited. Does that mean I'm going to have to shoplift again?* Paula shot a glance over to the back wall of the club where her roller bag and backpack were stashed. *Still there.*

She turned back to Gange. "I suppose you got along fine with your parents?" No response. He wore that distant, too-knowing smirk.

She probed, "And where exactly do you come from?"

The band played a soothing slide-guitar solo, while Gange remained eloquently silent. Paula attended to the words pouring from the stage:

> *"Standing like a stooge won't help*
> *you've got to play the game*
> *living joy and sorrow*
> *you're watching life*
> *through an hourglass*
> *and time still slips away*
> *just travelers through time and space."*

Paula pulled out her cell phone and Shazamed the song. "Hourglass," by New People. And it abruptly ended. Droning, clashing waves of sound bowled from the stage. Gange guided her to the back of the club. *Now he wants to talk.* Paula strained to hear.

"Why are you hating your parents?" Paula half-read his lips.

Paula felt her face cloud over. "Ever since I could remember, my mom always acted like I'm this great burden who ruined her life. She makes no effort to understand me. My dad, we get each other, but he humors her and her stupid cliches, and it drives me crazy." She shook her head. "I know we're not that always-loving kind of family. I don't understand their disappointments. All I know is it's just so draining to live with them. Again, and again, we get into the drama. Whatever I try to do, I can never please her. It's time I focus on myself."

Paula leaned her head against Gange's shoulder and neck. Abruptly, she pulled back. "You know what kills me? She keeps saying how lovable I was when I was growing up. So cute as a child. Such a joy. No trouble at all. As if the person in front of her is someone else entirely. If she doesn't like the way I turned out as a teenager, maybe she should ask herself why!"

Heads snapped, even amid the noise.

Paula hoped Gange would wrap his arms around her. Instead, his gaze turned more clinical. He said something she could not catch.

"Um, yeah…" Paula stabbed a guess. "Maybe. We all gloss our memories. Now here is what I want to know… Are you going to help me?"

Gange fixed his cold eyes on her. Paula reached up and in, lips parted, eyes closed.

*   *   *

Running breathlessly, Paula caught up with Gange in the back alley. A distant streetlight threw long, interrupted shadows. The music from inside the club throbbed, muted.

Paula pushed Gange up against the building and kissed him passionately. He participated in the kiss, but languidly. His arms remained at his sides. Paula pulled back, frustrated, without breaking contact.

"Give it up, Gange. You must know the dark web is buzzing with stories. It also explains a few things about you."

Gange's expression went quizzical. "Being what?"

"Well, the way you speak, for one thing. I might reach old age trying to have a conversation. Plus your clothes, your bearing… You have got to be one of those Traversers."

He shrugged.

"Why the hell won't you help me? What are you doing here then? Tell me! Everyone's wondering."

Gange stood, unmoving.

Paula pushed off the wall. She stalked around the alley, found a bottle with little effort, strode back to the wall near Gange. She lifted the bottle high.

"Please, take me to the future with you! Then maybe… my mother will understand what she missed."

Gange remained impassive.

She glared at him. "Take me away or I'll out you! I bet you won't 'be liking' that! You and all your Traverser friends."

Gange sighed, reaching for his wrist. A flicker of panic flashed in Paula's eyes. She let loose a scream. Then cut it off abruptly. Paula smashed the bottle on the pavement. She pressed a resulting shard against her wrist but only succeeded in cutting a finger.

"We'll just be at each other, without end. It's better that I am out of their lives." Paula's body hung in wired tension. Gange regarded her distantly. He stepped away from the wall. Paula dropped the broken bottle and strode forward. She loosened the top buttons of her blouse. She embraced him, hard, her last resort.

A siren chirped, nearby. An intense flashlight beam swept the alley. "Freeze!" came the command.

*   *   *

Sid's forays into brute force proved ineffective. He returned from the cellar with his dust-caked toolbox. Now he worked at tapping the hinge bolts up and out of their slots with a screwdriver and hammer. His neck hurt.

At least there were signs of progress. Gretchen stood by impatiently, biting her lips. Suddenly, inexplicably, came a muffled cry… They looked at each other.

"Am I going crazy or is that coming from Paula's room?" asked Gretchen.

"She's in trouble," said Sid.

"I'll run outside and look at her window. You get that door off!" Sid heard Gretchen scurrying downstairs.

Working on the door, Sid came to understand that Paula's violent slam had created a jam. The latch had jumped from its normal slot and become wedged into the wood of the frame.

He tapped the hinge bolts with renewed vigor. Doing his best to ignore the inexplicable wails, he concentrated. He removed the top one, relieving slightly the discomfort from craning his neck. He turned to the middle one, reasoning that removing this one would directly remove the pressure on the jam. Something in the change of pitch of the complaining wood told him he was on the right track.

Gretchen returned. "Paula's window is open. There's some grass disturbed just below. Someone's gotten inside her room. Get the door off, Sid, now. Paula's in danger! What's taking you so long!"

The second bolt came out. Sid, from studying and working on the mechanical issue, understood that the best course was to simply push the door in, even if more destruction resulted.

He pressed, rather than pushed, and with a final protesting groan, the door moved inward, not all the way, but enough to allow passage.

Gretchen entered the dark room first.

Sid followed, switching the lights on, looking on with amazement. His wife was lifting a baby into her arms, wrapped in Paula's old bedclothes.

*   *   *

They were returning from an impromptu visit to Calico Ghost Town, one of their spontaneous family road trips. The desert sun was setting. A happy day of adventure was slowly ebbing.

For hours, her long, skinny legs comfortably tucked in the front passenger seat, Paula listened to the old cassette tape over and over again, a gift for her twelfth birthday. Dad driving and Mom in the back, insisting that Paula sit up front. Paula was smiling now, sharing her favorite song of the album. The family's ancient Ford Fairlane sedan purred along the highway as they all daydreamed to the music.

Paula imagined a huge neon sign:

> ## S & G WELCOME
> ## THE ONE AND ONLY …
> ## PAULA LOBANUBIS!

Simon and Garfunkel reached out to welcome her on stage.

Confidently, Paula walked up to the microphone, her brand new acoustic guitar draped on her shoulder. The park was overflowing, and the crowd erupted in applause and cheers. Mom and Dad beamed with pride from the wings. As Paula pressed the strings on the fretboard, she struck the first chord with a bold, confident sweep of her right hand. The crowd went wild! Paula's impressive, high vocal notes wove in and out of the male vocal tapestry, creating a unique and timeless harmony reverberating through the warm air.

A flash of white light wiped out the scene. Armed with her ever-present Polaroid, mom captured a candid photo of her daughter: Paula the silly tween, frozen in time, playing her air guitar riffs.

Instead of smiling back, Paula blushed and recoiled in her seat. Her gaze diverted to the desolate expanse of the darkening Mojave Desert. Conflicting emotions surged within her, as she drifted into a restless sleep that lasted all the way back home.

* * *

"A baby," whispered Sid in disbelief.

"This is absolutely crazy! Who is this child?" asked Gretchen. "Why isn't Paula here? Is she supposed to be baby-sitting? Sid, you need to call her right now. And you just know she's not going to pick up when she's in one of her moods."

"Gretchen, please, I have to think!"

Sid regarded the tools he held in his hands. He laid them gingerly on Paula's bed. He retrieved his phone from a pocket, punched it, and waited. "Paula, it's Dad. You're not going to believe this… Well, maybe you are, because we're hoping you can tell us what's going on. There's a bundle of joy crying its head off in your room. Do you know whose baby this is? Call us back, please." Sid looked at his wife.

"That's all you could think to say?" asked Gretchen. "Text her right now, with the same message! She's gotten into trouble before, but this… and here we are, as usual, holding…"

Gretchen rocked the infant in her arms, lovingly. "Ssshhh."

They established they were dealing with a baby girl. Rummaging around the crib, they found baby clothing, a bottle, formula, a pacifier, diapers, a soft cotton towel… a basic infant care kit, tidily packaged in a small basket. Gretchen's quick inspection and ministrations revealed that the baby was running a moderate temperature and showing a case of splotchy skin.

Nevertheless, the little girl calmed down, contented. She gazed up at Gretchen, trusting her as if she were her own mother.

"Oh, Sid, she is such a gift. We can keep her for a little while, don't you think?"

"I don't know what to think," fretted Sid. "If Paula doesn't tell us something, we'll have to report her as a Baby Doe to the authorities."

"Sid, we will do no such thing! Those people are wretched, unfeeling."

"They have a job to do."

"I won't hear of it. Sid, don't you see? All the problems we're having with Paula. And now this baby just appears, out of nowhere?"

"And we're already having problems with her, too! She looks like she's sick... I have to think."

She held the baby out to Sid.

Sid took her, reluctantly. "There, there little one. Can you tell us, what is your story?" He was soon rocking the baby too, becoming spellbound. Sid shook himself, handing the baby back to Gretchen. "We have to take her to a doctor, get her checked out. Make sure she's okay before figuring out what to do next. Will you agree to that much?"

Gretchen looked up, after having quickly lost herself again. "I don't know. I guess that's all right."

Sid continued, "We're going to have to say something about who this baby is, and how we came to have her."

*   *   *

Sid and Gretchen crossed the parking lot and entered the Verdugo Hills Medical Professional Building. Paula's pediatrician was still practicing. They approached the young woman at the check-in desk.

"You say the baby is your daughter's?" asked the person with the Sheila name tag.

"That's right," said Sid.

"So where is the mother now?"

"She's out of town. She left the baby in our care."

"When is she expected to return?"

Sid glanced sideways at Gretchen. The baby was doing very well in her arms.

"When is the mother expected to return?"

"We don't know," replied Sid.

Sheila studied these scatter-brained grandparents. "And the baby's name is... ?"

"Um, Pamela. Pamela Lobanubis."

"Social security number?"

"933–" Sid began.

"Not yours," said Gretchen. "She means the baby's."

"Oh... I don't know."

"You don't know the baby's social, or you don't know if she has one?"

"Both – neither. Sorry, we don't seem to be of much help." Sid took a breath.

"Do you know if the mother has insurance?"

"She's actually still on our medical plan. That'll make things okay, won't it?" pleaded Sid.

"Not especially, and not if the birth hasn't been recorded." A silence dropped. "What is your concern regarding the baby?"

Sid was taken aback by the question.

Gretchen leaned into the window, instinctively shielding the baby well back on her hip. "She was crying a bit too much today. Better safe than sorry."

Sheila softened her posture.

*　　　*　　　*

Tomboy Paula calmly and carefully gathered the exotic "gum nuts" she was instructed to dry on the sun-bathed laundry room windowsill. Her tiny eucalyptus seeds needed just a couple of weeks to emerge from their hard shells. But in her perception, that stretch of time felt like years.

Rushing with excitement to the front garden, cradling the treasure in her palms, she knelt beside her father, who was diligently digging a deep hole.

Paula delicately placed the seeds at the bottom and piled soil over them. Dad handed to her a green, shiny, brand-new watering can. A gift, signaling the Lobanubis family seal of approval for her to preside over the cycle-of-life ritual. Paula was officially named custodian of the family tree.

She executed the baptism perfectly, sprinkling life-giving drops over the small, sacred plot. She promised herself not to disappoint her parents' trust.

Lifting her eyes, she saw her mother smiling from the porch, contorting her body in the effort to immortalize the moment with her Polaroid camera.

*　　　*　　　*

"Any other symptoms?" asked Sheila.

"Our baby girl is running a temperature, and has splotchy skin."

"How long has she had these symptoms?"

Gretchen looked at Sid.

He responded, "We're not really sure."

"We'll have to work up a full protocol. These are forms to fill out." Sheila pointed. "Please take a seat." Sid took the clipboard with its captive sheaf. He and Gretchen moved to the standard-issue waiting room chairs.

"I don't like her," said Gretchen.

"Did you hear our answers? They don't add up very well."

Sid dutifully worked through the forms while Gretchen babbled with baby 'Pamela'. Woman and child were not having any trouble bonding. *Father's profession.* Sid paused, wrote 'Handyman'. *Mother's profession.* 'Substitute teacher'. His eyes defocusing, and taking a deep breath, he scribbled his signature. When he glanced up at the desk, he saw another, stern woman engaged in low conversation with Sheila. One or the other would look over to them. Gretchen was oblivious. Sid tried to set aside the foreboding feeling creeping over him. A young medical professional approached them.

"Pamela Lobanubis? May I take her, please?" asked the female intern.

Gretchen stood and unthinkingly started to hand the baby over. In choreographed fashion, the woman who had been talking to Sheila swept in. "Mr. and Mrs. Lobanubis, would you come with me please?"

In an instant, the intern left Gretchen behind. She walked toward an entry door; infant cradled in one arm. With her opposite hand, she swung a badge out for the reader.

"No! I am going with her," shrieked Gretchen.

The other occupants of the waiting room, and one medical professional transiting the space, stopped, and stared. The intern paused in the entry, holding the door open with her hip. Sid was conscious of the stern woman holding his arm at the elbow. A curt nod.

The young woman smiled at Gretchen. "Mrs. Lobanubis? Absolutely, of course, please join us." Sid watched the heavy door swing shut after Gretchen, with a suppressed clang.

"Mr. Lobanubis, if you please."

*   *   *

The woman gestured to a seat facing her desk. Taking her own chair, she pushed a business card across the desktop.

> **Lydia P. Straitt**
>
> *Assistant Supervisor*
>
> Child and Family Services

Sid's heart sank. He looked around the small, spare office. Framed certificates hung on the wall, which he did not bother to study.

Without preamble, the investigator launched in. "Where is your daughter?"

"We don't know," replied Sid.

"How is it that you don't know? She's living with you, is she not? Sharing meals, on your insurance plan?"

"We had an argument. She left, rather abruptly," said Sid.

"You can call her?"

"Of course, we can call her."

"Your story seems a little off."

"Is that so?"

"Ever heard of Münchausen's syndrome by proxy?"

Sid offered a strained smile. "Isn't that a character from a movie?"

"That's what they all say, Mr. Lobanubis. Do you or your wife, or your daughter, have anything to gain from claiming that 'Baby Pamela' has certain medical symptoms, when in fact, she does not?"

"What the hell are you talking about?" Sid found himself leaning forward. He eased back but did not apologize.

"The hospital records indicate you and your wife had difficulty conceiving."

Sid glared. "I don't see how that is any of your business."

"In addition to the general work-up, I've asked for a DNA analysis. Those can be done rather quickly these days. Did you know that? It will be a simple matter to confirm whether or not the infant is your granddaughter."

Sid gazed at the dingy wall, past the investigator's head.

"Has your daughter ever been arrested?"

"She's gotten into her share of trouble, like most teenagers." Sid glared at the officer.

"What about last night?"

Sid opened his mouth but had to think what to say. Or ask. "What is she suspected of?"

"Oh, vagrancy. Prostitution. Amazingly, she cleared all tests. No charges were recorded. How does this news make you feel?"

Sid remained silent.

The investigator's eyebrows arched. "Maybe you just want to tell me what's going on."

*   *   *

A terrible shaking woke Paula. "Mommy! Daddy!" she cried out.

Then they were there. Dad's strong arms lifted her. Mom quickly tucked a blanket around her.

The lights flickered and died out, and the shaking got worse. Down in the kitchen, it sounded like milk bottles and marmalade jars were crashing on the floor.

"We'll stand in her doorway, Gretch! That'll be safe."

"What's happening?" asked Paula fearfully.

"Ssshhh, dear. Nothing to worry about. Just an earthquake. It'll be okay."

Paula closed her eyes. She curled her small fingers, concentrating on her dad's comforting smell. And her mom's too. She was slowly being swayed and could no longer feel the shaking. The noise was ending too.

"There, that's all over," said Mom. "You can sleep with us tonight, honey. Would you like that?"

Paula nodded.

All returned to quiet, except for the echoing of the grandfather clock ticking, which had never stopped.

*   *   *

Paula hesitated, seeing the majestic eucalyptus tree towering, already greater in height than the Lobanubis home. The tranquil moment was interrupted by the truncated *whoop* of a police siren. *Assholes.* She heard the squad car drive away, delivering one final accusatory burst before leaving the scene. Paula thought back to their treatment of her. Solicitous and harsh at the same time. *Message received. I need to get my shit together.*

Paula shakily keyed herself inside, then listened, at the entry. *No one home.* She plopped down on the weary sofa. She dug her cell phone out of a pocket, stared at it. Paula flipped through the log, sighed. She thumbed, steeling herself for she knew not what, then lifted the phone to her ear.

She shifted from anger to... delight. "Way to go, Gange. You surprise me," she murmured.

Then confusion, disbelief, and finally determination. She stood. "This is not what I wanted. You shithead. What a total cluster!"

*   *   *

"We have the results of the DNA analysis." The man smiled unconvincingly and offered his hand from behind a desk. "Forgive me, my name is Dr. Otsura. I am a geneticist."

Sid found his obsequious manner distasteful. He took the man's hand reluctantly. The silence was thick with combined distrust and attentiveness.

"I'm told the baby appears to be perfectly healthy. Temperature normal, skin normal, all indicators normal." Sid relaxed. "But the baby... I'm sorry to have to tell you this… she is carrying the genetic marker for a fatal blood disease."

Gretchen's composure collapsed. She clutched Pamela to her breast. "My baby!"

"Please understand that carrying the marker does not mean that the disease will manifest," continued Otsura. "And even if it does, typically this would happen in young adulthood. Far in the future.

A heavy silence descended.

"Mr. Lobanubis, when we conduct a DNA analysis, the software routinely searches existing databases for partial matches. That is how we establish familial relationships. The DNA results produced a perfect match."

Sid asked, apprehensively, "Do we need to provide a sample?"

"When I said a perfect match, I meant perfect, a hundred per cent." He stared. "This is actually unprecedented."

"I guess I don't understand."

"Who do you imagine is the perfect match?"

Gretchen picked up enough to pay more attention, suspending playtime with Pamela, who broke out into a wail. "Ssshhh. Mommy is here." Pamela slid back into contentment.

Sid glowered. "I'm sure I don't know."

"The match is with your daughter, Paula Lobanubis."

*   *   *

Paula opened the front door. Sid and Gretchen entered with the baby.

"Paula, honey, thank God!" said Sid. "We'll get this all straightened out now."

Gretchen said nothing, shifting to hold the baby more protectively. Then she exploded. "The hospital accused us of fraud, identity theft. And those are hardly the worst. They're even looking at abuse, kidnapping, all the way to murder! They even implied we had cloned you without your consent. I told them one of you is more than enough!"

Sid added, "Can you imagine, cloning? But they're

determined to get to the bottom of this. They're giving us twenty-four hours to sort it out."

"And then they'll issue a warrant for your arrest. And they do have the power to take the baby," said Gretchen.

Waves of emotion ricocheted around the small living room. No one had anything to say for a while.

Sid broke the silence. "Paula, what's going on? Where did you go? What do you know about this baby?"

"Dad, don't you know who the baby is?" Paula reached out and grabbed the infant away from the surprised Gretchen, hugging her closely.

"Don't you dare!" shrilled Gretchen. "Give Pamela back! She may be ill. What have you done to her? How could you, and we never knew a thing!"

Paula stared at her and turned away. "You love her more than you love me, isn't that right, mom?"

"What a silly question. How could I possibly answer?"

"Paula don't…" pleaded Sid.

"I want to hear her answer," insisted Paula. Beads of sweat stood out on her forehead.

"If you must know, I suppose I do, as of right now. As much as I can say I know her. You were never an easy one to love. Except back when you were, well, a child." Gretchen smiled at her memories. "You know, she reminds me of you."

Paula backed away with the baby, bumping into a tall hutch in the confined space. "She is me and I am her! Don't you understand? Gange… he's a Traverser. He traveled back and brought the baby here. Don't you get it? She is me, not her! There is no Pamela."

Paula rasped, "I am so sick and tired of hearing how you loved me when I was a child. What happened, when did things go wrong? Why do you always have to be in some kind of trouble? You can love *her* now. Until she disappoints you. Why are you surprised I wish to go to the future and get the hell out of here!"

Paula felt something shift inside her. A dizzying cyclone of birthday cards, adorned with family pictures and counting the years backwards, swirled around her.

She leaned back awkwardly, having trouble getting purchase against the piece of furniture. "It's like my life is flashing before my eyes." Even in her distress, she scrunched her face. "Now I sound like my mother." Struggling, she held out the baby.

Sid took Pamela just as Paula's legs began to buckle. She slid down in a steady, almost stately manner. Sid quickly handed the baby to Gretchen, then did his best to prop Paula up.

*   *   *

Paula drifted in semi-consciousness. She was dimly aware of a presence nearby. With an effort, she forced herself awake. She was at home, lying in her own bed, over-connected to fluids and sensors… which didn't look like anything she knew about. Harsh reality intruded by degrees. Gange stood in the bedroom.

"How did you get in here?" whispered Paula.

"I am moving about, when I am having the need."

Paula tried to reach out, but her weakened state and the profusion of tubing defeated her. Gange watched impassively, with that clinical gaze.

"Paula, you are having a rare, late onset, fatal blood disease. The spacetime traversal is triggering your disease."

Paula struggled to speak. "I don't… understand. I didn't…"

"Because you are encountering your own world-line."

Paula felt sure it wasn't just her debilitated and medicated state that was getting in the way of comprehension.

Gange continued. "Your requesting is granting permission. For bringing you forward in time."

Paula lay back, taking it all in. Unexpectedly, she felt empathy for her parents, trying to cope and assimilate all the mind-bending revelations. "I could never please them. We always ended up hurting each other. Pushing each other away. I've learned how to press their buttons, especially my mother's." Paula's vision blurred, behind an unaccustomed glistening.

"Your knowing is of no consequence. You are not forming memories, or you are dying. And consenting to the experiment." His eyes showed as ice.

"Experiment?" repeated Paula, weakly.

"The testing for Exclusion Syndrome." Gange projected impatience. "When looping, altering your deep molecular structure, to gene expression."

"Gange, you're scaring me now." Paula mustered herself. "You are a Traverser. I don't want to die hating my parents! You owe me that much."

Gange remained inscrutable. "You are having access." He reached for his wrist. A glow emanated from there and enveloped Paula.

*   *   *

After making sure Paula was comfortable, they departed with the baby, through the portal of their daughter's ruined bedroom door. In the master bedroom, Sid stumbled while trying to sit.

Gretchen wrapped Pamela in a hug. A muffled giggle seeped out. "Don't you worry, little one. Mommy and Daddy are here."

Sid covered his face with his hands. He was weeping.

Gretchen reached out to touch his shoulder and rub the back of his neck, not putting the baby down.

Sid pulled himself upright. "Paula never left us, Gretch... I mean, she was always here, growing up."

"Sid, you don't honestly believe... obviously, she had this child—"

"How could she have hidden the pregnancy? And what of the DNA results?"

Gretchen shook her head and held the baby tighter. Pamela squealed. "Having her, this beautiful baby girl, again... at our age. It's a gift." Gretchen gazed into Pamela's eyes.

Sid covered Gretchen's hand. He could feel through to

the baby's warmth, the little heart beating. "The true gift is knowing that we love Paula. And showing her, in the time that we... I mean the three of us... still have together."

"Oh, Sid." Gretchen buried her face against the baby's head, drinking in the scent.

At that precise instant, the grandfather clock chimed the midnight hour. They moved out into the hall.

*   *   *

A young man emerged from Paula's room. He was nondescript and hard to miss at the same time. Perhaps it was his bearing. Or his clothing, having a kind of metallic threading throwing glints from unexpected places.

"You must be Gange," said Sid.

Gange stopped and stood, evaluating. "You are being Paula's parents."

"Who are you, really? A time traveler? Our prospective son-in-law?" A knowing smirk flickered on Gange's face. Sid felt his impatience building. "Are you the baby's father?"

"Never. You are being the father."

Sid paused, silently elated. Gretchen adjusted Pamela back on her hip.

"I am being now here for the baby," announced Gange.

Sid said, "We'll take the baby to Paula. She'll know what to do."

Gretchen paused, then nodded.

"I am concurring," said the Traverser.

They all moved back to Paula's room, where Sid and Gretchen found their daughter lying on the bed, appearing exhausted, but awake.

"What is all that equipment?" asked Sid, horrified.

Gange said, "My sensors are monitoring Paula's disease."

Sid tried not to cringe. He moved to Paula, put a hand on her forehead. "Paula, should Pamela stay here, or go back?"

Paula's response was immediate. "There's only one possible way forward for Paula, Pamela, whoever makes this easier for you. There is no decision, no choice. We're only lining up with what already is. Like stepping off a curb." Her head fell back against the pillow.

Standing stock still, Gretchen stared at Gange. "Will Paula be saved?"

Gange stood there, dispassionately. "Paula always is dying young, approaching her eighteenth birthday. She is dying now. You are being with Paula in her final moments, and I am taking your daughter back to her days of infancy. The creating of new memories together – it is being forbidden."

"But... why can't we go back with her? We are ready to be alongside her. Please... We will do so much better! I promise," pleaded Gretchen.

Sid said, "And then Paula will never have need for this... fantasy. About running away to the future..."

"Say something!" shrilled Gretchen, her face contorted.

"I cannot be saying."

Sid took a deep breath. He held his arms out to his wife. Haltingly, the mother held out the baby, hands trembling with possession and loving care.

Sid carefully cuddled Pamela one last time. Then he placed the baby gently with Paula, and both parents leaned in. Then Sid stepped away, embracing Gretchen, turning her away.

A metallic flash. Even through closed eyes. A pulse of a breeze. An acrid smell.

*   *   *

Paula had settled back into a dreamy state, which so wanted to claim her.

Her eyelids fluttered.

They came to her, leaned in, and held her. Communicating, without words.

Mom and Dad. They're trying... but still... I so wish I could escape...

A light flashed over Paula's face, disturbing her.
Someone screamed. "Our baby!"

*   *   *

Paula turned on the bedroom light. The grandfather clock chimed the midnight hour.

She had just turned eighteen! That called for celebration!

Paula heard her favorite song playing in the living room, the old vinyl record. Bookends. That was the song title!

Going downstairs barefoot, she found Sid and Gretchen on the floor below, engaged in a slow dance, swaying to the soft, melancholy music.

Paula turned around, darted back to her bedroom. She retrieved her acoustic guitar from the closet. She remembered how to play the S & G song! A simple four-chord progression: F#m, E, A, E.

The bedroom window stood wide open, to a scented breeze, carrying the fragrance of eucalyptus, and a hint of rain. Beckoning with the lure of continuing adventures. Paula walked over and lowered the sash softly.

Back at the top of the stairs, she spun around to capture a selfie of the whole Lobanubis family. Through a burst of light, her eyes captured her aging parents' embrace, committing the image forever as a photographic memory. She could be with them whenever she wanted. Perfect moments and places could be held – and preserved.

Dizzy from the sudden turn, Paula closed her eyes. Something brightened and she opened them to see, in neon lights:

```
┌─────────────────────────────────────────┐
│      LADIES AND GENTLEMEN...             │
└─────────────────────────────────────────┘
```

Regaining her balance, she raised an imaginary microphone and reintroduced herself to her adoring audience below.

THE ONE AND ONLY...

Paula pressed the strings on the fretboard and struck the first F#m chord with a bold, confident sweep of her right hand.

PAULA LOBANUBIS!

Sid and Gretchen, holding wrinkled hands, went wild!

Paula pressed the strings on the fretboard and played the chords of a song by New People, the lyrics coming unbidden to mind, executing a bold and confident sweep with her right hand, propelling her entire body into motion... E, Cm#, Fm#...

> *"You're watching life*
> *through an hourglass*
> *and time just slips away*
> *there's nothing you can do or say*
> *the trick's on you my dear friend*
> *each day just flies away*
> *little time to think and learn*
> *the magic lies in you to share*
> *seconds tick away*
> *suddenly it's tomorrow."*

Sid and Gretchen unclasped their hands, raised them clapping, and let out a scream!

City of Dreams

Richard Christian Matheson

Frontispiece and illustrations by Alex Storer

Dear Professor Tovar,

As memory is subjective and fallible, it is seductively fluid. Perhaps time itself is even traversable; all anchorages of reality interpretable and prone to errors of measure.

Film is equally triumphant and culpable...it exists yet is false. And our spellbound hearts can detect no difference.

Such is magic.

RC

It was June when the Royal moved in.

I knew because high, metal fences started going up, perimeter shrubbery doubled, and two sullen Dobermans began patrolling. Then, overnight, an intercom, numerical keypad and security camera were mysteriously installed, at the bottom of the Royal's driveway, which ran alongside mine. Whenever I drove by, the lens would zoom to inspect me, staring with curt inquisition.

The Royal was obviously concerned who visited.

Had the Royal been hurt? Was future hurt likely? Were death threats being phoned in hourly? It seemed anything, however dire, was possible. I was already feeling badly for the Royal.

I didn't know if the Royal was a him or her. Rock diva? Zillionaire cyber tot? Mob boss? Pro-leaguer? My mind wandered in lush possibility.

But all I ever saw was a moody limo that purred through the gate and crunched up the long driveway. By the time it got to the big house, the forest landscaping hid it; a leafy moat. I found it all rather troubling. In my experience, concealment is meaningful; trees can be trimmed, the fears which lurk behind them are a different story. Ultimately, one cannot hide, only camouflage. Orson Welles certainly understood this; in *Citizen Kane*, tragic privilege never seemed so rapturous, nor incarcerated.

As days passed, I tried not to listen to what went on next door. I'd play jazz CDs, sip morning espresso, scan the entertainment section for reviews, to distract my attentions. But my community is exclusive and quiet, and bird's wings, as they groom, are noticeable. It made it hard to miss the Royal's limo as it sighed up the driveway, obscured by the half million dollars of pre-meditated forest.

Once parked, doors would open and close, and I'd hear footsteps, sometimes cheerless murmurs; the limo driver speaking to the Royal, I assumed. Russian? Indo-Chinese? Impossible to tell. Then, the front door to the house would slam with imperial finality.

It went on like that for two weeks.

I began to think, perhaps, I should be a better neighbor, make the Royal feel more welcome; a part of the local family. Which is somewhat misleading considering the neighborhood is an aloof haven and I barely know anyone. I'm like that; keep to myself, make friends slowly. I'm what they call an observer. Some dive, I float with mask and snorkel. But the instinct seemed warm; welcoming.

I was also getting very curious.

I was up late writing, one night, and decided to mix-up a batch of chocolate chip cookies. My new screenplay was coming along well, if slowly, and I thought about love scenes and action scenes as I peered into the oven, watching the huge cookies rise like primitive islands forming. They were plump, engorged with cubes of chocolate the size of small dice; worthy of a Royal, I decided.

I let them cool, ate three, wrapped the remaining dozen in tin-foil. Crumpled the foil to make it resemble something snappy and Audubon, the way they make crinkly swans in nice places to shroud left-overs. I wrapped a bow around the neck, placed the tin-foil bird into a pretty box I'd saved from Christmas, ribboned it, found a greeting card with no message. The photo on the front was a natural cloud formation that looked a bit like George Lucas.

I used my silver-ink pen that flows upside down, like something a doomed astronaut might use to write a final entry, and wrote "Some supplies to keep you happy and safe. Researchers say chocolate brings on the exact sensation of love; an effect of phenylalanine. (Just showing off). Welcome to this part of the world."

My P.S. was a phone number, at the house, in case the Royal ever "needed anything." I also included a VHS of François Truffaut's *Day For Night*, a film I especially love for its tipsy discernment.

I debated whether to include any exclamation marks, thought it excess, opted for periods. Clean, emotionally stable. Friendly but not cloying. Being in the film business, I knew first impressions counted.

It's one reason I'm sought after to do scripts, albeit for lesser films with sinking talents. But I'm well paid and it allows me to live in this secured community near L.A., complete with gate-guard, acre parcels and compulsory privacy. I'm an anonymous somebody; primarily rumor. I wish I could've been Faulkner, but there you are. I'm a faceless credit on a screen; my scant reply to a world's indifference.

I left the cookies and card in the Royal's mail-box, at the bottom of the driveway, and spoke tense baby-talk to the Dobermans, as I made the deposit, like one of those pocked thugs in *The French Connection*. The package fit nicely, looked cheerful in there. Too much so? I considered it. Every detail determines outcome; it's the essence of subtext, as Frank Capra once observed. And certainly, if the Royal were truly an international sort, I wanted there to be room for some kind of friendship. I could learn things. Get gossip that mattered; the chic lowdown.

I waited two days. A week.

Nothing.

I'd sit by my pool, every morning, read the paper, scan box-office numbers, sip espresso. But I wasn't paying full attention. I was watching my Submariner tick.

At ten-thirty, sharp, the heavy tires would crunch up the driveway and the door ritual would begin. I couldn't make out a word and tried to remember if I'd left my phone number in the P.S. Even if not, there was always my mailbox. Concern was devouring me by ounces and I disliked seeing it happen.

In self protection, I began to lose interest in the Royal; the inky sleigh, the seeming apathy, the whole damn thing.

At least that's what I tried to tell myself.

Sergio Leone says the important thing about film making is to make a world that is "not now." A *real* world, a *genuine* world, but one that allows myth its vital seepage. Sergio contends that myth is everything. I suppose one could take that too far.

Two weeks passed quickly and I'd heard nothing. I felt deflated, yet oddly exhilarated to be snubbed by someone so important; it bordered on eerie intoxicant, even hinted at voodoo. Despite efforts otherwise, the truth was I continued to wonder what the Royal thought about me, though it hardly constituted preoccupation.

I'm a bit sensitive on the topic because my ex-wife often said I paid unnatural attention to those I considered remarkable, though I found nothing strange in such focus. The way I see it, we all need heroes; dreams of something better; perhaps even transcendent. A key piece of miscellany: she ran off with a famous hockey player from Ketchikan, Alaska; a slab of idiocy named Stu. *TIME* and *NEWSWEEK* covered their nuptials. Color photos, confetti, the whole bit. A featured quote from her gushed:

"I've never been happier!"

Real pain. Like I'd been shot.

I feel it places things, as regards my outlook, in perspective. She certainly never could. Strangely enough, I've been thinking about her lately; how she drove me into psychotherapy after she left and took our African Grey, Norman, with her and never contacted me again, saying I'd made them both miserable. Over time, I heard from mutual friends that she was claiming, among other toxic side-effects of our marriage, that I'd caused Norman to stop talking, and that once they'd set-up house elsewhere, he became a chatterbox. I took it personally; couldn't sleep for weeks.

More haunting facts of my teetering world.

The fate of the cookies preyed on my mind for days, affecting work and sleep, a predicament rife with what my ex-shrink, Larry, used to term "emotional viscosity", a condition I suspect he made-up, hoping it would catch on and bring him, and his unnerving beard, acclaim. Still, I wrote half-heartedly and my stomach churned the kind of butter that really clogs you up.

Another few days went by and I made no move. Any choice seemed wrong; quietude the only wisdom. I was feeling foolish; mocked. My heartfelt efforts had been more irrelevant than I'd feared. I continued to work on my screenplay, and joked emptily with my agent, who seemed an especially drab series of noises compared to the person I knew the Royal must be.

It's true, I had no real evidence. The Royal might be an

overwhelming bore. Some rich cadaver in an iron lung, staring bitterly into a tiny mirror.

But I didn't think so.

In fact, I was beginning to think anyone who went to such trouble to avoid a friendly overture had something precious to protect. On a purely personal level, if cookies, a card and a badly executed foil swan could scare a person, their levels of sensitivity had to be finely calibrated. Perhaps the Royal had been wounded; given up on humanity. I've been there. I wish somebody like me tried to crack the safe; get me the hell out.

But when's the last time life had a heart. Let's face it, unsoothed by human kindness, souls recede. It's in all the great movies; pain, sacrifice, hopes in dissolution.

It's how people like me and the Royal got the way we are. We flee emotionally, too riddled by personal travail to venture human connection. Sort of like Norman. We're just recovering believers, choking on the soot of an angry world.

I understood the Royal. Yet I had to move on; get over it.

But it was hard. Maybe I was simply in some futile trance, succumbed to loneliness and curiosity. I admit I'm easily infected by my enthusiasms. You read about people like me; the ones who do something crazy in the name of human decency only to find themselves stuffed, hung on a wall; poached by life.

So, despite rejection, I found myself listening each morning, over breakfast, to the Royal's property, gripped by speculation. Awaiting the door ritual, sensing the Royal over there, alone, needing a friend. It was sad and nearly called out for a melancholic soundtrack; something with strings; that haunted Bernard Hermann ambivalence.

It made me recall a line I once heard in a bleak Fassbinder movie; this Munich prostitute whispered to her lover that a person's fate "always escorts the bitter truth." She blew Gitane smoke, pouting with succulent blankness and, to my embarrassment, it just spoke to me. I don't know why. It got me thinking, I suppose, the ways movies can; even the sorry, transparent ones.

It was the first time I began to consciously wish I could do a second draft of me, start things over; find my life a more worthy plot, tweak the main character. Maybe even find a theme. A man without one has nowhere to hide. Ingmar Bergman based a career on it.

Two days later, the note came. In my mailbox, dozing in an expensive, ragcloth envelope. It was handwritten, the letters a sensual perfection.

> *We must meet. How about drinks over here.*
> *Around Sunset?*

I must have read it a hundred times, weighing each word, the phrasing and inclusion of the word "must". It seemed not without meaning.

I debated outfits. Formal? Casual? I was able to make a case for either, chose slacks, a sweater. I looked nice; thought it important.

Before heading over, I considered a gift. Cheese? An unopened compact disc? Mahler? Coltrane? But it strained of effort and I wanted to seem offhand; worth knowing. The way Jimmy Stewart always was; presuming nothing, evincing worlds.

I used the forgotten path between the two driveways, dodging the Dobermans, who seemed to expect me, tilting heads with professional interest, beady-eyes ashimmer.

I walked to the front door. Knocked. Waited two minutes, listened for footsteps, and was about to knock, again, when the door opened. She was *exquisite*.

Maybe twenty. Eyes and dress mystic blue, dark hair, medium length. Skin, countess-pale. She wore a platinum locket, and gauged me for a moment.

"Hello," she said, in the best voice I've ever heard, up till then, or since.

We spent an hour talking about everything, though I learned little about her. At some point, she said her name was Aubrey and I'm sure I responded, though I was lost in her smile, her attentions colorizing my world.

It seemed she told me less about herself with each passing minute, which I liked; she was obviously the real thing. Genuine modesty looks best on the genuinely important.

She asked me about my work and carefully listened as I spoke about why I loved the music of words and the fantasy of movies; of creating perfect impossibilities. Her rare features silhouetted on mimosa sunset, and she said she'd always loved films, especially romantic ones, and when her smile took my heart at gunpoint, I felt swept into a costly special effect, a trick of film and moment, as if part of a movie in which I'd been terribly miscast; my presence too common to properly elevate the material.

She took my hand, and when we walked outside and watched stars daisy the big pool, I thought I must be falling in love. I still think I was, despite everything soon to befall me.

After a slow walk around her fountained garden, she said she was tired and needed her rest, that she'd come a very long way. I wish I'd thought to ask for details of that journey; an oversight which torments me to this second.

Aubrey slowly slipped her delicate hands around my waist and it almost seemed like loss had found us; a moment nearly cinematic in composition.

She said she had a gift for me, and led me to a wrapped package that rested, on a chaise, near the pool.

"I made it," she said.

"A painting?" I guessed, reaching to open it, until she gently stopped me.

"Tomorrow," she suggested. "When you're alone."

It seemed she was being dramatic. I wish it had been anywhere near that simple.

"Goodnight." Her full lips uncaged the word, as she looked up into my eyes, vulnerably.

I protested, wanting to know more about her, but she placed her mouth to my ear.

"I've always looked for you out there," she said, softly,

voice a despairing melody. "In the dark. I've wondered what you were like."

"What do you mean?" I finally replied, lost.

She never answered and I watched her disappear into the mansion, with a final wave, and what I would describe, in a script, if I had to tell the actress what to convey, as veiled desperation.

The next morning, I slept so deeply I didn't even hear the car that sped up my driveway. It wasn't until the knocking that I finally awakened.

When the detective spoke, I felt the earth die.

"A break-in?" I repeated in a voice that had to sound in need of medical attention.

He explained the missing piece was valuable, purchased in London, at auction. The chauffeur had told the police the owner of the house was a collector, but gave no further details.

"It was a gift. She gave it to me." I explained.

"She?"

"Aubrey." I could still see her plaintive eyes, desperate for connection. "The woman who lives there."

He said nothing.

Asked if he could see it.

I nodded and took him to my living room, where it leaned against the big sofa. He slowly, silently, unwrapped it and my world began to vanish.

The poster was full color, gold-framed.

It was from the thirties and the star was a stunning brute, named Dan Drake; unshaven and clefted. His beautiful co-star was Isabella Ryan, and she was held in his embrace as the two stood atop Mulholland Drive, windblown; somehow doomed. Behind them, a stoic L.A. glittered, morose precincts starved of meaning. Though striking, no splendor could be found in its image, merely loss. The movie was titled City of Dreams, but I'd never heard of it.

Isabella's eyes and dress were mystic blue, her flowing dark hair and pale skin more regal than the platinum locket adorning her slender neck.

From any angle, no matter how inaccurately observed, she not only resembled Aubrey, she was her.

It was shocking to me in a way I'd never experienced and I nearly felt some cruel director zooming onto my numbed expression for the telling close-up.

Both stars had signed at the bottom.

To everyone who ever loved. Yours, Dan Drake

Beside his, in delicate script was:

I've always seen you out there.

You're in my dreams. Love, Isabella Ryan

She seemed to be looking right at me, disguising a profound fear.

Charges were never brought against me, and the sunken-faced detective said I'd gotten off easy, that my neighbor, still unnamed, didn't want trouble and was giving me a second chance. The Royal only wanted the poster back, nothing more. For me, this generosity stirred further mystique; intolerable distress.

It's futile to determine who I'd actually spent the evening with; I don't believe in ghosts unless they are of the emotional variety; aroused by séances of personal misfortune, you might say.

But this thought brings no peace, no clarity.

I looked up *City of Dreams* in one of my movie books and found it; 1942, MGM. Black and white. Suspense. 123 minutes. There was a related article about Isabella, an airbrushed studio photo beside her husband, the obscure composer Malcolm Zinner. Zinner was bespeckled, intense. It appeared their marriage had been loveless.

The book said she'd had a nervous breakdown, but then don't they all? She'd never done another movie after *City of Dreams*, despite promising reviews, and died in a plane crash, in 1953. The book said her real name was Aubrey Baker.

Truffaut said that film is truth, twenty-four frames per second. Mine seems to be moving rather slower these days, my heart circling itself. I feel drenched by confusion; a lost narrative. I am drawn to unhealthy theory and wonder if perhaps I am dying.

Maybe I've just seen too many movies.

My ex-wife used to say the thing about irony is you never see it coming; that's how you know it's there. Also, the bigger it is, the more its invisibility and caprice. She used to talk like that, in puzzles. I'm not sure what she was getting at, but there you are.

All I know, is a movie poster with a long dead beauty, had been the most genuine thing I could remember in a lifetime of misappropriated and badly written fictions; it seemed a bad trend. Not even a particularly worthwhile plot, but I was never much good at that part.

Meanwhile, the Royal, it appears, is out there somewhere, hidden by lawyers; filtered and untouched. Bereft, bled by abuse and event; disfigurations of neglect.

It's been two months now, since that evening by the pool, and still no sign of the Royal, who remains at large in elite silence. I suppose I've given up thinking we'll ever actually meet, barring the extreme twist.

Sometimes, I find myself staring at the handwritten invitation, which I saved, though I have no idea who really wrote it. I stare until the words lift from the paper and fly away, scattering grammar into sky; an image Vittorio De Sica might have sparked to.

After considerable search, I finally found a copy of *City of Dreams* at a specialty video store, which had to track it down for me. When I watch Aubrey, despite her astonishing beauty, I keep thinking she looks trapped; not by bad dialogue or plot, but an apprehension of her life to be. Its imminent ruin.

Today, I tried to tell my agent why the dumb script I've been working on is late, and when he heard all of what had happened, he sighed and said writers were always getting themselves in crazy messes. He said he thought

I'd probably seen Isabella's movie when I was a kid and forgotten about it.

He nearly accused me of drinking, again, and wondered if maybe I'd had too much one night, wandered around the Royal's house and seen the poster; decided I had to have it, succumbing to stupid nostalgia. To bring back my only good childhood memory; going to the movies. The rest had been loveless, terrifying; an ordeal that lasted for endless seasons of pain.

I'm sure he's right. I do drink when I get lonely. I could take many evenings out of your life failing to convey the dread and hurt I often feel. I've had nights where I stared pointlessly, out at the world, and thought that no one could ever love me, just as, it seems, Isabella watches it from her lurid, heartbreaking poster, searching for the one face out there, in a heartless city, who will truly care.

Bunuel said every life is a film. Some good, some bad. We are, each of us, paradoxes in an unstated script; pawns who wish to know kings, souls divided, hearts in exile. We're all tragic characters, one way or the other; the vivid Technicolor glories, the noir hurts, the dissolve to final credits.

Fellini believed movies were magic, itself, awakened by light. That theaters were churches, dim and velvet; filled with incantation.

All I know is that when you feel lost and wounded, movies always welcome you, like a friend, inviting you to forget the painful truth; embracing your most lightless fragilities, the sadnesses which bind you.

To dream of better things.

Life pales.

Sync City

R. James Doyle and Rogelio Fojo

Frontispiece by Alejandro Burdisio
Illustration by Fangorn

Welcome to The Conflux. I am Madame Zelda, keeper of the Veil and consort of Traversers.

Tonight, we embark on a journey to commune with our foredescendants, performing a sacred ritual taught to me by the whispering lips of Eternalist Magicians.

Gather at the heart of this chamber, holding hands tightly as you form an unbroken ring around the Flickering Orb. Let not a single link in our chain falter, for together we shape the conduit through which we connect with Traversers.

Banish all distractions from the outside world. Allow only the dim glow of this Ghost Light, a phantasm of the full moon, to illuminate our gathering.

Now, we begin.

Repeat after me:

"Perpetuis Futuris Temporibus Duraturam."

Mighty Traversers, enigmatic wanderers of the spatiotemporal void, we summon thee to our midst.

Manifest yourselves in the ether surrounding us, revealing your presence in the shadows that dance at the edges of our perception.

We will now designate one among us to lead The Conflux.

You, sir! Step forth into the center of our circle, bearing the Ghost Light as your beacon. Touch the base of the light five times.

Finally, let us call for total silence.

Aidan? Please extinguish the Ghost Light and await –

"I am coming for you, motherfucker!" rumbled a deep, ominous voice, emerging from the darkness.

*   *   *

Access to the Carynx shop was through a narrow street-level doorway on the Vegas Strip – the seedy layer of the city, quite distinct from the elevated realm where the wealthy and beautiful indulged their vices and fantasies – buffered in an insulated world of depthless glitz and faux possibilities.

Madame Carynx sat at her reading table, idly shuffling her Tarot cards, with deftness and precision, a daily routine. Her eyes wandered over the various tired, thematic decorations which gave an otherworldly ambiance to the shop. Finally, she stood and walked briskly over to where an arrangement of dark-stained bookcases stood, with splitting spines, and gilt, unreadable titles. The shelves were additionally obscured with strings of beads, draped haphazardly.

Without hesitation, Cara probed through and retrieved an ancient leather-bound tome, an eighteenth century Latin edition, meticulously handwritten. Pliny the Elder's *Naturalis Historia*. From its aged pages, with the application of her fertile sense of the dramatic, she had derived some delicious words for her act, cryptic Traversermania terms. They fueled the popularity of her medium sessions these days. *Conflux... Sexus... Eternalists...*

She frowned. Someone had placed a peculiar metal bookmark in the book, bearing a numeric symbol surrounded by cryptic words. The design conjured thoughts of ancient runes in her Celtic mind.

Madame allowed the fragile tome to open at the location of a thin, dark bronzed rectangular plate, marking an undistinguished pamphlet. She drew out the document and opened it, delicately thumbing its contents, with increasing attention.

"Madame Carynx?" called Aidan from the doorway. She hastily replaced the book on the shelf.

*   *   *

"Madame, it is my pleasure to present Julie and… Grim. They would like to have their fortune told. They have kindly offered a generous recompense. Would now be an auspicious time?"

"The name is Julia," stated the young, cherubic woman.

Cara slowly, with a flourish, lowered her hand to the table, fingers splayed. She spoke with a husky voice. "I *am* a tad knackered, just so you know. Our foredescendants are gatherin' 'round just about now, and I will behoove them, respectfully, to be showing the way."

Cara Carynx gazed across the wood-worn table with a jaded eye, her vision well-adjusted to the gloominess. Her brother Aidan, who served as her right-hand man, bookkeeper, and occasional bouncer, brought in the hand-holding clients, and withdrew. Cara's world-weariness blended well enough with her crafted persona as a mysterious fortune teller. Which was convenient, saving her from having to work too hard on her performance.

Cara put her right hand to her forehead in a practiced, faintly theatrical gesture. She peeked through as her guests looked wide-eyed around the small, dim space. Celtic patterned cloths and tapestries, distinctive crosses, an incarnation of their eponymous ancient bronze war trumpet – all cluttered the limited confines of the shop.

Julia and Grim exchanged excited glances and shivered in sympathetic fashion. She was starry-eyed. Her more mature boyfriend was quiet, attentive.

Cara had seen it all over the years, and these two fit a familiar category. Both smart and capable. They would believe they could never be hoodwinked. Likely, they were eloping in Sin City, either coming from one of the brazen commercial wedding chapels or about to head there. Full of their power tinged with some guilt, they were looking for some form of affirmation as they stepped into a wide future.

Madame prolonged the silence, knowing her customers would not bear it for long, and soon say more than they should.

"I can hardly believe how much Las Vegas has changed since my childhood," Julia said, her excitement palpable. "I remember a dusty outpost in a vast desert landscape. Now, it's a glittering metropolis!"

"You two soulmates are not from this realm."

"You're right!" Julia blurted. "I was completing my engineering degree at Berkeley when I met Grim, I mean, Mr. Grimley. Now he's whisked me off to Nevada, in his most amazing automobile. We are going to collaborate on a bid for the re-architecting competition. What an incredible modern city! Replicas of famous buildings from around the world, transformed into hotel casinos – astounding! They don't waste time building things around here!"

Madame Carynx scoffed. "Me brother has work in this... construction boom."

"Being a fellow architect your brother?" inquired Grim.

Madame leveled her gaze at Grimley, summoning great dignity. "A... security contractor."

Julia was on a roll. "A skyline of towering skyscrapers! Neon illuminating the night! Bustling streets filled with sleek automobiles! Extravagant entertainment venues! The town has evolved into a modern marvel! Don't you agree, Madame Carynx?"

"If you set aside that it's all fake," muttered Cara,

under her breath. Then, smiling enigmatically, "Aye, 'tis a testament to the boundless ambition and invention of humanity, me dear."

"And yet, the potential is not being reached," noted Grimley.

Silence descended. Julia reached out, again taking her companion's hand in hers.

Without another word, Cara brought forward an oversized deck of Tarot cards, which she methodically and expertly shuffled, thoroughly mesmerizing her clients. She dealt out four cards from the Major Arcana. They seemed to float into place, lining up neatly on the table, rather than being deposited.

Judgment. The Hermit. The High Priestess. The Lovers.

She looked up, engaging her guests with direct eye contact, one, then the other. All the while, she casually tucked in graying wisps of hair which strayed out from her head covering. Cara waited while the uncertainty in their expressions grew.

"What do these cards mean?" asked Julia.

"I perceive that your future is holding before you… a choice. An important decision. Do these signs have any meaning for ye?"

"*Hermit*. We are going on a retreat?" offered Grim.

"Or we'll have a lovely home in a beautiful remote setting," countered Julia.

The *Judgment* card, with the Dead being called forth by trumpet to their reckoning, sat on the table like a tasteless, edgy joke.

The young woman stared at the *High Priestess* card. Cara took in how she stole glances at her companion, seeking a cue, while he kept his eyes only on the fortune teller.

"You are both of you fine things. The Traversers, they're telling me of your lantern of love glowing warmly, and of your carnal pleasure growing stronger."

Grimley's eye twinkled.

"Could *The Lovers* indicate joy in finding a kindred spirit?" asked Julia.

Time to bring this session to a close.

"May ye pass into your future together the same way you entered," said the Madame, becoming annoyed with these lovers. "Aidan will arrange for your coinage. You are free to return whenever you're feeling the need for additional guidance from the hidden world."

Cara bowed her head, placing her left hand fully over the crown of her head, breaking all eye contact. She listened as Aidan led the couple out, one following the other, dull beads swishing around them.

*   *   *

At City Hall, the chair of the Municipal Council spared no words outlining their reasons for reimagining Las Vegas's architecture.

"So many constituencies, even in this town with its very specific *raison d'etre* – of separating the masses from their monies by preying on the deep irrational human motivation to pursue false hopes," they said.

The mayor had to work at not rolling his eyes. His colleague on the council tended to wax philosophical, and sometimes, annoyingly ethical. Unlike them, he was eminently pragmatic. He sorely wanted to cut to the chase. Why won't others on the council acknowledge that the purpose of the elevated transportation system, with its internal and isolated connectivity, was simply to separate the haves from the have-nots? The high-rolling deep-pocketed tourists did not wish to experience the Strip at street level – unless they were seeking something they could only find there.

"Extending the moving sidewalks and monorail to connect every casino in the city, this should be a no-brainer," he said.

"Yet it is the duty of civic leadership to provide for a safe comfortable experience, and to keep the tourists coming back to drive the city's unique economic engine. Our mistake may be in being too obvious, telling people where we want them to go," replied the chair.

The mayor snorted, not trying to hide his annoyance.

"At least we have our green light to put out the call for architectural bids."

"Yes. An open call. All are welcome to submit projects and ideas. Let's see what we get."

*   *   *

Madame Carynx held tight the leather-bound book, tracing her elongated fingernails along its spine as she impatiently watched Aidan pore over the open pamphlet on the table.

"What is it, brother?"

"Appears to be a set of technical plans to build out the monorail."

"That much I could tease out. Are they any good?"

He looked up. Cara could see the interest in his washed-out blue eyes. "Quite good. How did this get here?"

"It's apparently been sitting quietly on the shelf, one more beat-up manuscript, contributing to the ambiance."

"But… ?"

"Today, it would not fade into the background." Cara paused. "What does your… contractor persona say about these plans?"

Aidan scowled. "You mean my on-again, off-again work for the casinos?"

He scanned the document with his cell phone, brightening. "One app says it's a concept to complete the monorail, with more seamless transfers from the moving sidewalks, and finally connecting all the casinos. Just as the city is promoting. The design includes a sophisticated routing system."

He looked up. "But there are portions I don't understand. Like this title above… Sync City?"

"A pun or a typo?" Cara sat, pondering. "Whatever, I know what we'll do with this."

Her brother raised an eyebrow.

"These are desperate times for us, brother. It's time for the hard-working proprietors, the honest – well, maybe not honest, but the *real* part of the Strip… it's time for us to fight back for our livelihoods – before the city squeezes us out entirely. We don't even have enough money to cover the permits for the parlor another year."

Madame tossed her shoulders, setting her shawls swaying. "This is going to be the Carynx Family bid."

Aidan smiled from ear to ear. "I'll work on getting us some backing from the big boys."

*   *   *

While she pitched, Cara flaunted her many bangles, rings, and shawls, knowing they bespoke Celtic earthiness, melancholy – and pugnaciousness.

"Thank you, Madame Carynx," interrupted the chair of the Municipal Council. "A most interesting concept. Although we wish we could have received more detailed answers to our questions."

"I'm not quite at me stoppin' point. Ye see–"

"We're ready for the next offer," interjected the mayor.

Madame remained rooted. "I understand, and begging pardons, Your Chair, Mr. Mayor, distinguished members. Me wee bruther is the technical one in the family. He's no slacker, but he couldn't be here today. I'll ask him to get back to ye with bang on answers to your questions. I'm texting him right now."

"Yes, but that would perhaps not be fair to the other bidders–"

"I'm not sayin' ye already know who the winner is…" said Madame, scowling, "…but I am suspectin' you're not much interested to be hearin' from the denizens of the Lower Strip."

A commotion at the door interrupted the proceedings.

An energetic man pushed into the chamber, shrugging out of the grip of a security person. A younger woman trailed the pair. The guard's substantial presence remained within grasping distance of the intruder, who wore a tasteful business suit over what resembled an acrobat's leotard.

Cara stared, aghast at seeing those two again.

The intruder launched right in. "Madame is not being able to answer your questions, because she is stealing my plans!"

Cara's guard and hackles went up together. The man seemed somehow younger. "Who's lettin' in this eejit?"

The mayor gazed out the window. The chair sighed and beckoned with their hand. The man proceeded forward, the security professional continuing to track him.

"You are?"

"We are Morgan and Morgan, Engineering Architects," said the woman.

"You have made an accusation, sir. Would you care to explain yourself?"

Grimley leveled a disdainful look at Cara. He turned to the head of the table. "Your Chair… ness. I am thanking you."

The interloper settled and addressed the room. "I could be describing how I am placing my plans at one of your quaint establishments, but I am acknowledging the difficulty to be explaining."

He shrugged, theatrically. "I am possessing, and sometimes catching myself on, an overdeveloped flair for the dramatic… I could be answering your questions, such answers being expressed, necessarily, within your understanding. The concept, after all, is being mine."

"A bit *loco*, aren't we?" observed Madame.

A few titters bounced around the chamber. The chair lifted their gavel, then replaced it on the table without striking.

Grimley continued. "But I am thinking it is being most expedient to be describing the purpose of my superior design. The accomplishment of that purpose being, as you are fond of saying: 'At the end of the day…'" He offered a smug chuckle. "…the intrinsic functioning of architecture. And I am being a most brilliant architect."

Cara wanted to cross the chamber and slap Grimley around. She could see the chair and mayor conferring, *sotto voce*, the mayor looking past their shoulder. Madame followed his line-of-sight to a view of the *Circus Circus* casino.

The chair sat up straighter. "Mr. Grimley, that purpose is… ?"

"The opposing of the scourge of a technological society, the challenge remaining when all others are being addressed, the final disease of the eminently accomplished, the–"

"Mr. Grimley."

His partner Julia intervened: *"Mesdames et messieurs… nous parlons d'ennui."*

Uniformly blank stares. Madame Carynx worked to keep a smirk off her face.

Grimley cleared his throat, with an air of great patience. "Boredom. This is being what you are having now, with your transportation system."

The stares continued.

"When one is knowing that all… *places* are being within reach, when all experiences are at the calling, how is one to be finding… the new?" Grimley leaned in. "How is one to be pursuing *meaning*?"

To Madame's dismay, she saw Grimley had their attention, even if no one had the thread. Time to interrupt.

"It's been donkey's years since I've seen such a pathetic–" countered Madame.

Grimley leaned back into his speech. "They are knowing their destinations. They are taking the moving sidewalk from *Excalibur*, they are going to *Luxor*. They are taking the monorail from *MGM Grand*, they are going to *Bally's*. You are telling them where they are wanting to be going."

The chair frowned.

The mayor enjoined, "What do you mean? Telling who where who wants to go?"

"The passengers traveling via your monorail system," said Grimley, evincing a deep sense of being put upon.

"In no way are we telling them where they want to go," returned the mayor. "We are only making it easier for them to get there."

"That is being exactly the genius of my design. One is

boarding the train, and one is arriving... knowing not... *where*."

Cara watched Grimley pause at self-congratulation, perhaps self-adulation.

The mayor spoke again. "And how do you accomplish this... sleight-of-hand?"

The technologist bristled. "Now, there is being no magic here."

Madame Carynx evenly returned the gaze that Grimley leveled at her.

He continued. "Topology is being dynamic, not being fixed. Passage is being accomplished by the spontaneous generation of synchro–"

Grimley stopped. For the first time he seemed to be thinking before speaking. "I am standing on my trade secrets. But I am pointing out, and surely you are agreeing, there is being no better *venue* for this new type of travel experience than in this glittering, always-unpredictable, clock-banishing, endlessly hope-bearing, City of Chance!"

Madame Carynx scowled. "Oh, stop now. Is anyone else here thinking the man's too much in his whiskey?"

The chair and mayor conferred in hushed tones. Madame strained to earwig.

The chair lifted their head. "This is by far the most intriguing, but also the most confounding bid received. There is also the matter of possible intellectual property theft. Keeping in mind the future interests of our city, the mayor and I concur as to the following... We ask that you, Madame Carynx–" A nod in Cara's direction. "– and you, Mr. Grimley and..."

"Ms. Julia Morgan."

Another nod. "...confer and make every effort to combine your bids into a single project. If you are successful, we are willing to–" They inclined their head. "– look the other way. As to the unresolved difficulty. We offer you one week, and we wish you the best. We believe that your success would become our great town's success."

"Your Chair, I must protest with all–" began Cara.

The chair rapped the gavel. "We are adjourned."

Madame Carynx whipped her head around to glare at Grim and Julia, making no effort to hide her fury.

*　　　*　　　*

The reluctant team emerged onto street level, proceeding stiffly. Out of the side of her eye, Madame Carynx watched Grimley shake his head, muttering. Julia walked a pace ahead.

Cara spoke first. "I did not steal your plans."

Grimley gave her a baleful look. He moved his right hand toward his left wrist, turning to face Madame. Cara saw an odd bracelet there, mostly hidden by his jacket sleeve.

A man stepped between them, bumping, roughly separating Grimley's hands, taking a separate elbow in each of his, such that the twosome became a threesome, moving briskly along the sidewalk.

"Aidan!"

She felt the strong grip of her brother's left hand. She could only imagine what Grimley was feeling.

"Mr. Grimley, you have harassed my sister quite enough today," said Aidan. "You and I are going to come to terms. We'll talk privately."

Aidan let go of Cara, keeping his implacable hold on Grimley. Her brother half turned. "I'll take care of this."

The Carynx team would prevail. She would follow her brother's lead.

She caught up with the stunned Julia. "Dearie, we'll let the lads flaunt their testosterone," Cara said. "While we have a chat between lassies. I'm sure this is all just some misunderstanding."

Over Julia's shoulder, Madame watched her brother lead Grimley into an alley. She guided Julia in the opposite direction, escorting her to a nearby café. They took a table on the sidewalk. A waitress approached. Cara ordered two cappuccinos.

"Doin' a bit of time travelin', are ye?" she questioned Julia.

"Beg your pardon?"

"You're a Traverser, too, aren't you?"

"Traverser?" Julia seemed genuinely surprised.

"Was it meself who summoned ye to this realm, Ms. Morgan?

"To Las Vegas? No…"

Madame sighed, allowing one more minute to pass, her annoyance simmering beneath a composed exterior.

"Aye, forget it then. May the best team prevail. Farewell, and may luck be with ye."

Cara legged it out of there, leaving Julia to deal with the check.

*   *   *

Madame peered around the corner, trying not to be conspicuous. She saw Aidan glance quickly up and down the length of the alley. He pushed Grimley against a brick wall.

The endlessly annoying technologist seemed unworried. He said something Cara could not catch.

"Why didn't you simply retrieve your plans?" Cara had no trouble hearing her brother's baritone across the distance.

Grimley started a movement of crossing his hands.

Aidan moved swiftly, his prosthetic hand fastening onto Grimley's throat, and squeezing, to an awful crackling sound. Grimley's eyes widened in disbelief and agony as his assailant plunged a hand into his chest with brutal force. Aidan dragged Grimley behind a dumpster, checking sight lines to both ends of the alley.

"Now you've underestimated both members of the Carynx Family," he said with a snarl.

Cara saw her brother roughly handling Grimley's clothing. Traversal would deliver no antidote against the finality of passing. Glints faded, and what had seemed a sleek, skin-tight fit became rumpled, unkempt. Aidan worked at something, which he pocketed.

All Madame could do was back away. Quickly, efficiently, stealthily.

Without looking back, Cara picked up her pace, her heart pounding in her chest. She could hear the faint sound of footsteps behind her, growing closer with each passing second.

"Grimley will be no more trouble," said Aidan, catching up to her.

"You're sure."

"I was convincing."

Cara breathed a sigh of relief. "All right, I don't want to know more."

Aidan handed a roll of coins to Cara. "A souvenir."

Cara unwrapped the paper covering. Inside were tokens, not coins. They were metal, but of a strange dark color, almost black, without luster. They reminded her of the bookmark. Like iron, but not iron. Heavier. "How odd," she said, putting the tokens away in a hidden pocket of her shawl.

*   *   *

Cara and her brother stood together to represent the Carynx Family bid.

The chair rapped the gavel to call the Municipal Council meeting to order. "Madame Carynx, would you care to make the introduction?"

"Yes, Your Chair. Grand. This fella here is me bruther, Aidan Carynx. He'll see to the fine details of the city's new project."

"Very good. We may have some questions for you, Mr. Carynx. In the meantime, we appear to have a straightforward outcome for the monorail bids. Mr. Morgan Grimley has withdrawn?"

"No, your honor," replied a bewildered Julia. "He's gone missing. I haven't been able to reach him. Please, would you grant us more time?" She looked around the walls to check the hour, to no avail. "Oh, right, no clocks here. I wish Grim had provided a clearer explanation of his plans for the re-architected city." She glanced at Cara and Aidan. "I am a competent painter and sketch artist, and I helped him to visualize his concept. I also contributed engineering blueprints for the monorail, but…"

"But?"

"Grim has been rather tight-lipped lately. He asked me to shift focus to our next project – in California."

The mayor took the floor. "Honorable Chair. If I may speak plainly, this entire affair smells off."

"Carynx Family, either of you, would you care to respond?"

Cara raised her finger. The chair nodded.

"Your Fine Chair, we stand here with nothing to add, other than our disappointment at poor Mr. Grimley's no-show. The city needs its monorail, and it's been too long since such work was awarded to the working class. Me bruther and I are no chancers. We're ready to build out the transportation service our fair city needs, in a timely manner. Wherever Mr. Mayor may be poking his nose, I'm thinkin' this may be another time when all interests are best served… by lookin' t'other way, as 'twere." Cara watched the mayor's eyes narrow.

Another round of titters ricocheted around the council chamber.

The chair rapped the gavel. "Order… order now!"

The hubbub subsided.

"Ms. Julia Morgan: Your partner Mr. Grimley made some curious remarks about his design allowing passengers to travel to… unknown destinations. Can you illuminate?"

"Mr. Grimley's vision, as I understand it, revolves around a novel concept of removing all landmarks from the city. His core idea is to encourage people to get lost in Las Vegas, as in a game of chance… and, in so doing … find themselves."

The chair turned to the Carynx siblings. "Can either of you edify us?"

"I cannah, Madame Chair, said Aidan. "I'm only havin' the account of Mr. Grimley's words from me darlin' sister. Perhaps he had a few bats in the belfry? The man's a tad breathless too, one might be sayin'."

More titters.

"Thank you, Mr. Carynx. We will strike that last remark from the record."

Cara sat down with her brother, impatient. The chair leaned over and conferred with the mayor in inaudible tones. Presently, the two settled back.

The mayor spoke. "A city without signs? You push a button before crossing a street and random instructions light up? That sounds very Las Vegas, but... we would need more clarity on how such a system would function and its potential impact on navigation and safety within the city. And given the absence of the principal architect..." He shook his head.

The chair picked up the thread. "But the City needs its monorail completed, with or without additional fantastic capabilities, and noting the underwriting associated with your bid, we are pleased to award the contract to the Carynx Family." They smiled, a politician's smile. "Madame and sir, congratulations!"

Applause resounded around the chamber. Cara and Aidan stood and firmly clasped hands. Madame put on her world-weary cast, but a smile peeked through. She saw that Aidan looked uneasy, but showed no signs of irony, or diffidence.

The chair continued, "Recognizing that this will be your first undertaking of this order – generous bond notwithstanding – the city will retain approval authority for subcontracts, and provide oversight, at least until the project is confidently underway."

"Thanks a million, Your Chair," said Madame. "We welcome the partnership. Me bruther will crack on to construct the system to specifications. We are grateful for the opportunity to contribute to the welfare of our fine city – from the ground up."

More applause. The gavel rapped once more, and the meeting dissolved into mingling, handshaking, and good cheer. Madame Carynx drank in the triumphant scene, a long time coming.

Julia Morgan departed, shoulders both slumped and tense.

*   *   *

The Carynx team managed to build out the monorail system steadily, to Julia's precise specifications. Madame was more than pleased when Aidan showed hidden skills and talents to keep the development project on schedule and on budget.

"With an iron fist," Cara joked, pointing to her brother's management style – and anatomy.

The first new stations opened to great fanfare and acclaim. Everything worked flawlessly. City Hall was impressed, and pleased.

Sin City residents learned that the station turnstiles possessed a coin slot, but the opening did not seem to fit any domestic, or even foreign currency. The media applauded the quaint retro touch. Soon the dream of connecting all the casinos – well above ground level – would be realized.

Riding the strength of unqualified success, Madame returned to her roots with a new lucrative venture. Exorbitantly priced seance-like medium sessions, aimed at contacting Traversers, the craze sweeping the nation. Cara embraced a new role as Madame Zelda, assisted by her faithful sibling, each contributing unique talents to a successful new act which the city's casinos vied over.

*   *   *

Cara unpacked boxes at Madame Zelda's new digs in the upscale part of town. Despite its luxurious setting, the space was already as cluttered as their former establishment on the Lower Strip. But she was thrilled to have a larger, gleaming reading table, its polished surface inviting her touch. On impulse, she sat and released the drawer slung on its underside. She withdrew a paper roll, bobbing it in her open palm to remind herself of its heft.

She placed the roll on the table, carefully opening one end. Lifting out one token, by its rim, she placed it on the surface. The same dark metal she recalled, striking in color, dull in luster. Symbols adorned the face of the coin – 1M*t* – with lettering reminiscent of Celtic runes. Cara replaced the roll, pocketed the token, and closed the drawer. She leaned forward and punched the intercom button.

"Yes, Madame Zelda?" answered Aidan.

"Hold my meetings and calls. I'm going for a ride."

*   *   *

By unspoken agreement, City Hall was one of the first new stations completed and opened for business, a simple enough extension of the extant monorail line. This station would never receive as much traffic as the ones at the casinos. Moreover, it was mid-morning, a reliably low-activity period in the city.

Nonetheless, Cara peered around to verify the station was deserted. Satisfied, she withdrew the dark token and moved it to the coin slot on the turnstile. Satisfyingly, it fit perfectly. She deposited the token and was disappointed to see it simply drop through into a little well where she could retrieve it.

She repocketed the token. On a whim, Cara placed her hand on the turnstile bar anyway and was surprised to find that it rotated and clicked with a clear *thunk* to admit her. She pushed on through and looked up.

The space of the station was subtly altered. The lighting had shifted, to become more diffuse, and the overall palette was… stronger. The station remained deserted and was utterly silent. But the quiet did not last. The *whoosh* of an approaching train sounded and intensified.

The train pulled into the station at a frightening speed. It not so much slowed and halted, but simply became… stationary. The doors snapped open, faster than Cara could see.

Madame moved, feeling drawn forward, but she willed herself to pause. She had no ticket and had no idea where this train was going.

Cara took a few breaths. Setting her shoulders, she boarded the train.

The doors shut. Cara looked out the window, but there was nothing to see. Nothing to make sense of. Instinctively, she hooded her eyes and looked at the floor of the train. Soon, she sensed the doors were open again. She had not experienced any sensation of acceleration.

She disembarked to another deserted station. Cara hesitated at the exit turnstile, but it did not resist her, and she pushed on through…

…to the mild bustle and returned normalcy of a sparsely populated monorail station. Cara looked around in vain for an identifying sign.

*   *   *

Outside, at the elevated level, Cara took in the view down the plaza to the *ARIA* hotel and casino, a view she had always found to be curiously off perspective and rescaled, as if one were looking into the future. But the palette was normal, and she saw no other indications of… displacement.

On impulse, she twirled, rising and dropping on her toes, giving herself over into exuberance. Her signature shawls – more finely made now – floated and twisted about, responding to her motions.

Madame Zelda was already recognizable along the Boulevard almost as an icon. Passersby gathered at the spectacle. They were soon applauding, in heartfelt fashion. Cara dropped from her twirl and took in the scene around her. A seasoned performer reading her audience, she segued neatly into a curtsy, much to their delight.

Madame threw back her head and arms and shouted. "My eternal city!"

*   *   *

Cara made her way along a pre-existing moving sidewalk to the *Bellagio*. The paths now extended to cross the Boulevard in several places, compact: elegant colonnades. She soon found herself at *The Venetian*. The painted ceilings there offered another perspective-distorting illusion, for all the world convincing as a sky canopy. Even clouds seemed to move and evolve if one looked from the corner of the eye.

Madame ambled along a curving, lushly carpeted corridor, giddy from feelings of delight, and… possibility. The light dimmed as she followed the trajectory of narrowing walls. She heard voices and slowed. The voices grew sharper, clearer. She halted, peering around an extravagantly long row of planters holding cypress trees.

"You dirty cheat! You know what they do to people like you in this town."

"I can explain… please."

A man sitting on the floor tore bills out of his wallet and tossed them at his assailant. Cara watched, horrified, as the angry man suddenly plunged his hand into the chest of the other. Blood spurted and spilled.

Her street instincts took over. All Cara could do was back away. Quickly, efficiently, stealthily, driven by pure self-preservation.

As she turned to flee, Cara felt a cold chill down her spine. She sensed the killer's eyes on her, a sinister presence looming behind her.

Without looking back, Cara picked up her pace, her heart pounding in her chest. She could hear the faint sound of footsteps behind her, growing closer with each passing second. Catching up to her.

She looked at the token in her hand.

Emerging from a primal haze, Cara found herself outside, at street level. People on the sidewalk, some sitting, nodded at her, smiling. She hardly noticed. Harrah's station was at hand, and she hurried to the entrance. With no thought of alerting the authorities, Madame pushed forward until she was at the turnstile, on a crowded platform.

Madame paused, glancing around. She was in a queue, with few options and freedoms, and celebrity status or not, people were impatient. Breathing heavily, Cara scanned the crowd behind her, but the killer was nowhere in sight. Still, a shiver ran down her spine as she wondered if he was watching her from a distance, waiting for another opportunity.

She dropped in the token, but this time it was retained by the system.

Cara pushed through the turnstile. Silence. The shift again, as before. The train came, for her alone. Noisily, abruptly. She boarded and shaded her eyes. Presently, she disembarked at City Hall station.

*   *   *

'Perpetuis Futuris Temporibus Duraturam.'

Now, extinguish the Ghost Light.

In the darkness, allow our minds to merge as one, a beacon of hope against the void.

Repeat after me: 'We call upon the Traversers… to join us in this moment… at this Sexus of time and space… in Sync City.'

When time travelers breach our reality, they may signal their arrival via subtle disturbances… never with direct communication. Be vigilant for chronological irregularities… dimensional rifts… Their presence may be discerned in myriad ways.

Once contacted, you may pose your inquiries. But heed well: Understanding their responses requires focus, patience, and belief.

Those who harbor doubts about Traversal, heed this warning: Depart from this parlor if you dare question our veracity. For Traversers appear only where truth reigns and is sought.

Do not falter. Only through desperate commitment and perseverance will you gain their assistance to unlock the secrets of the ages.

Commence.

*   *   *

Madame took ample time to assimilate her experience on the monorail, choosing not to share it with her brother. She carefully counted tokens and determined that forty-six remained.

She put out word that Madame Zelda would further expand her fortune-telling service. The fee would be greater than before – more even than her Traverser medium sessions – and would include a ride on the 'Sync City Express'. Madame told her select new clients, with her usual cynicism, that their fortunes would be fulfilled 'on the other side'. The generated buzz was entirely word-of-mouth, and quite effective.

The intercom hummed.

"Yes?"

"Your client is here," said the latest assistant.

"Enter," commanded the Madame.

Cara adjusted her shawls, and her facial muscles. She knew from experience that the distance from true weariness to a practiced mantle of bearing a great burden of knowledge was not far.

She recognized the young woman who entered.

"Madame Zelda... Ms. Julia Morgan." The temp retreated quickly.

Cara waved to a chair on the other side of her desk.

"I didn't know where else to go. You may not remember me," said Julia.

"Oh, but I do. One of *The Lovers*." Cara's smile bordered on genuine. "But I'm a tad surprised to see ye again. Did *The Hermit* ever say why he skedaddled rather than bid on the project?"

Julia dropped her gaze. "I've not seen Grim since. But... you offered that we... that I... could return for additional guidance."

"That I did, and you are welcome to it," added Cara. "Ye know, me brother is taking his sweet time getting back too..." Madame sighed.

"We didn't tie the knot after our earlier visit. My parents caught up with us. I'm being sent overseas to a school in Europe," explained Julia. "To make a long story short, they agree that you, Madame, would cast my fortune again – which they're paying for – and that I would abide by the outcome."

"Your ma and your da are unusually supportive," noted Cara, sincerely.

"Well... My father Charles wanted me to stick with engineering, following in his footsteps. But Mama Eliza, she always ran our household like a royal castle. She surprised me by understanding why I wanted to pursue architecture."

Madame reached into her desk, rummaging, but in a precise manner. She produced a deck of dusty Tarot cards. And a dark token, which she placed pointedly in the middle of the table surface. She shuffled the cards, and soon, one by one, they floated out as an assembled array of four, facing her client.

The Lovers. The Wheel of Fortune. Temperance. Judgment.

Madame addressed her charge. "This time, you are thoughtful of your path forward, and the comin' responsibility."

Madame pushed the token to the edge of the desk, within reach. "The period is most auspicious. I'm workin' now with Traverser entities. You will ride the Sync City Express, and all will become clear."

Julia Morgan looked at the coin, wide-eyed. "How does it work, exactly?"

"You place the token into the turnstile. You proceed on an illuminating journey and answers come to you... if your heart be truly open."

Julia had the look of someone who suspected she was being taken for a different kind of ride. But she took the token. "That sounds eerily reminiscent of Mr. Grimley's enigmatic concepts. Do you recall?"

Madame simply smiled. "There's the matter of me shillings."

*   *   *

Julia deposited the token and pushed on through the turnstile, her excitement barely contained. Feeling a vague discomfiture, she closed her eyes. She reminded herself, "This is meant to be a journey."

Hearing a rushing sound, she opened her eyes to find Grimley standing there, waiting for her. He beckoned her on to a train – of which there had been no sign a moment before. Julia couldn't contain her excitement at the sudden turn of events.

They emerged at the *Rio*, one of the newly connected casinos. They entered, Julia still catching her breath, and made their way onto the glittering, chaotic floor, with its lack of references for day or night.

Grim collected an impressive tray of chips at a cashier. Hardly noticing their trajectory, they arrived at a roulette table.

The evening was not yet at full swing, and they took two seats at the partly occupied table. A well-dressed, middle-aged couple acknowledged them perfunctorily, on their way to becoming drunk, if not already there.

"Red or black, I can never decide," said the woman.

"That's being you, all over. Not deciding," returned the man.

"Well, since you're clearly seeing red, I will go with black."

The woman pushed forward a stack of chips and spoke to the table host, who paddled her stack onto *Black 22*. Other players placed their bets. Julia and Grim watched as the wheel whizzed and spun down in its usual mesmerizing fashion. The ball began to clack, then bounced and settled.

"Double Zero."

The woman groaned. The man of the couple gestured in a disgusted manner. Julia watched, fascinated.

Through several spins, the couple did fine, in the up-and-down winnings sense. But they would steal uneasy glances at each other. Their dialogue did not improve. If anything, their snipes became more bitter, making the other table occupants, who came and went, uncomfortable.

Julia assessed the woman to be, in the vernacular, well-preserved. Once beautiful, still striking, and certainly dressed elegantly. But past her prime, most evident from attitude, and a certain practiced manner of ignoring her partner while not giving him an inch.

The man worked through another bourbon and soda. His hairline exposed a well-shaped forehead. Crow's feet radiated from his eyes. One might say he was 'rugged' – not the worst place to land. But he seemed deep in malaise, with a settled habit of finding fault.

Looking at the woman, Julia saw herself twenty-five years hence. The same hair color (faded), the same way of leading with the shoulders, first one way, then the other (now tiredly), the same enviable breasts (more ample and drooping). However, she took a liking to the woman's glasses. *Pince-nez*, lacking earpieces and staying in place by pinching the bridge of the nose. The style was becoming increasingly popular in her circles, a symbol of status. Julia thought they would suit someone like herself. Far-sighted.

The man presented a similar picture. The hairline no doubt matched that of his maternal grandfather (receding), with brown eyes (unlit), and strong hands (grizzled knuckles).

Not difficult to see how those two could have been powerfully attracted to each other – once.

*   *   *

Julia and Grim reemerged onto the glitzy upper level and made their way back to the monorail station.

"Let's not be worrying about my plans for this city," said Grimley. "I am being confident that my architectural concepts are being taken up. I am hiding the pamphlet inside the thirty-seven books of Gaius Plinius Secundus and scattering them about. Someone can be finding my plans one day and building it."

"But–" protested Julia.

Grim held up a hand. "I'm being more interested now in applying my ideas to your Castle."

"The one commissioned by Mr. Hearst? Thank you, Grim! I don't imagine revealing the secret additions I plan to make now. Hearst wouldn't understand anyway, even if I did explain them."

"I can be showing you how it is appearing," said Grimley. "With a range of inspiring sights, being for you alone."

"How?" Julia was incredulous.

"With this birthday present," he said. "Be using this coin to board the train, and you are seeing. You are going alone on this trip. I am promising to be meeting you later, at a random halfway station. But your ultimate destination is being uniquely yours."

*　　*　　*

Julia deposited the special token and saw it returned to her this time. She pushed on through and turned to wave goodbye to Grim, but he was gone.

The station was deserted, silent. The lighting shifted, becoming more diffuse. Julia appreciated the European design. The *whoosh* of an approaching train sounded and intensified, as it pulled into the station at a frightening speed and then froze on its tracks. The doors snapped open.

She took a seat and gazed out the window, but there was nothing to see between stations. And somehow unfathomable to look. But she could sense when the train approached one station after another. At each stop, she looked around in awe for the station names.

Stazione Centrale, Milan
Wien Hauptbahnhof, Berlin
King's Cross Station, London
Estació de Sants, Barcelona
Amsterdam Centraal
Zürich Hauptbahnhof
Roma Termini
Madrid Atocha

The full journey ignited Julia's newfound passion, with each historic site and architectural landmark shaping her burgeoning interests and sensibilities.

On the twentieth of January, the train arrived at *Stáisiún Heuston*, the sun washing Dublin in a calm, golden glow. Despite weariness from the lengthy journey, Julia wished to mark her twenty-second birthday with something memorable.

She felt the call of the nearby historic campus, knowing its features would further inspire her as an engineering-trained architect – a sentiment reinforced throughout this extensive tour of Europe. The haunting medieval castles and other magnificent edifices she had seen overwhelmed the innocent replicas found in Las Vegas.

Pocketing the token, Julia stepped out of the train station on a windy afternoon and made her way to the entrance of Trinity College. The facades of the campus buildings thrilled her. Her excitement turned to disappointment when she made to enter the library to view the famous Book of Kells only to find it closed for the day. As an artist, she felt a pang of regret for missing the opportunity to see the illuminated manuscript, created by Celtic monks in the ninth century, and renowned for its intricate illustrations, decorative motifs, and calligraphy.

Disheartened, Julia wandered the deserted campus. She reached a central sculpture – a globe. She began spinning it, as if battling against the forces thwarting her plans. She removed her hand, and the sculpture spontaneously revolved in the opposite direction. Julia sighed and bent to read the description.

Sfera con Sfera is the artwork of Italian sculptor Arnaldo Pomodoro. The bronze sculpture encompasses a large spherical structure with another smaller sphere inside, floating or rotating within the outer one.

The surfaces of both spheres were intricately textured with patterns and symbols. Then Julia understood intuitively what it all meant: the complexities of the universe... the interplay of order and chaos... the fragility of existence.

The sign she had been searching for all along! The fortune she had hoped to find in the Tarot cards. She had been looking in the wrong place. Or in the wrong way.

Julia returned to the station. With sudden conviction, she resolved everything. She would apply to the architecture program at the *École des Beaux-Arts*, in Paris. Grim had warned her about the historical absence of female students there. He had also turned out to be unreliable. She knew her moment had arrived.

Julia placed the token and retrieved it. She wondered about getting home to California to arrange her affairs. Later. Soon she would be disembarking at her intended destination: *Gare du Nord*. Gateway to *La Ville des Rêves*, the City of Dreams.

*   *   *

The intercom buzzed. Madame looked up with annoyance. At the second buzz, she stomped from her desk and yanked open the door.

A mature woman stood there, peering over pince-nez glasses.

Without skipping a beat, Cara stepped back, gesturing. The woman entered. She appeared happy, striding more purposefully than Madame recalled.

"Quaint touch with the spectacles. And you're tellin' me you're no Traverser."

Julia's forehead wrinkled. "Madame Carynx–"

"It's Madame Zelda now."

The woman got straight to the point. "Julia Morgan. You may not remember me. I'm here to thank you."

"For what, if I may be askin'?"

"For delivering my fortune, just as you said."

Cara, impatient, knew she would have to hear her out.

Julia continued. "I did not rush into marriage with Mr. Grimley."

"Oh? Ye found him then? And the reason bein'?"

"Well, not exactly. We did love each other, but maybe not in the way that's meant to last... lifetimes. For starters, we were both dedicated to our careers as architects. Our work defines us, and we put our professional goals first. Plus," Julia continued, "as a woman in a male-dominated field, it's not easy to find someone who really sees you. I focused on breaking barriers and making a name for myself." She paused. "The best way to put it is that we looked into the future and saw ourselves and all became terribly clear."

Cara stood still, drawing out the moment from habit. She stirred. "Good for ye, lass. Let it be stewin' in your heart then. But there's really no need to be thanking me."

"Oh, but there is."

Cara imagined how she might demur, and wrap up this conversation, but Julia pressed on.

"You see, when you sent me off on the Sync City Express, you helped me discern that my career was, for me, the most important thing. I have never regretted my choice. I wanted you to know. And I suspect your clients rarely get around to thanking you. I'm just sorry it took me so long."

Cara found herself uncharacteristically without words.

*   *   *

Madame Carynx pushed through the whitewashed iron gate giving access to a sturdy exterior stairwell. She knew the stairs would take her down to street level, near the old shop. She listened for the heavy, one-way gate clanging shut behind her. At sidewalk level, Cara soon spied the narrow storefront, pleased that it looked even seedier than her memory of it.

As she fumbled for a key no longer in frequent use, the door opened.

"Aidan!" Cara smiled. They had not seen much of each other lately.

Aidan stepped aside to provide space for her to enter. His features were set.

"You know, I pay you well as my assistant. I'd like to see more of you."

"I like it here," he snapped.

Cara waited.

"This business of the fortune telling again. And that ridiculous Traversermania crap. What are you thinking?"

"Why, I'm honoring a Las Vegas tradition. Separating the marks from their dollars. Only more so. I came to collect that special Tarot deck we rarely used. You know the one I mean, the gilt-edged one."

"It's unseemly."

"But Aidan, what they're willing to pay! I keep upping the fee, and it makes no difference. I'm thinking of going to open bidding."

"It wouldn't hurt for us to give something back," growled Aidan.

Madame Carynx came up short. "To whom?"

"To the real inhabitants of the Strip!" Aidan gestured. "They're right out there!"

"Is that what this is about?" Cara felt her features harden. "They're just a bunch of losers! If they want to improve their lot, they can figure it out, using smarts, and opportunity. Like we did. Otherwise, the hell with them. We don't owe them a thing!"

Aidan shook his head slowly, muttering, "After all I did for you."

Cara fixed him with a look. "What did you do?"

He returned the glare. Then made an exasperated gesture in her direction, with both hands. Madame flinched. The prosthesis seemed momentarily threatening.

Cara felt an unaccustomed unease. Not from clashing with her brother, which was normal enough. "All right Aidan, I can tell we're not on the same team anymore."

The fortune teller gazed past his shoulder and spotted her old, worn reading table, its surface etched with faded mystic symbols hinting at a past both distorted and better forgotten.

"Just hand me the cursed cards, Aidan. I'll divine the Tarot once more for me wee brother. And then ye can decide how ye want to be movin' forward."

*   *   *

Aidan strode along the sidewalk, his steps heavy with the resentment of heading back to his assistant job at Madame Zelda's, his gaze turned inward and distracted.

On a hunch, he turned a corner, not far from City Hall, and kept moving. A red glow brought him up short. His way was blocked by a large man, wearing a leer and a strange, form-fitting jumpsuit, both unappealing.

"Aidan Carynx, you are being under arrest."

"Who the hell are you?"

"Marshal William Arp. I be now and here in the matter of Morgan Grimley, deceased."

Aidan's street instincts kicked in, and he tensed. A knife flew from his powerful hand, on an unerring trajectory.

The man had been ready, hand on wrist. Aidan saw motion there. A flash, and the knife dropped to the ground between them, a fused lump.

Aidan looked at his formidable adversary. "Are you going to kill me?"

"Being something like that."

Another playing of the fingers. Aidan crumpled to the ground.

*   *   *

A flash.

"Cara, I haven't much time."

Aidan's sudden appearance inside her luxury parlor caught Cara off guard. Her eyes widened.

"I had to beg to see you. He said it 'be not mattering.'"

As she often did during awkward moments with her brother, Cara glanced at his prosthetic right hand. She saw a strange, faintly glowing bracelet there, on his wrist.

"It's best if I show you." Aidan gestured to his cell phone.

After a series of efficient taps and swipes, Aidan presented an image on the screen. A fat face looking straight into the camera.

"You've never wanted to know details of what I do for us," he said. "The City of Las Vegas basically invented modern surveillance technology. I've had contacts with the casinos for years."

Madame settled more easily in her chair. "Thank you, Aidan. What am I looking at?"

In response, he unfroze the image. Madame Carynx watched the ugly man mouth something at the camera in exaggerated fashion. Aidan tapped through, several times, to similar sequences, all with different backgrounds.

"Given several opportunities, casino security was able to arrive on the scene within *seconds* of these recordings being captured. But they never found him. They thought they might be dealing with hacked images, but they appear to be genuine."

"What is the man saying?"

"Not a problem for lip-reading apps. Arp says the same thing each time."

"And?"

"First, he says, 'Where is being Aidan?'"

Cara's breath caught.

"He then says, 'I am coming for you.'"

Somehow this last revelation was less shocking, almost expected. There seemed to be nothing more to say at the moment.

"Cara, please, I don't know how much time I have."

She nodded.

"I was trouble back then, aimless. On the Boulevard, leaning to the wrong side, or the wrong level you might say. I needed to know if there was something else... I was here for."

Cara listened, intently.

"I still remember the cards you turned for me: *The*

Hierophant, *Strength*, *The Emperor*, *Justice*. I thought I should know better, but… that sequence felt like a real sign, a call to action. On my way here I decided to place a quick bet, on a hunch our luck was about to change. But I never got to a casino."

Madame felt their dynamic shifting.

Aidan looked her straight in the eye. "Now I knew what I was here for. To protect you. There's a name for this kind of thing. I get it now. *Synchronicity.* From the title of the pamphlet, Grimley's plans for the city's architecture. Arriving at unexpected places, at unexpected moments. No matter if we got lost. We would always find a way out or a way back. But… my dear sister… now you've lost *your* way." His prosthetic hand tenderly touched her heart. "I can't find you anymore."

Cara did not trust herself to speak.

Her brother vanished in a flash of light.

*   *   *

Madame Carynx sat there, through dusk gathering, into the night. Except that the night in this city, especially along the Boulevard, was always a spangled wonder. She watched images washing over the Sphere, mesmerized.

Cara reached forward and turned on her desk lamp.

Cara placed her head in her hands, no longer able to hold back the sobs. "Aidan, I am so sorry. Forgive me, my brother."

She reached under the table and brought forth the Tarot deck. The confined pool of light on the table allowed her to draw cards without first seeing them. And then revealing them, flashing, into the illumination.

The first card: *The Tower*.

The second: *Justice*.

The third: *Death*.

The last: *The World*.

Cara reached once more into the drawer. She held a dark token in her hand.

*   *   *

Madame proceeded along the streets, moving between pools of light thrown by streetlamps, finally to City Hall station. She had a sense of being shadowed.

But Cara walked upright, steadily, peacefully, with an unaccustomed feeling of... *direction*. She paused at the station entrance. "Life is a sad progression of closed-off possibilities. Sorry to say, I'd become such a wonted purveyor of mystery that I lost my way, too... forgotten how to care."

Madame reached the turnstile. "Not an escape, whoever you are... a journey." Cara shook her head. "Meaning? Purpose? Destiny?" Her voice echoed softly in the deserted space. She could hear the hint of irony within her habitual disdain. She smiled. "One may hope for adventure."

She placed the token into the turnstile. When it dropped into the well, she was somehow not surprised to find it transformed to conventional bronze – flat, larger, unadorned. As worthless as any of a million other slugs to be found around the city. She left it behind and pushed through.

*   *   *

The night was gone, replaced by diffuse, endless daylight. Madame looked around, drinking in the larger-than-life colorings. She proceeded into the station, adjusting her shawls, looking straight ahead. The train rushed to a stop, in the blink of an eye. The doors opened.

Cara Carynx crossed over from the platform, ready to embrace her fate.

She was not alone in the car. The ugly man was there, sitting in the back, waiting.

"You are really one of them," she said. "I should know... I summoned you. I am Madame Zelda, keeper of the Veil, consort of Traversers."

She strode fiercely toward him, demanding, "Now, take me to me bruther, ye bollocks!"

*　　　*　　　*

I sense restlessness stirring among the Traversers. Let us not bid them farewell but entreat their return, a millionfold, to grace us, at a special juncture in the grand tapestry of existence.

We give thanks for the precious moments they bestow on us... We treasure their fleeting presence... and beseech another rendezvous at another time and place.

Our temporary odyssey in Sync City draws to a close.

'It will last into endless future times.'

The Man Who Broke Time

David Gerrold

Frontispiece and illustrations by Alex Storer

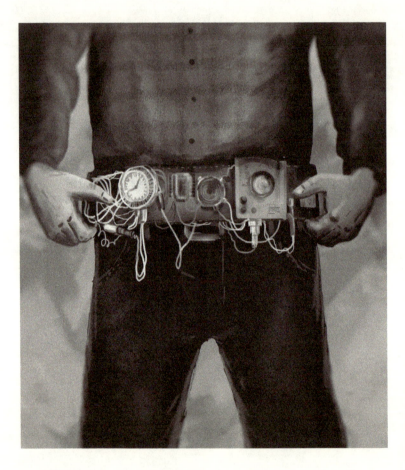

Tovar:

I don't have anything new to say.

David

Even after Steve graduated, we stayed in the apartment on Romaine, partly because it was still a good office for me, but mostly because we'd spent so many nights here wrapped up in each other's arms, it was our private little hideaway. It wasn't very big, just a bedroom, a bathroom, a kitchen, a small closet, and a diagonal space that served as a living room. The furniture was leftovers and hand-me-downs – but it was all we needed right now. And even though I never said it aloud, it was my escape plan – if maybe Steve and I didn't work out.

Which was why I felt invaded when I came in the front door and found three strangers sitting in the living room.

No, not strangers.

Not exactly. Harlan Ellison and Dorothy Fontana on the green couch. And the third one, sitting in the blue chair. That was the real shock. Dog was parked in his lap.

"What the hell–"

And then I had to stop mid-sentence, because why would Harlan Ellison and Dorothy Fontana come visiting me? We weren't friends. We weren't even acquaintances. They were writers, I wasn't. I'd seen them on a couple panels at the Writers Guild, how to break into the business, and then again at a local science fiction convention. I was surprised they even knew who I was.

The third person? He was me. An older version of me. Short hair, going gray, puffy face, a paunch – I hadn't aged well. He looked exhausted. In fact, they all did. They looked a lot older than they should have been. Harlan had white hair. Dorothy's was an artificial dark red. Dog looked confused. He got down and trotted over to me.

I think I handled it well.

I went into the apartment's little kitchen. Dog followed. I put down the grocery bags. I put the sodas and eggs in the fridge. I put away the cans of dog food and the other items too. I gave Dog a cookie.

I leaned on the sink to catch my breath and tried to make sense of what I'd walked into. I turned it over and over, upside down and inside out. It was impossible, but there it was – the only possible explanation.

Finally, Dog and I walked back into the living room. "Dorothy, do you want some tea? I think I have some Lipton's or something. Harlan, you want Perrier, of course. And you, Older Me, do you want a Coke?"

"Sit down, kiddo," said Harlan.

"Please," said Dorothy.

"I'll explain," Older Me said.

"You're time travelers, right?" I picked up Dog and held him in my lap.

Older Me looked to the others. "Told you he'd get it. I'm smart."

"Yeah. That's why we're here." Harlan was a lot more mellow in person than on the stage, but he was still Harlan. He said, "Look at him. He's too young. He's not going to believe us."

I looked from one to the other. "Why should I?" I didn't know any of them very well, only from the occasional run-in at some fannish event or other. So why were they here? Why me? "You let yourself into my apartment. What do you want?"

Older Me said, "Well, first we need you to trust us. You know who I am. It's not too hard to figure that out. And Harlan and Dorothy – they're two of your best friends in the world."

"Uh. I don't think so. Maybe they're two of yours–"

"Shut up, kiddo." That was Harlan. He pointed to Older Me. "That man – the one you might become – is one of the most courageous men I've ever known. You might be him someday. But right now, shut up and listen."

I shut up.

But I was tired of listening. I'd heard all the explanations. Too many explanations. It had taken a while, but I'd finally figured it out. Explanations are the booby prize. They don't produce results. I had lots of explanations. And no results.

My television career had fizzled out for reasons I never understood. Maybe I just didn't understand the industry. The only show I had wanted to write for had been cancelled after its first season. Right now, Steve was supporting both of us while I struggled with the Great American Science Fiction Novel and the occasional small pitiful sale to *The Staff*, the local underground weekly. I was desperate.

But Steve still believed in me. Sometimes I wondered how long that would last. He was beautiful, he was successful. I was neither. And it scared me. One day, Steve would probably figure it out, he'd realize what must have been obvious to everyone else. And then I'd be left alone with no one but Dog. Dog was loyal, not judgmental.

Older Me said, "You have no idea, do you?"

"I have no ideas at all," I said. "Do you want the whole list of producers who've shut me down. Even my agent gave up–"

"It's Chinatown, Jake." That was Harlan. I had no idea what he meant.

"Please listen to us. This is important," said Dorothy.

Older Me leaned forward, steepling his hands in front of himself. I recognized that gesture. I did it myself. "You're important."

"I don't think so. Almost everyone I know tells me that I'm not. The only one who thinks I'm special is Steve. So why should I listen to anyone else?" I held Dog close.

"Because everyone else is wrong," said Harlan.

"And you're the only one who can do this," said Dorothy.

Of all of them, it was Dorothy – something in her voice – that made me shut up. I looked to her.

"It's that article you wrote," she said.

"The one in *The Staff*," Harlan said.

There are people who believe in alien space lizards, Sasquatch, yeti, and Nessie. There are people who think the Earth is flat and others who insist that Hitler is still alive and living in Argentina. There are people who are so disassociated from reality they shouldn't be allowed out of the house without a keeper. They assume every unexplainable fact is evidence of something impossible – and the lack of evidence is evidence of a conspiracy. The more bizarre the idea, the more they embrace it.

I said, "This is about the murders, isn't it?"

Harlan nodded. "Yeah, kiddo. This is about the murders."

Older Me said, "I know you meant your article as a joke, but... well, here we are."

He was referring to a piece I'd written for L.A.'s second most popular underground weekly. The most popular had been The Freep, (short for *The Free Press*) until it ran into financial problems. Most of the staff had quit to start a competing weekly, appropriately called *The Staff*. I'd sold a few small articles to them, but I'd never been able to bootstrap that into a regular column.

The most recent article – I'd intended it to be a semi-satirical speculation, so of course, most of the paper's terminally-stoned readers immediately accepted it as hardcore truth, a revelation of the way things really were.

There had been murders – murders are always page one stories. But these were particularly interesting. The FBI had been tracking a serial killer for almost a decade. He (or maybe she) seemed to kill at random. If there was any kind of a pattern, it remained unknowable. And apparently, there were other murders not publicly included in the official count.

It was a very odd list. There was no sense to it.

Charles Whitman in Texas, Thomas Hagen in New York, James Huberty in San Ysidro, John Wayne Gacy in Chicago, Ted Bundy in Washington State, Lee Harvey Oswald in Texas, James Earl Ray in Memphis, Sirhan Sirhan in Los Angeles – all of them apparently killed with the same 9mm weapon. The rifling on the bullets was a forensic match. The imprint of the firing pin on the shell casings was a forensic match.

Some of these were explainable. Somebody had pissed off somebody else. Maybe the Las Vegas casino magnate had offended another mob boss. Maybe the Australian broadcaster had angered a business rival. Maybe someone with a grudge had hired a prolific hit man and that might explain a few of the others. But then why the movie star's fiancé? Why the draft-dodger? Why the favored son of a rich Saudi family?

It had to be random. Except somebody had gone to a lot of trouble to get to some of the victims. A random killer wouldn't do that. But the forensics matched up, so it wasn't random – that was the problem. It looked like the same weapon had been used all over the world, but mostly in the United States.

The prevailing theory – at least the only one that fit the available facts – was that it was not the same gun. It couldn't be. There had to be some quirk in the manufacturing process of that particular model of gun, whatever it was, something that allowed multiple copies to all produce the same rifling and firing pin impressions. That was the only logical possible explanation.

But just for the fun of it, because that was the way my mind works – and because I had always wanted to write science fiction – I postulated that an aggressive time traveler was taking out murderers and assassins and terrorists before they could commit their terrible acts of violence.

It was a joke. Really.

Because if there really were time travelers, weren't there bigger and better targets?

Good questions, Right?

But not to be taken seriously.

Until three time-travelers showed up in my living room.

"Yeah," said Harlan. "You have questions. It's kinda brain-melting, isn't it?"

"Yeah," I said. "If you're really time travelers, then why are you here? Why didn't you kill Hitler?"

"Because if we had, you wouldn't have been born. Neither would any of us. Now stop being so smart."

"It's complicated," said Dorothy. "It'll take a while to explain."

"And even longer to understand," said Older Me. He held up what looked like a briefcase. "This will help. It's a laptop."

"What's a laptop?"

"It's a personal computer. It fits on your lap."

"Bullshit. Computers are as big as refrigerators."

"We're time travelers, remember? This is future technology. Don't panic, you'll figure it out. There's even a book of instructions. *Laptops For Dummies*."

I folded my arms around Dog. He grunted, he knew the gesture, he knew what it meant. I didn't believe a word of it.

Older Me said, "I know it's hard to accept. I didn't want to believe it either. But this laptop contains a whole library. All the resources you'll need. Books, articles, videos, documentaries." Older Me put the bag on my desk, next to my treasured IBM Selectric typewriter. "It's going to change your life."

"It'll do more than that," said Harlan. "It'll change the world."

"Um, wait – wait a minute," I said. "Do I understand this correctly? You're giving me the resources to change the future?"

"No," Harlan said. "We're giving you the resources to unchange the future."

Dorothy cleared her throat. Both Harlan and Older Me looked to her. She was holding a thick spiral-bound manuscript. Very thick. "This is the important part. You need to read this first."

"What is it?"

"It's a printout. The whole file is on the laptop too. It's a history of the 20th century that didn't happen. It's not your history, it's not this history, but it's the one that might still happen."

"If what?"

Harlan said, "If you don't listen." He looked annoyed.

Older Me said, "I know you like alternate histories, but you're not gonna like this one. It's a very scary read." He took it from Dorothy and put it on my desk next to the case containing the laptop.

"Okay, fine. You're giving me a science fiction book. Is there anything on that laptop thing that you wrote? That I'm going to write?"

"No, there isn't."

"Why not? You could have saved me a lot of work."

Harlan interrupted. "Because if you don't write them yourself, you won't learn how to write."

"That doesn't make any sense."

"It will after you write them."

"I don't believe you. I don't even believe in that laptop thing. If I know anything at all it's that everyone has an agenda."

"Yes, we do," said Older Me. "But it's your agenda. Or it will be soon enough."

Dorothy spoke then. "We went to a lot of trouble to get here. That's how important this is – not just to us, to you too."

"Okay, fine. Whatever." I don't know why I felt so annoyed. Maybe it was because they'd interrupted my frustration. I had my own plans. I didn't want theirs. "What else?"

Older Me said, "We've outlined it all for you, the steps you need to take. You'll read the history, then you'll know what's next – what we need you to do."

"Okay." I pointed to the black case at his feet. "What's that? What's in that box?"

He picked it up carefully and held it on his lap, but he didn't open it. "A 9mm pistol. A Sig Sauer with padded grip and a laser sight for targeting. And ammunition too. Seven magazines, seven rounds each. Don't play around with this. Read the instructions carefully. Spend some time practicing with the dummy rounds until you get–"

"Wait – stop. What? Why are you giving me a gun?"

"A 9mm Sig Sauer with a padded grip and a laser sight for targeting. There's a custom holster too. And extra ammunition, and a speed loader too." He pointed to a dark metal box tucked under my desk. I hadn't noticed it before. "You'll need it."

"No, I won't. Take it away. I'm not–"

Harlan leaned forward, a hard look on his face. "Yes, you will. You're going to save the world, asshole."

Coming from anyone else, I would have bristled. But when Harlan calls you an asshole, it's a term of affection.

"Please," said Dorothy. "It wasn't easy arranging any of this."

"It's complicated," said Older Me. "This timeline doesn't exist yet. We're trying to make it happen."

Dorothy said, "That book, the terrible history of the 20th and 21st centuries, the book – that's what's going to happen. That's what we want to stop."

"Wait. Stop. I'm confused." I wasn't confused as much as I had a terrible suspicion. "Is that what the gun is for?"

"Yes. I'm sorry, but yes."

"The people in the article – ?"

"Yes."

"But those people are already dead–"

"Yes. And no," he said. "They won't be dead until you kill them."

"If they're already dead, then why do I have to kill them?"

"Because you already did. That is, you will."

"No, wait. That can't be true. I'm not a killer. I can't be. That would make me just as bad as them. Maybe worse. Because I'd have a real justification. Like a holy mission. No, there's gotta be another way–"

Older Me said. "There isn't any other way. We tried. It didn't work. You're the way, the only way."

Harlan interrupted. "Kiddo, this is on you. You might be an asshole, but you're the asshole we need."

"Thank you for sharing that," I said. Sarcastically.

"David," said Dorothy. "Please read the documents we've provided."

"You think that's going to make a difference?"

"We think so, yes."

"Um…I think you're wrong. I'm not exactly a big fan of guns."

"We know. Yes."

"So why me? Why not one of you?"

Older Me said, "We're not from this timeline. You are."

Harlan said, "Your timeline can't exist until you do what you have to do."

"And then what happens to you?"

"Dorothy and Harlan become two of your best friends," said Older Me.

"This was your idea, wasn't it?" His expression was answer enough. "Then you should know–"

"I know," he said. "Much better than you. I know your past, you don't know your future. I'm doing you an enormous favor here–"

"Fuck you," I said.

"Yes," he said. "I wrote that one too. With a timebelt it's possible."

"What's a timebelt?"

"It's a belt that lets you travel backward and forward through time."

"Sounds convenient. I'd like to see that."

"You will. We're going to give you the timebelt."

Harlan made a face, he looked to the others. "He'll believe in a timebelt, but not a laptop? Oh, yeah – he's the right kind of asshole."

I shrugged. "I can only believe six impossible things before breakfast. That was the seventh."

Dorothy said to Harlan, "Please stop calling him an asshole. It's not helping."

"Okay, I'll just call him a schmuck. Because that's what he is until he accepts the responsibility."

Older Me reached around to the hidden side of the chair. He brought out a flat box and passed it over. "This is the timebelt. It's the only one we have. We all had to share it. Now it's your turn. Take good care of it. When you're done with it, put it away in a safe place. Maybe get a gun safe."

"Don't you want it back?"

"I'll get it back, don't worry."

"And don't play around with it, kid," said Harlan. "The timelines are fragile enough."

Older Me looked like he wanted to put a hand on my shoulder, but he didn't. He said, "I wish I could sit and talk with you for as long as it takes, but – I can't. That doesn't work. Read the printout. Read the letter with the laptop. Read all the documents. There's everything you need to know. And a lot more. Then you'll understand. And then you can decide. Will you do that much at least?"

I nodded, a noncommittal assent.

"There's really only one good choice," said Dorothy.

"Good for who?"

"Good for you. Good for everyone," said Harlan.

"But especially good for you," said Older Me.

I didn't answer that.

I was tired of people telling me what would be good for me. Most of the time, they were telling me what would be good for them if I'd just please cooperate.

So yeah, I was pissed.

Pissed at the intrusion. Pissed at their presumed authority. Pissed for no reason I could identify.

There are a lot of emotions for which there are no words. I was experiencing several of them. Maybe several dozen. Confusion was at the top of the stack, but there was also annoyance, anger, upset, fear, curiosity, and even a sense of relief. Because whatever else this was all about, apparently I was important enough for Harlan and Dorothy and Older Me to travel through time to tell me to do something.

The problem?

Well, that's where the other emotions came pouring in. Resentment and outrage.

I'm not a killer.

I've never fired a gun. And I doubt I ever will.

I'm a strong believer in rational discussion as an alternative to violence. Except, of course, if you're dealing with Hitler. Maybe that was an exception. Maybe that was why they were here – ?

There was still too much I did not understand.

"Look," Older Me said. "You don't have to decide anything tonight. You don't have to do anything tonight. Sleep on it. Read the documents tomorrow, or this weekend. Take your time. There's no rush. You literally have all the time you need. So do yourself a favor. Be the writer you want to be and allow yourself to imagine the possibilities. Will you do that?"

Dorothy added, "Please."

I thought about it. Finally, I said, "Okay."

They stood up then, ready to leave. Harlan said, "You gotta do the right thing, kiddo."

Dorothy said, "We believe in you."

Older Me said, "I wish there were an easier way. I really do. I know this is going to be hard for you. But…trust me, it's important. It's necessary. We need you to be a hero. The hardest kind of hero."

And then they were gone. Pop, pop, and pop. One after the other, they vanished.

I went into the kitchen, Dog followed and I fixed his dinner without the usual conversation about how lucky he was to have the expensive wet dog food instead of the usual dry kibble. It didn't matter, he'd eat whatever I put in front of him. Even salads. Especially salads.

I called Steve. I hardly ever bother him at work. I hate the telephone. I've hated it since I was four. My mother had one surgically attached to her ear and getting her attention while she was on a call was impossible. I learned at an early age that I was nowhere near as important as whoever she was talking to.

But talking to Steve always made me feel good – like everything was going to be okay, no matter what.

I told him I had some serious reading to do, so maybe he could pick up a pizza for dinner. That confused him – he said, "I thought we were going out tonight."

"Oh, right – um, I must have forgot."

I didn't ask for details. Maybe he had planned something. We'd sort it out later. He had to get back to work. He never objected to having me check in, but we tried to keep our calls short anyway.

I opened the bag and took out that thing they called a laptop. It didn't weigh very much. I put it aside. Whatever it was, I didn't trust it. Most future tech was a lie. Flat screen televisions had been predicted in 1955. They were still ten years in the future.

I picked up the spiral-bound manuscript instead. The pages were crisply formatted and there were pictures on almost every page, many of them in color. However this thing had been printed, it was an impressive piece of work.

Dog and I curled up on the couch and I began to read the horrifying history of the 20th Century that hadn't happened. Not just what could have happened in the past, but also what could have happened in that future. I paged ahead to the end. This thing even predicted what the 21st Century had become – oh, come on. That's just ridiculously stupid. We'd never –

Okay, I've read bad science fiction. I've even written bad science fiction. Maybe that's why I didn't have a career.

But I've read stuff by so-called professionals that was so bizarre, so deranged, so terminally stupid that even some of my worst efforts made more sense.

This book – this "printout" – this thing went from bizarre to insane to surreal to simply unhinged.

But it was so convincingly written. And supposedly there was even more evidence on the laptop, documentaries and videos and interviews.

If it was a hoax, then somebody had spent way too much money creating all of these pictures and photocopies of news articles. And if that laptop really had a couple thousand hours of video – hard to believe that – then the cost of that kind of fakery would have been in the millions. You couldn't have done it anywhere in the world, except here in Los Angeles – and if you had, the whole town would have been employed in the effort. And there would have been all kinds of chatter everywhere about the effort involved.

So no.

And there was one other reason it couldn't be a hoax.

Harlan and Dorothy and Older Me were the evidence that this thing –

A single sheet of paper fell out of the book. It said, "You want proof? Test the timebelt. Here's how."

I read the instructions. I put on the belt. I popped backward. Three hours. The bright sunlight of midday dazzled in the window.

Older Me was sitting in my living room again. Or still. Or before. Not certain of the phrasing. This time he was alone. Dog got down from his lap and trotted over to me. I appreciated that. He was going to get a special dinner tonight.

Older Me pointed to the desk clock. "Convinced?"

I swallowed hard and nodded.

He said, "Here's a thousand dollars. More than enough to pay off all your debts. But more important, before you do anything else, take Steve out to dinner tonight. You have a reservation at 7:00pm at Musso and Frank's. Splurge. Order off the expensive menu. Have a great dessert. And tell him how much you love him. That he's the best thing that ever happened to you. There's the phone. Call him now."

I didn't need any encouragement for that. I called Steve and told him we were going out for dinner. Oh, now I understood our mutual confusion on the earlier – later? – other call.

After I hung up, Older Me said, "I want you to know something. Just you and me." He took a deep breath. Maybe he was figuring out how to say it.

I waited.

"What?"

"You're stronger than you know. Remember that."

"Why? What do you know?"

He shook his head. He wouldn't explain. "You have to go now. You'll be home soon. You don't want to meet yourself, that would freak you out." Hmm, that was an interesting idea, maybe I could write a story about that.

Back in my own time, I picked up the printout and started reading in earnest. Each chapter had a summary, followed by a longer narrative, and then a thoroughly detailed timeline.

It was not comforting. Particularly the assassinations. And the mass shootings. And the – ohell, whoever had taken out these bastards was a hero. One of the greatest in history –

Oh, shit.

I put the manuscript down as if it were something evil. I stared at it for a long moment, then slid it into the desk drawer.

I stood up slowly, went into the bathroom, peeled off my clothes and stood in the shower, letting the hot water rain down on me – hammering on my head, splattering across my shoulders, draining down my back – letting it do its steaming best to soothe an ache that would not go away. Those terrible images, those disturbing words, they'd been stamped indelibly into my soul.

Damn them, damn them all! Older Me knew me too well. He knew I would want to do something – anything to end the pain in my head. Damn that bastard! Damn me!

I got dressed.

I met Steve at Musso and Frank's. He lit up when he

saw me. And I let go of all my worries when I saw him. Steve had the brightest eyes and the most beautiful smile. He was my joyous red-haired completion. He was soul-filling. Conversation was unnecessary. Smiles were enough. Anything either of us said, the more important message was how much we relished being together.

Steve shared his day at work. I listened as if it was the most important news in the world. When he asked me how my work was going, I said, "Really hard to explain. I have this thing I have to figure out."

"Can I help?"

"I dunno. It's a story problem. Well, more of an ethical one. Would you kill Hitler?"

Steve's expression darkened. There were some things he didn't like to think about. "Killing is a mortal sin," he said.

"That's the problem. What if you could save many lives by taking one? Is the lesser evil acceptable?"

"The lesser evil is still evil. That's what Father Byrne says."

"I know. But what if those are your only choices. Big evil or little evil?"

He smiled, and I knew what he was going to say even before he said it. "You're the writer. You choose." He quoted my own words back to me. It made me laugh. I told him how much I loved him and he smiled and put his hand on mine, his way of saying it without words. He lit up my soul.

We went back to the apartment and spent the entire night wrapped in each other's arms. For just a little while longer, I didn't have to care about – the decision. When we were naked together in bed, just looking into each other's eyes, he sang to me. "You're just too good to be true." It made me cry. Now I know why there are love songs.

In the morning, I made him breakfast. The refrigerator was filled with a lot more food than I remembered buying. So we had bacon and eggs and hash browns and toast and jam and coffee and orange juice. He smiled in delight, hugged me tight, and kissed me deeply before heading off to work.

Leaving me alone with – that printout. That book. That decision.

The gun.

I hadn't opened the case.

I didn't want to kill anyone. I didn't know if I could.

Everything I'd read – sociopaths do it without caring. But real people, the kind of person I tried to be, wouldn't recover from the emotional trauma. It would become a permanent part of who you were.

On the other side of that equation – if there ever were crimes worthy of capital punishment, I now had a list. The crimes and the perpetrators and the days when they were supposed to have happened. And I had the power to stop them.

If I didn't stop them – the world I lived in today would not be the world any of us would be living in.

I kept reading, looking for a way out.

There wasn't one.

If there had been an alternative, then wouldn't Harlan and Dorothy and Older Me have done that instead?

I'm very good at overthinking things.

There were detailed instructions in the box. How to handle the gun safely. How to load and unload it. How to take it apart and clean it. Everything.

Older Me had thoughtfully included dummy rounds. I practiced loading the magazines, I practiced putting the magazines into the gun. I practiced dropping them out again. I practiced everything but firing actual rounds.

It was an alien experience. And yet, curiously satisfying on a mechanical level.

The instructions included the address of a target range north of the San Fernando Valley, just off I-5. I wasn't certain it was a good idea, but not going was a worse idea.

The range safety officer questioned me about the gun, he'd never seen one like this. I couldn't tell him it hadn't been invented yet, so I said it was a prototype, designed for inexperienced users. I was testing it for the company. He accepted that explanation and told me that the gun was clearly built on the 1911 platform, whatever that meant, and would certainly serve well.

I told him I didn't have a lot of experience, that was true, so taught me how to hold the gun – how to place my hands, keeping my finger out of the trigger guard, and using my left hand to provide a firmer grip. He showed me how to load a magazine, slam it home, how to drop it out one-handed, use your thumb on the button, and finally how to check that the chamber is empty – and then double-check that the chamber is empty. Then everything all over again.

Then when he thought I was finally ready, he put up a paper target for me. I practiced shooting at the silhouette of the alleged criminal. The first time I shot, the recoil startled me, but after that I began to get used to aiming and shooting. By the end of the afternoon I felt almost comfortable loading and shooting, reloading and shooting again. I surprised myself – I could hit the target in the chest at least five times out of seven. The misses were the head shots.

I drove home with my fingers stained with gunpowder residue and my whole hand aching. My index finger was sore as well.

But I could do this – the physical part, that is.

The emotional?

I tried to imagine what it would be like to shoot someone – to face a man and kill him.

I couldn't.

This wasn't a movie – death wasn't a convenient plot point.

Something someone said to me once – all great stories are about revenge. Maybe that was what was missing from this – I couldn't see these shootings as vengeance.

And maybe that was what was missing from my writing too. I couldn't do revenge. Is that what was missing from my psyche?

But according to Dorothy and Harlan and Older Me, if I didn't find a way to do this, we'd stumble into a much worse future.

It was the classic grandfather paradox, only turned inside out. If you don't kill your grandfather, you inherit a shitshow.

The book of horrors scared me. There was no shortage here of men (and a few women) the world would be much better off without. Serial killers. Mass murderers. Assassins. And a couple of billionaires who'd put their thumbs on the scales of liberty. Promoters of bigotry and corruption and greed, creators of ignorance and poverty and despair. It was a horror story.

But here – I was living in a world where they never had a chance to commit their atrocities. Didn't I want to save this world?

President Robert F. Kennedy had inherited a booming economy from his brother, President John F. Kennedy. The cold war was over. We had a base on the moon. We had the first legs of high speed rail running up and down the eastern corridor. We had the minimum wage pegged to the cost of living. We had government insured health care. We had expanded civil rights and voting protections for all citizens. And the Beatles were talking a reunion album.

The alternative –? This goddamned printout was a great argument for becoming a serial killer.

Just not me.

And I really couldn't talk to anyone about it. Couldn't share the problem. They'd think I was crazy. Or they'd think I was trying to plot another dreadful sci-fi novel. "You still haven't given up, have you? Still trying to write your little stories?"

The only one who believed in me was Steve – and I wasn't going to drop this on him. I couldn't have him doubting me.

There was only one thing to do. I'd known it from the beginning, I just hadn't wanted to admit it to myself. I had to find out for myself if I could face a monster and squeeze the trigger.

I picked one. Not at random. Someone local. Not the worst, but bad enough. It would be a test.

Then I practiced with the timebelt.

I could target a specific moment, even a specific place. I would arrive at an instant of stopped time. I could find a clear space to pop in – like right in front of my target. Then I could raise the gun. I could fire it two or three times, however many times I thought necessary. The bullets would hang unmoving in the air. Then, if I was satisfied with my aim, I could pop in and out of real time – inserting myself and the gunfire for only the briefest fraction of a second, but in that tiny flicker of time the bullets would be traveling at 900mph. They would penetrate the target instantly, tumbling through their flesh like jelly. In stoptime, I would see only a frozen explosion of bloody bits.

In theory, anyway.

What actually happened – I saw three rounds suspended in front of me, all poised to send this someday killer into oblivion, this sad little man who would never know what hit him or why –

But he looked so pathetic, like a poor dumb homeless hippie.

– so I walked around the motionless rounds and pulled him sideways. My bullets would shoot past him and thump into the distant hillside beyond.

I popped in and out of real time. The sound of the gunshots startled him, he jumped sideways, then I popped out and he became a statue again.

I didn't know what he might someday do to deserve this, and I didn't care – but I couldn't be the agent of his destruction. I was not going to kill Charles Manson or anyone else.

I hit the return button and sank down on my bed, shaking and gasping and sobbing. I couldn't do it.

I couldn't.

Dog came over and put his head in my lap. I picked him up and held him tight, rocking him like a baby. I kept telling myself, it's not a weakness. It's a strength. But it still felt like a failure.

Whatever his eventual crime, he had to be stopped. But not this way. There had to be a better way. But if Harlan and Dorothy and Older Me hadn't been able to come up with a better way, how the hell could I?

And if he was already dead, then why did I have to do it?

None of this made sense.

I dropped the clip out of the gun. I put it and the gun in the box. I shoved the box under my desk.

By the time Steve showed up, I was almost human again. He looked at me oddly, then just held me for the longest time without talking.

He finally asked, "Are you all right?"

I shook my head. I wanted to tell him everything. I didn't have the words. I couldn't speak. I just sobbed into his shoulder while he held me tight. I felt safe in his arms. And scared as well. I never told him how afraid I was – about everything, but most of all that I wasn't good enough for him and that maybe one day he'd feel that way too.

"I don't know what this is all about," he said. "I don't need to know, but I can see you're hurting. Whatever it is, I'm here for you." He held me tighter and whispered in my ear. "I'm not going away. You can stop worrying about that. I'm not leaving you. I'm here forever."

Eventually we crawled into bed and Steve held me close all night. I relaxed in his arms, finally accepting his certainty, and drifted into a dreamless oblivion.

Slivers of light replaced the dark. Sparkles of dust floated in the light. Morning invaded the bedroom, demanding a trip to the bathroom and then coffee.

Stretching awake, I felt strangely at ease, as if everything had sorted itself out. As usual, Steve and I showered together without much talk, still drifting in the land of afterward, punctuated only by the usual fits of giggling in surprise as we soaped each other up. It was clear now, Steve was important, nothing else.

After he left for work, I gathered up everything. The gun, the laptop, the printout, the extra ammunition. I put it all in my battered old suitcase and zipped it up. The suitcase sat in the middle of the living room floor, almost an accusation.

"You're the writer," Steve had said. "You choose." They were my words, but now a shared joke.

Choice. That's the question.

We all have choices. Every day. Every moment.

Those people, the ones listed in the printout, they'll choose whatever they choose. They'll be whoever they choose to be.

I choose not to be one of them.

Dog and I got in the car, the suitcase in the trunk.

We headed south to Santa Monica. I bought a round-trip ticket on the ferry to Catalina Island. Halfway to the dock at Avalon, I dropped the suitcase into the water. It disappeared in the ferry's wake. A nearby steward looked oddly at me. I said, "I'm not diving in after it."

Dog and I walked around Avalon for an hour, then caught the ferry back to Long Beach.

We drove home and I gave Dog a belly rub and a cookie.

I went to hang up my jacket –

The closet was half-empty. All of Steve's clothes were gone.

I stood there, staring at the emptiness. He'd promised me –

The bathroom, his toothbrush, his razer, his shampoo, everything, that was gone too –

No, this was wrong. All wrong.

I deserved an answer, an explanation. Into the living room, my desk, I picked up the phone, dialed his work number. An unfamiliar voice answered, a woman. She said there was no one there by that name. That didn't make sense. Wasn't this his company? No, you must have a wrong number –

Maybe. I dialed again – same woman. Sorry to bother you, and hung up confused.

The car – I fumbled with the keys, panicking now, driving recklessly, impatiently across Hollywood, straight to the office – except it wasn't there. The building was gone. Instead, a decaying strip mall filled the lot.

I felt odd. Headaches and double vision. Hallucinations like memories, but not – ugly fragments of thought –

Terrified, hurting, screaming, crying, the bottom dropping out of the world, a screeching pain in my gut, somehow got back to the apartment, grabbing Dog and holding him close. Fearing the worst –

I woke up, as if from a dream, my mind churning with bad memories. Terrible ones. Things that happened in 1963 and 1968 and 1969 and –

Oh, no, no, no, no, no!

*

The day I decided to kill myself, they came back.

Older Me was playing with Dog. "I missed him," he said. "He was always the best."

Dorothy and Harlan were sitting in the only two chairs I had. Nobody was sitting at my desk. That was my sacred space. Older Me must have told them.

They had the timebelt – the laptop, the book, the gun case, and the ammunition – all of it, on the couch.

I didn't offer him a Coke. I didn't offer them anything.

"I threw all that in the sea," I said.

"You threw a later iteration," said Harlan. "This is an earlier instance."

Dorothy added, "The timebelt you threw overboard had several hundred years of experience before it got to you, including this visit."

And Older Me finished the thought. "There's a story idea you might want to consider. Time machines always uninvent themselves."

"What do you want?" I said.

"Do you want a second chance?"

I didn't have to think about it. "Yeah, I do."

"You sure about that, kiddo?" That was Harlan.

"Fuck you," I said.

Harlan shut up. It might have been the first time in his life.

Dorothy said, "We know you're hurting–"

"Stop it! Just stop it! Nobody knows anything. And I can't tell anybody. Nobody understands – I can't even tell anyone who he was, what he meant to me. Not now, not here, not anywhere. Nobody knows how alone I am!"

"I know," said Older Me.

"Fine. Then just give me the gun and get out. Everyone else can just eat shit and linger."

They understood. They stood up.

"Write like that," Harlan said. "Write like that and you'll do okay."

Dorothy said, "We know. And we care. And someday, you'll know it too."

Older Me looked – I don't know how he looked. He was unreadable to me. Maybe he was sad. Maybe he was something else. I couldn't tell. "It's gonna be a long hard road, but – well, I'll see you on the other side."

"You knew from the beginning that this was going to happen, all of you? Didn't you?"

Older Me nodded. "I knew. They knew. I was you."

"So you know how this is going to work out?"

"Yes, we do."

I picked up the gun case, opened it. Looked inside. Closed it again. "Okay, give me the timebelt."

Dorothy didn't look happy. She said, "Go find out who you are."

Older Me stood up, leaving everything on the couch. "I'd say, let me know how it all works out, but I already know."

Harlan stopped at the door. He looked like he wanted to say something else, but he stopped at, "Seeya, kiddo."

After they were gone, I sat down at my desk and put my head in my hands. Yes, I was going to do it.

And I did.

The details don't matter. I went after that bastard and his so-called family. I popped up in front of them like a demon from hell. I didn't bother to freeze time. I wanted them to know terror. And they did. They screamed and died.

I set the timebelt for home. I was barely able to press the button. I was shaking. I felt a familiar dizziness. The timeline was rewriting itself.

Steve's clothes were in the closet.

I unpacked my gear and pushed it all under the bed.

I took a long shower. And a nap.

When I woke, it was dark, Steve was lying next to me. "Are you okay?" I could hear concern in his voice.

"I don't know." I rolled over and looked at him. I was still feeling it. All of it. "You have no idea," I said. "You do not know what I have done for you. You will never know."

"What are you talking about?" He looked at me strangely.

I didn't know what to say. I wasn't going to explain. I rubbed my eyes. "I had a bad dream." It was a lie. The first lie I'd ever told him.

"Oh, okay–" He pulled me into a hug. I relaxed into his arms. But I couldn't feel complete. Not now, not yet. Not while I knew that reality was so fragile.

I held him tight. I wanted everything to be all right again.

Only it wasn't. It couldn't be.

Because now that I knew I could do it, now that I knew it was necessary, I had to go after the rest – as many as I could. I didn't want to do it – and I did. I needed to prove something to myself. To Harlan and Dorothy and Older Me.

Every afternoon, while Steve was at work, I went to work. I set myself a quota. Three, six, ten. I wanted to get it over with as soon as possible.

I went after the assassins first – presidents and candidates and civil rights leaders survived. And then I took out the mass murderers – the massacres didn't happen and families thrived. The most violent murderers went next – she lived, they all lived. And then the kidnappers too – the children got to grow up with loving parents. The arsonists – the buildings stood, the people survived. The child molesters – the children deserved a chance to grow. The abusers of all kinds – their victims lived. The drunk drivers who killed families and children, they survived – I just shot out their tires, the first time anyway.

I went down the list methodically. Sometimes I

screamed at them. Sometimes I didn't. Sometimes I was incoherent with rage. I didn't care who was on the list or why. If they were on the list, it was enough. Someone – my older self – had decided that these lives were dangerous to others and that was enough.

After the first few, I fell into a terrible rhythm. I won't say it was easy, but after a while it wasn't hard either – I won't say I was good at it, but after a while I was efficient. I wanted to get in and get out, get it over with as fast as possible. My days became a blur of splatter and gore. Familiar and different every time. I wanted to believe that I'd made the world a little better, but all I'd seen of it was death and horror.

And every time, I felt the same strange dizziness as the world rewrote itself. I'd lie in bed waiting for my heart to slow, waiting for the memories to reassemble.

I couldn't stash anything under the bed anymore. I didn't want Steve to find it. I had no better place, so I put it all in the trunk of my car. Not just the gun and the ammunition and the book and the laptop, but the cash too – thousands of dollars, from all their wallets. I had made the killings look like robberies. Where I could, I grabbed their wallets and took the cash. Maybe I'd donate it somewhere. Maybe I'd burn it. But I'd probably spend it stupidly. Consider it my fee.

I weakened. I bought a new television. I bought a new stereo. Steve didn't ask where the money came from. He asked other questions instead. He asked me why I smelled of ammonia. He asked me where I was going during the day. He asked me why we weren't making love anymore. "Is something wrong?"

I just shook my head. I said, "It isn't you, it's me. I'm working something out."

"Are you trying to solve a writing problem? Maybe I can help. Do you want to talk it out?"

I hadn't written anything in weeks. I hadn't even tried. I shook my head. "No, it's not that. I'm sorry, I can't explain."

Steve looked hurt. I should have apologized, but no.

Sorry is not an eraser. I couldn't be with him right now. I didn't know what else to say. Finally, I blurted, "I just need to be alone."

He didn't say anything. He just got up and walked out. I heard the front door close behind him. I felt abandoned and empty. It was my own fault, but I didn't know how to fix this. I felt so bad I wanted to kill someone. I went and got the timebelt and the gun and the list. At least that was something I could do.

Later, much later.

We hadn't given up. We still had moments. But the chasm between us was growing wider – and you can only build bridges if you're building from both sides. I'm not sure who gave up first. Probably me. I don't know why. I just didn't feel love any more. Not even lust. Nothing. Where once we were lovers, now we were strangers.

It was inevitable. Steve said, "You've been spending a lot. Where is all that money coming from."

"Odd jobs," I said.

"You're not writing. You haven't shared anything with me in weeks."

"I'm working it out," I said.

"No, you're not." He faced me, he was still the most beautiful man I'd ever known, red hair, green eyes, porcelain skin, all of him, but now his expression was the most painful I'd ever seen. He was sad and hurting. I wanted to grab him and hold him, but I couldn't. "You're not the same person anymore. I don't know what happened. We used to be special. Now, we're nothing. There's something happening here, I don't know what it is, and you won't tell me. I think I should move out."

"I know," I said. "I'm sorry."

He packed his things the next day.

I wanted to hate him. I couldn't.

I sat alone for a long dreadful time, I don't know how long. Then I put on the timebelt.

I went after the serial killers. I'd been avoiding them, I didn't know why. They were strange broken men. I watched them from a safe distance. They looked like normal human beings. But they weren't. They were monsters. So I shot them in their beds. I splattered their brains across the walls. I walked away, shaking. And then I reloaded and consulted the list. It was something to do. Something no one else could do, so I had to do it. Over and over again. There were just too many of them –

Until one horrible night, lying alone in my own bed, staring at the ceiling, the recognition hit me, washed over me like a wave of acid fear.

I was no better.

I was one of them.

Dog whined at me. I pushed him away. I got up, took a shower. A long hot shower. It didn't work. I couldn't wash the pain away. I couldn't wash the guilt away. I had become a bigger monster than any of them.

I should kill myself now. It would be justice.

I put on the timebelt. I chose the setting carefully. I gathered everything. All of it. I pressed the button.

I found him sitting alone in my apartment, playing with Dog. Older Me.

"You're a monster," I said. "A bigger monster than me. You knew what I would become and you let me do it anyway."

"You had to know what the choice was," he said.

"I lost Steve again."

"Sit down," he said.

I sat. I waited. I held Dog on my lap and buried my face in his fur. He smelled doggy.

Older Me waited until I looked up again. "There is no timeline where you and Steve can stay together," he said. "Believe me, I tried."

"The timeline we were in. If you had left us alone–"

"That timeline was already broken. It was an illusion. Untenable. I've been trying to fix it."

"You've just made a bigger mess."

"It looks like it, yes."

Something about the way he said it. I stopped. "But – ?"

"But nothing is ever what it looks like."

"I don't understand."

"Most people don't. We don't see things as they are. We see things as we are."

"Fine, thank you. It still hurts."

Older Me looked at me sharply. "What kind of a person do you want to be?"

"I don't want to be this person. I want to be a good person."

"Are you willing to pay the price?"

"Is there a price worse than the one I'm already paying?"

"That's up to you to decide. This part of the timeline – this loop. Now that you know where this choice goes, do you want to get out of it? This is where we choose. What do you want to do?"

"I don't want to be a killer. I want to go back – but that's not possible, is it?"

Older me nodded. "Actually, it is. But I needed to hear you say it."

*

The day I decided to kill myself, he came back.

I didn't offer him a Coke.

"What do you want?" I said.

"Do you want a second chance?"

I didn't have to think about it. "Yeah, I do."

"So do I," he said. "But there aren't any. We stumble through life and we get what we get. Then we either learn to live with it – or we don't. That's the harder choice."

"That's it?"

"That's it."

"It sucks."

"Yes, it does. But this is it. There isn't any other." He stood up. "But I can tell you this much. You're going to be okay. I know you don't believe it, I know you won't feel it for a long time. You still have a lot of stupid mistakes to make first. None as bad as the ones you've already made, but you are going to be okay. Maybe even better than okay."

"Yeah, right. Thanks. Now go to hell."

"There isn't anything I can tell you that will make any of this easier. But I know this much. There are possibilities in your future that you have yet to imagine. One day, you will ask the right question and one day, you will make the right choice. And one day in 1992 – well, just do it."

"What happens in 1992?"

"Your chance at redemption." He made as if to go. "Oh, and one more thing. Take good care of Dog. He might be your only friend for a while." He stopped at the door. "You won't be seeing me again."

"Promise?"

"Well, not until one day a long time from now, when you look in the mirror and say, 'Oh, there I am.' And you'll laugh. It'll be good."

I wanted to believe him. Maybe one day I would. But right then, I just crawled into bed and cried. Maybe it was a good cry. I don't know. But Dog snurfled next to me and that had to be enough for now.

The Stooge

Christopher Priest

Frontispiece and illustrations by Elle Kelly

A ROGELIO FOJO FILM

FROM THE AWARD-WINNING WRITER OF "THE PRESTIGE"

ROBERT **PICARDO**   PAT **SCOTT**   WHIT **HAYDN**   CARISA **HENDRIX**   ADAM **SONNET**   HERBERT **SIGUENZA**

I want you to look closely at this...

CHRISTOPHER PRIEST'S

THE ST⬤⬤GE

2288 STUDIOS & DANDERULET CREATIVE PRESENT A FILM BY ROGELIO FOJO
BASED ON THE STORY "THE STOOGE" BY CHRISTOPHER PRIEST

ROBERT PICARDO PAT SCOTT CARISA HENDRIX POP HAYDN AND ADAM SONNET WITH HERBERT SIGUENZA MUSIC BY PERLA EDUNEVA SONGS BY ARIEL E. IGLESIAS EDITED BY EDWARD MORENO
PRODUCTION DESIGNER SBOLKENJE SKOLASKIN ADAM SONNET DIRECTOR OF PHOTOGRAPHY KEITH JEFFERIES CO-PRODUCERS ELLE VIANE SONNET KARA HUME CHRISTINE BERGERON ELIAS P. ONTIVEROS
PRODUCED BY ROGELIO FOJO EXECUTIVE PRODUCERS MIGUEL A. DELGADILLO & JOSE CASILLAS SCREENPLAY BY CHRISTOPHER PRIEST DIRECTED BY ROGELIO FOJO

One evening some years ago I went along to a live magic show to see how things were done. I was researching for the novel I was writing then – this book became The Prestige, which was filmed in 2006 by Christopher Nolan. I'm a writer not a magician, and I wasn't trying to find out secrets, but I wanted to get the look and feel of how pro magic was performed.

The secrets of magic are usually well concealed, mainly because magicians are conscious that many of the greatest tricks depend on some careful preparation – a hidden device, a marked card, etc. – that most people would find disappointing if they knew about it. Magic is all about illusion! We judge a magic performance not by how well the secret is kept, but by the quality of the performance. This is one of the main themes of The Prestige.

During that most enjoyable evening one act in particular impressed me.

Two young women, dressed in bare-minimum costumes, performed some amazingly impressive high-speed escapes, one from a straitjacket, the other from ropes. The final illusion brought all these elements together with an extra twist – a young man was invited up on stage from the audience and became their hapless victim in a rather spectacular, and sexy, way. He took it all in good part, but was clearly somewhat embarrassed. He was cheered enthusiastically at the end.

When I was home I spent a lot of time trying to figure out how these two women had done their tricks. I said just now I wasn't interested in exposing secrets, but by this time I had learned that all magic is based on six basic principles: disappearance, transposition, and so on – the full list is in the novel of The Prestige. I therefore knew that those principles must have been in use. With a lot of thinking I could just about see how most of the effects had been achieved, but the final one, with the guy from the audience, went on baffling me. Those young women with their ropes and their minimal costumes had done some attractively naughty things to him.

Finally, I had it. The guy must have been a plant, a stooge. He wasn't an ordinary member of the audience, but was on the payroll. His part of the illusion was to 'volunteer' to go up on stage, but he did so because he knew exactly what was to happen. And that knowledge, that silent collaboration, made the act perfect.

The book of The Prestige was written, the film came out. Then one day I started thinking about the role of a stooge in magic. Who becomes a stooge? How does he or she get involved? What do they know about the tricks? What do they have to do to earn their money? And what becomes of them later ...?

The story came alive, and now Rogelio Fojo directed The Stooge as a motion picture, with a lot of magic and just a little naughtiness ...

– Christopher Priest

FADE IN:

INT. A DARKENED ROOM

CLOSE on a baize-covered card table, held in a pool of light.
A pair of hands on the table. They are never still.
They belong to MILTON, now a mature magician, who speaks in a reflective, contemplative voice.

>   MILTON
> Many years ago, a beautiful young woman
> said to me the words that are the key to
> every magical illusion ever performed.
> She said, "I want you to look closely at this."
> Those words were to change my life.

As he speaks, Milton expertly performs a piece of close-up magic: a brilliantly deceptive vanishing or production, right there in front of our eyes.

Now Milton comes into view, sitting at the table.
Somewhere behind the table, not brightly lit but readable, is one of Milton's publicity posters.

>   MILTON (to camera)
> Those words led me indirectly to
> becoming a magician. That was my
> beginning. But magic is all about
> endings. When you see a trick what you
> remember about it is the climax. For
> example, can you remember the first
> thing you saw just now, not the last?

A REPRISE. We see again the first two or three seconds of the close-up magic. This time, because we know how it will end, we see Milton's hands expertly preparing for the trick.

MILTON (to camera)
So let me tell you how I began. I was a
young man who loved magic, but who
didn't know much about it …

INT. MEETING ROOM - NIGHT – CONTINUOUS

A public hall, or rooms over a shop, sparsely furnished,
bleak. Two men sit on wooden chairs on opposite sides of
a card table covered in green baize. Behind them is a
large but slightly faded showcard, advertising
SPLENDIDO THE ILLUSIONIST!
The showcard has a large picture of Splendido in full
magical regalia, surrounded by smaller pictures of
rabbits, top hats, wands, flags, swords, etc.

One of the two men is SPLENDIDO himself, but he is
not in costume. In fact, he is hardly recognizable as the
man on the showcard. He is in his 40s, slightly
overweight, has untidy hair.

The other man is BARRY HENSON, an ordinary young
bloke, early 20s.

Splendido is expertly shuffling a pack of cards.

SPLENDIDO
Remind me of your name.

BARRY
Barry Henson, sir.

SPLENDIDO
Thank you for applying for this job, Mr
Benson. Have you worked as a magician's
assistant before?

> BARRY
> It's Henson.

> SPLENDIDO
> I beg your pardon?

> BARRY
> It's Henson, sir. My name is Barry Henson.
> And no – I haven't worked in magic before.

> SPLENDIDO
> We'll sort out your name later.

With a flourish Splendido finishes shuffling, then fans the cards across the table-top.

> SPLENDIDO (cont'd)
> All right, Mr Benson ... choose a card,
> please. Any card you like.

Barry leans forward and regards the cards intently. His hand hovers over them, moves from side to side. He is briefly distracted when a young woman, ANGELA, walks behind Splendido and exits the room through a side door. Barry looks back at the cards. Then he touches one with a finger.

> SPLENDIDO
> Turn it over, please.

It's the Three of Clubs. Written across the face in clear red ink are the words: *Harry Benson gets the job!*

> BARRY
> Wow. That's brilliant.

> SPLENDIDO
> No ... you have to be REALLY surprised.
> Do it now.

BARRY
Wow!

SPLENDIDO
More.

BARRY
WOW! That's amazing!

Barry gets up and leaps backwards, kicking the table so that it shakes all the cards.

SPLENDIDO
Perfect, Mr Benson. The job is yours. In a moment I'd like you to go into the room next door, and my assistant Angela will give you all the practical details.

BARRY
Thank you ... sir.

SPLENDIDO
You should always address me as 'Splendido'. Now, there are two vitally important things you must remember at all times. The first is that if ever I do any trick in front of you, you will react with amazement. You're bowled over, absolutely flabbergasted. Got that?

BARRY
Yes, sir ... I mean, Splendido.

SPLENDIDO
Secondly, if I ask you your name, you will say 'Milton'. Is that clear? Your name is Milton.

                    BARRY
OK.

                    SPLENDIDO
So would you tell me your name, Mr
Benson?

                    BARRY
Actually, it's Barry *Hen* –

Barry sees the expression on Splendido's face.

                    BARRY (cont'd)
Milton.

                    SPLENDIDO
Excellent.

Splendido stands up, and indicates the side door.

                    SPLENDIDO (cont'd)
Angela will give you the money. *Next!*

As Barry moves away towards the side door, GEOFF
(also an applicant for the job) enters. Geoff is another
ordinary bloke, same sort of age as Barry.

CLOSE on Barry's face as he opens the side door, and
FREEZE.

SUPERIMPOSE TITLE CARD:

                    THE STOOGE

INT. SECOND ROOM – NIGHT – CONTINUOUS

ANGELA is waiting for Barry.

Barry reacts when he sees her: she's pretty and has a
lovely figure.
There is a small table there, with an accounts book, a
cash box, some pens, etc.
At the back of the room there are three wooden boards,
about six feet high, and hinged together so that they can
fold, like a screen.

> ANGELA
> Congratulations! I assume this means you
> got the job!

> BARRY
Yes.

> ANGELA
> So it's Mr Harry Benson? Otherwise known
> as Milton?

> BARRY
> Actually, he got my name wrong. My real
> name is *Barry* –

> ANGELA
> Oh, he's always doing that! He's
> terrible with names. It doesn't matter,
> Harry. From now on you will be Milton.

Barry is enchanted by Angela, and is barely listening to
her. She speaks breathily, intimately.

> ANGELA (continuing, in a breathy voice)
> Now, I want you to look closely at this.
> Everything you need to know is in this envelope.
> Details of how to get to the theatre.

> You mustn't be late. Some notes to remind you
> of what Mr. Splendido wants you to do.
> There's also a ticket for a seat in the stalls.
> You must be in that seat, so we know how to find
> you.
> Oh, yes, and the money.

Angela opens the cash box and takes out some notes,
which she passes to him.

> ANGELA (cont'd)
> It's twenty dollars for the first
> performance, and if we need you again
> there will be another fee of thirty
> dollars. Is that all OK?

Barry, holding the money in his hand, just nods dumbly.

> ANGELA (cont'd)
> So if you would sign the receipt book,
> and we're all done.

Barry signs, his hand shaking slightly.

> BARRY
> Thank you! So now we ...?

> ANGELA
> Yes, there is one more detail.
> I have to make sure you will fit inside the cabinet.

> BARRY
> Cabinet?

Angela leads him across to the three hinged pieces of
wood.

As she takes hold of them they hear a muffled voice from
the next room.

GEOFF (V.O.)
Gosh! Well done!

Barry looks questioningly at Angela, who simply smiles.

She turns Barry so that he stands with his shoulder
against the central plank. She then closes the other two on
him, but his shoulder gets in the way.

ANGELA
Would you turn slightly to your right,
Milton?

She helps him turn, her hands first touching his arm, but
then his hand.
The two outer planks now meet, and Barry is contained
inside.
She quickly releases him, again touching his arm as he
steps out.

ANGELA
That's perfect. We'll meet again.
Tomorrow evening at the theatre?

From the next room there comes a crash of a table falling
over.

GEOFF (V.O. shouting)
God Almighty! That's just BRILLIANT, Mr
Splendido! How did you do THAT?

Barry and Angela have turned in the direction of the
noise.
Angela squeezes his hand, and leans towards him.
Her face is up against his ear.

ANGELA (breathily)
He's overdoing it a bit.
Always a mistake.

INT. THEATRE (AUDITORIUM AND STAGE) –
NIGHT – CONTINUOUS

A theatre, long past its prime. Most of the AUDIENCE is
sitting in the front five rows of the stalls, but there are
other people further back.

CLOSE on Barry, sitting in an aisle seat, about ten rows
from the front.

Splendido is on-stage, completing an illusion. There is a
huge flash, smoke, and a large number of flags suddenly
appear.
A trickle of applause.
Splendido walks to the footlights to take a bow.

Upstage of him, ANGELA has appeared. She looks
sensational!
She wears a tiny bra with narrow straps and two tiny
sequinned triangles, and a microscopic G-string, also
sequinned.
At her appearance the applause starts to include wolf-
whistles.
Splendido takes no notice.
Barry's gaze is locked on her.
While Splendido acknowledges the applause, Angela
rolls forward a tall cabinet, and moves it to centre-stage.

> SPLENDIDO
> Ladies and gentlemen! I need a volunteer
> for the next illusion. Would some brave
> young man care to step up on stage?

Angela has stepped forward too, and she is posing
invitingly.
Barry cannot take his eyes off her.
The house lights go on. Several men in the audience
move hesitantly. One chap stands up nervously.
Splendido appears not to notice him.

SPLENDIDO
There must be someone here who will come on
stage!

Angela is looking straight at Barry.
Barry suddenly jerks into life! This is his moment!
He walks down the aisle. Some steps lead up to the stage.
Angela holds out her hand towards him. Music plays
from the pit.
As Barry goes up the steps, Angela leans forward to take
his hand, and Barry is rewarded by a close-up glimpse of
her breasts.

SPLENDIDO
Ah! A hero amongst us!

Now a brilliant spotlight bathes both Barry and Angela in
a flood of white light. Music is louder.

ANGELA (whispers)
Well done, Harry! Do what he says
and we will meet later!

She takes him across to Splendido, who grabs hold of
Barry's wrist.

SPLENDIDO (into microphone)
Good evening, sir! May I ask you your name?

BARRY
Milton.

SPLENDIDO
Good! Let me show you something, Milton.

Splendido pushes his hand under Barry's jacket, and pulls
out a live dove.

>   BARRY (shouting)
> Wow!

Splendido reaches into Barry's trouser pocket, and comes out with a live rabbit. Barry looks amazed.

>   BARRY (shouting)
>   How did you do that?!

Splendido then seems to set fire to Barry's hair.

>   BARRY
>   Waaah!

Splendido moves away to the cabinet Angela brought forward. This is on casters and can be rotated.
Splendido spins it slowly.
He opens the two doors, one at the front and one at the back, to show it is completely empty.

>   SPLENDIDO (into microphone)
>   Now, if you would be so kind, my dear –

He takes Angela's hand and helps her step inside the cabinet. Her sequins flash in the spotlights.

>   SPLENDIDO
>   And you too, please Milton, if you would
>   join the lady?

The music from the pit ceases, and is replaced by a roll of drums.
Barry steps into the cabinet, and we briefly glimpse him having to press up intimately against the almost naked Angela.
Splendido slams the door at the back of the cabinet, then slams the one at the front. He spins it with Angela and Barry inside, so the audience can see there is no escape for them.

INT. MAGICAL CABINET – NIGHT

Inside the cabinet almost nothing can be seen of Angela
and Barry – just dark hints of their shapes.
The drum roll continues, more muffled now.

>   BARRY
> What do we do now –?

>   ANGELA (fiercely)
> Keep still! You'll enjoy it more!

She is doing something with her hands – at high speed.

INT. THEATRE – STAGE – NIGHT

Splendido is striding around the cabinet, making
theatrical gestures towards it. The drum roll is getting
louder. We can see the cabinet is shaking from all the
movement inside.

INT. MAGICAL CABINET – NIGHT

The drum roll reaches a climax!

>   ANGELA
> Bye, Harry!

Suddenly light bursts into the cabinet. We glimpse
Angela stepping out on to the stage.

INT. THEATRE – STAGE – NIGHT

Angela has moved quickly away from the cabinet, and is
already out of view. Both doors are now open, and it
looks as if the cabinet is empty.

Splendido walks behind and can be glimpsed through the two open doors.
Meanwhile the audience is going wild – clapping and cheering, and a lot more wolf-whistling!

INT. MAGICAL CABINET – NIGHT

Barry is still inside, locked in a secret inner compartment. There is a breathing hole. Barry's eyes are pressed to it. Dangling in front of him are Angela's tiny bra and G-string.

Barry's POV: A restricted view of the stage through the hole.
Music is playing loudly, the spotlights dazzle. Angela's legs pass in front of Barry's eyes as the men in the audience whistle and cheer.
The legs sashay sexily and the cheers grow louder.
Barry is desperate to see more!

EXT. THEATRE YARD – NIGHT

Two or three WORKMEN are pushing and lifting the magical cabinet on to the back of a small truck. It's held in place by ropes, but doesn't look too secure.

> BARRY (V.O. inside the cabinet)
> Help! Can anyone hear me? I'm still inside!

Two of the men get in the driving cab, while the third bangs on the side of the cabinet, then leaps down.
The truck drives slowly out of the theatre yard.

> BARRY (V.O. inside the cabinet)
> What's happening? Help! Help!

EXT. MAIN ROAD – NIGHT

The truck drives along at high speed, the cabinet perched precariously on the back.

INT. FURNISHED FLAT – NIGHT.

The two men manhandle the cabinet into the living room of the flat. They set up the cabinet in the centre of the room.
One of them operates a secret release, and as one of the doors slowly opens he reaches in and quickly grabs Angela's tiny costume.
Then both men exit quickly.
Barry emerges from the cabinet, looking confused and worried.

INT. FURNISHED FLAT – NIGHT – CONTINUOUS

Barry explores the flat. He discovers in a montage of brief shots:
He is locked in.
There is a bathroom and toilet.
A fridge filled with food.
A television.
Shelves with many books and LPs.
And lying on the carpet in front of the cabinet is a note written in red capitals on pink paper:

> *Harry – You will LOVE what happens next.*
> *Be inside the cabinet by 6:00 pm*
> *tomorrow. Make yourself at home!!*
> *Angie XXXX*

The "O" in "LOVE" is a big heart, and there is a glittering sequin glued to it.
Clipped to the back is $30 ... Barry's next fee.

He stares at this in wonderment.

INT. FURNISHED FLAT – CONTINUOUS

Montage: Barry passes the day. He sleeps, eats, watches
TV, tries to read, yawns, scratches, showers.

Finally he climbs inside the cabinet. At first he finds it
difficult to close it from inside, but then the mechanism
operates itself and the door closes emphatically on him.

>   BARRY (muffled – inside cabinet)
> Ouch!

EXT. MAIN ROAD – NIGHT

The truck is driving in the opposite direction.
The cabinet stands perilously on the back.

INT. THEATRE BACKSTAGE – NIGHT

The cabinet has been dumped in an untidy backstage
area.
Angela taps gently on the side. She is dressed in street
clothes.

>   ANGELA
> Harry? Are you all right in there?

>   BARRY (muffled – inside cabinet)
> I can't breathe, I'm thirsty and I've
> got cramp.

>   ANGELA
> You're fine, then. Not much longer now.

She puts on the sexy, come-on voice.

>   ANGELA (continued)
>   Harry ... I hope you'll enjoy what we do
>   together. It's a treat, I promise you.

No reply from Barry.

INT. THEATRE (AUDITORIUM AND STAGE) –
NIGHT – CONTINUOUS

Onstage with Splendido, seen from behind.
He is producing his smoke and flags, as before.
The audience starts to whistle and cheer.
Angela comes up behind Splendido, trundling the cabinet
into place.
As before, her costume is extremely revealing.

Barry's POV, through the breathing hole in the cabinet:
Splendido calls for a volunteer.

>   SPLENDIDO (muffled)
>   Ladies and gentlemen! I need a volunteer
>   for the next illusion. Would some brave
>   young man care to step up on stage?

General POV:
The house lights go on.
Someone steps forward, and walks up on the stage.
ANGELA greets him. It is Geoff!

>   SPLENDIDO
>   Ah! A hero amongst us!

A brilliant spotlight bathes both Angela and Geoff in a
flood of white light. The music is louder.

> SPLENDIDO (into microphone)
> Good evening, sir! May I ask you your name?

> GEOFF
> Milton.

CLOSE on Barry's eyes, through the breathing hole.

> BARRY
> Milton?

Splendido performs the same tricks as before: a dove, a rabbit, flames.
Geoff over-reacts.
Angela is standing close beside the cabinet.
She leans towards the air hole.

> ANGELA (coming on)
> You ready, Harry?

> BARRY
> You bet!

Splendido takes over. He rotates the cabinet, opens front and back doors.
Angela sashays for the audience's benefit, then climbs into the cabinet. Splendido slams both doors closed.
The drum starts to roll.

INT. MAGICAL CABINET – NIGHT

All is dark. The drum rolls, slightly muffled. The only glimpse we have of Angela and Barry is their dark shapes.
Barry is pressed against a wooden wall. Angela is moving at high speed: her arms and head are darting about.

> BARRY (over Angela)
Here – what are you doing?

> ANGELA (over Barry)
Keep still!

> BARRY
Oi! That hurts!

> ANGELA (breathily)
Feels good, Harry! Ooh – that feels SO GOOD!

> BARRY
I like that!

> ANGELA
Let's go!

INT. THEATRE (AUDITORIUM AND STAGE) –
NIGHT – CONTINUOUS

The drum roll reaches a climax! There is a flash of light!
Barry stumbles out of the cabinet on to the stage.
He is dazzled by the lights. The audience claps loudly.
Behind him, the cabinet appears to be empty.
Splendido is next to the cabinet, with Geoff nearby.
Splendido slams the cabinet door closed.
Almost at once the door opens again, and Angela steps
out into a flood of light. The music blares. The audience
goes wild.
Angela is completely naked.

> GEOFF
Gosh, that's amazing, Mr Splendido.

No one is listening to him. Angela strikes a sexy pose,
and a gale of wolf-whistles rises.
She seizes Barry's wrist, and together they go down to

the footlights to take a bow.
Now the audience is laughing too. As Barry bows and
looks down at himself, he understands why.
He is wearing Angela's microscopic bra and pants,
pushed on over his clothes.

> BARRY
> Bloody hell!

> ANGELA (with stage smile)
> You're overdoing it, Harry.

She releases him, and runs across the stage to Geoff. She
throws an arm around Geoff's neck, and he quickly lifts
her up.
Angela whispers to Geoff, and still carrying her he runs
towards the wings. With one arm around Geoff's neck,
Angela raises the other to acknowledge the cheering
audience.
The curtains close quickly, hiding Splendido and the
cabinet.
Barry is alone in front of the curtains.
The Audience starts chanting.

> AUDIENCE
> Off! Off! Off! Off! ...

FADE TO BLACK.

> END

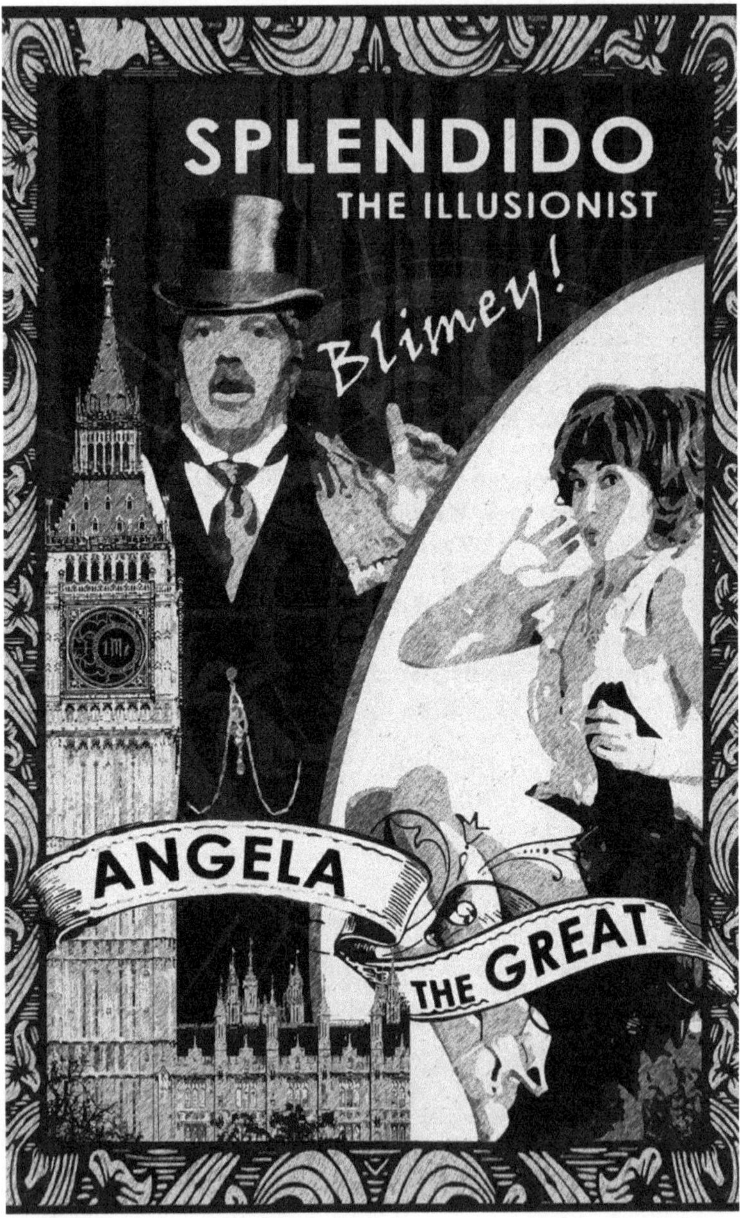
SPLENDIDO
THE ILLUSIONIST
Blimey!
ANGELA
THE GREAT

Race Machines

R. James Doyle and Rogelio Fojo

Frontispiece and illustrations by Alejandro Burdisio

My name is Eva. I live in the twenty-first century.

A question that puzzles many scientific minds of our era is the possibility of time travel.

I devised a simple experiment to verify its existence.

Von Browne's 'All Amazing Almanac'
Trends in Sports History

Given humankind's long-standing lust for greater and greater speed, and its equally insatiable desire for competition, it was a foregone conclusion that the advent of Spacetime Traversal would result in a fresh technological reshaping of the sport of vehicle racing. But it was recognized early on that an ability to leap around in spacetime could defeat the very notion of a finish line and render the sport a severe yawn prospect.

This self-defeating outcome was avoided by invoking that mostly invisible but essential element of any professional sport – the rules commission. The commission members formulated an approach to spacetime racing based on known physics, and on the emerging technology of *spacetime viewing.*

Spacetime viewing – relating to, but distinct from, spacetime traversal – involves *observing* a selected volume of spacetime, as distinct from *relocating* to that locus. Spacetime viewing is about *knowledge*; spacetime traversal is about *movement.* It was already known that spacetime viewing had its limits. When accessing a volume of spacetime, a viewer can choose to observe a larger volume at poor resolution, or sampling, or a smaller volume at high resolution.

Under the agreed-on rules of Spacetime Racing, each driver and support team are allowed to preview the designated spacetime volume – the racing venue. By stipulation, the less experienced and skilled are required to gather more information, while the more experienced and skilled, by virtue of both success and survival, are constrained to collect less information – and perform at greater risk.

Furthermore, each racing team is unaware of what their competitors are learning about the venue. They instead factor in their best models of competitors' strategies. In this head-game aspect, Spacetime Racing is much like any other serious sport.

The inspired treatment of Spacetime Racing restored true competition, corralled cheating, and ensured that *danger* would be an integral aspect of the sport. The prospect of a spectacular crash between racing vehicles, or between a racing vehicle and some local object, inanimate or not, occupying the same spacetime coordinates, was always present. Such a crash would be a most unusual kind of inside-out collision, with matter itself arriving at head-on and instant collocation.

For what is the point of any sport if not to channel the uglier aspects of human nature in a way that gratifies both participant and spectator? Risk must be present, or the entire enterprise is a sham.

New sports provide the means to expose latent human talents. Spacetime racers need off-the-scale excellent reaction times, for that critical moment when they drop into the racing volume and possibly encounter an obstacle that must be appraised and dealt with in a flash. The skill of *anticipation* is key. Every racer has this ability to some degree, or they have no business racing. But it remains mysterious.

Somehow, certain spacetime racers know what is coming, beyond utilizing instrumentation, and they turn their advantage to success.

Mysterious? Always, and unavoidably so. But dangerously reckless? No longer. Thanks to the inspired, human-centered designs introduced by ace Traverser Royce 'Race' Halliday. Under his inspired humanitarian and technological guidance – and brilliance – Spacetime Racing became the one sport that could be enjoyed safely – in all eras.

The following account is historic and provides a record and origin story for the legendary perennial champion and true hero of enduring Race Machines competition.

ONE

The place was essentially a desert. The road, such as it was, was marked out more by yellow mustard plants in bloom along its rough border than by any defined, hardened surface. The route stretched vaguely southeast to northwest. A conveyance of any sort passing along *El Camino Real* would kick up dust clouds.

The spacetime racer in the lead approached the designated finish line with precision. It was common wisdom that the winner would be the one dropping in at the right place and at the right time, as nearly and as briefly as possible. The win went to the most discerning competitor, possessing that uncanny sense of knowing what happens next.

The driver had a preview floating on the pop-up holographic display, above the control panel, but she made little use of it. She adjusted the temporal throttle and manipulated the temporal clutch. With a feathering touch. Lightly now... *here*.

The display began flashing the *locked* indicator. The moment of crossover – always exhilarating. The racing venue opened, end-to-end, backward-and-forward, visceral, complete. A warm, bright spring day. Mostly flat, slightly ridged terrain. A mountain range in the distance.

The future site of the *Misión San Gabriel*. Only two California missions were built: *Misión San Diego de Alcala*, and *Misión San Carlos Borromeo de Carmelo*. Ground had been broken for the *Misión San Antonio de Padua*.

El Pueblo de Los Angeles was ten miles away and more years in the making.

*   *   *

The remaining racetrack was delineated on the display; there were no usable landmarks within the scene itself.

The equivalent of a straightaway, three city blocks long. With the full-throated roar of internal combustion engines as a quaint add-on, always sexy.

The driver was perceiving a crash. She calculated; felt instantly how she would negotiate the course. If a racer showed up too early, or too far away, she might not reach the finish line quickly enough or might give too much ground to another racer. The ideal strategy was to drop in directly in front of another racer who was daring to taste victory.

She depressed the temporal clutch fully, adjusted the throttle and... dropped in. Crossed the start line. Clutch again; and gone. A ghost, a hallucination. Quick pivot around the crash. Same sequence next, at the finish line, barely an instant later.

Another racer. Popping in and out. But short of the finish line. An easy adjustment. Slicing in now, plenty of margin. Cleanly, no need to jostle. And... gone, over the line.

Behind her lay the crash, resolved now, as one vehicle had been pulled out of the race. The driver looked at her panel and posting. *No one would beat that.*

All the other spacetime racers showed poorer times. Only one had made a respectable play. Her victory was official. But one of her colleagues might be injured. The temporal clutch was designed to automatically withdraw a racer on contact, but there were continuing questions about the fail-safe.

The winning driver, savoring the moment, was the last to jump away from the past, severing the spacetime link for spectators viewing from the future. As far as those enthusiasts knew or cared, nothing remained here to indicate the intrusion into the historical scene except some anachronistic dirt tracks, and some slowly settling dust.

The locals, however had become aware of invisible forces tearing through *El Camino Real*, phantom whirlwinds leaving a wake – mangled bodies of Indigenous laborers and Spanish missionaries. Their lifeless forms lay strewn along the dry and occasionally muddy trails like forgotten relics.

These inexplicable tragedies had become disturbingly familiar during the Christmas season of 1799 – soon hardly provoking more than a whisper of shock and mourning. A few would invoke divine judgment or ill omens, muttering that the deaths were punishment for forgotten sins or the dark workings of restless spirits. With solemn conviction, priests would speak of *la voluntad de Dios*, urging survivors to pray harder and repent more fervently. The nearby Chumash elders retreated to their sacred Pimu islands, issuing hushed warnings about ancient curses and disturbed spirits roaming the mainland in retribution.

Numbed by loss, the locals wished each other *Feliz Año Nuevo*, choosing to turn away from the sorrows crisscrossing *Alta California*, vague tales and the seeds of legends in their wake.

TWO

Eva Fontana sat on her bed in her pajamas, cell phone to ear, doing her best to remain gracious in a longer than usual conversation with her thesis advisor.

"Yes, I've got it right here. Santa himself dropped it off at dawn, rang the bell, woke me up, then drove off in *your* car, Professor. Nice touch with the Christmas wrapping. Thanks!"

She fumbled with the package, pulling a semi-professionally bound manuscript from the crumpled envelope.

"Yes, it's a nice title, maybe a bit long. '*Revive the Past Through the Language of the Future.*' You probably mean 'relive' rather than 'revive.' A translation thing. But I rather like 'revive.' The root does mean 'relive' and it also makes me think of something like… 're-excite.'" She suppressed a chuckle. "Remind me, please… what is your new article about?"

Eva pulled the phone away from her ear as a loud exclamation burst through.

"Oh, that's right. I remember now. '*Male Traversers: A Theory of Time Travel.*' Hmm. *I* know what you mean, but with that title, readers may think *you're* the misogynist, my dear *Professore Testosterone*." She giggled. "Give me a week to proofread it, okay?"

The frequency-limited sounds went shriller.

"I still need to figure out a practical experiment. Yes, yes, I get it – you're desperate. I'm your last hope. No pressure, right? But don't worry, I caught the urgency when you left your life's work abandoned on my doorstep. No, Professor Tovar, I haven't forgotten the image of my praxis pairing with your theoretical framework – how could I? I promise, I'm working on it, brainstorming day and night."

She paused.

"Speaking now colleague to colleague Professor, wouldn't any treatise like this one need to answer the much more central question 'Where are all the time travelers?'"

Jabbering.

"Okay, that's interesting, and maybe obvious, now that you've said it, although you didn't quite answer my question. Once time travel is invented, Traversers will come from different future eras, with different worldviews, different agendas... That makes perfect sense."

More chattering.

"Yes – I'm still listening. Why are you including an appendix now? What exactly are you trying to show by adding extra data? Go ahead. Read it to me while I brew a cup of coffee."

Eva punched the speaker, setting her phone down on the kitchen counter.

"*Christopher Columbus. Marco Polo. Ferdinand Magellan. Vasco da Gama. Amerigo Vespucci. James Cook. Hernán Cortés. Francisco Pizarro. John Cabot. Henry Hudson...*"

A long pause.

"Okay, okay, I see your point… All men, right? Then I'll bet you one thing won't change… *especially* if Traversers are exclusively male, as your list clearly implies.*"

Query.

"Well, for starters, the same hormonal drive that allegedly pushes your Alpha Men to become explorers – past, present or future adventurers, it doesn't matter – will lead them to making mistakes and leaving behind traces of their typical bravado-fueled, reckless, risk-taking behaviors."

More jabbering.

"Be careful, or you'll have women from every era clamoring to hang you! Again, I know that's not how you meant it, but no offense – you're not exactly equipped to understand. Yes, I know, Professor. But you love me also because I'm your fearless and outspoken conscience! And if anyone needs time travel to exist, it's you – with your anachronistic views."

Enthusiastic sounds.

"I fully agree. This must be a scientific inquiry. I'll help devise a way to test your hypothesis. Come around on New Year's Eve. Yes, you can bring a bottle of champagne to celebrate. I will have something ready for you."

"What?" Deep breath. "No, it's not that kind of party – I'm not inviting a friend as your date, forget that! We'll just officially mark the advancement of your project! My gift to you will be a testable experiment – which you can include in your book."

Loud sigh.

"Okay… this has been a very, very long conversation. See you next week. Merry Christmas, Professor. *Ciao!*"

Eva held out her phone at arm's length, shaking her head, smiling.

THREE

The setting sun cast warm late afternoon rays into Eva's apartment on the last day of December. She was about to take a shower when a series of sharp knocks – *tat-tat-tat* – interrupted.

I have nothing ready yet! It had better not be Tovar.

She quickly threw on her bathrobe and cracked open the front door.

A scrawny, weather-beaten man stood there, his skin creased, hair greasy, beard bedraggled. He stood next to a Harley.

"Being mine, um, yours, the privilege to answering the invitation... very much."

Eva lingered in the doorway, hand on her hip, eyes narrowing.

"Be thanking for one night with your body–"

She slammed the door in his face and stormed back to the bathroom, fuming.

*   *   *

Eva emerged from the shower, pensive.

She toweled away the moisture. Gazing at her reflection in the mirror longer than usual, she decided she looked more alluring with her hair wet.

Another *tat-tat-tat*.

She cracked open her front door, this time ensuring the blockchain slid securely into place.

A man stood there, over-brimming with hauteur. He wore an expensive-looking sport coat over a... jumpsuit. Form-fitting, threaded through with odd metallic glints.

"The name being Grimley. I am being 'in the neighborhood' as you are saying so quaintly, and I am thinking your charming offer of diversion is being most compelling. As an advocate of the use of the human form in architectural design, I am being open to experience your body–"

"Buzz off!"

Eva found the slammed door to be more than satisfying. At least this jerk didn't have a motorcycle.

She sat at her piano to unwind, puzzled by the persistent banging on her door all day long.

Who are all these weirdos?

Eva began playing a melancholic tune, though it did not align with her agitated mood. Her inquisitive mind prompted her to pause and scan the room for a psychological explanation.

Her gaze drifted to the tall Christmas tree she had picked out herself at the seasonal lot, on the first day of December. Rows of pines had stood upright on wooden stands, filling the air with the sharp scent of fragrant needles. A tradition from her small family childhood – choosing the tree, bringing it home, and decorating it with twinkling lights and ornaments.

Her eyes returned to a framed photograph sitting on top of the piano – an image of her mother and herself as a child, with a similar living tree in the background. A year after her mom's absence, the pain still lingered, as sharp as ever. She recalled the final struggles at home with dementia and fought to keep at bay the old fear of what might lie ahead in her own future. Biology was not her field, and the uncertainty of genetics frightened her.

*   *   *

Eva stood purposefully at her makeshift computer console, set up on the fold-down panel of an antique hutch in her dining room. She forced herself to refocus. She pounded the keyboard and finished with a key jab flourish. She heard the pushing and clacking sounds of the printer.

Eva retrieved the single page of notes from the caddy and signed it at the bottom with a blue pen. The full description of her experiment concept was now ready for Tovar's review. She had labored to counteract its inherent silliness with statistics, mathematical formulae, and graphs. What more could she do to make this *Gedankenexperiment* legitimate and scientifically sound?

What if... I test this idea... on myself? I wouldn't be the first serious scientist to do exactly that.

Composing herself, Eva opened the camera app on her laptop. She frowned.

I need a box. Of the right size. Where to find one, around the house?

Her mind raced, synapses firing a flurry of ideas. Eva recalled Alexander Halliday and his obsessive search for his brother. His relentless pursuit to recover a missing motorcycle and find its rightful owner. She thought of her mother's struggle to reclaim what had been lost inside her brain.

She made her way to the bathroom and turned on the tap. Returning, she reexamined her image, now with wet hair. Satisfied, she settled herself again, hit the record button, and began speaking.

"My name is Eva.

"I live in the twenty-first century.

"A question that puzzles many scientific minds of our era is the possibility of time travel.

"As a straightforward test, I am making this recording, which I will leave to be discovered in the future. If a technological society one day develops a working time machine... some bold Traverser will be able to travel to the past and stand before me... bearing a special gift."

Eva allowed the top of her robe to slip to her waist, all the while continuing to record.

"I am burying this recording as an artifact. I only ask whoever finds this, please bring it back to me – as empirical proof."

She watched as the rest of her robe cascaded to the floor, in slow motion. *The final curtain falling – in a magic show.*

Gradually, Eva lifted her eyes... *Mesmerizing, even to me.* Her captivating gaze held the lens.

"In return, I pledge my body to the Traverser. For one night. No strings attached, no demands, no expectations, only memories. No yesterday, no tomorrow, just an enduring *now*."

*   *   *

Eva stopped the recording and located the video file.

Digging down into a drawer of the hutch, she retrieved a white box that had once held discarded pairs of glasses, sitting there all this time. She picked out a jump drive from the assorted items inside and inserted it into her laptop. Once the file transfer was complete, she ejected the oddly shaped device, removed it from the port, and held it in her hand.

She chuckled at the sight of it, shaped like a toy motorcycle – not her kind of vehicle!

The cardboard box would now be repurposed from collecting electronic detritus to fulfill its final, historic role as a *bona fide* time capsule, carrying her secret message.

Inspired, Eva grabbed the blue pen she had used earlier and wrote an inspiring quote on the reverse side of the box lid.

Her alma mater's motto: '*Learn by Doing.*'

*   *   *

Later, Eva stepped into her dark backyard, determined to follow through with her time travel experiment.

The air was seasonably cool, storm clouds clearing. Stars sparkled above, drawing her gaze from the Pleiades to Orion, then to Gemini, with Castor and Pollux. She shifted north until her eyes landed on Polaris – her guiding amulet in the sky.

A high smallish half Moon cast a soft glow over the garden, reflecting off the surface of her small pool. Once she finished her task, she would drop her robe and dive in, despite the chill, skin against water, celebrating her scientific accomplishment. What would Professor Tovar think, reading her experiment description? Would he choose to incorporate it into his book? Smiling, Eva briefly considered recording her skinny dip swim as a consummation for her time capsule video. The sight of the Moon troubled her. But not enough to alter her mood.

She would rescue her Celestron NexStar 6SE telescope from gathering dust in her bedroom. She would align the computerized mount to precisely track the Moon and savor the dramatic play of light and shadow along the lunar terminator. *The first astronaut of the New Year, exploring the rugged alien landscape.*

Satisfied with her plan, Eva went back inside, returning to bury Tovar''s manuscript within the white box in the shallow hole where earlier she had placed the motorcycle-shaped jump drive. She carefully placed the document inside a hermetically sealable plastic envelope, intending to ask Tovar for a replacement, with a casual excuse about spilling coffee on the original.

Wielding a spade and kneeling at the foot of her garden statue – the *Winged Victory of Samothrace* – suitable to mark the historic spot, Eva wondered how the manuscript would fit. She heard a distinct, hair-raising *knock-knock*.

Her pulse quickened. Looking up, she saw a blurry figure standing in her living room, silhouetted behind the glass patio door. Heart pounding, still holding her package, she dropped the spade and moved carefully toward the figure.

Did one of those weirdos break into my home?

She stopped at the edge of the pool, frozen, her mind racing through the most logical possibilities. Without her eyeglasses – set aside earlier to record her video message – and with reflections in the way, she could not make out the intruder.

Am I in danger?

Eva took a steadying breath before stepping cautiously toward the patio door. The feel of her bare skin beneath the robe made her acutely aware of her vulnerability.

Someone was holding an object up against the glass, obscuring their face. Eva hardly registered how sources of light – the living room lamp, glints, even the Moon above – were strangely limned, splintered, and alive. There was not enough ambient glow for Eva to read the title on the object – a book – held by the figure. She could make out that it was a beautifully bound volume, possessing an inner life, worthy of a magnificent archive.

The other figure lowered the book, revealing herself as an older woman, and placed her free left hand against the glass. Eva saw pressure whitening the skin at spots of contact. Instinctively, she mirrored the gesture, first pressing Tovar's manuscript against the leather-bound book, then raising her right hand to align with the other woman's. Their hands matched in perfect symmetry – almost touching but thinly separated by glass, converged from opposite ends of an unfathomable journey.

FOUR

After visiting her mother at San Gabriel Valley Medical Center, fighting back tears, Eva walked out into the bright summer sunlight and cloudless blue sky of greater Los Angeles. Dementia had created an unbridgeable gap between mother and daughter, leaving them unrecognizable to each other. To make matters worse, her *mamma bella* now spoke only in her native Italian. Eva regretted now working hard to distance herself from her heritage.

The holiday season intensified her feelings of loss. She couldn't wait to return to the comfortable family house on the coast and breathe in the salt air, far from the exhaust fumes of the city freeways, and the source of her mental anguish and heartbreaking pain.

She waited stoically at a bus stop, watching a motorcycle rider weave through the traffic inching along Valley Boulevard, crawling from east to west. A road repair activity was underway in the middle of the day, taking down a lane, backing up cars for several blocks.

"Fai attenzione ai segnali stradali," warned a voice inside her head. *I remember.*

The young man was trying to be inconspicuous, never an easy task for someone on a bike, especially a Triumph Boss, with its distinctive rattly sputter, striving to expand into a clashing symphony.

Eva saw one of the frustrated automobile drivers, top down, wearing an angry scowl. He was play-shifting through the gears, fingers fluttering over hand paddles. The driver revved the engine of his BMW M3 to a roar less appealing than the Triumph's – but he had nowhere to go. She looked around at the parked cars, cluttered storefronts with foreign signage, and faster-moving pedestrians.

Another vehicle, a Ford Mustang 5.0, inched forward audaciously, maneuvering as two lanes constricted to one. The first driver lurched his M3 forward and braked, as a single action, all the while not offering eye contact to the other driver, who responded much the same, refusing to give way.

Something coming...

Eva glimpsed a shadow and a flash of blue metal, dropping from above. *There.* And then not there. Now the shadow came closer, surrounding the M3, enveloping the vehicle. *Whumps* of displaced air made punching sounds, accompanied by angry screeches of rending metal. Low bass rumbles emerged as from an earthquake, but not coming from below. Then the disturbance, just as suddenly, was gone.

Eva hadn't eaten for hours, but she ignored the scent of street food and even the arrival and departure of her bus, remaining on high alert.

The Mustang pulled over to a hard stop, unscathed. Eva watched that driver get out, gawking. Spectators bled toward the scene of the crash. The M3 was a complete wreck. A deep gouge ran diagonally across from the driver seat to the engine block, back to front, left to right. The edges of the ugly scooped-out scar glowed. Hot dust swirled.

The destroyed vehicle made an extraordinary sight. As if a T-Rex had chewed its way in to extract some hapless prey. The driver could not have survived. No remains were visible, except perhaps some dark splotches that persisted as the torn metal slowly cooled in the strong sunlight.

Eva shook her head sharply, remembering her earlier target. She looked around to relocate the man on the motorcycle. She found him, on the sidewalk now too, regarding her with frank interest. His gaze moved to take in both her face and her body.

Eva boldly returned his gaze. The seated rider walked his bike forward, maneuvering, concealing himself behind shifting movements of the sidewalk crowd, four or five rows deep now. She glanced back at the wreck on the pavement, torn between two quarries.

During this cat-and-mouse, a news van appeared on the scene, arriving along the west-to-east lanes. The motorcycle slipped behind the van. A siren wailed, approaching. Eva pursued. A flash of light, which might have come from the news crew's gear, but did not.

*   *   *

Eva rounded the van. The motorcycle and rider were nowhere to be seen. She decided she must be patient, not easy for her. She scanned the area. A narrow alley led away, mid-block. The space was shadowed in the mid-afternoon light. She smiled when another flash of light appeared there, creating momentary stark shadows. She moved quickly up against the wall of one of the buildings framing the alley entrance. A moment later, the motorcycle reappeared, being walked forward.

"Are you a Traverser?"

The biker wheeled around, startled. But from his wry smile, he was not entirely surprised.

"I mean, I watched you… disappear," said Eva. "And then come right back, after the cops arrived."

"I've been watching you too," returned the young man. "Somehow, you're always present when the machines are dropping in."

Eva studied the rider for the first time, her growling

stomach twisting at the sight of a disturbingly familiar face. The young man instantly inspired a strong dislike in her.

After a moment, he extended his hand awkwardly.

"My name is Royce."

Eva ignored the proffered greeting.

"You didn't answer my question," Eva pressed.

"I'm not saying yes… I'm not saying no. What are you knowing about Traversers?"

"They represent the controversial theory of my thesis advisor, and rumors are flying."

"What do you believe?"

"I'm following the evidence."

"I'm liking you already."

She smiled, deciding to encourage him. "Shall we go for some lunch? I want to know what you mean by machines dropping in. And my name is Eva Fontana."

Royce glanced at the scene of the wreck, at unfinished business. But he turned back to Eva, nodding.

*   *   *

Eva sat comfortably with Royce, elbows resting on a small round table on an open-air patio, below street level. She sat back to wall, working a mortadella and provolone demibaguette. She tried not to look askance at Royce's iced green tea latte. Eva was confident she could handle him. She let the moment draw out, inviting him to speak first.

"Please tell me about your ability."

Eva squeezed the features of her face quizzically.

"You're knowing when and where a race is happening. How are you knowing?"

Eva considered the question. She looked Royce in the eye. "I don't much like you. You remind me of someone who insulted me once. So, before we start, are you going to answer *my* questions?"

Royce leaned back. He was not put off. She liked that, but quickly filed the feeling away.

"Yes, but please… do you value the truth?"

"Of course," Eva responded, impatiently.

"Even if the truth is leading somewhere dangerous?"

She gave a quick nod, then berated herself when she realized Royce must have caught the flash in her eyes. He smiled, more genuinely.

"Yes, Eva, I am answering your questions. But I forgot whose turn it is."

She peered back. And decided she could get more out of him if she gave something first.

"It's not too difficult to figure out where the phantom crashes are occurring. With the media all over them. They're strung along the old *El Camino Real*, near where I live, in Cambria."

Royce's eyes widened slightly.

"Very good, Eva. But in this city, every neighborhood is claiming that a piece of *El Camino* is running through."

"I said, the *old El Camino Real*, the original. And before you ask, the incidents are spaced evenly apart – more or less."

"Right." Royce paused. "There's also the *when*."

"Same answer." She watched him mull her responses.

"And yet, your ability to be predicting... even with the uncertainties, it's near *perfect*. How?"

"I'm a good guesser."

He looked at her steadily.

Eva knew how she could turn that look. She would be revealing something private, but maybe this... Traverser was the one who could tell her something about herself.

She closed her eyes momentarily. Reopening them, she knew they were flashing again.

"I have a... talent. Something like premonition. I guess I was born with it. But like any kid with an unusual gift, at first, I thought everyone else must have it too. Slowly it dawned on me that I was special... Basically, no one gets the drop on me."

Royce leaned in.

"Do you know how you are doing this?"

Eva nodded. "You know how our eyes collect scenes, something like thirty times a second, and how our brains put them together to make it seem like we're seeing the world continuously, without any breaks?" She had Royce's full attention now.

"But how is this connected to your skill?"

Eva assembled her words. "I am able to vary how I look at the world… normal, fast, slow. My brain has a kind of… plasticity, filling in the blanks, the in-between. I can't do it for very long."

Royce closed his mouth, which had dropped open. "You're able to be slowing – or speeding – your subjective passage through time… at will?"

Eva leaned forward. "That is a really unusual way of putting it, but… yes."

He stood up. His sudden motion nearly knocked over his latte.

"Royce, slow down."

His eyes were sparking now too.

"I think it's your turn to answer my questions."

"Even better if I show you."

Royce extended a hand across the table. She took it, warily. He pulled her up and along, and they departed the cafe. They reached his motorcycle. He mounted and invited her to join him. She hopped on but sat stiffly apart.

"You should put your arms around me. For your safety."

Eva rolled her eyes, although she knew Royce could not see her. She held herself to him, formally.

"Don't you want to hold on tighter?"

Eva ignored him.

Royce started the Triumph and throttled the engine until it settled into its characteristic clattering sputter. Eva saw that the compact dash was not factory. Royce manipulated something. Eva felt a… shift. She closed her eyes reflexively.

FIVE

When Eva opened her eyes, they were in a… high-tech

racing pit. Two workers looked up from their tasks. A racing car formed the unmistakable centerpiece.

They dismounted from the motorcycle and Royce led her over to the racer. The vehicle was gleaming, possessed of evocative lines. The exterior was all aesthetics – most strikingly an anodized blue metal surface. The cockpit was aggressively high-tech, a molded environment with all information and control compactly accessible. A holographic projection hovered in the space immediately in front of the driver. Oddly, there appeared to be a second clutch.

Immediately, Eva was a kid in a candy store.

"Are we in the future?"

Royce shrugged.

"This looks like the future," she pressed.

"I'm maintaining a workshop… now and then."

Eva could no longer deny the best explanation to the available evidence. The phantom crashes, the rampant rumors, and now this… workshop. They all made the most coherent sense if… Traversers *were* real. Tovar apparently was right. He was to be congratulated, but it was *she* who was actually exploring.

"Why?" After her blurted query, Eva composed herself.

"There are reasons. But we're getting ahead of ourselves." Royce held out a hand. "Please…"

Eva took his hand and interlaced their fingers, deliberately.

Royce winced slightly but did not adjust the contact. He led her to a different vehicle against one of the walls, a two-seater, similarly equipped, but not nearly as sleek.

"This is the trainer car. All racers must take my training and become certified."

He gestured to the passenger seat. The vehicle was equipped with dual controls, in the driver's cockpit and in the second seat, the familiar driver's education set-up.

Eva got in. Seat-belt-like restraints enveloped her, almost lovingly.

Royce climbed into the driver's seat. "Want to be going for a ride?"

*   *   *

Royce went through a checklist, verifying the readiness of each control in the trainer car. "Steering, accelerating, braking, clutching and shifting are all just as you're familiar with."

He pointed next to a throttle-like device. The spacetime joystick – another of his inventions. Royce borrowed the concept from the helicopters of his own era. The stick moved freely left-right, forward-back, up-down. The racer accessed the time dimension haptically through the strength or lightness of touch – one of the most critical elements of training. "That's the STJ. It sets the rate at which you preview the environment. Novice racers sample at high resolution and expert racers at low…"

"That's how my brain works!"

"…the difference being – Wait, which one?"

"Either. Both. I choose!" she exulted.

He appraised her, then continued. "The difference being a kind of handicap. In an actual race, the available range is preset and locked." Royce looked at her squarely. "I'm thinking about how to test your abilities… safely."

Eva pointed into the well at Royce's feet, past the helmet tucked into the space. She dropped a hand to his thigh and rested it there.

"What's the second clutch for?"

Royce now looked like he was the kid in a candy store.

"That's what makes this car one of my Race Machines. That's the temporal clutch."

"Is that what it sounds like?"

"Yes. When operating that pedal, you're dropping in and out–" Royce paused.

Eva could press his buttons further. But for the moment, she felt satisfied. "What are we waiting for?"

"One thing. You need to put on your helmet." Royce reached for the one at his feet and pointed to similar headgear in the passenger seat foot well.

Eva removed her hand from his thigh. She hesitated. "Please, won't that ruin it?"

"If it's any consolation, during an actual race, the entire cockpit provides protection, and there is no need for the helmet."

"Protection from what?"

"That's a long story."

"Tell me."

Royce studied her. "The lack of reference points."

Eva raised her eyebrows, dragging out the moment.

Royce watched her carefully. "Are you putting on your helmet?"

She shrugged. "Anything you say, Royce." Eva donned the headgear.

Royce inspected the fit, then followed suit. "We're able to hear each other. The helmet shows you what a racer sees in the pop-up holographic display." Royce reached forward, adjusted the throttle. "We'll start easy, but I'm thinking soon you'll be able to handle more. Maybe much more."

*   *   *

Royce finished the checkout. Eva watched as he pressed the accelerator. An exhilarating throaty roar filled her helmet.

"Oh, please. Given what this car is made for, what is the point of all that noise?" Eva imagined Royce blushing. "You've got me there. But it's my design and I have nothing more to say."

She watched attentively as Royce manipulated the conventional clutch and accelerator. The vehicle eased forward to a large garage door which… simply vanished. Bright sunlight spilled in. Royce maneuvered the car out of the workshop, along an alley. Eva admired that the display was sufficiently crisp and faithful, enabling the helmet's presence to be almost forgotten. *Almost.*

Royce emerged onto a moderately busy street. The view opened up, and Eva went goggle-eyed.

Vehicles moved everywhere. Not only on the ground but stacked into the air. Proceeding smoothly, following lanes or more generalized vias without apparent delineation. Vaguely, Eva registered soaring skyscrapers as a backdrop, but her eyes were for the cars. They were not as futuristic as she was expecting – especially given the aesthetics of Royce's design. They were delightfully retro. Heavy grilles, ample chrome, piled-on metallic protuberances. Some seemed more like railcars than private passenger vehicles. They zipped, leaped, and danced.

"What is the year?" Eva asked shakily.

Royce considered before answering. "We are in the year 2288."

Next, he engaged the temporal clutch, made a final feathering touch on the temporal throttle, then eased it out.

The crazy external environment, projected within Eva's helmet, changed subtly. An approaching car became smeared, unusually washed out on approach and then curiously darker on passing. At the extremities of its trajectory, the other car faded, phantom-like, going transparent. The same smeariness and see-through aspect applied to pedestrians, pets being walked, birds, vehicles high overhead, anything in motion.

"Eva, you're seeing my constructs, not actual–"

"I didn't think so Royce, because it's not what I'm used to seeing when my brain is doing its thing."

He let out a breath. "The display is coupled to the vehicle's viewer, which is sampling forward and backward. The images overlap, stretching what you see. By my convention, images from the near past are fading to white while images from the near future are fading to black. Lots of information to work with – once you're trained! Like flying by instrument."

"Yeah, it's different. What my brain sees – and I'm guessing at some of it – I perceive as normal motion. But it's like I can take more slices when I need to. It's hard to explain. You know how people talk about the world slowing down when they're in a crisis, like in an automobile accident. It's like I can turn that on and off. And it's not so much that things are slowing down or speeding up, it's more like I can know more when I crank it up."

"Eva, hold that thought – and remember what you're seeing now."

Royce settled in behind a car going the same direction. Along the ground – rather disappointingly. As the other driver sped up, the image of that car in her helmet spread out.

Eva was fascinated to see them enter the light part of the smear – where the car had been, if she understood the conventions of Royce's display correctly. She inferred he was manipulating the temporal throttle. She watched the smeared image stretch less and also become less... blinkered.

She appreciated the logic of the display but yearned to apply her own talents to interpret the landscape. She could not possibly... *not* take the opportunity.

Eva removed her helmet.

*   *   *

At first... what? Royce was right... no reference points. But that didn't begin to describe what Eva was experiencing.

The other car was there, and she could ask, within her mind, where was it going, where had it been... and get an answer. Not exactly *see* the answer but collect information she could interpret. But beyond answerable questions within her mind there was... great depth. *Out-there-ness*. No end to it.

Eva closed her eyes, or some equivalent action, and focused on what was happening around their vehicle. A better defined task. Once in that frame, she had no trouble inferring that Royce had engaged the temporal clutch expertly, jumping instantaneously past the car ahead. From her expanded viewpoint, she knew the maneuver was safe but imagined Royce indulging a smirk when brakes screeched behind, wherever... *then*.

She could already interpret more: forward, backward, around... and confident she would get better at it – quickly. Ahead, she *willed* the landscape to slope up, such that she could perceive more. To the sides, in response, the scene sloped away… preserving a kind of balance. *A conservation law.*

But the urge to gaze directly at the *out-there*, it was alluring. And no doubt dangerous.

From a very long way off, "How do you like this, Eva?"

Eva held no interest in reacting or responding. In this boundless place, there was so much to explore… In her short time here (how long?), she sensed her mind partitioning for different tasks. She should allocate one of those compartments to answering the annoying query…

"Eva?... Eva!"

*　　　*　　　*

Royce quickly pulled over. Curses flew out at them as the car behind passed. Royce yanked off his helmet.

From the wrong end of the binoculars, Eva watched him looking at her, sitting in the passenger seat. *Unprotected.*

"Eva! Are you hearing me?"

Eva turned but her eyes, her being, were focused elsewhere. Settling slowly, she saw her hand out in front of her, reaching toward Royce. The hand was unnaturally straight, bent as if pressing against something. She dreamily pulled it back, turned it. White pressure spots on her palm faded.

Royce reached out and grasped her hand. The contact melted her back into the moment, both of them again occupying the same now and here.

"You took off your helmet!"

"Your display was… informative, but I had to see for myself."

"People looking… at the bare environment…some are going insane!"

Eva felt fatigue, but also exhilaration. "Well, it was a roller coaster ride! I saw more than I ever have before. And…"

"And what?"

"It's like I belonged there."

A scowl and concern marched across Royce's face. He pushed himself back into his seat. "We're going back to the workshop, and then we're talking this through."

He put the car gently into conventional gear and headed back to the garage, driving like an old lady.

SIX

"You have to allow me to race... Royce!"

"In good conscience Eva, I must say no."

"Why?!"

"Because you have insufficient training. Racing, of any form, is inherently dangerous. One has to have a healthy understanding of the risks, and the means to manage them."

"What if I told you I've done some racing?"

"Eva, I can check easily enough."

"It's true! I've taken vehicles out on proving grounds – obstacle courses. On the Utah salt flats, during breaks while on a paleontology field trip. Before I met my current advisor. Intense, and kind of scary." Eva reminisced. "Oh, and mountain biking too – seriously off-road stuff."

Royce chuckled. "How did you do?"

"I kicked ass, Royce. You should have seen the lines I cut. My times were way better than anyone expected. But still, they were so far off the expert times, I felt discouraged." She smiled. "But not now!"

"Eva, please, my instincts still say *no*." Royce's face clouded over. "These risks... because of other attempts to understand them, I became separated from someone I care deeply about. And there are... barriers which prevent us getting back together... maybe. I need to be careful. The point being..." Royce's eyes had gone moist. "...safe Traversal is my life's work."

After a respectful pause, Eva continued. "Royce, I know you'll keep me safe. But think of how I can help you learn.

Not only about the risks of the environment, but new data that will help you make racing safer – for everyone!"

"There is my fail-safe…"

"What's that?"

"Pulling the driver away when a collision is imminent."

"But I saw–"

"The capability does not protect the locals. For that, I cannot forgive those… Eternalists."

"Milton the Eternalist? The magician?"

Royce frowned. "Eva, I'm saying too much!"

"Royce, please. After what I experienced! You can't be leaving me with only a memory…"

"Eva, stop. I need to think."

She backed off with an effort of will. Eva knew where she had been, even if Royce would not name the place. Her inmost being screamed to go again. She *belonged* there.

She knew Royce was torn between his fear for her, which was touching, and his curiosity, which had driven him already to amazing accomplishments. Now she understood he had demons too.

Why did everything have to be so difficult? She was smart, not unattractive… and she had this amazing *gift*. She could call it a gift now. Her special talent was not some defect that would result in her doom. Eva felt the presence of a half-formed tear and wiped it away. She forced herself to wait.

Presently, Royce looked up. "All right Eva, we're starting your training. But at the first sign of trouble, I'm calling a halt. Are we agreeing?"

Eva threw her arms around Royce's neck. As an afterthought, she pecked him lightly on the cheek, then quickly withdrew. He grinned from ear to ear.

*   *   *

Eva settled into the trainer vehicle, this time in the driver's seat, with Royce in the passenger seat.

"This is a simple first course. I'm maintaining dual control, and I will intervene if there is any need."

Royce pointed to the helmet sitting awkwardly in her lap, matching the one in his hands.

"If you sense any trouble at all, promise me you will put on your helmet. I'm your backup. There's nothing to prove today, we're learning only."

Eva waited impatiently for Royce to secure his helmet. He had explained they would not be able to communicate easily. With face hidden now, he gave her the universal thumbs-up sign. The next time he did so, she would have control.

Royce ticked through the checkout procedure. Eons later, it seemed to Eva, he feathered the temporal throttle, then depressed the additional clutch and... just like that, they shifted. They were moving along a racetrack.

Right. Why bother wasting time moving to the track? Just jump there and get on with it.

He took them around a few circuits. The track appeared to be a simple oval. As they gained conventional speed, other racing cars joined them, altogether three now. Suddenly, someone was waving a flag, and off in the distance a finish line beckoned. Eva watched, ramping up her sampling. One of the other racers signaled clear intent to leap ahead. That vehicle skipped forward well down the track. Royce's hands and feet moved briskly. Their vehicle also shifted, and Royce competently edged in front of the other vehicle and crossed the finish line. Eva sensed, without having to look, that the remaining driver had also executed a jump, but an inadequate one, not competitive.

Royce took a victory lap, rather tediously, and entered their designated pit area in the center of the oval. Eva imagined Royce wearing a juvenile grin behind his helmet. After another wait – lengthened by Eva's special perception – he gave her the anticipated second thumbs-up.

I'm ready. Eva entered the environment... *spacetime. Royce is such a careful person.*

Slow on the uptake, the other two race cars entered the track. Then, the person with the flag. Eva chuckled to herself. *I'm going to throw off established rhythms.* Her mind immediately calculated several lines for cutting around the other vehicles. All arrayed in her blinkered and compartmented awareness. *All that physics and math at Cam Poly serves a purpose too. Grounding my native talent. Now it's time to have some fun.* She focused on the more competent of the two drivers. *Feather the throttle, lock in the line, depress the temporal clutch, and...*

From a long way off, as if behind walls, not quite claiming her attention, she thought she heard, "...Eva."

Yes! Away from here... the line I see... jump there. All about being unpredictable. *Just a jostle, no worse than a friendly slap on the rump.*

Eva was surprised when the other vehicle – which she had barely kissed – jumped away. She sensed it reappear in the pit area.

Must be Royce's autonomous fail-safe. Even *she* could not see all around and react so efficiently.

From a great distance, as if underwater: "...Eva!"

Now to the other driver, the less skilled one. *This will be fun.*

Eva took her sampled observations, made one adjustment to her slicing trajectory. Her pattern and line crystallized. *Making conservative jumps will never win a race.*

Eva almost felt like yawning when she jumped in front of and blocked the other driver. One, two, three times...

Again, that tedious interruption. "...Eva, that is enough!"

I'll just ignore him. Except she felt control of the racer being taken away.

And I was just beginning to have fun.

*   *   *

"Eva, I'm worrying about you. I'm thinking this is not a good idea."

"But Royce–" Eva decided against telling him to stop acting like a grandmother. "I did better than you were expecting."

"Well…"

"Admit it! And what better way to achieve your goal of making racing safe for everyone, including locals, than to show that *your* racing cars, with all the additional safety measures, will *win* the race! And with my help, by a convincing margin. What's not to like?"

Eva could see that Royce did not like her argument, not at all. *Precisely because of its inherent logic.*

She waited while he explored different angles and counterarguments. He could still simply say *no*, but Eva was confident she was dangling the right carrot.

"All right, Eva. We're going ahead. But I'm watching you closely."

She smiled, while he frowned.

"You're needing a pit crew. You've seen the workshop. I'm introducing you to Cayla and Donn. We're prepping you for racing."

*   *   *

Eva zipped, zinged, and zagged.

Royce had explained to her how the fail-safe worked, how a driver would be plucked autonomously with the racer cockpit and deposited gently in a trainer whenever releasing the temporal clutch and dropping into the flow would result in a collision. He used the term *look-ahead* when talking proudly about his spacetime viewer. Eva thought it sounded limited. Her way of perceiving was something more like *look-around*.

He had wanted her to experience the fail-safe, to be familiar, but Eva was certain her instinctive skills would invariably circumvent a collision. *No matter how carefully he staged one.* She drove him crazy with her signature "kissing" bumps, which harmed no one, but nonetheless dispatched her opponents to the trainers, one after the other. She was gaining quite a reputation with the crew. They were deliberately leaking buzz now to the competing racing teams.

*   *   *

Eva and Royce approached the Race Machine. She kept physical contact with him, shoulder to shoulder, as he leaned into the cockpit to make some final alterations. Up close, the anodized exterior coloring showed more as turquoise. Eva wore a new uniform, not subtle, straight from twenty-first century automobile racing culture. A real leather garment, with a wonderful scent, adorned with badges of various sizes, shapes and colors.

"Some changes are necessary because the racing commissioners are handicapping you, given the unprecedented data from your trials," said Royce. "They're limiting your preview more severely. Even as they understand how valuable you are to the sport."

"I can handle it," avowed Eva.

"I'm updating the temporal throttle to comply with their edicts. I'm also modifying the fail-safe to track these changes, but its basic function stays the same. At the very moment a crash is unavoidable, the fail-safe kicks in and rescues the losing racer." Royce expanded ever so slightly, talking about his inventions, his underappreciated contributions to Spacetime Traversal technology.

He strained within the confined space to access a device at his wrist. He depressed two fingers. A holographic display appeared, but in place of a spacetime preview, engineering diagrams floated.

Eva withdrew from the cockpit, with an extended sliding of leather along skin, one of her fingers tracing the back of Royce's neck until contact finally was broken. "I'll leave you to your work, Royce. Let's go win the Ultimate Spacetime Rally."

SEVEN

The first Spacetime Racing season was a resounding success. The commissioners determined to stage an additional event, to raise the excitement to another level.

The Ultimate Spacetime Rally would utilize multiple racing venues in the historical City of Angels. Each racer must negotiate all specified venues, free to choose the order, except that the final venue – the true finish line – was designated. Up to a hundred competitors could qualify, making the scale of the event unprecedented. Due to the complexity of the course, each racer would be allowed one pit stop for repairs or adjustments, lasting no more than two minutes real time. Going past this limit would result in a penalty being applied to the racer's overall competitive time.

The commissioners engaged the era's premier topologist to architect the circuit, one Morgan Grimley. Who did not disappoint. The truly dramatic change – the insane factor that had everyone hopping – were his route and era selections. Notoriously crowded streets, intersections, and high-volume roadways of the twenty-first century Los Angeles urban landscape.

Blood boiled, especially given that Eva Fontana, an unknown from the present era, emerged as the spacetime racer to beat.

*   *   *

Eva expanded her awareness away from the mechanics of executing the last trial heat. She was living a thrilling new life, and sometimes the old one felt… remote. She could go anywhere, *anywhen*. But mostly, she reveled in being *out there*, where she could sense the boundless vastness, feel the endless possibilities…

She was getting better and better at moving about. *Traversing,* Royce called it, but *projecting* was a better word. *I simply imagine going somewhere, somewhen, and I go.*

On a whim, Eva realized she might trace out Royce's life. His *world-line*. She hesitated. *Would that be an unforgiveable invasion of privacy?*

As she developed her skills – and they were already beyond what she was revealing – a great responsibility began to settle on her. Having to do with what she was coming to *know*. *How* she was coming to know. Her knowing sometimes had a ring of finality to it. Possibilities being taken away…

There was so much to see, to learn – and to know. *It is well beyond me, even with my advantages, to know everything. There is really nothing to worry about.*

Eva forced herself to refocus on the race trial. More and more she knew she was just phoning it in. *Dropping back in now…* Royce was watching over her, as always.

Too tempting. Eva projected out to Royce, touching his world-line. She began tracing backward. Faster now. Sampling broadly to get the broad picture first, searching for meaningful events…

She operated as delicately as possible. *But still… disturbances. Events congealing. That can't be good. But so much is out there, what difference would they make… in the whole?*

No way. Royce has a brother?

Not that ass-wipe.

She took in their story and got lost in its tragedy.

Eva moved in the other direction. But it need not end badly, in… *exclusion.* Rather… in the twin paradox.

Eva forced herself to withdraw. She did not want to… she could not know more.

I will not make this mistake again.

From down a long, twisty tunnel, "…Eva, we're done for the day."

Royce… She quickly unwound from his world-line. *Now… here.*

Eva felt herself swinging with all her might. Dimly, she felt Royce catch her wrist.

Confused, she murmured, "I'm so sorry."

Royce's urgency pulled her all the way back. "What are you saying?"

Such intensity in his eyes. Eva lapsed into silence.

"Are you angry with me?"

"I'm not, Royce."

"Why are you mentioning my brother?"

"Your brother?"

The silence stretched.

"Royce, it's... there's so much to explore. Being back here, now, it's... boring."

Royce studied her carefully.

"No offense," she offered.

"None taken... Truthfully, a part of me is envious."

Eva wandered again. Then, from farther off, farther than ever...

"...my whole life... dedicated to making Traversal safe. Ever since losing my brother. Milton and the others... they never cared..."

"...I have to suspend your racing..."

He does not understand. He cannot stop me from becoming... who I am. I need to go... out there.

"...I'm sorry too, Eva. This is all my fault."

*   *   *

"Boss, you're sure you're being ready?" asked Cayla.

Royce Halliday tore his gaze away from Eva. She sat placidly at his desk chair, against a side wall, commanding a full view of the workshop. "I have to race. We must win. Otherwise..."

"Boss, you're the first to be saying that psychological readiness is being most important."

Royce frowned and did not answer.

"You and Donn please keep an eye on her."

"We're watching. She's seeming hardly now and here anymore."

Royce directed his words. "Eva, I'm going to win, *with* the new protections. I'm going to show them. After, I promise... I will find a way to include you, to help you."

He gazed at her, too long. His assistants stood by him patiently. Then, he entered the racer cockpit. Proceeding through the checklist, his focus sharpened by degrees. He was slowly harnessing his emotions to the purpose at hand. He looked up at Cayla and Donn.

"Remember, the fail-safe now delivers the entire vehicle from a collision, not just the cockpit."

They both nodded.

He gave the thumbs-up and the cockpit hatch closed over him. A throaty roar filled the space. Royce and his Machine vanished in a burst of light, jumping to the start line of the Ultimate Spacetime Rally.

"Don't be worrying about me."

Donn startled, and looked over at Eva, then exchanged glances with Cayla.

*   *   *

Royce let his mind go, into the flow, to work freely and easily. He brought up his preview. The first venue was the Sepulveda Pass. The steep terrain forced a racer to deal with all three spatial dimensions. He felt his touch on the STJ going more organic.

His mind built up a picture. He wondered if he was pushing his sampling rate too far, effectively bringing perception to a standstill. But a quick check of the console and his semi-professional feel for the environment told him the jammed-up vehicles were, in fact, not moving.

That's the Sepulveda Pass all right!

This segment of Grimley's course started at the crest of the pass, and ended down the hill on the other side, at the hopelessly inefficient interchange between the 405 and the 101 Freeways.

*   *   *

She could see that two of the competitors – and their vehicles – were already out of the race. Collisions were impossible to miss when the traffic was packed this tightly. A flash of blue – behind which a glimpse of the future cityscape was briefly visible – and a local car's trunk wobbled and rocked, nothing worse, and soon struggled to move forward again through the jam.

Another spatter of blue – this time revealing a glimpse of a hardscrabble desert landscape – and Eva watched, fascinated, as a too-fast approaching cargo hauler jack-knifed, the massive trailer sweeping through several smaller vehicles, creating localized mayhem.

*   *   *

Royce descended into severe disappointment. He could eliminate the physical crash, but not the reactions.

Another vehicle was entering the race, unauthorized. He gestured sharply, manipulating his displays. *Stolen my design!*

*   *   *

Eva targeted her opening. She found pockets of open space appearing intermittently between the closely tracking local vehicles – behaving almost as if they were tethered. She zipped into and out of one pocket, at the apex of the roadway. She had already selected a paired opening down at the messy interchange, and she jumped there now. *In, out. Only a fraction of a second after my dip at the top of the hill.*

She pivoted to DTLA, the next venue in the circuit. The start line for this segment of the Rally was near Dodger Stadium – appropriate enough in a game of *now you see me, now you don't.*

*   *   *

From the constrained but globally thorough view, and reconciling his personal experience, Royce now better understood LA Downtown to be defined more by its relentless vehicle traffic patterns than by its geography, or by any definable urban neighborhood boundary.

He played with the STJ, especially the temporal

throttle, striving to ascertain what was happening. He feathered more finely for greater resolution.

*   *   *

Eva picked her opening near the crush along the 110 at the stadium. *In, out.* A flash of... red this time, a pitch-black vehicle dropping in, a dimly seen other place, a vague sense of menace, another crash. *The racing commissioners must be urinating in their jumpsuits by now.*

This collision involved a motorcycle, mounted by a driver and one other. The passenger careened in free flight while the driver tumbled and scraped the road surface, wrapped around the bike.

*   *   *

Royce's dismay knew no bounds. While creating his latest round of protection, he had accounted only for the physical, not the psychological.

He needed to complete this portion of the race and jump to a pit-stop.

*   *   *

Eva had already formulated a strategy for this segment – taking account of the time of day, with the finish line at the interchange of the 110 and 5 freeways. She knew that in a pathetic attempt to regulate the local traffic, a second lane opened in the interchange at the advent of rush hour. She pounced on the moment. *In, out. First in line.* Just before the altered-purpose lane became overwhelmed.

*   *   *

Cayla and Donn were already running toward him as the cockpit cover slid into its recess. Royce scrambled out of the racer. He glanced quickly at Eva. She looked like she had never moved.

"Boss, something being wrong? You are having the lead!"

Royce shook his head. "The entire Race Machine is pulled out by the fail-safe, not just the cockpit!"

"We're knowing, boss."

"It's not enough! The changes aren't working as I intended. The local drivers are reacting to the spacetime collisions anyway. They're surprised, flabbergasted, and all hell is breaking loose. People are still dying!"

"Boss, we're having less than two minutes…"

Royce looked again at Eva, pale and distant in her unsettling inertness.

He grimaced. "I have to withdraw. It is the only responsible thing to do. And there's a copycat out there!"

The throaty roar of the racer filled the space. Royce whipped his head around. Eva was no longer against the wall. He pivoted back to the launching area, catching only a glimpse of her in the open cockpit before all vanished in a bright flash.

*　　　*　　　*

Eva settled in. Royce had performed credibly on the first two segments, but now it was time to get serious. She examined the final venue every which way.

Century Boulevard at the entrance to LAX, the Los Angeles airport. Always a mess. *Well chosen.*

Private cars, ride-hail vehicles and limos seeking to enter the airport were stacked up for more than a half mile. Red and chartreuse emergency vehicles attempted to reach a prosaically local crash scene. News and police helicopters flitted above. Varying her sampling, Eva enjoyed how the strobe lights and rotors lurched differently around their cycles.

A flash, again red. The feeling of threat was palpable, unreasonable, like being chased by a bad cop. *Whatever, bring it on!* Eva attended to the developing collision, ignoring its local details, exploring spacetime around the event, characterizing competitor trajectories – including the black racer.

She drew on another of her honed survival skills – her ability to get inside the head of an adversary. Something that Royce, bless the dear man, sorely lacked.

Eva watched, in her expanded view, while the second-place racer made his move, utilizing the local crash as a distraction, an obstacle, a convenience. *Interesting, but predictable.* She had already played it all out. Her countermove was going to be exceedingly clever – even for her.

Eva dipped through the start line, at the tremendous bottleneck of the interchange between Century Boulevard and the connector to the 105 Freeway. She then cut and sliced and jumped and... crossed the finish line. As foreseen, the trailing driver tried to divert but was not up to the task. He and his racer were plucked away. But his final maneuver set up a cascade, disrupting the third-place driver, who reacted similarly, and on and on. A beautifully choreographed, ineluctable domino sequence. Royce would be declared the winner, simply because *his* racer, returning to him now, would be the last one standing.

She was both exhilarated and dead tired and was no longer tracking the impostor. She stepped out of the Race Machine and whapped it with all her might.

*   *   *

Eva stood at a desolate bus stop, near downtown, a few transfers away from LAX. *Sorry, Royce. I didn't want to face you after breaking so many of your rules. But you deserve to be the winner. If you're not too angry at me, you know where to find me.*

The last bus of the day soon arrived for the long ride back up the coast. Eva worked her way down the aisle. She made to sit down next to a morose young woman with magenta hair, who looked like she needed a friend. As Eva was about to sit, the girl jumped up, realizing it was her stop, and rushed off, pushing past.

*   *   *

Donn popped his head up from the holographic display serving as a play-by-play monitor. He pumped his fist and with Cayla executed an unconventional, twisty, backhanded high-five. "A clean sweep! Woo-hoo, that Eva is being good!"

Royce's frown relaxed into a grin. "I should have known." He clapped his hands. "Eva was always several steps ahead. Now that she is demonstrating how to win with my modified racers, the commissioners will have no room to object to additional protections."

Yet inevitably, it would be another arms race, with the usual veneer of civilized discourse. But with Eva's help, he had won this round.

"Incoming!"

A blue light washed over the interior of the workshop, accompanied by a squelching noise of displacement. Royce put on a wide smile, preparing to congratulate the true winner.

The triumphant Race Machine sat on its platform, empty.

Royce's smile crumpled and he sat heavily, dropping to the floor. "Where is Eva?"

Another flash, red, emanated from a different location in the workshop.

Marshal William Arp emerged from the fading light, red-faced, wearing a poorly fitting jumpsuit. He reached behind his back. A moment later, a doughnut shape lay on his palm.

"Royce Halliday, you be being under arrest."

Royce sat there, no reaction, other than repeating, "Where is Eva?"

Cayla intervened. "Who the hell are you being? We are celebrating, and you're interrupting!"

Arp ignored her and advanced.

Donn blocked his way. "What are being the charges?"

Arp erupted with an offensive guffaw. "For going Rogue. Unauthorized disclosure, destruction of private property, intellectual property theft. That be being enough for you? Oh, and… murder."

The final declaration elicited a response from Royce. He looked up blearily. "Murder?"

"Being truly." Arp dipped his chin at Cayla.

Silence dropped over the crew and its boss. Royce raised his arms stiffly, holding them out.

"One hand be being enough," said the marshal.

Arp twisted the toroidal device in his hand, and it began to glow. He applied the device to Royce's right wrist. He shook out his left arm. A similar device emerged at his left wrist, from under the retracted sleeve. Arp manipulated and the two appliances now pulsated in sympathetic fashion.

The agent, or enforcer – whatever he represented – moved swiftly forward. Arp made a yanking motion. Royce was lifted roughly to his feet. He offered no resistance.

Donn attempted to reassure. "Boss, we're contacting the Racing Commission. They're clearing this up."

Arp snorted.

Royce offered only, "It's true. The locals. Even I was forgetting them. I deserve punishment. I only wish I could see her one last time…"

"Nice if all my prisoners be being this cooperative. Royce Halliday old boy, you and me, we be going for a ride – a nice, old-fashioned flight to Ireland!" He burst into an offensive laugh that took ages to subside. "We be resuming your interrupted journey."

Arp moved his right hand over his left wrist, fingers playing.

Captor and captive disappeared in a flash of blue light.

EIGHT

A gentle *tat-tat-tat* sounded from the front door – soft enough to be ignored.

Eva shook her head, dispelling the dreamlike images swirling in her mind. She felt dizzy with excitement.

"I can't believe I won... or will win one day... a speed race!" Eva laughed, sitting with the female Traverser on the sofa squeezed between the piano and the Christmas tree. "I tried going on a track once, and honestly, I felt terrified. I'm just a theoretical scientist!"

"You'll be honored by being first," said the older woman, who appeared to be in her fifties.

"But then someone always thinks they can beat *you*."

"Then you simply have to be better. And relentless about it. Don't worry, Eva, it's what *we* do best."

They sipped hot tea, served for the momentous occasion in delicate, old-fashioned cups from her mother's antique Italian set. "But I don't even own a car! These days I take the bus to the university and ride my bicycle. Fast enough, it's true, but not at racetrack speed!"

"You will soon find your true calling, Eva. Applied Physics. And remember *The Flying Mantuan*."

The curious name sparked a faint memory from her childhood. The name evoked a superhero, but she couldn't recall which comic. Eva's curiosity deepened.

"So... what about this Royce, or Race? Did we have a... romantic affair after our victory? Where is he now? All I know is that his brother is going mad trying to find him."

The Traverser smiled softly. "Patience, dear. The story is not yet finished."

*   *   *

The doorbell chimed, snapping Eva out of the moment. "Excuse me, Wilhelmina," she muttered, rising from her seat.

She opened the door cautiously, keeping her hand ready to close it quickly... and there stood the last person she wanted to see.

"Happy New Year!"

"Really, Professor?" Eva said, pulling the belt on her bathrobe tighter. "You're very early!"

Tovar beamed. "Really, my precious Eva! I simply could not wait to hear how you're planning to test my theory."

"I'm working on it, Professor, I promise." Eva forced a smile. "In fact, I may already be getting some early results. Success is literally knocking on my door. But now is just not a good time…"

"Forgive my anxiousness, Eva, but I'm losing all my supporting witnesses! The motorcycle guy, Axel, isn't at home in Barstow, and I can't reach him. The magicians have all left town in a hurry. The police – even Detective Conklin – look at me like I'm a dangerous nut, claiming he doesn't know what I'm talking about. Even his suicidal stewardess friend, Linda Scarlett Bradley, is back to flying back and forth from Ireland as if nothing ever happened. Every case I cite in my manuscript is being dismissed as lies. I hesitate to call it a vast conspiracy cover-up, but… no, they won't be able to stop Traversermania from spreading. Not if I publish a book that proves I'm sane, correct, and smarter than all of them – with your experimental evidence to back it up!"

"Don't lose hope." Eva paused, gathering her thoughts. "Your book is going to be famous."

Tovar's chest swelled with pride. "Thank you, my dear. I never doubted it."

Eva nodded, but her mind was elsewhere. "I'm sorry, Professor, but I really can't do this right now. Can we meet later? We agreed to gather around midnight, remember?"

"I totally lost track. What time is it now?" He chuckled. "What day? What year?"

"You're way too early!" She gently pushed the door to close it. "I have a special visitor here, and I need to say goodbye to her first."

"Oh, *enchanté*, madame!" Tovar exclaimed, swiftly sidestepping past Eva before she could react. He produced a bottle of champagne from a brown paper bag and, with surprising grace, kissed the older woman's hand. "Are you family? Of course – I can tell by the shared beauty."

The woman smiled, seemingly amused. "Her name is Wilhelmina," Eva interjected.

"Among others," the woman added.

"Eva?" a voice called out from the other side of the front door.

"This is getting ridiculous," Eva muttered under her breath.

She opened the door and found a young man standing there – no motorcycle, no helmet. Her heart skipped a beat. "I was starting to think the magician really had made you disappear." Her voice softened as she studied his disheveled appearance. "You look awful." *Does he really look like Race?*

The man shifted his weight and nearly lost his balance. Eva instinctively reached out, steadying him as their faces came within inches of each other.

"I was thinking we might spend the night together," he said, his voice low and tentative. He fumbled through the pocket of his leather jacket and unfolded a well-used white cardboard box. "I brought you this."

Eva's eyes widened. "When… where did you get this?"

Professor Tovar appeared behind her, grinning widely and holding two champagne glasses. "Ah, Axel, finally! Glad you could make it, my boy. We're having quite the New Year's party here!"

Peering over Eva's shoulder into the open box, Professor Tovar's eyes caught sight of the jump drive shaped like a toy motorcycle. "Does that have what I think it does?" he asked.

"Well, time to go!" Wilhelmina clapped her hands. "I have a job for you, young man," she declared. She stepped over to Axel and handed him a set of keys. "Could you drive my old Alfa Romeo to Hearst Castle? I always make a point to visit when I'm in the area, but my eyesight is not good enough anymore to negotiate the road to *La Cuesta Encantada* at night. They're expecting me, and it's not far from Cambria. You'll be rid of me in no time." The elderly woman regarded Axel. "Who knows, it might become a regular gig…"

Axel hesitated. "Well, it's been a long walk, and I just got here–"

"Nonsense," Wilhelmina interrupted, smiling. "We need to give the professor and his student some space to discuss their crazy time travel theories… right, Hector?"

"Milady, time travel can wait," Professor Tovar proclaimed, his eyes twinkling. "And since I'm still single, I'd be honored to take young Axel's place. How about I drive you up to the Castle to welcome the New Year in style, Wilhelmina?"

The woman raised a playful eyebrow. "No time for flattery, Professor. You need to start working on your second book."

"You mean my first book."

"I mean your follow-up. Please do publish your research on the Traversal cases too. Very important. I've already shared a story with Eva for your collection."

Turning to Eva, Wilhelmina smiled warmly. "Goodbye, dear. Find your speed through life and… pay attention to the road signs."

"*Fai attenzione ai segnali stradali,*" Eva repeated under her breath.

"Exactly! You're going to love what happens next."

With a wink, she added, "Dig under the Christmas tree, professor. I left something for you there. A global, all-time bestseller."

Tovar blinked, startled. "You brought me a present?"

"Yes! I hope you like it, my handsome young scholar," Wilhelmina said, twinkling.

Tovar's voice faltered. His throat tightened with emotion. "If I'd known you were coming tonight, dear lady, I would have brought you something worthy."

Wilhelmina smiled. She turned and held out her arms.

Eva stepped into them for an enduring maternal hug, which she did not wish to end.

"Happy 2288, everybody!" Wilhelmina called out as she waved. "Come on, Axel, let's go. Chop, chop! Have you ever heard of the Italian driver Tazio Nuvolari?"

The door fell shut, and her words faded into the night. Silence hung in the living room.

"Wait… what *year* did she say?" asked Tovar.

Eva W. Fontana shrugged, snatched a champagne glass from his hand, and gulped it down, bracing for impact as the Professor crouched under the Christmas tree to retrieve his present.

Hector J. Tovar paused, confused, turning to Eva with a furrowed brow before opening the handsome leather-bound book and reading the title page:

**REVIVE AND RELIVE THE PAST THROUGH
THE LANGUAGE OF THE FUTURE**
by
Professor Hector J. Tovar
Foreword by
Susan von Browne
Experiment Design by
Eva Fontana

then flipping straight to the last pages:

APPENDIX: THE TRAILBLAZERS

- Leif Erikson (c. 970-1020): Norse explorer, possibly first to reach North America.
- Marco Polo (1254-1324): Traveled to Asia, wrote "The Travels of Marco Polo."
- Zheng He (1371-1433): Led Chinese expeditions to the Indian Ocean.
- John Cabot (c. 1450-1500): Explored the North American coast.
- Christopher Columbus (1451-1506): Discovered the New World in 1492.
- Amerigo Vespucci (1454-1512): Recognized America as a separate continent.
- Ferdinand Magellan (1480-1521): Led the first expedition around the globe.
- Vasco da Gama (c. 1460s-1524): Established the sea route to India.
- Francisco Pizarro (c. 1475-1541): Conquered the Incan Empire.
- Hernán Cortés (1485-1547): Conquered the Aztec Empire.
- Henry Hudson (c. 1565-1611): Searched for the Northwest Passage.
- James Cook (1728-1779): Explored the Pacific Ocean, charted eastern Australia.
- Meriwether Lewis (1774-1809) and William Clark (1770-1838): Explored the western US.
- Sir Ernest Shackleton (1874-1922): Antarctic explorer, known for the Endurance rescue.
- Roald Amundsen (1872-1928): First to the South Pole, navigated the Northwest Passage.
- Evangeline Wilhelmina Fontanarrosa (2001-): First Traverser, Spacetime Explorer, all-time champion of the Ultimate Race Machines Grand Prix Rally, established the One Million Times Trophy, crafted from Corinthian Bronze.

Calegüinas

Fernando Sorrentino

Frontispiece by Alejandro Burdisio
Illustration by Ryan Doyle

My esteemed Professor Tovar,

While I haven't had any personal contact with the subject of your interest (time travelers), the perambulations of my readings has allowed me to come across a review (in Spanish) of a certain book (in German) by the scientist Ludwig Boitus.

The review is titled "An Enlightening Book."

I must confess that, having an exclusively grammatical and literary background, my ornithological ignorance can be considered close to perfection. For this reason, I dare neither to confirm nor deny the veracity of Dr. Boitus's information.

However, in the toponym "Huayllén-Naquén," I seem to discern a – let's say – Araucanian "sound" that makes me think that the mentioned lagoon is located somewhere in Argentine Patagonia.

Alas, as yet I have not found mention of such a toponym in any of the meticulous world atlases published in London and New York by the cartographic publishing house Rosencrantz & Guildenstern; hence, my legitimate suspicion about the probable non-existence of said lagoon and, consequently, also the birds that inhabit it.

My penchant for delving into fables and narrative inventions led me to discover a writing by a namesake of mine titled "Los opiliones de San Fernando." A footnote in that text provides the following information about Dr. Ludwig Boitus:

On page 498 of Arachnida, the section titled "Note on collaborators" unfolds. Boitus's entry – brief as the others – notes these details: "Born on November 8, 1142, in Sohrröntingen, a small German-speaking village in the Sacrum Imperium Romanum Germanicum, Dr. Boitus has, over more than nine centuries, developed a notable body of work as a polygraph, widely recognized in the scientific and humanities world. Prior to his birth, he collaborated with Pliny the Elder in the drafting of the Naturalis historia, and his study on Cicadella viridis is commendable."

Dear Professor Tovar, here my knowledge concludes. I, therefore, limit myself to sending you "An Enlightening Book" with the exhortation to use that text as your judgment deems most appropriate, not excluding the possibility of discarding it and consigning it to the basket of useless papers.

May a cordial greeting fly from the Buenos Aires plain, with wishes for success in your research.

Fernando Sorrentino
Martínez (Bs. As.) Argentina

An Enlightening Book

Translation by Gustavo Artiles and Alex Patterson

In his brief prologue to *Stelzvögel*, professor Franz Klamm explains that Dr. Ludwig Boitus travelled from Gottingen to Huayllén-Naquén with the sole purpose of studying *in situ* the assimilative attraction of the long-legged bird popularly known as calegüinas (this name has almost unanimous acceptance in the specialist literature in Spanish and it will be used here). *Stelzvögel* fills an acute gap in our knowledge of the subject. Before Dr. Boitus' exhaustive investigations – the presentation of which takes up almost a third of the volume – little was known for certain about calegüinas. In fact, except for fragmentary qualitative studies by Bulovic, Balbón, Laurencena and others – works plagued by whimsical, unsubstantiated claims – before *Stelzvögel*, the scientific community lacked a reliable basis on which to base further research. In his work, Dr. Boitus starts from the – perhaps debatable – premise that calegüinas' main character trait is its very strong personality (using the term *personality* in the sense established by Fox and his school). This personality is so potent that simply being in the presence of a calegüinas is enough to induce strongly calegüinas-like behaviour in other animals.

The calegüinas are found exclusively in the Huayllén-Naquén lagoon. There, they flourish – some estimates put the population as high as one million – helped both by local by-laws, which make hunting them illegal, and by the fact that their flesh is inedible and their feathers have no industrial use. In common with other long-legged birds, they feed on fish, Batrachia and the larvæ of mosquitos and other insects. Although they posses well-developed wings, they rarely fly, and when they do, they never go beyond the limits of the lagoon. They are of a similar size to storks, though their beaks are slightly larger and they do not migrate. Their back and wings are a blueish-black; their head, chest and belly, a yellowish-white. Their legs are pale yellow. Their *habitat*, the Huayllén-Naquén lagoon, is shallow but wide. Since there are no bridges across it – in spite of many representations to that end – the locals are obliged to make a long detour in order to get to the opposite side. This has had the effect of making complaints to the local newspaper almost continuous but communication between the shores of the lagoon rather scarce. To the uninformed observer it would appear that residents could cross the lagoon quickly and easily by using stilts and even without them, at its deepest point, the water would barely reach the waist of a man of average height. However, the locals know – although perhaps in a intuitive way only – the assimilative power of the calegüinas, and the fact is that they prefer not to attempt the crossing, choosing instead – as already stated – to go around the lagoon, which is encircled by an excellent asphalt road.

All this has not stopped the hiring of stilts to tourists becoming the single most important part of the Huayllén-Naquén economy, a circumstance that is perhaps justifiable in view of the scarcity of basic resources in the region. The absence of serious competition and the lack of official pricing has made the hiring of stilts a very costly business indeed; inflating prices to outrageous levels is the only way tradesmen can recoup their inevitable losses. In fact, there is a rather limited Huayllén-Naquén by-law stipulating that shops hiring stilts should display a sign, positioned in open view and written in bold lettering, warning that the use of stilts may lead to fairly serious psychological alterations. As a rule, tourists tend not to heed these warnings and, for the most part, treat them as a joke. It should be noted that it is simply not possible to make sure that the notices are read by every single tourist even when, as is undeniably the case, the shopkeepers comply with the by-law punctiliously and place the signs in highly conspicuous places. The authorities are notoriously inflexible on this point. It is true that inspections are not very frequent and are always preceded by a warning sent a few minutes beforehand – but the inspectors are known to perform their duties conscientiously and it can only be coincidence that there is no recorded case of a shopkeeper being sanctioned under the by-law.

Once in possession of their stilts, the tourists, either by themselves or in cheerful, chattering groups of two, three, five or ten go into the Huayllén-Naquén lagoon with the aim of reaching the opposite shore where they can buy, at very reasonable prices, tins of exquisite fish – a product that provides the main source of income for the population on that side of the lagoon. For the first two or three hundred metres, the tourists advance happily; laughing, shouting, playing practical jokes and frightening the calegüinas, which, like all long-legged birds, are extremely nervous creatures. Gradually, as they penetrate deeper and deeper into the lagoon, the tourists become more subdued while, metre-by-metre, the density of calegüinas increases. Soon the birds are so numerous that progress becomes extremely difficult for the tourists. The calegüinas no longer run or fly away nervously – as their numbers rise, they appear to grow in confidence, although their behaviour could also be explained by the fact that, by then, most movement is physically impossible. Whatever the reason, there comes a moment when shouting is no longer enough and it becomes necessary to use sticks and hands to shoo the calegüinas out of the way. Even then they concede very little ground. This is generally the moment when the tourists fall silent and the joking and laughing comes to an end. Then – and only then – they notice a dense humming emanating from the throats of the thousands of calegüinas, filling the entire lagoon. In its timbre, this humming is not very different from that of doves – it is, however, considerably more intense. It enters the ears of the tourists and resonates inside their heads, it fills their minds so completely that, gradually, they too begin to hum. To start with, this humming is a poor imitation of the birds, but soon it becomes impossible to distinguish between the humming of the humans and that of the calegüinas. At this point, the tourists often start to experience a choking sensation, they can detect nothing but calegüinas for as far as the eye can see and soon lose the ability to differentiate between land and the water of the lagoon. In front and behind, left and right they see an endlessly repeating, monotonous desert of black and white made up of wings, beaks and feathers. There is usually one tourist – especially if there is a large group of them on the lagoon – who perceives the wisdom and convenience of returning to Huayllén-Naquén and sacrificing their prospective purchase of exquisite fish at very reasonable prices from the opposite shore.

But where is the opposite shore? How can they go back if they have lost all notion of the direction they came from? How can they go back if there are no longer any points of reference, if everything is black and white, an endlessly repeating landscape of wings, beaks and feathers? And eyes: two million blinking, expressionless eyes. In spite of all the evidence that returning is no longer an option, the tourist who is most lucid – or rather, least delirious – addresses his companions with some pathetic exhortation: 'Friends, let us go back the way we came!' But his companions cannot understand his strident croaks, so different are they from the gentle humming they are now accustomed to. At this point, even though they themselves answer with the same unintelligible croaks, deep down they are still conscious of the fact that they are human. Fear, however, has unhinged them and they all begin to croak simultaneously. Unfortunately, this chorus of croaks has no meaningful content and, even if they wanted to, the tourists would be unable to communicate their final coherent thought: that they are all calegüinas. It is then that the elders of the calegüinas community, who up to this point have kept knowingly silent, begin to croak with all their might. It is a triumphant croak, a cry of victory that starts from that inner circle and spreads quickly and tumultuously through the length and breadth of the Huayllén-Naquén lagoon and beyond its limits to the remotest houses of the nearby town. The locals put their fingers in their ears and smile. Happily, the noise lasts barely five minutes, and only after it has completely stopped do the tradesmen get back to making as many pairs of stilts as tourists have entered the lagoon.

A Rest Stop For Weary Travelers

R. James Doyle and Rogelio Fojo

Frontispiece by Alejandro Burdisio
Illustrations by Fangorn and Emma Howitt

PART I

A projectile is on its way tonight. Ineluctable. I can't fathom why it hasn't struck yet. I distinctly saw the gun barrel pointed straight at me, less than three feet away, and the flash from the shot.

What's going on, Lisbeth the Lovely? Did we execute a perfect escape act routine? Should we leap out of this worn-out magic cabinet, take a bow, and relish the applause?

I've been delving into the intricacies of magic illusions performed by people like yourself. According to Professor Tovar, panicked eye movements can induce saccadic suppression of our visual field, arriving at spatiotemporal stasis, in extremis! Our brains deceiving us into believing that we've become invisible, or time has frozen. All under the veil of hypnosis.

Well, it sounds like ophthalmo-babble, to me. I simply don't believe in your magic. It's all tricks and hoaxes – smoke and angled mirrors. Not to mention those tall tales about your lot being time travelers! A mass hallucination among impressionable youths, dismissed by sophisticated adults – like me – as just another silly fad: hysterical 'Traversermania.'

And yet, here we are, you and I, locked inside a yellow box dotted with tiny round holes which allow us to breathe. Feeling woozy and nauseous from that brutal spin.

What do you see in our future, Lisbeth? Tell me. I don't think I've heard your manner of speech before. Did you know I took a course on Social Communication Techniques? I hold a degree in Linguistics from TCD. Nuances of the tongue are dear to my heart. And I have a knack for spotting fake Traverser-speak.

Why are you guys so secretive?!

Earlier today, I observed your boss the illusionist hire a suspicious stooge for the show. Harry or Barry if memory serves... maybe Peter? – a 'volunteer' for your tricks. I must confess I was later spying on you too, while you put on that flattering, form-fitting, sequined jumpsuit. I saw you gather your pet and contort your lithe forms to fit into a secret compartment of this apparatus.

I know, I know, it's unprofessional. But I wanted to understand the trick behind the grand illusion of the magicians I'd hired! I wanted to assess the reputability of your act.

People think of me as a pompous control freak, but I see myself as more of an amateur debunker – the proud possessor of a bright, rational, and objective mind. Albeit, regrettably, ensnared within a psyche governed by irrational fears and fierce carnal desires.

Oh well, we all play with the cards we are dealt.

*   *   *

The twenty-sixth of December began with brilliant
sunshine and a gentle breeze wafting the dust of the
nearby *El Camino Real*. The temperature on the central
coast of California was delightful, inviting everyone to
head outside and enjoy the day.

McGready examined his multi-purpose monitoring
console at leisure, noting the approach of the first of the
day's expected guests.

The Director of the exclusive and secretive retreat,
known simply as a Rest Stop for Weary Travelers, smiled
as he left his private Control Room, semi-consciously
practicing his lines, knowing that soon he would be
turning on the charm.

A clap of thunder reverberated along the coastal cliffs,
startling McGready from his peaceful reverie. His gaze
instinctively shot skyward, but the vast expanse of blue
held not a single wisp of cloud.

He resumed his musings on the guests, including Mrs.
Evangeline Wilhelmina Fontanarrosa, a septuagenarian.
He would place this VIP guest in one of the Rest Stop's
high-end short-term residences.

*   *   *

Let me rewind my story clock a bit.

*The Hi-Hat's back door slams open. Within the dim
glow of the Ghost Light, I see a menacing shadow hurtle
forward. The silhouetted figure – with its cat-like
movements and broad shoulders – must be one of the
many guns available for hire. Did he come all the way
from Las Vegas to murder me? Oh well. Big debts like
mine aren't easily forgiven in Sin City.*

*I scramble onto the stage in a foolish attempt to hide
inside your magic cabinet. The soft click as you secure
the latch of your refuge compels me to discreetly close
the main door too.*

*Total silence. Then, the threat nears. I hear his
footsteps.*

The assassin spins the cabinet violently on its casters.

That's when I lose my composure and cry out to you in sobbing whispers: "Help me, Lisbeth! If you really are a Traverser... help me now!"

But you remain silent to my pleas.

Gyrating at a disorienting speed, our haven is peppered with a barrage of thunderous gunshots, piercing the blackness with crisscrossing beams of light. Bullets strike relentlessly on all sides, chipping away at the decrepit wooden prop.

When the magic cabinet finally spins down, the man yanks open the door, his face contorted in a wild frenzy, a sight seared into my brain. He's shocked by his inexplicable misfires, but what happens next catches him even more off guard: a white dove materializes and clumsily flutters away from the box.

He swats at the disoriented bird with his wool cap, his fury palpable. He struggles to cover his shaven head again. All I can do is nervously smile and execute a magician's flourish with my hands, as if presenting a spectacular trick, desperately trying to buy time to delay the inevitable.

Slowly and deliberately, he levels the gun at my chest and recites an incantation of his own:

"Abracadabra, motherfucker!"

*   *   *

The woman driven by her ash-bearded chauffeur ascended *La Cuesta Encantada* – in a Race Machine equipped with a Traversal Engine. The powerful vehicle was an upgraded Alfa Romeo P3 two-seater, straight from the 1935 German Grand Prix at the Nürburgring, the historic event famously won by legendary racing figure Tazio Nuvolari.

The woman regaled her long-suffering driver. "The Flying Mantuan, that's what we called him! He was my hero, driving this old Alfa against those fancy German Silver Arrows from Mercedes-Benz and Auto Union."

Pride in her history found expression in the woman's

chosen conveyance. Of Italian descent herself, she regarded her countryman's triumph in the German race as a pivotal moment in motorsport history, powered by Nuvolari's extraordinary talent behind the wheel – a shared trait.

The chauffeur cut a striking figure in his meticulously maintained garrick coat, embodying the professionalism and timeless elegance required by his discerning employer. Beneath the heavy, dark wool, thermoregulation processors adjusted his comfort, embedded sensors cooling or warming as needed. Multiple shoulder capes draped gracefully over his strong shoulders, adding authority to his silhouette.

His gloved hands, encased in supple black leather, gripped the steering wheel with practiced ease, the gloves' sheen catching ambient light from the dashboard displays. The coat's wide collar, partially turned up against the morning breeze, framed his ruggedly handsome face.

Alexander's eyes, under the brim of his chauffeur's cap bearing the 1M*t* insignia of his employer's society, flicked between the road ahead and the hovering displays. He maneuvered the Alfa Romeo P3 with the deftness of a seasoned driver, blending the high-tech nature of the Race Machine with the historical gravitas of his attire, anchoring him in a tradition of service and excellence.

"You should take some piloting cues from him, Alexander! Tazio was the underdog but showed amazing skill and strategy, winning against all odds. A memorable victory!"

The chauffeur regarded his charge affectionately, his experienced eyes easily processing the information from the complex set of displays.

The mature woman exuded sophistication in a tailored ensemble which complemented the chauffeur's classic attire. She wore a sleek, fitted dress in baby blue velvet, its rich texture catching the light. The dress featured a cinched waist and a high collar adorned with a delicate brooch. Over it, a long, peach coat draped elegantly, its lining visible with each movement. Polished black ankle boots and matching gloves added a modern touch to her vintage-inspired look. Her gray hair, styled in soft waves, framed her face, accentuating her confident and poised demeanor as she spoke.

The vibrant red car flickered in and out of view as the expert driver negotiated the ancient hills, listening attentively to his passionate passenger.

There wasn't a sharp edge to be seen anywhere. The land to either side of the road was covered with naturally low-cut golden grasses, soothing to the eye. The view to the horizon showed the brilliant cerulean sky melded seamlessly with the dark, equally rich blue of the limitless Pacific Ocean.

*   *   *

Split seconds – that's all it takes for your life to change course.

My memory blurs between that point-blank flash of blinding light, the deafening shock wave of the projectile breaking the sound barrier... and the engulfing darkness and silence that followed.

It seems we've been stuck here together for quite a while now, Lisbeth... and still not a single word escapes your lips. I fear – though I cannot discern the telltale sign of blood streaming from your hideaway – that you may have already departed this space.

My poor girl... dust to magic dust.

I too must be in a state of demise. I am uncertain as to why I continue to ramble on.

*   *   *

The woman placed her hand against the dashboard with rigor while her chauffeur skillfully navigated the gently undulating terrain. She relished the open road. The poorly delineated byway hugged the land while moving travelers along all dimensions: forward along the axis defined by the road itself, rolling softly up and down, swaying almost lovingly side to side, and, if one chose to complete the picture, which she did without effort, inexorably forward in time also, the lot of almost all travelers.

"Not being far now, Mrs. Winnie," said the driver.

"Thank you, Alexander," she replied, breathing in the bracing, salt-strewn air. Her gray strands snapped deliciously in the wind. The sounds of crashing surf made for a source of drama in the landscape. A scene of sea lions flopping and basking among glistening, haphazard rocks failed to soothe her.

The views were pleasant, but the circumstances surrounding her trip did not allow her to relax.

Soon, an arresting sight came into view as they cleared the next rise.

* * *

Thin light flickered through the bullet holes, casting eerie patterns on the cabinet interior. A chill breeze whispered through the openings. According to my smartwatch, the temperature inside the box was a frigid twenty degrees Fahrenheit. Shivers traversed my spine.

I contemplated my next move.

My eyes adapted to the dimness, and I conducted a survey of my immediate surroundings.

No sign of Lisbeth.

Through the mist of my breathing, I resolved two shiny suspended objects: A single high-speed 9mm hollow point bullet – trailed by the stainless steel, full-size Luger that had propelled it. Amazing how one notices specific details when given enough time. The handgun was reddened and still clutched by the severed hand which had pulled its trigger.

Instinctively recoiling from the weapon still pointing at my chest – and still in the path of the bullet – I backed against the cabinet wall with no room for further retreat. I opened the door partway, stealthily, so as not to alert the assailant outside – now surely more agitated and dangerous after the loss of an appendage. As a precaution, I retrieved the hovering pistol, with its remaining ammunition, plucking it from midair with less effort than I expected. I cocked the weapon.

Disgustedly disentangling the severed extremity clinging obsessively to the trigger, I tossed the hand outside ahead of me, as both bait and unconventional peace offering. Holding the gun steady, ready to defend myself, I cautiously pushed the door open.

What I saw next stopped me dead in my tracks.

*　　*　　*

Mrs. Winnie gazed at the elaborate apparition of Hearst Castle, as it appeared in her younger days, but expanded. Reaching backward and forward. The multi-towered structure, with numerous dazzlingly white spires, was unmistakable – all architectural opulence, standing out dramatically with energetic surfaces and angles from the rolling scenery.

"The Rest Stop is becoming even more spread out by blending Blarney, Gillette, and Pittamiglio," said Mrs. Winnie. "What an unprecedented design! Beautifully integrated into the setting, don't you think, Alexander? I must be thanking the architects."

The complex was indeed sprawling. Mrs. Winnie watched her taciturn driver find the way easily, working with subtle spatiotemporal landmarks.

*　　*　　*

No walls lined with sound systems, no ceiling rigged with Fresnel lights, no stage for magicians. I was somehow transferred from the familiar setting of the Hi-Hat Club to a desolate beach.

Up in the night sky, a too-small moon spun in place, cycling rapidly through its phases. I blinked, certain my eyes were deceiving me. Only when the orb wound down into a normal full moon, did I finally breathe and dare to step outside.

"That's one small step for a man, one giant leap for Malcolm."

I dropped my eyes to the moonlit shore where I'd landed, trembling in response to the engulfing frigid air. The panorama of a gritty, icy beach stretched before me, with frosty gravel dunes rising to meet the silhouette of a looming structure atop a nearby hill.

Consulting again my watch, I got a reading of twelve degrees Fahrenheit now! The bone-chilling conditions outside the confinement of the box spurred me to seek refuge in that nearby edifice, without delay.

I felt compelled to glance back one last time. The distressed planks of the cabinet provided no hiding place for a concealed figure – or a frozen cadaver. Lisbeth had truly vanished into thin air.

I was utterly alone.

*　　*　　*

There. The woman and her chauffeur passed the perimeter. Also elusive – except for those to whom it was meant to be an impenetrable barrier.

The main structure's embracing wings evoked a grand hotel of another era. Along the approach, the grounds became increasingly well-tended until they were rolling along an exquisite red brick roadway, bounded by verdant manicured lawns. Copses of leafy trees dappled the environment.

Another building, white, with a more functional aspect, appeared in the middle distance, before becoming eclipsed behind the looming principal edifice.

Mrs. Winnie thought she caught a glimpse of a young woman at a window watching their arrival: long flat hair, unspeakably sad. But in the shifting perspective, glare overwhelmed her cataract-challenged vision, and the sight disappeared behind the main building.

They reached the terminating circular drive.

*　　*　　*

The gun was freezing my hand. No visible threat, so... I jogged back and tossed the weapon back into the cabinet. My mistake! It landed on the floor with a loud thud, causing the firing pin to strike and fire a bullet that blasted another hole in the walls.

The shot thundered along the cliffs like the proclamation of a war drum. Not the most advisable way to announce my arrival.

Oh, well.

How could this possibly be the California coastline I knew so well? What was this landscape?

Was I having a bad dream? Had I traveled through time within the enigmatic cabinet? For the sake of expediency, I decided to adopt the second hypothesis. No more skepticism about Traversers, no further questions – just unwavering belief in an extraordinary possibility.

As I climbed, I paused to catch my breath and take in my surroundings. Was I suddenly transported to a prehistoric era? Amid the persisting eerie silence, I half-expected to witness pterodactyls soaring overhead.

The imposing castle stood ahead of me, a solitary beacon of civilization, beckoning.

*   *   *

A festive banner hanging directly above the double doors of the main entrance shouted:

> ## "Welcome Mrs. Winnie!"

A well-dressed man in coat and tails, accessorized with a deep burgundy silk bow tie, approached at the vanguard of a welcoming committee. His high forehead was bordered by well-coiffed hair, and he sported a closely cropped red beard. He waited at ease as the arriving car cruised to a gentle stop.

The chauffeur applied the brake, exited, and came around to offer a sturdy arm.

The greeter bowed. "Mrs. Fontanarrosa, my name is

Mr. McGready. I am the Director here, and it is my distinct pleasure to welcome you to the Rest Stop for Weary Travelers."

He offered his open hand, palm up. Somehow the gesture was not anachronistic. The woman felt an almost impish smile twitch on her face before she dropped her barriers back into place.

"Call me Evangeline."

*   *   *

I pressed on, driven by the relentless Arctic cold that seeped straight through my inadequate attire: a navy blue summer business jacket, paired with a crisp white guayabera shirt, designer sunglasses... and very expensive, and too slippery leather tassel loafers.

A splitting headache throbbed my head. Sensing I might have only minutes to live, I concentrated on reaching shelter.

I negotiated the final slope and approached the building. Despite the perilous weather conditions, I couldn't help but stop and admire the towers and turrets, their overall harmony and coherence. The somewhat familiar facade evoked a sense of relief, tinged with curiosity.

Shivering not only from the cold but also from awe of the castle, I pushed open the massive wooden doors and stepped into the grand entrance hall.

I'd survived!

My gaze was immediately drawn to a display hovering behind the empty concierge desk.

Eleven thousand – ?

*   *   *

Mrs. Winnie and Mr. McGready proceeded on tour, arm-in-arm.

McGready informed his guest. "The residences are along the wings, but the central public spaces and our beautiful grounds are where guests enjoy their lives to the fullest."

They were in the main hall, a large space lit by tall windows. The ceilings were high and wainscoted in their recesses; the paneling, in the bright light, leaned toward blond tones, well-polished; the carpets were exquisitely threaded; artwork hung in numerous locations to complete the environment with excellent balance.

A concierge desk stood right of center, staffed by a uniformed attendant. The view straight ahead opened to a huge ballroom with a central chandelier appearing as if it could throw enough illumination to rival the sun – even the brighter version here, several miles inland from the limning coastal haze. Along the main hall stood other portals inviting investigation. In the distance residential wings angled out of sight.

As they approached the desk, Mrs. Winnie's eyes were drawn to a stunning calendar prominently displayed. The date of her arrival, December 26th, 1799, had been specially marked by McGready with pulsing multicolored lights, making her feel warmly welcomed and appreciated.

Mrs. Winnie noted, with some annoyance, her favorite colors, baby blue and peach, in glowing neon, matching the elegant ensemble she was wearing.

*   *   *

I moved closer for a better view and conclusively established it was, indeed, a calendar. One day was highlighted, pulsing slowly blue – the twenty-sixth. The month was December.

And yes, the year appeared to be... 11799.

Although I was immensely grateful to find warmth and sanctuary within the Castle, regardless of the year, an unsettling sense of dread lingered, impossible to shake.

I turned back to close the door as the chilling wind howled outside, its icy fingers still clawing at me. Darkness rapidly enveloped the room, deepening the eerie stillness. Luckily, I found plenty of candlesticks scattered around and had several Hi-Hat Club matchboxes in my pockets.

Despite the total lack of electricity, I found much-needed solace in the grandeur of the building and even reassurance in its enduring presence through the passage of time. I soon wandered through the corridors, illuminating my way with a handheld candelabra. The furniture was shrouded in dusty white sheets, and vines crept into every crevice.

Surprisingly, there were no spiderwebs or signs of rats and other vermin. The silence was absolute. I struggled to hold at bay a creeping loneliness.

Instinct born of my experience as theatrical manager of the Hi-Hat Club led me to a small stage, flanked by a larger space filled with costumes. A wooden sign with faded letters had fallen to the ground. Squinting, I could make out the word 'Wardrobe'.

Still shivering from the bone-deep cold, I grabbed a hooded jacket from the neglected racks. It seemed like an authentic Eskimo Inuit parka, lined with Arctic fox fur. Soon, it warmed my body, preparing me for whatever lay ahead.

*   *   *

Director McGready sat in the passenger seat of the Alfa, gesturing. "You know, Alexander, a very long time ago I was one of those skeptics who would ask, 'Then where are all the Traversers?'"

No response came from the chauffeur, who seemed unnecessarily focused on his driving along the short but labyrinthine path to the concealed parking garage.

The Director continued. "I don't know who posed the objection originally, but when over-enthused Traverser-maniacs would attempt to sell their time travel conspiracy theory, I would scoff, put on a smirk, and ask that same question. And be quite impatient with the stock response: 'They are among us, but they do not wish to engage.'"

Alexander carried on, ignoring McGready.

"Then I came to know the different answer." He paused. "They are right here! Unwinding their biological clocks at the Rest Stop for Weary Travelers. Which I've prepared for them," the Director concluded.

The chauffeur drove forward carefully.

Nothing to say, like a good Traverser.

One needed to appreciate, psychologically, whence most of his guests were coming, and whereto they were going. Any experience can become routine. The über-experienced Traversers – over time – became desensitized to risks, dangers, causes, consequences, even life and death. They became jaded, going as they pleased around spacetime – up to the Corinthian Bronze limits, of course.

The Rest Stop for Weary Travelers was the means by which Traversers met for fun and camaraderie. At this coastal resort assembled near Cambria in the past, they could drop their guard and relax.

The enclave was a superb 4D-printed scale reproduction of the famous edifice on *La Cuesta Encantada* at San Simeon. Fashioned from enduring materials, rooted in former times, with inspired additions. The structure owed its existence to the brilliance of Dr. Morgan Grimley, named in honor of – and worthy successor to – Julia Morgan, the architect of Hearst Castle.

McGready's role was to operate this powerful Traverser hub, keep meticulous records, and maintain order at the Rest Stop – while personally lacking the privileges to partake of its transportation possibilities.

"Oh well. Here we are, Alexander. You can leave your vehicle here at the Carriage House," said McGready. "Mrs. Winnie will occupy the Guest of Honor suite in 'La Casa Grande,' and you can choose one of the nearby garden guest cottages, either 'La Casa del Monte' or 'La Casa del Mar.'"

Alexander proceeded straight through the ostensibly solid door, and they were inside. The chauffeur quickly opened his door and stood straight, cap in hand, fixedly studying the array of vintage vehicles.

McGready, catching new details of the chauffeur's classic

uniform, felt a surge of satisfaction. The Director had recovered from a negligent period in his youth of dressing poorly. He was now welcoming guests with an impeccable appearance, befitting the elegance of those he hosted.

He noticed with approval the chauffeur's shiny black trousers, sharply creased, leading down to knee-high leather boots. Their surfaces were meticulously maintained to a glossy finish. These jackboots, sturdy yet elegant, completed the ensemble, ensuring Alexander was not only protected from the elements but also presented a sartorial splendor.

Most of the parking spots were occupied by colorful, anachronistic automobiles. Alexander took in the panorama, no doubt having little difficulty identifying some as Grand Prix Race vehicles, like the one he was driving for Mrs. Winnie. The chauffeur scanned the array of sleek muscle cars: the formidable Mercedes-Benz W25 Silver Arrow; a pair of dark green-hued Type B and Type C Auto Union racing cars; an elegant Bugatti Type 59 racing car in resplendent blue finish; and the sleek red chassis of the powerful Maserati 8CM model.

"I hope our garage meets the prestigious standard expected for Mrs. Winnie – owner of the prized Tazio Nuvolari auto," said McGready.

Alexander nodded, impressed.

The spacious garage accommodated not only bygone cars but also a few historical train engines resting on short railroad tracks.

Now McGready beamed with special pride, exulting in the Rest Stop's impressive and recently acquired Traversal Locomotives collection: the Russian Armored Train Zaamuret; the Soviet-era Hungarian train Magyar Államvasutak; and his favorite *choo-choo* train – the Australian steam engine 3801. The Director easily got lost in its sleek and streamlined design, its polished brass fittings gleaming under the garage roof lights, the vibrant green and yellow paint contrasting beautifully with the black detailing and…

"A Triumph!" gasped Alexander.

"Indeed, my dear fellow! Quite a sight, yes?" remarked the Director. Then he noted with disappointment that Alexander's attention was elsewhere. The chauffeur gazed at the most modest vehicle in the Carriage House – a small black and white machine nestled between a huge vintage locomotive and the proud body of a classic Ford Model T car.

"Can you tell me when that arrived?" asked Alexander, pointing to a dusty and worn-down motorcycle.

"Oh, this month," said McGready, slightly flummoxed.

"Why is it here?" Alexander pressed.

The Director was unprepared for this conversation with a Traverser. "It was… confiscated," he stammered out, regretting his words immediately.

Alexander's hand trembled slightly as he reached into his shirt. His fingers carefully pulled out the weathered key of a 1954 TWN Triumph Boss motorcycle. He swiftly inserted it into the lock of the black toolbox mounted over the rear wheel. Inside, all he discovered was a hammer, a screwdriver, and a wrench – which he discarded without a second thought. He rummaged at the bottom.

McGready peered over the man's shoulder. A small, engraved plate read:

> **'Property of Axel-H.'**

"This is my old stolen bike!" exclaimed the chauffeur.

*   *   *

"Crackpot!" I called.

While exploring the bookshelves of the Gothic Library, I came across books by the eccentric Professor Tovar, renowned for his theories about Traversers and stage magic – all in the realm of what I used to hold, consider, and finally discard, like expired theater tickets.

Appraisals of this individual, mostly fringe, ranged from prophetic to deluded. I knew this much: Traditional book publishers rejected his manuscripts. Even indie publishers shied away from his work, fearing legal issues. Wary of accusations of Traversermania having the effect of inflaming vulnerable young minds, leading to suicides and other tragedies.

No, thanks. I'd rather look for some graphic novels if I wanted to entertain myself with fiction.

Still... what about my own present circumstances?

A chill ran through me as I suddenly remembered where and when I was, wondering if his tales connected more to me than I had initially thought.

*   *   *

"Mrs. Winnie, do you enjoy dancing?"

"Evangeline, please. Well, it's been many years…"

"I insist on a first dance, before the younger bachelors around here start crowding in."

"Mr. McGready! Perhaps, we shall see." Mrs. Winnie followed the Director to the next chamber, left of the ballroom.

"Is reading one of your hobbies?" He pushed on the tall, well-balanced double doors. "Do you ever get lost in a good book?"

"Oh my, I should say so."

The space within presented a classically elegant library: floor-to-ceiling bookshelves, rail ladders, indirect light, a range of comfortable desks, plush upholstered chairs. Another uniformed attendant sat at the ready.

"I know you will like what you see here," McGready said. "I understand that reading truly became something of a lost art. I guarantee you will find volumes here that you have never encountered before."

"A bit of trivia, Mrs. Winnie… Evangeline," he continued. "One of the antique lamps from the Gothic Library was found to be missing its original shade. The lampstand was relocated to the theater, where it now serves as a traditional, bare Ghost Light for the performers."

Mrs. Winnie was intrigued but the Director whisked her gently onward.

"Can you guess where we discovered the missing lampshade?"

They reemerged into the main hall. She reset her expression into a studied nonchalance and pursued the Director through the next portal.

*   *   *

Tools! They always come in handy!

I located a hammer, screwdriver, and wrench in the garage, relieved that such still existed.

Determined to restore some semblance of order, I rolled up my sleeves and got to work.

First, I repurposed an exquisite parchment lampshade to create a new sign. Carefully unrolling the parchment and using a red marker I borrowed from the front desk, I inscribed two words over faded Latin verses – a palimpsest, no doubt speaking of ancient knowledge, wisdom, and literature. Oh well, apologies to history.

Then, I affixed the new sign over the 'Wardrobe' label and reattached the wooden plaque above the door of the neglected dressing room.

After lots of hammering and twisting, I stepped back to admire my handiwork. A sense of accomplishment washed over me, as I read the evocative new name.

*   *   *

Mrs. Winnie's eyes twinkled upon spotting the scroll displayed above the entrance.

"We call this The Armoire," said McGready.

Mrs. Winnie could not help catching a breath.

The room was roughly the same size as the Gothic Library. The walls held not books but authentic period costumes, recessed into alcoves, all linked into a conveyance system. The place resembled a colossal dry-cleaning establishment. Any one of the beautiful vestments could be brought to hand on demand.

The racks were arrayed as: Indigenous America... Victorian Britain... Pacific Oceania... The Crusades... Aboriginal Australia... Shogun Japan... Imperial Rome... Ancient Egypt... Classical Greece... and many more.

"You must host quite the masquerade party," said Mrs. Winnie.

"Any day here can be an opportunity to indulge in a bit of fantasy... anything you like, at most any time at all."

The doors, which had closed silently, opened again. A couple entered, dressed in curious close-fitting garb, odd-looking fabric which threw off rippling glints in the indirect lighting.

The woman gazed at the interior of the Rest Stop for Weary Travelers with bemused appreciation. She strode forward. "Director McGready, we are Julia and Morgan, ready for our journey."

The man glanced at Mrs. Winnie, then stepped back and bowed, hands held outward. Julia quickly followed suit. "Being an honor," said Morgan, whispering to his companion.

"Beautiful work here," said Mrs. Winnie. "Thank you."

The Director added, "Delighted! Now be telling me, how is being your journey, so long and so far? Off now to Imperial Rome if I am recalling? I am welcoming you on your way."

The woman could not take her eyes off Mrs. Winnie. "Director, no... we decided the bread and circuses have become tiresome. We are happy to be here and now in Indigenous America."

"An excellent choice," said McGready.

"But there is a tour presently that may be worth catching. Maybe you'd both like to take it, too? We'll bring back a brochure."

"Oh, I wish," said McGready. "But thank you."

Mrs. Winnie felt the Director smoothly disengage his arm.

He moved a step away. "Mrs. Fontanarrosa, we are a multi-function institution. Regretfully, it is not possible that I continue with you right now, but I promise to make it up to you later."

"Did they say they were on holiday?" asked Mrs. Winnie. "Mr. McGready, I would like to remain right here in The Armoire a while longer."

He hesitated. "As you wish, dear lady." The Director turned back to his new charges.

Mrs. Winnie watched the group depart and felt the slight pressure change as the exquisitely balanced doors shut.

*   *   *

Behold the sanctuary of fire!

I discovered it the following day as I resumed my exploration of the complex.

I stumbled upon an unexpectedly immaculate hall – I'll call it the Assembly Room – buoyed by the eternal hope in my chest for companionship. The space was adorned with pristine armchairs and crackling flames warming a central fireplace.

"Where are the people who lit the fire?" I wondered aloud. My voice reverberated off the walls.

Undeterred by the lack of answer, I proceeded through the corridors, ascending and descending stately, ornate stairways, gathering speed with each stride, repeatedly calling out, "Hello? Where is everybody?"

The silence enveloped me like a heavy cloak. I felt a twinge of embarrassment as I continued to call out in vain.

*   *   *

McGready sat in his office. A soft chime heralded the arrival of Dr. Alunn Lance, Clinical Psychologist and Principal Attending Psychiatrist at the Mind Recession Clinic. Time for their weekly session to review the status of the inmates. The Director touched the virtual button that lit a green light on the exterior wall panel and simultaneously released the door latch.

The psychologist brought McGready up to date. They turned to the final, most interesting case.

"Linda Scarlett Bradley," said Lance. "Former flight attendant."

"Any additional breaks?"

"None."

"Has the other personality remanifested?"

"Negative."

"Do we have a name? Any identifying parameters?" asked McGready.

"No name being given, but definitely male. The other was threatening in manner, being delighted to portray Linda as naughty, dangerous, or worse."

"What is Linda saying?"

"She is giving no indication of having any active memory of the manifestation," noted Lance.

"Unconscious memories?"

"Always being a tough call. She is being more nervous, blood pressure elevated, appetite depressed, but still being within normal for her. She is being a remarkably intelligent and sensitive person, capable of picking up cues from others, even professionals."

"Asymmetric memories, then?" the Director asked.

"Apparently. I am detecting markers of temporal displacement indicative of early Eternalist experiments. But there are not being clear records of Linda traversing."

"Based on general behavior and progress, we had identified Linda for performance therapy. What would you recommend now?" asked McGready.

Lance considered. "Generally, I am leaning toward pushing for progress. Her case is being unusual. The commitment records are citing something dreadful in her past, which fits what the other personality is insinuating. But there is being only ambiguous evidence of an incident involving Trinity Airlines. She is becoming obsessed with it, and one isn't really blaming her."

"With a duplicate personality manifesting, are we medicating her?"

"Being standard protocol. She is fitting parameters for potential harm to herself or others."

McGready paused. "Wouldn't that suggest *not* proceeding with performance therapy? With other guests present?"

"I'll be having security on hand, and I am being present with a fast-acting sedative. She is being a physically slight individual."

"We have responsibility for our other guests. We must not allow any collateral trauma."

"A fair point, Mr. McGready. I would say it is being your call."

"All right, Alunn. Without some risk, there is less progress... and less understanding. We'll go ahead. With all due caution."

"Very good. I am making the arrangements."

*   *   *

I was never alone! Or rather, no longer alone. Or, at least, not anymore. It was becoming increasingly challenging here to be thinking clearly with verb tenses and temporal adverbs.

I caught sight of other human beings along the beach in the afternoon, a coveted sight indeed! Through the large, stained glass windows of The Castle, I saw them strolling leisurely under the moonlight, showing little curiosity about the decrepit magic cabinet.

I experienced a sense of displacement. Sitting at controls... trying to watch a recording. A comfortably enclosed space, brightly lit, a wraparound set of displays, hovering in the air...

I blinked. The others were still down there, strolling along the dark beach.

The extreme cold didn't seem to affect them. Or perhaps... I remembered Lisbeth's exotic outfit. Their similar, strange, glittering jumpsuits no doubt provided high-tech warmth.

I made to call out to them, but some were already climbing the slope towards the building, having little trouble with the icy pathways. I figured they'd appreciate patience as a virtue, so I kept quiet.

Surely, they could explain much to me.

I'll also ask their help to book permanent accommodation for myself at this fancy hotel at the end of the world, where the hired assassin chasing me would never, ever find me.

The future now appeared luminous within the frosty landscape.

*   *   *

McGready presided within his clandestine workspace, enjoying a moment away from his duties. His various guests and colleagues (excepting those from other times) never entered here. When a need existed, they met him at one of his conventional offices: the one in the Rest Stop for Weary Travelers, rather ornate; or the one in the Mind Recession Clinic, austere and functional.

The Director sat comfortably, embedded in a wraparound console, viewing the bank of holographic displays which enabled him to monitor the facilities, the grounds, the garage (with his treasured collection of Traversal vehicles) and beyond. The circular chamber was punctuated along its curving wall with various brass fittings, including portholes. The helm column stood a few easy strides from the console. More brass and glass – wheel, levers, panels, gauges. All indulgences of his recently developed fondness for naval history.

Behind the helm sat two elaborate chairs, comfortably cushioned, dressed in brass also, and in a darker metal. The helm was fully functional – the means by which McGready sent Traversers on their way.

Adventurers were encouraged to sample sanctioned destinations, selected primarily for their stability. There was always risk associated with Traversal, and occasionally, a Traverser did not return, having met some unknown, or perhaps elected, fate.

From the vantage point overlooking the vast expanse of the Pacific Ocean, the tales of the untamed, rugged Pimu Islands served as a constant source of inspiration.

McGready brought to mind an image of Julia in her period Indigenous garb. *Fetching.* Morgan, on the other hand, had looked fairly ridiculous. No sense or concern for the temporal variance of fashion. Earlier, the Director confirmed they had taken their linguistic and cultural conditioning to an adequate level. Morgan had been quite put upon. Granted, it was unlikely they would encounter any native Chumash along the sparsely populated early Pacific Coast region. But the destination was becoming popular. Something about simplicity, and harmony.

Julia inquired about traversing ahead to one of the Pimu Islands to comfort the young Lone Woman of San Nicolas Island – who would spend eighteen years stranded at *Ghalas-at* after her Nicoleno tribe's evacuation. Her request struck a personal chord with McGready, stirring old but still painful memories of loneliness. The Director faltered, saying, "It's not the right time," then swiftly excused himself to ensure Mrs. Winnie, their Guest of Honor, was receiving proper treatment, deflecting Julia's request.

A sensory bundle, carrying personalized and finely differentiated meanings, roused him from his nostalgic reverie. It was not intrusive, but impossible to ignore. In the present circumstance, an old-style buzzer might have sufficed, but that would have been crude.

Director McGready came fully alert. A marshal was arriving, with a Rogue in tow.

*　　*　　*

It was such a disappointment. I'm invisible to these people, these impolite Traversers.

Nevertheless, I made a sincere effort to understand their attitude. So, I hurried back to the Gothic Library and quickly pulled from the shelves all the books by Professor Tovar.

Now in my hands, I held two exquisitely bound volumes of Tovar's mad fancies: His theoretical treatise, packed with graphs and equations, Book One: 'Revivisci praeteritum cum lingua futuri.' And Book Two, filled with real-life anecdotes bolstering his theories, titled cryptically, '1Mt: Perpetuis Futuris Temporibus Duraturam.'

I glanced through the Table of Contents, Book One:

> • *Observable and Objective Effects of Spacetime Traversal.*
> • *Portals of the New World: Gillette, Hearst and Pittamiglio.*
> • *Portals of the Old World: Blarney, Lovrijenac, and Neuschwanstein.*
> • *Boxes, Tori, Jumpsuits, Engines.*
> • *The Deleterious Health Effects of Traversal: A Summary.*
> • *Etc.*

Then Book Two, listing several reported cases (both anecdotal and documented):

> • *Exposed Avian Brains.*
> • *Serial Time Breakers.*
> • *Scripted Stage Acts.*
> • *Traversal Artworks: Authenticity versus Forgery*
> • *Traversal VIP Tickets.*
> • *Etc.*

I scribbled some of my own personal insights in the margins of the first chapter, noting that déjà vu and synchronicity appear to be subjective 'felt effects' of Spacetime Traversal. And from my own experience, I've observed objective effects such as the moon cycling through its phases in an instant.

What else?

I must find answers on my own. These so-called companions, these ghostly new people – well, I suppose they're still human – are the least communicative beings I've ever encountered, now into my fourth decade!

It's unsettling, especially considering we're all residents of the same hotel, and who knows for how long. Their complete silence is driving me crazy.

Oh well, something positive came of it. I love reading now, I get lost in a good book and time just flies by.

* * *

"What is being this one's name?" asked McGready.

Before replying, the marshal continued with the process of releasing his prisoner into the Director's custody. The man placed his right hand over a glinting torus wrapping his bruised left wrist, making pressing and tapping motions. The device faded to a dull appearance. A matching torus on the prisoner's right wrist followed suit, a moment later going bright again. The prisoner's hand jerked slightly – in toward his body, then out again, as if under puppeteer control.

"Transfer complete." Marshal Arp looked up. "This specimen be calling himself Royce Halliday. I be strongly suggesting you be watching him closely. I be having one hell of a time getting him here. But that being another story…"

The marshal flexed his wrist. "Being given the nature of your ancillary enterprise, I be suggesting you also be considering placing Mr. Halliday on suicide watch. I be not recommending lightly."

Every Rogue Traverser was inevitably a special case, but Director McGready took careful note of this unusual debriefing. He focused on the prisoner. "All right, Halliday, here is being the drill. The wrist wrap now is being under local control, my control. You are being under continuous surveillance. If you are approaching any perimeter, you are feeling the consequences. Other than that, you are being free, and you are having access to the facilities, the grounds, and the considerable resources now and here, with the exception of the Rest Stop. I am hoping sincerely that you are enjoying your time with us."

McGready turned back to Arp. "And concerning the reason for his being here…"

"From what I be receiving and observing, he is sure being single-minded to be telling all the locals as are listening about Traversers. That they be traveling to his present frame, and he be offering his own twisted self-serving notions about why that be." Arp shook his head in exaggerated fashion. "I be impounding the mis-appropriated equipment, being already delivered."

McGready nodded. "A 1954 TWN Triumph Boss model, two strokes, 350cc?"

Arp rumbled, "Being the one."

"I am thanking you, Marshal Arp, for your servicing. You are being welcome to the diversions of the Rest Stop for Weary Travelers before you are returning."

"Being much obliged, Director McGready. But I be getting around. Energy is being Corinthian Gold, as they be saying."

Arp shook lustily, too pleased with himself. He vanished in a flash of blue light.

"You know I will try to escape," said Halliday.

McGready appraised his new ward, looking for signs of displacement symptoms. Despite Arp's odd warnings, he saw none. "You are being welcome to try. But you are indeed staying. Let me be acquainting you with your new life."

The Director smiled, genuinely. "You are being free to move about, within defined boundaries. You are being placed in our ward which specializes in your type of… delusion. You are being free to interact with other inmates. In some settings, there is proximal supervision, for your protection, and for the protection of certain other residents, some of whom are capable of doing harm."

McGready continued. "Are you being familiar with the meanings of 'Be my guest'?"

Halliday sat impassive.

"It means, 'Welcome to my domain and be giving your best effort. You won't be making any difference.'"

Halliday kept his counsel.

McGready softened his voice and gaze. "Some free advice, Halliday. Life here... diversions and even dalliances are being limited only by your desires, and your cooperation. But be making no mistake. You are found going Rogue, and you are in prison. You are being evaluated periodically. How long you're being now and here is depending on you."

"You try but you don't really talk like a Traverser," said Halliday.

McGready elected to offer trust. "It's true. I'm from the present era, like yourself."

Halliday's eyes turned hard. "You're one of those damned Eternalists!"

A door in the back of the office opened. A burly man entered.

"Halliday, this is Dr. Alunn Lance. Alunn, I present our newest guest, Mr. Royce Halliday."

Lance came forward, taking the clipboard the Director handed him.

"Alunn will escort you to your new residence."

*　　　*　　　*

Lonesome nights, Lisbeth.

I've been gazing at the sky, trying to catch the moon performing its shenanigans again. But it quickly hid behind dark clouds, and then it began to rain continuously, occasionally turning into a loud hailstorm which made a racket against the stained glass windows.

According to the front desk calendar, only a few days had passed since my arrival, but to me, they felt like months, years, and occasionally even eternity.

Time after time. Through time. Across time. Within time. Endless stretches of unmodulated duration. Again and again. One Million Times.

Though I encountered other hotel guests, I discovered with great disappointment and discomfiture that they continued to ignore me. Not only did they dismiss my anxious questions... but also my presence. I began to wonder again if I was dead, a ghost, invisible, a fleeting dream.

To test this supposition, I attempted to get their attention with shoulder taps and by abruptly stepping in front of them. They would raise their eyes to me, ostensibly listen to my questions... and then look away, continuing with their activities.

Conversations among them were mostly non-existent. When they did occur – usually as an annoyed response to my attempts to communicate – they used language with odd constructs. Largely indecipherable, notwithstanding some recognizable words.

Who are they? I don't know, but from now on, I will use Professor Tovar's label for these guys: Traversers.

I truly believe that's what they are – mysterious beings capable of jumping through time and space. I can't say they're simply from the future; I'm from the future too, now! And with no further future in sight for me or this frozen planet, I might be the most advanced human specimen in the universe!

Oh well.

So I don't know where these Traversers come from, and I can keep asking them until my last breath, but they won't answer.

Driven by desperation, I attempted to pursue and physically stop one of them... the Traverser simply touched a wrist bracelet and vanished in a flash of light.

Very rude people.

*   *   *

Hearing the chime, McGready examined the monitoring display in his Clinic office.

Mrs. Winnie and her chauffeur.

He let them in. But before the Director could utter a word of greeting…

"Alexander has a request of you," said Mrs. Winnie.

The middle-aged man's eyes held a new intensity. "I'm

quite sure now you're holding my brother Race here...
You know, Royce. His full name is Royce Halliday."

McGready sat back. He drummed his fingers on the
traditional desk.

"I won't lie to you. If this Race or Royce is being held
here, it's because... he is branded a Rogue." The Director
hesitated. "I'm afraid I have obligations to... certain...
Enforcers."

Alexander bristled. "I demand you let me see him!"

"Careful, Alexander," Mrs. Winnie interjected.
"Director McGready... look, my chauffeur's younger
brother disappeared under mysterious circumstances in
Ireland, right after his graduation. He's been searching
high and low, far and wide, through and through, round
and round for him! Imagine his shock to learn that he
may have located him alive now, on the old coast of
Califia of all places... right here in your own
establishment."

"I'm taking note of your request," said the Director.
"And I am empathetic. I will consider what I can do on
your behalf. But I feel... the time is not right. Patience."

"We understand, Director, this must be approached
with the risks in mind." She engaged Alexander with her
eyes. "The Exclusion issue."

The chauffeur corralled his emotions with difficulty.
He nodded. "That's the only reason I'll agree to wait." He
turned to glare at McGready. "But make no mistake,
you're asking a lot."

"Acknowledged." McGready sat straighter. "Exclusion...
I have heard of such a thing, but it was a young poet who
was involved."

*   *   *

Food for thought,
Sustenance for body,
Auspicious discov'ry,
Feeds soul mind and belly,
Raising spirits wholly.

Oh well, poetry was never my strong jumpsuit. Therefore, I turned my focus to a more practical pursuit now: satisfying my hunger.

During my solitary explorations of The Castle, I stumbled upon an impossibly large pantry... an underground catacomb teeming with provisions, including fresh fruits and vegetables and clay pots of cheese. Despite the lack of electricity in The Castle, the cold from outside had been ingeniously channeled into this expansive, ice-box-like dungeon, keeping the provisions fresh. An impressive feat of nutritional engineering!

I found no alcohol of any kind (I'll miss my whiskey and elaborate cocktails) except for amphorae filled with wine. There were also caskets of tobacco, but I don't smoke.

I couldn't help but wonder about the origin of all this food. Could there be a hidden vegetable garden somewhere on the premises? An abattoir? A bakery? The mystery intrigued me, but ultimately, it didn't matter. My basic nourishment needs were met, allowing me to focus on other concerns.

In that respect, my satisfaction was short-lived. The other guests continued to do little to fulfill my social needs, and I kept longing for meaningful interaction.

All I encountered was their oppressive silence and vacant looks.

As I stated earlier, Lisbeth, I pride myself on possessing a rational, objective mind. I could explain away and even justify the failure of my overrated 'Social Communication Techniques' course to assist with interaction here. But did I also mention my carnal desires?

These, too, went unfulfilled in the frigid, isolated atmosphere of The Castle.

*　　　*　　　*

Another Rogue.

McGready eyed the robust, head-shaven man, while Arp executed the transfer procedure. The Director glanced idly at the wrist torus to verify the sequence of glows: on-off-on. He was taken aback.

An ugly, prosthetic right hand.

He drilled the new arrival with a hard gaze. "Do I know you?"

The Rogue, up to that moment self-possessed, stammered, "No... no, of course not."

McGready turned to Arp. "What is being his crime?"

"Murder. I be saying, parricide," the marshal said sternly, with little sign of his usual irreverence.

"What is being this one's name?"

"Aidan Carynx."

McGready completed the transfer. "I'll be keeping a tight leash."

The man winced. "I expect nothing else."

The Director's eyes narrowed. "Mr. Carynx, I assure you, you are being treated humanely."

Aidan looked doubtful.

"I be bringing his sister anon," Arp muttered smarmily while twisting his wristband. "Being another long story."

Wincing at the departing flash, Aidan muttered, *"Adiós, Marshal."*

*   *   *

A bloody robotic hand – a harbinger of fate. This recurring nightmare refused to release its grip on my nights at The Castle.

But lately, even during the day, I've been haunted by visions of my self-inflicted demise.

I tell you, Lisbeth, these blasted, stubbornly tight-lipped, mute Traversers are messing with my head!

I needed to protect myself from falling apart. Back at the Gothic Library, I searched for books on human psychology.

I read Maslow and recalled an illustration hanging in my Hi-Hat office, meant to inspire me when managing my club. It dawned on me that by escaping my assassin and seeking refuge in The Castle, I had reached the second level of his hierarchy of needs: 'Safety and Security.'

I sighed. The third level of Maslow's pyramid, 'Love and Belonging,' on friendship, family, intimacy, sense of connection... none of these would I find here.

I decided to skip number three and focus instead on the next level. My self-esteem. 'Confidence and Achievement.'

I imagined dedicating myself to restoring order here by undertaking the task of maintaining the place. As far as I could tell, I represented the sole fixture of permanence amid otherwise transient comings and goings.

Could I take on the task of preserving the legacy of The Castle, ensuring its continued availability for these mysterious yet ungrateful and undeserved visitors? You bet!

Yet, I remained hopeful for companionship, of the talkative type.

You're right, Lisbeth, I could definitely learn to converse in Traverser. Did I mention my degree in Linguistics from TCD? It was a huge deal back in Dublin.

*   *   *

The Armoire was reconfigured as a small, intimate theater. Two rows of comfortable seats were set out. The racks of period clothing, shrouded now in dimness, created a pleasant and mysterious backdrop. As of a rich tapestry, with colors and details obscured.

Mrs. Winnie occupied a seat in the front row. The performances tonight would be given by inmates from the psychiatric wing, as a form of therapy. A splendid idea.

At the end of the row sat a large man, attentive. Inmates sat among the audience members. She perceived signs of Traversal. *Rogues.*

Mrs. Winnie swiveled gracefully, looking along the row behind her, picking out a man and a woman wearing wrist wraps. Endeavoring not to be impolite, she noted the man's prosthetic right hand. Both were clearly shades of their past selves. Easy to imagine the former physical power of one and the psychological power of the other. These apparitions left her unspeakably sad.

She returned her gaze to the stage to the distressed cabinet with the cracked yellow paint – bullet holes and all. The eye-catching box was finding good use as a piece of showcase art in the Rest Stop for Weary Travelers Museum, and as an occasional stage prop.

The lights dropped and a spot darted. Music issued forth, with a historical feel. A harpsichord.

A voice burst out. "Ladies and Gentlemen, your favorite emcee, and our very own... Greedy Mack!"

Mrs. Winnie clapped heartily, recognizing the charming Director, decked out in coat and tails, a buttoned-up sequined vest, and a top hat, wielding the traditional cane of an entertainer.

He moved briskly into the spot as it whipped to front and center on the small stage. "Thank you, thank you, one and all. Tonight, none of us are to be weary, but rather full of life, and healing. I guarantee the performers will all be memorable."

McGready gestured with both hands held wide, then seemed to skip a beat, looking into the row behind Mrs. Winnie. She glanced there. The Rogue, sitting alone now, had his left hand up in a friendly greeting.

The emcee collected himself. "Without further ado, I present to you, an operatic talent... Zelda!"

Entering, bounding in, came a large, flushed, high-energy woman. Needing no amplification, she began belting out the Italian lyrics of a familiar *aria*. Mrs. Winnie recognized it, but she deliberately kept her thoughts flitting, not wanting to retain these new associations. She put on a convincing and encouraging smile and enjoyed Zelda's mercifully short rendition.

*   *   *

A treasure, behind The Armoire!
I was searching for warmer clothing during one of my random yet determined explorations of The Castle (all

right, you could say desperate) when I stumbled on a remarkable discovery.

After moving aside a stack of wooden stilts and navigating a hidden portal, a display flickered to life, in the shape of a hovering pink note. The source of its power? Unknown. But the text message was clear:

'Malcolm – you will LIKE what happens next!'

Finally, a breakthrough.

Much of the capability in this control room simply responded to my presence. But the technology was totally obscure. I felt stymied trying to figure out how to get any of it to do my bidding. And with no one here to be my mentor... now this message appeared, but I had no idea why, or how.

'Locate the white box. But leave the gun.'

White box?

I recalled how I had rolled up my sleeves, determined to accomplish a deep cleaning of this place, so full of dust and decay – even vines growing through the walls. I had found storage spaces...

I went to the walls and started waving my hands around. Shelves emerged, unfolding. A multicolored chest opened, brimming with strange contents, large and small. I meticulously sifted through them: a creepy ventriloquist dummy, scratched vinyl records, silly wigs, crumpled pink notepaper, punched theater tickets, rusty coins, sealed decks of cards, a ridiculous jester hat...

There! A small white box. Intrigued, I reached out and removed its cover.

I recognized the archaic object inside the box, disguised as a plastic toy motorcycle... incredibly, an old – no, ancient – flash drive.

I experienced a sense of déjà vu. This very room... a comfortably enclosed space, brightly lit, a wraparound set of displays, hovering in the air... but not quite the same.

*   *   *

McGready knocked and immediately strode in.

Royce Halliday looked up from a plush, comfortable

bed. "I see you're not needing my permission to enter."

The Director evinced cheerfulness. "Mr. Halliday. Being good morning to you. I am having on your schedule that you are being due in group therapy. Is that meaning anything to you?"

Halliday stared back blankly, then asked, "Do you take such a personal interest in all your wards?"

McGready pushed past the remark. "It is being simple. You are meeting with other guests, and discussing whatever you and the others are wishing to discuss."

The Director watched Halliday finger the torus on his right wrist. Despite its metallic appearance, the substance was soft and pleasantly warm, its presence easily relegated to background.

"Let's be going then. I won't be accomplishing anything here."

"Very good, Mr. Halliday. Be following me, please. We are going to the Mind Recession Clinic."

They left the well-appointed bungalow and ascended a spiral staircase to a room situated in a corner, a tower, with vistas west and north. Thin sunlight entered through tall narrow windows but failing to dispel the somber ambience. Nor did the sconces, feeble light sources only. Arcane alchemical symbols adorned the walls – and names: Asclepius, Erasmus, Galen, Newton... In the western view stood the other large structure in the complex, with elegant architecture, and more towers.

They reached a comfortable sitting area, where soft crimson chairs were arranged in a circle. Embedded in the center of the floor lay a rod with animated twisting serpent, framed by moving mottoes: *Do no harm... Care for mind, brain, and body...* An idealized set of moving, intertwined brain waves rippled through.

The chairs numbered seven. Lance was seated at the vaguely defined top of the circle, with his back to the windows. Two of the other seats were occupied, by the Carynx siblings – also wearing wrist devices. McGready watched Royce studying the torus on the man's right hand and waited on his reaction. *That's right, artificial.*

The pair noticed Royce immediately. Halliday, on the other hand, clearly had no desire to take the implicit relationship anywhere.

Royce took one of the remaining seats, one which maximized views and avoided proximity to the Rogues. In the northwest direction, blue – the ocean. In the late afternoon, the scene often turned spectacular. To the north and northeast, golden hills rolled away.

The woman with the wrist wrap rose, shawls swaying, and sashayed over to sit next to Royce. He leaned away. She settled, looked around, and soon placed her focus into catching the eye of the newcomer. Royce ignored her, in her usual over-stimulated state.

A final patient joined the group. Halliday had to stop himself from staring. A young woman of indeterminate age, for her challenged state of health advanced her years. Linda was rail-thin, with points and surfaces of bone visible, notably along her cheeks. Her black hair was stringy, unkempt, falling across her face. Royce would not be able to see her eyes. Her movements were unnaturally slow, yet she possessed a wired tension. Frail and almost frighteningly downcast, she nonetheless had more presence than anyone else in the room. Dr. Lance guided her gently to a seat open next to Royce, who averted his eyes with effort.

*   *   *

I pondered the cryptic message: 'Locate the white box, leave the gun.'

The gun?

The stainless steel, full-size Luger handgun! I had left it behind in the magic cabinet!

Donning my parka, I hurried down to the beach, with a sense of apprehension.

But amazingly, when I wrenched open the cabinet door, the gun sat there on the floor, bloodstains darkened with age.

I decided to leave it all to rot and decay, as instructed. But... I didn't want to get rid of it. Somehow, that awful weapon had meaning for me. I bent down, lifted it delicately, between finger and thumb. I deposited it within Lisbeth's secret space. No one would ever find it there.

I hurried back to The Castle, shivering from the increasingly biting 'Californiarctic' winds, tucking my cold empty hands into the pockets of my parka. At least the rain and hail had stopped, but now they were being replaced by the flurries of the season's first major snowstorm.

The winter of 11799.

*　　　*　　　*

Director McGready gestured to Lance to carry on.

The psychologist took charge of the room: "Ladies and gentlemen, we are having a new guest today, Mr. Royce Halliday." Lance took note of the newcomer's focus. "Mr. Halliday, this is being Linda and I am assuring you she is hearing everything that is being said. She is talking when ready and is being always worth listening to."

While all eyes turned to the thin woman, McGready took the opportunity to whisper in Lance's ear. The psychologist nodded to his boss, then extended an open hand to the woman to Halliday's right, the one with the shawls.

"Zelda I am," she addressed Royce, "very pleased to make your acquaintance. Would love to hear more of your story."

She made no show of her bracelet, neither concealing nor highlighting it. The torus was lost among bangles, necklaces, and the shawl. She offered her other hand, dangling it in a provocative manner. Royce took the manicured hand reluctantly, clasping it as briefly as decorum allowed. He looked past her to the other Rogue.

"Aidan," said the head-shaven man, his fingers fiddling with his wool cap. He looked capable but resigned. He dropped his wrist out of sight to the side of his leg.

McGready stiffened involuntarily when the man looked at him.

"Aidan, would you be caring to begin?" asked Lance. "Are you feeling you are making progress?"

"I do, Dr. Lance." Aidan's baritone came out softer than expected. "I've spoken here about the terrible things I've done in my life. I justified them at the time as necessary, for survival, out of love for my sister Cara." He glanced at Zelda, who inspected a garish, tapered fingernail.

Aidan now stared more purposely at the Director, who swallowed hard. "But I no longer make such excuses." He held up his prosthetic hand, flexing the digits unconsciously. "I accept my loss as just, as restitution for my crimes."

All stared at the prosthetic device, including McGready. Clearly artificial, not aesthetic in any way, and as a consequence, threatening. Aidan seemed well aware of the effect. He stopped the fingers from flexing, and put the hand away, out of sight.

Lance waited for an acknowledgement or response from Zelda, but there was none. He prompted, "How is Aidan's admission making you feel, Madame?"

"Ravings, methinks," she said. "All I know is my brother needs protection. From the Conflux."

Aidan lifted both his hands, seemingly about to thrust them forward in exasperation. However, something made him halt mid-motion. Swinging around, he pointed a mechanical index finger at the Director.

Startled, McGready awkwardly smiled and waved hello – a flourish of his hand.

"Hi-Hat." Aidan mumbled.

McGready stood and hastily departed.

*   *   *

I smiled and waved hello – to no avail.

They're all staying indoors now because of the snow blizzard. But screw them!

If the Traversers prefer not to speak to me, so be it! I

no longer felt the need to chase after them desperately. Quite the opposite.

My new home was renewed. Shining. Although all done solitary, I came away with a huge sense of accomplishment. I am a worthy and unique individual. I am having an impact.

I felt a rush of renewed confidence. I was the boss again.

I marched back to my favorite place, the Control Room. It could be a lengthy journey to the Armoire and beyond, because this immense castle is a true labyrinth, seemingly designed to ensnare and lead you astray, helping you stumble upon unexpected places.

Breadcrumbs don't work. I tried, even by shredding the shirt on my back. The markers would simply disappear. In fact, Professor Tovar made note of these anomalies in his chapter on 'Observable and Objective Effects of Time Traversal.'

I lean on my memory to navigate The Castle. And hope it proves reliable.

Now, where is that damned Control Room?

*   *   *

The psychologist turned. "Not to be putting you on the spot, Royce, but please be telling us about yourself."

Royce scanned the ring, uncomfortably conscious of Linda beside him. He realized he wanted to see her eyes. He turned.

And there they were, black, with compelling depths, but despairing. Her locks fell again, obscuring.

Royce collected himself and decided to put it out there.

"I'm from the future."

Ripples passed around the circle.

"Another one. Just what we need," said Zelda, shaking her head. "Lad, I know ye are not from the future. I did not summon you." The sharp look she gave him carried considerably less interest than before.

Royce felt genuinely confused. Then he glimpsed where this was heading.

He had to give McGready credit. He could rant and rave about spacetime traversal all day long, and the next day. As other Rogues no doubt have done. But no one here would ever take him seriously.

Royce was trapped, cleverly and effectively. Still he had to try. "Since I'm not the first one, doesn't that tell you something? You need to be paying attention. Traversers are coming to our era… There is a reason. They're coming to exploit us. And people are dying."

Royce paused, swallowed. He wished he could be more eloquent. "The reprehensible part is that no one is telling you. You have a right to know but it's all concealed from you!"

He glanced around the circle.

Zelda continued looking at her fingernails. Aidan was barely listening now, his brow furrowed in silent struggle, seemingly wrestling with his thoughts. Lance was professionally detached.

Royce took a breath, crestfallen… then started, feeling a hand placed on his knee.

Linda's eyes were peeking out between limp tresses. Interested, intelligent. The thin high voice fit her appearance.

"I would like to know more."

* * *

At long last, I reached my destination!

I retrieved the toy-motorcycle flash drive from storage. I held it in my palm. What secrets here? On impulse, I presented the device forward… into the open air. Its power light went on. I withdrew my hand awkwardly and the drive hovered, engaged with a kind of virtual slot.

The bespectacled face of a young woman appeared, hovering, looking straight at me!

Blame it on my relative youth and the overwhelming isolation, but I totally disregarded the technological marvel. A sudden rush of hormones swept over me.

Forgive me, Lisbeth, but I spent hours alone with her.

That night, as I lay in bed, tingling with excitement, I immersed myself in the pages of Professor Tovar's first book. And, as is often the case, synchronicity unveiled a remarkably enlightening chapter – 'From Freud to Jung: Exploring the Human Urge, Desire, and Temptation to Mount a Time Machine'.

Here, the author placed emphasis on the sex drives of pioneering Traversers, those willing to risk the dangerous time jump without a safety net. His impassioned arguments stirred memories of my college days in Dublin and the adventurous antics of my rowdy friends: how the TCD dorms provided countless opportunities to refine our... social communication techniques in intimate ways.

Sunrise cleared the shadows from my ornate master bedroom as I closed Professor Tovar's book. I pulled a nightcap over my eyes, one adorned with a fluffy pompom, using it as a makeshift sleep mask before finally drifting into slumber.

The bespectacled young woman lingered in my dreams, her gaze fixed on me.

*   *   *

McGready admitted Dr. Lance. Soon, the Director was brought up to date on details of inmate care and progress, including incidents.

"Thank you, Alunn. I would like to have your preliminary evaluation of our newest guest, Mr. Halliday."

"Royce appears to be adjusting well. Another Rogue to be treated for the time travel delusion."

"Those are our instructions from Arp and his cohort," said McGready.

Lance put on a smirk. "Being an interesting form of hysteria."

"Would you consider Royce to be suicidal?"

Lance sat back. Although surprised, he gave the question its proper professional due. "I am saying no. Royce is harboring feelings of guilt, and he is not yet opening up.

This is being well within a normal adjustment progression. I am having no particular concerns."

"Mr. Halliday is forming an association with Linda Scarlett Bradley. Any reservations?"

"There is appearing a mutual attraction. No, Director. I am rather believing that Mr. Halliday can be doing her some good."

"Very well, then."

"Anything else?"

"One more thing," said McGready, "The new rogues, brother and sister…"

"Aidan and Cara Carynx."

"Where are they from? I mean, originally."

"Las Vegas, Nevada," replied Lance. "Why?"

McGready swallowed another gulp of déjà vu, leavened with a bitter taste of certainty this time.

"How did Mr. Carynx lose his hand?"

"He is saying it is being caught in the rotating door of a moving machine."

PART II

Tovar cited scientific arguments in his book: a dreaming brain cannot create faces; they are always people you've met… at another time.

I pondered this as I wandered through the winding passages of The Castle, my mind elsewhere, until unexpectedly, I found my way back to the Control Room: I didn't recognize the woman in the hovering display from my past. Was she from my future?

Professor Tovar was really getting into my head.

I reached out to cycle through virtual controls I had stumbled on over the years – but hardly understood. I made a twisting motion with my right hand. The video quality improved.

The young woman said, "…in the present year. A problem –"

Finally, I got sound!

She was visibly shaken, but her voice remained calm: "...initial – please, come back to your past... proof."

The time-ravaged sequence pixelated and broke up. I panicked. "No, no, no!"

I gestured wildly to the left and brought my motion to an abrupt, confident stop. The effect was to rewind the recording back to the beginning. But the glitches multiplied.

"...I live in the twenty-first century, in the year..." *The woman was becoming more beguiling to me.* "Our best minds... time travel... possibility..."

The image and sound would not stabilize.

She continued. "No more todays, yesterdays, or tomorrows..." *Distortion and shifting refused to settle out.* "I just ask whoever finds this recording in the future..."

Yes, me! Me! I was living in the Year 11799. She couldn't get someone more futuristic than me! What did she want? Malcolm is here, waiting...

At last, the video and audio locked up, in sync.

She took off her glasses... Her big eyes filled the space. "Please..." *she said.*

The transmission halted on a frozen image of her mesmerizing face.

I waited, taking an enduring, longing glance at her. "Please – what?"

*　　　*　　　*

McGready was true to his word.

Royce did indeed have the run of the complex, including, now, the venerable Rest Stop for Weary Travelers – all its nooks and crannies. He reached the Armoire, looking for something different to wear. *There!* His roving eyes halted on the perfect leather jacket. On his way out, he bumped into a lovely older lady, who had a smile for him, and a twinkle in her eye.

Now Royce and Linda were perched on a rolling hilltop, partly hidden in the golden grasses. In the early spring, the air could be bracing, from intermittent land breezes tumbling west. But when they sat far enough down in the lee, on the slope facing the ocean, they could bask in the temperate sun, and enjoy the distant view of the Pacific. While being mindful of stiff plant material, irritating to bare skin.

He had been at the Clinic for some weeks now. In the first days, Royce had systematically tested the perimeter. When he ventured out far enough, a slight tug developed on his right wrist, which became a buzzing weight, then prickly waves interfering with wakefulness and cognitive coherence. None of this had crossed over into pain, more the promise of pain. He filed away these experiences.

Royce had not abandoned his mission to spread knowledge of Traverser intrusions into the local era. Nor his goal, ultimately, to escape this place. Linda had been unexpected. Not only did she readily accept his premises, but she assimilated effortlessly an understanding of the principles and practices of spacetime traversal – almost as if having a head start. She was a disturbingly quick study, and clearly knew her physics.

*   *   *

I swear, Lisbeth, I'm making a valiant attempt to shake her from my mind.

I returned to the Gothic Library and cooled off by delving into different books, steering clear for the time being of Tovar's work on that one particular Traverser Wave. For quite some time, I became genuinely intrigued by his idea that different future eras would embody different values, priorities, social constructs, aspirations, and inevitably, agendas. In fact, it was one of those insights which once gained, is so compelling it cannot be put aside.

So I absorbed Tovar's speculations about there being a Wave akin to a police force. And one made up of experimentalists, who viewed past humans as mere specimens. And the inevitable colonialists, fully entitled to exploit whatever resources they might find, or define.

*And another focused on the seeking of knowledge –
perhaps close to Tovar's heart. But that led me straight
back to that first Wave, which was clearly close to his
heart, and again I was lost...*

*As a kind of defense, I developed obsessive interests in
certain adjunct traditional disciplines, such as
Linguistics, Psychology, and now... Architecture.*

*I became fascinated by the building itself. I roamed the
restored corridors of The Castle – its gleaming floors,
walls, carpets, and furniture. I could finally and fully
appreciate the beautiful design of my new home.*

*I discovered records about one of the architects
responsible – Morgan Grimley. 'Devoting his life to the
architecting of cities and transportation systems, Grimley
was driven by deep philosophical principles for the
creation of endlessly fresh spaces and experiences.'
Principles based in synchronicity – a concept to which he
deeply adhered.*

*I viewed with new interest renderings of exquisite art
from antiquity appearing on the exterior of The Castle.
'The Winged Victory of Samothrace' was a personal
favorite. Entering a large salon empty of furniture, I
discovered a stained glass version of the same statue,
positioned overhead. The window's hues of gray and
silver cast a moonlit glow throughout the room,
transforming the scene into a haunting vision of triumph
over nostalgia.*

I could start a museum here!

*Excited by the idea, I ran down the stairs to the Grand
Hall, searching for markers and scrolls to fashion a new
door sign. 'What should I name it, Lisbeth? The
Galleria? The Exhibit? The Archives?'*

*Again, that feeling of displacement. Through a dark
blood haze: a frozen body, something in the ice nearby. I
hacked it free with the claw of my hammer.*

I need to get a grip.

*At that precise moment, a figure rang the bell at the
Concierge desk.*

Beyond peculiar.

No Traverser ever bothered to check in. I had to track down each reticent newcomer and determine which room they had chosen. For my own amusement, I assigned them invented names and wrote the aliases into the guest book, noting date, time, and guest room.

I attended to my guests with care, even making their beds after they departed. I chose to never begrudge the total lack of acknowledgement, much less compensation. All part of my newfound generous disposition.

In stark contrast, this guest rang the bell insistently. I lifted the hinged counter and hurried to the other side of the desk.

"Welcome to The Castle, Mr. ... "

"Dr. Morgan Grimley, being at your service."

*   *   *

Royce had given up trying to work with the members of the therapy group. Not much there beyond dimness and despair. He chuckled inwardly, having learned how some patients were told the wrist entrapments administered special medicines in controlled doses.

With Linda, things had turned intimate. There seemed to be no concerns among the staff or guests. Royce had asked Dr. Lance about Linda's age, which seemed so confusing. The psychologist assured him she was twenty-six, and with a smile, encouraged him.

The first time had been odd, the physicality, all bone points and taut skin. He had been gentle, but soon found that concern misplaced, for Linda possessed wells of energy, even surprising muscularity. Now he found the uniqueness of her body exciting. He knew they would go there before heading back to the Clinic, scratchy grass, and all.

Linda asked, "What could it be about our present era that is drawing Traversers?"

Royce pondered, "I have my speculations. Some say there's a tangle of world-lines converging at the local spacetime, a concentration of energy. Others say simply, and more mystically, that all paths lead now and here. But whatever is the actuality, many object to Traversers exploiting the inhabitants of a local frame without their knowledge. It's the old conceit of treating the past with disdain."

"Do you believe the past can be undone?"

"That's a central question, Linda. Everyone has something in their past they would change. I lost my brother, and I would dearly love to see him again. I've heard arguments against the possibility. But a part of me is unsure, wondering if we're missing something."

"Royce, you see things clearly. You are noble. I would undo an event in my past if I could, even though I do not remember. They say I killed hundreds of people."

Halliday stared at Linda, wide-eyed. "They say the same about me."

"Then we can help each other."

Royce couldn't see how Linda could help him, but he loved her for having such a thought. He reached toward her, placing his hand on her cheek and then on the back of her neck, tugging. She moved to him readily.

*   *   *

I no longer felt alone! Now, I had a real, erudite, learned companion with whom to delve into discussions of historical affairs and spatiotemporal conundrums.

"Dr. Morgan Grimley, being at your service," he had said, filling the void in my soul with the sound of a human voice again.

Soon, we were roaming the halls together like old pals, chatting about the Castle, the bad weather and everything. The unique Traverser manner of speaking began to rub off on me, until I could readily mimic the odd phrasings and cadences.

Professor Tovar and his Traversermaniacs were not far off, after all. Speech patterns were indeed a marker of visitors from the future. Traversers overemployed the present imperfect tense – a result of their worldview of time lacking divisions, and actions never needing to be considered complete.

"You're seeming more loquacious than other Traversers," I noted.

"Not being really," returned Grimley. "But you are being correct too, Malcolm. The typical Traverser is being taciturn – for good reasons. I am choosing to be otherwise."

I frowned. The architect winked.

"And I am discovering that although I may be revealing more than is being wise, the frame locals are hearing, but not listening, even less understanding."

I smiled awkwardly. "Now you are having me lost here, Morgan."

"Good! I am designing and building always to be enabling the unpredictable. For the getting lost, and the consequent finding of oneself. No less should I be stepping outside my psyche, stretching beyond myself."

I missed these chats so much, during the architect's long and frequent absences from The Castle.

But in a way, he was, is and always will be here, there and everywhere. 'Hiding in plain sight' being the apt aphorism for a Traverser as extraordinary as Morgan Grimley.

*   *   *

It was open mic night at The Armoire theater.

Mack announced the next number, with a subdued voice. "And now, ladies and gentlemen, an interpretive reading of verse from the young and sadly late poet, Paula Lobanubis."

He made an unexpected exit into the magic cabinet.

A wraith-like figure entered the spot, long strands of dark hair falling across her face. Mrs. Winnie expected Linda to flinch in the bright beam, but she did not. She stood there, with unnaturally unblinking deep black eyes, monotonously reciting from *Hamlet*.

"To be, or not to be: that is the question–"

Restlessness stirred within the audience as her face contorted into a grimace.

A lower and louder voice fought through her words, imposing the darker verses of Paula Lobanubis. "Reflect mortality, where shadows are bred."

Linda kept on, not acknowledging. "Whether 'tis nobler in the mind to suffer…"

Mrs. Winnie caught a movement to her right and saw the large man at the end of the row sitting up in his seat.

Linda's voice was cut off by the harsh, clearly male voice, spitting gloom:

"Vanish, spectral echoes boast."

Linda pressed on, unfazed. "…and by opposing end them? To die: to sleep…"

The growling voice interjected again, more forceful, "In a moonlit shadow, find your true ghost!"

The large man leaped from his seat and in two steps was upon Linda. Audience members gasped and yelped. Mrs. Winnie stayed silent – riveted. She watched the man move to restrain Linda gently with one arm, and immediately have his hands full with a kicking, jerking whirlwind.

The thin figure broke free and spun the magic cabinet violently. Gunshots rang out. People screamed.

Linda held a gun and fired into the cabinet. Bullet holes appeared in a sprayed pattern.

A guttural voice rasped, ugly, from Linda's mouth. "Mirror of celestial dread: The undiscover'd country from whose bourn no traveler returns…"

The large man moved in again and contained Linda, who slumped, dropping the gun. He quickly carried her off stage, into darkness.

Mrs. Winnie, unaware when she had stood, slumped back into her seat.

The audience gasped again.

A figure struggled to emerge from the magic cabinet, holding a screwdriver, hammer, and wrench, and wearing a hooded parka more suitable for Arctic cold than mild Central Californian nights.

The man appeared to be in his thirties, with fiery red hair and a beard which glowed in the spotlight, casting a warm glow around him, in a caricature of an Irishman.

His abundant mane, like strands of vibrant copper, framed his round face with a touch of comedic wildness, giving him an air of untamed charm.

He seemed absurdly happy, yet his face was frozen, eyes bulging and mouth agape. The only features missing were painted-on tears and a clown nose.

The audience breathed a collective sigh of relief, breaking into nervous giggles.

The man stepped away from the worn-out magic cabinet, took a bow and waited for the applause.

*   *   *

I remembered one of my last conversations with the great architect, in achingly distant times.

Now talkative by default, Grimley explained how Traversers referred to the magic cabinet which had conveyed – no rescued, me – now and here, as a 'Traversal Engine.' A device capable of traveling to the future – the path of least resistance – and to the past, within limits. Its most exquisitely fabricated technological elements were 4D-printed in Corinthian Bronze, an obscure alloy. Attempts to push the engine beyond the time of the alloy's first rendering, in ancient Greece, risked breakdown. The metal amalgam weakens and disassociates via an un-annealing process, scattering shards of the exotic material.

I found all this fascinating, but Grimley had abruptly changed the subject.

"I am being more interested in your experiences of 'Sin City.' Being my next destination," he stated.

*   *   *

"Is Linda Bradley back on suicide watch?"

Dr. Lance nodded. "With increased medication. We are following the standard protocol after the dramatic dissociative episode."

"Indeed," said McGready.

Lance continued. "Intake and history are not providing insight. As if the hidden personality is coming out of nowhere or nowhen. Not at all typical. Usually there are being indicators, even if not being recognized at the time. The circumstances leading to a manifestation are being difficult to understand. Classically, the 'strong' personality is appearing when the primary but weaker personality is feeling threatened. But Linda's case is being highly unusual."

The Director inquired, "A traversal döppelganger?"

"Maybe. That theory about bifurcation points during personality development. Informally, key events may be moving an immature personality along one path rather than another. But vestiges may be remaining, and in the right circumstances, reemerging. The memoryline being not taken."

Lance raised his eyebrows. "Are you thinking it is bearing on the Bradley case?"

The Director sat back, considering the unpredictable side effects of Spacetime Traversal. Dissociative disorders, including multiple personalities, were within scope to be treated at the Mind Recession Clinic. The psychologists on staff – Lance prominent among them – were among the best anywhere. McGready's vision may have created this facility, but he deferred to the experts.

"I am being interested in your opinion, Dr. Lance."

The psychologist continued. "Thanking you, Director. But again, a history of Traversal is not being evident. Linda is being a kind of prodigy, before being sidetracked. Overall, a tragic case." He caught the Director's eye. "There is being the matter of the gun."

"Right." McGready tapped his fingers. "Any idea how she... or he, managed to acquire a weapon?"

"None whatsoever," replied Lance. "Security is looking into it."

"Appropriate. Thank you, Alunn, for your insights, and your diligence. Let's continue on the present course and hope there can be healing."

With a nod, Dr. Lance turned to the exit, and left the room.

*   *   *

As far as Mrs. Winnie was concerned, the practice of pairing Clinic wards with residents of the Rest Stop was an enlightened one, benefiting all who participated. She had the arm of Linda.

"My dear, I would like to show you something truly special."

They moved spiritedly through an obscure passage connecting the Clinic and the Rest Stop. Mrs. Winnie noticed that her young companion, though heavily sedated since the open mic incident, seemed to have more energy lately. No doubt something to do with that dear young man. Mrs. Winnie smiled to herself.

"That sounds like fun," said Linda. "Where are we going exactly?"

"It's in the Rest Stop for Weary Travelers."

The air cooled down during California nights but remained faultlessly comfortable in the ideal climate. They had nearly closed the distance between the buildings when Linda came to a stop.

"What is it, my dear?"

"Mrs. Winnie, I'd like to tell you more about myself. I mean, why I'm here."

"Please do not feel there is any obligation to do so."

"I know. But Dr. Lance says that doing so can also be a form of therapy. I think he's right."

"Then of course, my dear."

"Do you know what a paranoid schizophrenic is?"

"Not exactly."

"I am someone who suffers delusions. Even hallucinations. And I often feel the world is against me, and that I'm in danger… It's very hard to live this way."

"My dear, I am so sorry. But I believe you are doing better. That young man?"

Linda's face lit up slowly.

"It's important to have someone to share life's journey," added Mrs. Winnie.

Then Linda's expression dropped. "You know, they restrain me at night, because they believe I may harm myself."

"Do you think you ever would?"

"I don't know. I don't think so... May I tell you a secret?"

"If you wish, my dear."

"I can slip the restraints. It's easy, really."

"Oh my."

"I didn't mean to upset you Mrs. Winnie... Are you afraid of me?"

Mrs. Winnie caught her breath. *I can honestly say I am not afraid. I have lived long, and well.* "My dear, I see only a beautiful, talented young woman, and I wish I could help you."

Linda's eyes tried to glisten, but her medication got in the way. "You wanted to show me something special?"

"Yes, dear. It's inside."

They reached the Rest Stop for Weary Travelers. An attendant held a door for them. They passed inside, crossed a transverse hallway, proceeding left and then right, to the residences. They made their way down a corridor, which gave out onto the Grand Hall, next to the concierge desk. They turned right, into a bright airy space.

"My dear, we are going to The Armoire. I recall your recent dramatic performance there. Do you remember?"

"No, Mrs. Winnie."

She took them past the Ballroom and the Library. Mrs. Winnie pushed open the well-balanced doors of The Armoire, and they entered.

Linda took in the revealed sights: the period costumes, the organized and mechanized racks, the sense of function in the place. Her scrutiny intensified.

"Didn't I say it was special?" asked Mrs. Winnie.

Linda continued drinking in the details.

"Is there something you would like to try on?"

"Oh, no thank you... But it is special, Mrs. Winnie. I would go so far as to say it's the missing piece."

*   *   *

Morgan was gone. Lisbeth had disappeared too.

Then, at the moment I needed it most, the Castle provided me with Shakespearean tools of writing – quill, ink, and parchment – vessels for the emotions tearing at my soul.

I sat down to write these memoirs, determined to master the art of literature now, eager to capture both the stories left behind and those yet to unfold.

Feeling more lonesome and helpless than ever, I found myself repeatedly drawn back to the Control Room, where I would sit at the console, pining.

I returned not so much in pursuit of insights, but out of desire to see that intelligent and sensual woman, unattainable. The frustration of being unable to clean up the corrupted signal became unbearable. Dizzy, I would eventually rise to my feet and exit, looking for other ways to divert my thoughts.

Venturing outside the Castle seemed pointless, as it was now almost perpetually shrouded in a thick, swirling fog. At times, the mist would intensify, plunging the surroundings into a complete whiteout, where visibility vanished entirely, leaving only an opaque barrier pierced occasionally by the eerie shapes of wandering Traversers.

I resumed my methodical exploration of the Castle's interior until twilight descended, the soft glow of a candelabra in my hand casting shadows along the ancient walls. Once more, I found myself lost, wandering through labyrinthine passages until I stumbled upon an unseen portal, disguised behind a magnificent tapestry. Gently, I pushed aside the heavy fabric, revealing yet another hidden room. It was no surprise – the Castle seemed to be full of such secrets. This particular thrill never grew old. It was always fun.

With some effort, I pushed open its thick, vault-like door.

Entering this new chamber, I was enveloped by a sense of confinement, almost suffocating, as if the walls *themselves were closing in. They were covered by too many artworks, from oils and acrylics to black-and-white sketches and mixed media and collage pieces. Bright depictions of Earth's four seasons contrasted with dark, ominous seascapes, while charcoal studies of the human form mingled with vintage posters of Hollywood movies unknown to me.*

I couldn't help but suspect I had stumbled upon the most prized treasures of an art collector. On the spot, I christened this sanctuary of beauty... L'Atelier!

I felt a new stirring within me – an awakening of sorts. The paintings seemed alive, each brushstroke pulsating with vitality. As I moved the candelabra about, colors danced, and shadows whispered of forgotten tales. A veil had been lifted, revealing new beauty to appreciate.

Each piece vied for attention. But it was a triptych of mechanical bronze spheres that caught my eye, evoking memories of my old college campus. The arrangement was deliberate, each panel forming a cohesive composition while standing alone as an independent piece, collectively dominating the room.

I stood there in tears, entranced by this piece of art. Was all this a coincidence? I couldn't shake the feeling that this artistic arousal was somehow connected to the bespectacled woman whose gaze had ignited a spark within me. I needed to go back to her!

A sudden cold draft extinguished the candles as I pushed the door to leave. Lo and behold, the triptych became transparent – a triple stained-glass window revealing glimpses of the well-lit... Control Room!

L'Atelier also served as a monitoring station!

I could keep an eye on my platonic sweetheart, the most precious artwork of all, from here!

*   *   *

Royce was jostled awake. In the lack of light, he sensed rather than saw Linda at his bedside.

"Royce, let's go."

He sat up, rubbing the sleepiness from his eyes, his skin slick with sweat in the stifling room. He didn't understand how she was here. Once, early on, he had gone looking for her in the evening, and Lance had intercepted him, explaining that Linda did not leave her room at night. Royce had wanted to challenge the silly declaration, but something in the way the physician held himself convinced him to leave it alone.

Yet here she was.

"Where are we going?" he asked.

"Wherever you want."

He barely had time to pull on his jeans and throw his leather jacket over his worn-out v-neck. She took his hand as he stumbled outside, hurriedly slipping on his running shoes. Together, they soon left the Clinic building, greeted by a refreshing ocean breeze.

Linda was sure-footed on the moonlit grounds. They made their way to the Rest Stop for Weary Travelers via a dark passage, negotiating corners Royce could barely see, ultimately entering through a nondescript door. Two connecting hallways later, they stood in the main thoroughfare dominating the building's entrance. Moonlight penetrated through the high windows, strangely fluctuating, although there hadn't been any clouds. Linda went directly to one of the large portals along the hallway, and they entered.

Despite the dimness, Royce recognized this space as The Armoire, prominent in conversation during the recent celebration of Mardi Gras. He tugged at a sleeve of his leather jacket.

"I can send you home, Royce."

"What do you mean?"

"I can reunite you with your brother."

"Oh Linda. It's not that simple."

For the first time, Royce sensed a kind of disappointment emanating from Linda.

"There must be a time travel capability here," she said. "It only goes to reason. You told me how Traversers come here as a waystation and go on to destinations in the past. The Armoire is a giveaway. You get your period clothing here, and…"

Linda moved to one of the costume alcoves. With that surprising strength, she reached in and took hold of the floor-to-ceiling structure. Following a click, she pushed. The panel swung inward, revealing a space behind the wall.

Linda disappeared inside.

Royce followed. Lights came on. He stood blinking, taking in the sights with a critical eye, equipment everywhere.

Linda gestured impatiently. "This is the Control Room. You must know how this works. Royce, I want you to send me back, and then I will know what I have done."

"Linda… please, whatever happened, it does not need to rule you. With the help available to you here…"

"All right, Royce, you go first. Take one of the chairs."

He looked where she gestured. Two seats, throne-like, with brass fittings.

"Go!"

Royce reluctantly sat down in one of the chairs. His thoughts flew. He glanced at his right wrist. Whatever surveillance he was under would trigger an alert. The situation would be resolved soon, one way or another.

"How can you possibly know how to operate the Engine?" he asked.

"I've figured it out. I'm pretty smart."

Royce had always been charmed by that high-register voice, sometimes tense, other times plaintive, always painfully innocent. Now there was an unaccustomed edge creeping in.

Linda continued. "Don't you want me to help you? I can send you anywhere. Back where you came from. Somewhere else? To our era, where you can continue your mission? I love you, Royce. Please tell me where you wish to go."

"Linda, I am good to be right now and right here, with you."

Something was happening to his wrist. Royce realized he couldn't move. He watched Linda's eyes transform, becoming hard. Then he was horrified to hear a male voice issuing from her mouth.

"If you won't choose, I will choose for you."

Linda examined the hovering displays, studying them briefly. Then she approached the brass column standing prominently in the center of the room. She placed her hands there and manipulated.

Royce vanished in a flash of green light.

*   *   *

I was blinded by a flash of green light.

I had just found my way back to L'Atelier after some meandering, one hand laden with a stack of weighty tomes on art and film, the other clutching several brushes and a palette.

From here, I could paint and also remotely monitor the Control Room. I'm embarrassed to admit, even to myself, that I've planned to do so extensively, hoping for a glimpse of the bespectacled woman, wondering if my apparent absence might somehow encourage her to return...

Earlier, I had set up a comfortable chair in front of the triple window, flanked by ornate amphorae filled with wine. A small table beside me held a casket of cheese and a humble clay cup. Now, I was ready to keep watch, perhaps paint a masterpiece, or more likely, just get drunk.

The unexpected light burst disrupted all those artistic plans.

I rubbed my eyes and reopened them. In the Control Room, I beheld a seated man in a black leather jacket. The letters 'TWN' were emblazoned on the back. He was engrossed in studying my girl – my platonic future sweetheart. Even seeing him only from behind, I did not appreciate his level of focus.

Who was this leather-clad Traverser?

The man impatiently waved his hands about and fluttered his fingers. Footage flowed. When the video refused to advance, he deftly darted new motions into the air and fixed the problem.

In a matter of seconds, with quick jumps and quality adjustments, the mysterious man then paused, his shoulders evincing pleasure, and emphatically gestured with his open hand, palm up – what must be the virtual equivalent of PLAY.

A final, stray rational thought passed through my mind. The man was using a gestural language. Signing! All I had to do was observe him carefully and let him unlock all the secrets of the console – and of The Castle!

*   *   *

"How are we being today?" asked Dr. Lance.

"First person plural is rather insensitive… don't *we* think?"

Lance snapped fully alert and tuned into the unexpected presence. The rough masculine voice was nearly impossible to reconcile with the slight figure. Linda weighed less than a hundred pounds. The wrists and ankles protruding from the extremities of her clinic-issued garment looked like they might snap before they could apply any appreciable force. But he wouldn't make that mistake again. He didn't fully know what he was dealing with, but he remembered too well the transformation on the stage of the Rest Stop for Weary Travelers…

The eyes being the window to the soul.

In place of Linda's fleeting, self-effacing glances, he saw a feral tracking, probing for weakness. *Careful.* The depths of strength hidden personalities can summon… even from a frail body.

Lance casually endeavored to determine – from a distance – whether the restraints were in place. But Linda was settled in a way as to thwart verification. He felt the intruder's drilling gaze. Almost against his will, he locked glances, only for a moment, but long enough to see the mockery in the eyes. *The hatred.*

The intruder rolled Linda slowly in place on the bed, pointedly, to allow Lance to see that the straps were where they should be. A loud laugh issued, a grating rasp.

Lance elected to not entirely trust his eyes. He would follow safety protocols to the letter.

"You are being quite right, that is being terribly insensitive. I am apologizing. May we be starting over? My name is being Alunn."

"I know who you are. Call me Brad."

The intruder shaped lips and eyes to signal who had the upper hand.

Lance thought furiously. Linda did not seem to be aware of Brad's presence. On the other hand, the intruder was already exhibiting access to Linda's memories. He likely retained her high intelligence.

But why would Linda feel threatened?

Given her developing relationship with Royce, Lance would have expected the opposite. He took another calming breath, aware that Brad would take it as a sign of weakness.

* * *

Monitoring all the boring technological activity in the Control Room through the triptych window, I found myself yearning for Morgan Grimley's wisdom.

I recalled one of my last conversations with the great architect, from times that now seemed achingly distant. He had asked for my advice on visiting 'Sin City.' I told him all about the casinos and how to move between them without ever stepping outside onto the Strip.

He listened attentively as I waxed wistfully about my old playground of Las Vegas.

My troubling memories compelled me to be honest with him about my gambling addiction. How it had caused me immense trouble back in the day.

But the architect unexpectedly absolved me, proclaiming that games of chance reflect the essence of the philosophical foundation he sought – to design the perfect habitat for all humanity of all times.

I blinked back to reality. Yes, I missed Grimley deeply, but even he couldn't fully cure my yearning for the woman with the big, captivating eyes. And now, the mysterious man in the TWN leather jacket seemed poised to render her presence permanent!

I poured myself another cup of wine and took a bite of cheese.

The cleaned video and audio finally locked up, perfectly in sync!

The girl took off her glasses. Her big eyes filled the screen.

At that moment, who wouldn't fall forever in love with her?

*　　　*　　　*

McGready burst in, saving Lance from having to determine his next move.

"What have you done?" the Director demanded of Linda.

Brad settled his menacing gaze. "I've sent Royce away."

Lance shot McGready a warning glance.

The Director shook his head, gathered his resources, and engaged the intruder – glare for glare. "Where?"

"I do not know," said Brad simply.

"What do you mean, you don't know?" McGready saw Lance looking aghast at the exchange. Standard protocol proscribed engaging a dark personality in anger.

Brad responded with insouciance. "Pure random number generators utilize spontaneous nuclear decay events and leave no trace."

McGready checked himself, slipping from anger into consternation.

Lance shouted, "Director, the classical concept is being wrong here. The hidden personality is not coming forward to protect Linda. Brad is appearing because *he* is being threatened."

Linda's head swiveled back and forth. "I'm going to let you in on a little secret, gentlemen. Poor Linda, always fretting about what it was she had done. What if I told you that she has done... nothing?" An awful cackle emanated from the distorted face.

The intruder continued. "But that won't help her. She has only her memories, like any one of us. And they make her reality."

Brad's hard countenance began to withdraw.

"Wait! Not yet!" yelled McGready. "Where are you going?"

"Where you cannot follow. I have an appointment... in Linda's past. I am off to create more memories. She'll never know the difference. I'm done here."

Linda was present again, dropped in. She stared at them, and their unfiltered fright. Then the horror began leaking in from the sides of her eyes.

The two men could only goggle at her.

McGready dropped his head, clutching his left shoulder. *I've failed Royce, utterly. As my ward, I have responsibility for him.*

Mrs. Winnie burst in with her chauffeur.

"Where is Royce?" demanded Alexander.

*   *   *

I peered from my remote alcove, catching tantalizing glimpses of my girl over the shoulder of the mysterious young man clad in the leather TWN jacket.

Her words were audible over the feed.

"My name is Eva... I live in the twenty-first century. A question that puzzles many great scientific minds today is the possibility of time travel... I came up with a simple experiment to verify its existence."

I was taken aback by what unwrapped next.

"I'm recording this video today... which I leave to be discovered by fellow scientists of the future... if our society develops one day a working time machine..."

I stopped listening, missing the main point – whatever it was. The images alone had never been more captivating.

Eva, the young woman on the screen – some kind of rocket scientist – was undressing as she spoke!

When she was fully exposed, I gasped! The TWN man suddenly stood and turned to look directly at me.

I swear, Lisbeth... shame and a sense of modesty compelled me to avert my gaze from such a spectacle devoid of scholarly merit.

"Pseudoscientific nonsense!" I exclaimed, reverting to my old pomposity.

But as shocking as those racy Traverser images of Eva may have been, they would linger with me through the long days of winter, sustaining my will to survive in this world of the future.

*   *   *

"I'm sorry Axel, that Director McGready has to be such a stiff bureaucrat," said Mrs. Winnie, from the passenger seat of the red Alfa Romeo P3. "He worries too much about minutiae and his own twisted interpretations of Professor Tovar's writings. But he's right about the potential dangers of being placed in an exclusion. There are real risks to consider before arranging a meeting between you and your brother Race. Give him time. We've obviously left our grumpy Director deep in thought."

Alexander steered the sleek, powerful vehicle with silent precision, guiding Mrs. Winnie to a secluded viewpoint atop a cliff. Below, the desolate sandy beaches stretched out, the rhythmic thunder of ocean waves crashing against the shore, creating a symphony of nature.

As the sun began its descent, painting the southwest sky with hues of orange and pink, he turned to Mrs. Winnie with a respectful nod. "This is a lovely spot."

"You might take some time alone to reflect too," she suggested gently.

The faithful chauffeur nodded. "To engage the right mood... tradition holds that the last sunset of the year offers a chance to glimpse the mythical 'green flash.'

You've told me you've wanted to catch sight of it since you read a book about it in childhood. Perhaps tonight will finally bring you that moment, Evangeline."

"The Green Ray? I love Verne's books, but I guess my brain operates on more scientific fuel these days. But thank you all the same, Axel. This is a lovely spot. Pick me up at nightfall. I won't need your services again until then."

With a solemn nod Alexander started the car and quietly drove away, leaving Mrs. Evangeline Wilhelmina Fontanarrosa to her solitude. Yet his mind was not idle; his skilled hands, accustomed to the mechanics of fine machines, were already sketching imaginary plans. He couldn't just be a silent witness to history. He had his own preparations to make.

Back at the Carriage House, he chose a spot next to his prized, though temporarily confiscated, Triumph motorcycle. He muttered to himself, a hint of defiance in his tone, "Eva, I believe our maverick Flying Mantuan would bless my cannibalizing."

Without hesitation, Alexander opened the hood of the Alfa Romeo P3, its Traversal Engine gleaming. He set to work, his hands deftly dismantling the complex machinery, transferring the powerful Corinthian Bronze motor into the frame of his vintage 1954 TWN Triumph Boss motorcycle. The tools he had left scattered around earlier – the wrench, hammer, and screwdriver – lay ready for the task at hand.

He smiled, the timing was perfect, and nobody was around to bother him. He could hear the Traversers in the distance, gathering at the Rest Stop for Weary Travelers, singing and igniting the first fireworks of the night.

He soon finished his task, clearly satisfied, and admired his beloved motorcycle, wiping grease from his hands. "*Perpetuis Futuris Temporibus Duraturam*, indeed," he muttered under his breath, collecting his tools. Fitting words of self-congratulation for the moment.

A stern voice shattered his concentration. "What are you doing?" barked Director McGready. "Do rogues run in the Halliday family? Stop right there!"

Startled, Alexander froze, his tools dropping to the ground like surrendered weapons. Without turning, he spoke softly, his voice smoldering with barely contained anger, "I've told you a million times, Director. Nothing will stop me from finding my brother!"

For the first time, the chauffeur noticed the soft ticking of an antique clock on the garage wall.

McGready's silence was heavy, his authority palpable, leaving Alexander to ponder the consequences of his defiance stretching across past, present, and future.

*   *   *

Realization struck me like lightning, and I snapped my gaze upward! Please – what? WHAT?

Naked Eva took off her glasses. Her big eyes filled the space.

"Please… bring it back to me!"

The video sequence faded to black. Urgent knocks snapped me back to reality.

The rooms were adjacent! I guess the configurations of hidden spaces exist only in the eye – or the mind – of the beholder.

I opened the door to the Traverser in the leather jacket.

He held in his hand the little white box containing the toy motorcycle flash drive.

My cherished, sacred white box! No!!

Trembling with conflicting emotions, I swung the door wide, prepared to confront the thief!

Give me that box back! It's mine! She belongs to me!"

For what felt like an eternity, I stared at him, futilely trying to bring his young face into focus. He returned my gaze searchingly, agitated.

"Director," he greeted me finally with a shaky voice which sounded oddly familiar. "I just wanted to say… thank you for this!"

He landed a seriously energetic punch on my left shoulder. He tucked away the white box deep into a pocket. Then with a sudden, forceful shove, he pushed me aside and dashed away, leaving me stunned and heartbroken.

"It's not fair…" I cried out, chasing him through the door and out into the Castle's courtyard. "It's not fair!"

*　　　*　　　*

It was always New Year's Eve at A Rest Stop for Weary Travelers.

The serene landscape calmed Eva's eyes. And her being.

Rippling low grasses blanketed softness over rocky terrain. Braided streams of water slipped off the jumbled, splintered faces of the boulders, refreshed by new crashing breakers, the wave energy coming from an ostensibly infinite source.

To commemorate this incarnation of the special occasion, someone produced a vintage vinyl record to play quaintly on antique equipment requiring hand-cranking: the traditional *Auld Lang Syne*. Popular at all times, sung to bid farewell to the passing year and to welcome the approaching one.

> *Should auld acquaintance be forgot,*
> *And never brought to mind?*
> *Should auld acquaintance be forgot,*
> *And auld lang syne!*

*　　　*　　　*

I followed the intruder all the way outside into the frigid night, rubbing my shoulder, struggling to keep pace as the young man swiftly began descending the perilous precipice, taking a shortcut to the beach.

It was neither raining nor snowing on New Year's Eve, 11799, and the fog had cleared. I paused in astonishment, momentarily distracted by the breathtaking spectacle above, the night sky pristine for the first time since my arrival.

The star patterns and constellations had shifted in the most breathtakingly starry night imaginable. But that was not all!

Mesmerizing hues of green and blue painted the sky, right across the Milky Way. An improbable sight, so far south.

My neck hurt. I dropped my eyes to the large full moon, mercifully unanimated, continuing its overnight descent into the dark expanse of the ocean. The surface reflected the vibrant ribbons of the Aurora Borealis.

Together, the two light sources cast an otherworldly glow upon the waters – and on the true spacetime oddity of this place: my magic cabinet, looming on the beach, an enigmatic yellow monolith, nearly frozen into the inexorably encroaching ice.

The few Traversers milling about my beloved 'Winged Victory of Samothrace' statue on the ramparts, ignored the Northern Lights, instead gathering around... a motorcycle roaring up to them! They viewed the relic of transportation and its black-clad pilot with collective amazement.

The rider's uniform, from my distance, evoked the sinister image of a WWII German officer: a dark blue coat with multiple shoulder capes, black leather gloves and jackboots, a round, flat-topped hat with a short visor bearing a small insignia that, from the far perspective, disturbingly resembled that of the Luftwaffe.

Who was this apparition? A visitor from another Wave of Traversers, perhaps? He looked disoriented, desperate... an outcast like me! But they treated him distinctly unlike me, surrounding him as if he were a celebrity. An animated conversation ensued.

Soon, the Traversers pointed across the expanse of frozen sand. The uniformed man glanced in the indicated direction and quickly spotted the yellow cabinet. With a clear sense of purpose, he roared his motorcycle to life and sped down The Castle's icy drive toward the device.

Meanwhile, the younger man in the TWN jacket, leaping down the final cliff, converged on the location of the same magic cabinet.

*   *   *

Battling the bitter cold, I arrived at the edge of the cliff and observed the scene taking place down on the beach. My poor eyesight was barely able to discern the TWN white letters, the two figures by the cabinet, and the motorcycle parked nearby.

The pair approached each other, cautiously. Were they about to engage in a fistfight?

The younger one held out his hand. Likewise the other, forming a mirror image. They arrived at grasping distance. Then they paused, hands and fingers fluttering.

A peace gesture?

I'll never forget what happened next. The aurora brightened, unnaturally. Purple, magenta, sea green, cobalt blue – colors blazed across the heavens. Sibilant sounds showered down.

When I dropped my eyes again, the men held each other in a full brotherly embrace. The other Traversers, despite themselves, were clapping wildly. Now they were showing emotion?

The two slowly released.

They stepped to clear away snow and icicles hanging from the cabinet's roof and attempted to free the door. Together, they grasped its submarine-like wheel firmly with four hands, leaning hard to turn it counterclockwise. But the door of the magic cabinet stubbornly refused to swing open.

The Traversers gathered around them, fingers dancing over wrists. To a creaking sound, the wheel slowly spun. An aura seemed to emanate from within the box, possibly a reflection of the fading lights above. I could not be sure.

Then the door was open. The older rider in uniform quickly straddled the bike and restarted the engine. The younger rider swung onto the passenger seat and did not hesitate to clasp his brother firmly. Together, they roared down the beach between jets of spouting icy sand. The driver expertly turned in place, revved the bike, and returned headlong for the magic cabinet. The two entered at speed, to a blinding flash and a rushing sound.

I winced, bracing for a loud crash! But silence settled. I opened my eyes to find the door shut and the two of them gone.

In the sky above, a shifted Moon finished spinning in place, cycling rapidly through its phases, finally landing on gibbous.

The Traversers returned to their idle activities. I gazed in awe at the inert apparatus until the threat of frostbite made it impossible to stay any longer.

What if, Malcolm?

I hurried back inside The Castle, wondering about a potential escape route for myself!

*   *   *

The following afternoon, bundled in my parka, I made my way down the slippery pathway to the beach. The cold was almost unbearable now. I estimated having maybe fifteen minutes to reach hoped-for relative warmth inside the magic cabinet, before freezing to death.

An idle thought loomed: The possibility of finding the frozen corpses of the TWN and Luftwaffe men inside the cursed yellow box. One way or another, I needed a definitive answer.

I felt a certain pang for the eyesore yellow apparatus, standing alone on the hard sand. Having served as the portal of my arrival at The Castle and, hopefully, a safe departure portal for the Traverser brothers in the leather jackets. In my way of thinking, the humble cabinet had attained historical significance, worthy of preservation.

I skidded down the icy trail to the barren beach of the future. A rifle crack heralded massive chunks of ice calving from the encroaching glaciers, then crashing into the sea. Thunderous booms echoed along the coast.

The sea was slowly freezing. Stretching from the abandoned yellow landmark to the distant horizon, the ocean was strewn with immense icebergs, under a weak sun, jumbled together in the frigid waters. The scene put me in mind of a massive ice cube tray, twisted to yield up faceted turquoise treasures.

I reached my destination with five minutes to spare. I turned around to examine the exterior of the building I called home. The iconic Castle, perched majestically atop its hill, grappled within a landscape of draped, advancing ice. Its walls and turrets were coated with thick layers of rime. Icicles hung from the eaves, evoking a fairy tale fortress.

I assessed the yellow magic cabinet with a measuring eye, noting its height surpassed mine. Carrying the box on my back would be out of the question. Naturally, the guests wouldn't help. However, I could dismantle it into manageable planks, making several trips to The Castle, carrying my prize. For the purpose, I had collected my trusty screwdriver, hammer, and wrench, and some rope.

Large snowflakes began to drift down. With a sense of urgency, I reached for the cabinet door.

*   *   *

I tried to turn the wheel, but it was stuck. I inserted the screwdriver along the edges of the door and managed to open it, rather easily.

There lay a frozen corpse! A man, his face entirely concealed by a black ski mask. I gasped and stepped back, stumbling, falling onto my back on the rock-hard beach. I tried to calm myself.

Slowly, I got up.

No sign of either man in the leather jackets. I needed more light. With surprisingly little effort, breaking ice around the casters, I rotated the box toward the ocean, permitting weak afternoon sunlight to enter and illuminate the interior.

The projectile suspended in the air had vanished. My eyes followed its imagined trajectory. But there was no hole or bloodstain marking the rear wall.

My wristwatch beeped. One minute left before frostbite!

I could gain some time by enclosing myself in the cabinet. But the thought sickened me. No, rather my thoughts were becoming increasingly languid. Must be the cold.

Could I drag the corpse to the ocean and get back here in one minute? The old gambling thrill filled me. Yes, I bet I could do it!

In a blur, I took hold of the body and dragged it violently from the box, clothes tearing.

In a haze, I noticed a dark lump of crystallized blood, stark against the man's chest, and a detached body part encased in the ice nearby. I hacked it free with the claw of my hammer, shoved it inside the clothes, and heaved.

In a fog, I catapulted the ugly bundle into the ocean. Cracking sounds told me the waters would accept my gift.

In a torpor, I struggled to keep my feet under me. I crawled, scraping skin badly. I tumbled, rolled, reached...

I wanted to live!

Warmth surrounded me. They say that's what it feels like when you freeze to death. Oh well.

*   *   *

The echoes of my hammer blows were the only sound rolling across the beach. But no sea birds took flight. Here, in the remote future of planet Earth, my actions captured no audience.

I succeeded in hauling away the several planks comprising the magic cabinet. There remained only the base. More awkward, due to its size and weight. But I not only lifted it, I caressed it, feeling its lingering warmth.

The housing of the Traversal Engine which had saved my life.

Twice over, to be accurate. I was also cured of my gambling addiction!

Inside The Castle, I reassembled it all, nailing the parts back into place. I positioned the reconstructed relic in a place of honor within the new Museum. As with my other restoration projects, I felt a deep satisfaction... yet also overwhelming, exhausting fatigue.

Honestly, it was wearing thin. The incomprehensible Traversers. The Motorcycle Stunt. The Aurora Borealis Display. The Naked Woman Show. It all seemed so unreal. A ghastly nightmare!

I felt myself teetering on the brink of insanity. A persistent sense of dread haunted me. Tovar's theories of time travel paradoxes, my encounters with zombie-like guests – all swirled in my mind. Could that corpse on the beach... be me? An older version of myself? Why hadn't I dared to look at its face?

I couldn't stay here any longer! I needed to find a way out!

On a mad impulse, I stepped inside the cabinet, closed the door behind me, and began hitting every inch of the walls, roof, and even the floor with the hammer, desperately hoping to find a switch or some mechanism within the total darkness.

I lost track of time as I continued hammering away, unsure if it was seconds, minutes, hours, or days that passed.

Then suddenly, at the end of my rope... I was deafened! And engulfed in a flash of multicolored light.

*　　　*　　　*

The leonine man stumbled as he emerged from the worn-out magic cabinet, enveloped in light. Confused at first, he looked around and soon began smiling with delight at the rows of people.

The audience breathed a collective sigh of relief, breaking into nervous giggles.

He took a bow and waited for the applause.

His joy was short-lived as a pair of slender, toned female arms grabbed him from behind and pulled him back inside, slamming the door shut.

The audience erupted in laughter and clapping for these buffoons.

The lights abruptly shut off, plunging the stage into darkness.

A split second later… the lights went up again. With a crash, the door slammed open!

Director McGready emerged from the magic cabinet, still in immaculate coat and tails. He teetered, then planted his feet and stood firmly at center stage.

"Ladies and gentlemen, remain calm, and please accept our sincerest apologies…"

Mrs. Winnie found herself standing, hand over mouth.

*　　　*　　　*

My brief visit had lasted a split second and ended abruptly. No more than a time glitch. And it definitively broke my heart.

I was again stranded here and now, in the bleak year of 11799. My eyes welled up with tears.

Oh well, this was it. I had long ago chosen the stained glass window in front of me, a grim depiction of 'The Winged Victory of Samothrace,' as my final escape. The only way to end it all and soar free.

I gathered my strength, coiled my leg muscles, braced myself for impact, and let out a final, anguished scream.

But the flutter of wings and a voice calling from behind held me in place:

"Daisy, come!"

Someone else stepped out of the cabinet, slammed the door, and spun the maritime wheel clockwise. Each rotation was accompanied by a faint metallic clicking, until the locking mechanism latched into place.

"Lisbeth? Lisbeth the Lovely!" I shouted between sobs.

It was really her. Alive!

"Malcolm the Eternalist!"

The petite illusionist looked as healthy, young, and plucky as ever. "You scared Daisy!"

"What did you call me?"

"Being your new title," she said. "By Grimley's orders. In return for many years of faithful service at The

Castle. Being time for you to be gathering your belongings and embarking on a journey through the epochs once more."

She whistled for Daisy, and her pet dove flew down obediently from the Castle's rafters, settling on her shoulder.

"Anytime now, Malcolm the Eternalist. Soon."

Lisbeth calmly counter-spun the wheel, stepped back into the cabinet with Daisy, and closed the door behind her, vanishing from my sight forevermore.

The last word I heard reverberated from the Castle's stone walls.

The air grew heavy with silence, and I was left alone once again, a fading echo of her departure condensing out of the chilly air. Perhaps only imagined.

*   *   *

The sun set without producing the elusive, hoped-for green flash. Eva waited for her chauffeur to arrive.

She heard the distant honking of a seal, invisible among the rocks. At first distracting, she decided the creature's voice blended wonderfully, both in pitch and rhythm.

> *...And surely ye'll be your pint stowp!*
> *And surely I'll be mine!*
> *And we'll take a cup o' kindness yet,*
> *For auld lang syne.*

She swept her gaze around the landscape. Not a single point of light or sign of human life. Yet she wondered about eyes nearby, watching.

Eva knew the environs surrounding the Rest Stop for Weary Travelers to be home to Native American tribes – fishing, hunting, gathering – enjoying and sustaining the bounty of the land. The coastline remained pristine, untouched by European colonizers. But the encroachment of Spanish missions and settlements was underway.

But today, in December 1799, *El Camino Real*,

reaching from a southern terminus well below San Diego, had not yet reached The Castle. Eva had experienced this particular reality during her arrival, when her chauffeur shifted gears and applied controls, successfully traversing to *La Cuesta Encantada*, deftly negotiating the absence of roads.

Where was Axel now?

Where is Race?

Five years hence, the expansion of *El Camino Real* into the Santa Ynez Valley would enable the Santa Inés Mission to become the nineteenth of the Franciscan mission chain. But the Rest Stop for Weary Travelers would endure, with the help of some trivial optical confusion. Grimley had done his homework.

Eva reclined on the soft grass, her eyes lifting to the twinkling brilliance of Polaris, the North Star. The night sky stretched vast and infinite above her. She felt a serene connection to the cosmos, the ancient beacons guiding sailors across uncharted waters, now guiding her thoughts through the Conflux and remaining mysteries of Spacetime, Traversal, and the Universe.

The Tipsy Traversers, somewhere in the Rest Stop for Weary Travelers, were singing louder now. Eva closed her eyes, listening to the drunken, dissonant chorus. She pictured them hugging each other. A sorry lot. Bored. Dissipated. All enabled by that... architect. Granted, his is the philosophy born of Traversal. *But how does it help one to live? To find meaning?*

What must the natives think? When we're not here. Which is most of the time. I'm not convinced they do not perceive The Castle.

Where were her steadfast Axel and precious Alfa?

Celebrated as the Guest of Honor was flattering, even enjoyable, and that tour was simply wonderful, if tiring. But now she felt a growing impatience to depart. She exhaled a long, whistling sigh... her breath caught.

The soft, lapping waves of the ocean mingled with a chorus of singing insects, the sharp cries of seagulls, and the occasional call of a loon.

She waited contentedly – feeling like forever – for that green flash. Then Eva Fontana, Mrs. Winnie, and Evangeline Wilhelmina Fontanarrosa… passed peacefully, with the whole world whispering a serene farewell.

PART III

I resigned myself to linger by the fireplace, spending the last hours of the Year 11799 in the company of the few Traversers remaining at The Castle – the youngest ones, for reasons unknown. They were engrossed in a strange video game which rendered them immobile for extended periods, with closed eyes and inert bodies. So I took the opportunity to tell them my story… again and again.

"Let me rewind it a bit for you, guys," I began. "The Hi-Hat's back door slammed open. I scrambled onto the stage in a foolish attempt to hide inside a magic cabinet. Then, I heard his footsteps…

"The assassin spun the cabinet violently on its casters. A barrage of thunderous gunshots pierced the blackness with crisscrossing beams of light. Bullets struck relentlessly on all sides. When the magic cabinet finally spun down, the man forcefully pulled open the door, reciting an incantation of his own…"

The Traversers opened their eyes, casting cold gazes in my direction, tired of the grand finale. Together, we recited the incantation aloud: 'Abracadabra, motherfucker!'

I clapped enthusiastically. Annoyed, the youngsters paused their game, stood, and left the Assembly Room – and the Castle, one by one.

I let out a lengthy, audible sigh and once more found myself entirely, utterly alone in the vast, ice-bound Castle. The only illumination came from the flickering fire, casting eerie shadows which danced along the walls. The howling wind carried scary and mysterious sounds from far wings and towers, echoing through the icy corridors. The last time I had stepped outside, the towering spires of The Castle were barely visible through the icy mist. I would not venture forth. I feared becoming lost and succumbing to exposure. I had learned my lesson.

*   *   *

McGready sat back in his Clinic office, contemplating the upcoming New Year's Eve party. His mind drifted to another similar event at another time – the failed one: announced as a secret and a challenge, with the invitation published *after* the event. And reprinted in Book Two of Professor Tovar's opus.

You are cordially invited to a Reception for
Time Travellers
Hosted by Professor Stephen Hawking
To be held in the past, at the University of
Cambridge
On the twenty-eighth of June, the Year 2009,
at the Noon Hour

But no one attended. Zero Traversers.

Nonetheless, McGready happened to be aware of something unknown to Professor Tovar. The great physicist's idea had inspired renowned architect Morgan Grimley to create a special space for Traverser private gatherings. Thus, the Rest Stop for Weary Travelers was born.

Now, the Director would send his own invitation to every guest staying at the Rest Stop during the last week of December 1799. And this time, plenty of time travelers were sure to show up!

TRAVERSERS!

YOU ARE BEING INVITED
TO A CELEBRATION OF THE WORLD-LINE OF

MRS. EVANGELINE WILHELMINA FONTANARROSA

HAVING CONTRIBUTED TO THE INVENTION OF
SPACETIME TRAVERSAL EX NIHILO AND
HAVING UNIQUE SKILLS OF SPACETIME PERCEPTION

WE ARE ASSEMBLING AT
THE REST STOP FOR WEARY TRAVELERS
AND PROCEEDING TO A SELECT ERA

McGready reviewed the VIP invitation. Satisfied, he sent it out.

Composing that text had demanded his utmost concentration. Now his thoughts struggled to set aside the dangerous rogue, Aidan Carynx.

He well knew how the Sin City guy had lost his hand. And he didn't trust him.

He needed to act before it was too late. The assassin would be sure to try to kill him again. Malcolm McGready could not count on a third chance to escape.

Fortunately, he had a plan – of the best kind. One that had already happened.

But first things first…

He checked the large clock on the wall, its face resembling a ship's wheel. It indicated that he still had time to fulfill the promise he had sworn to Alexander.

*   *   *

Time slipped away, my thick red hair a distant memory now, years blending into each other until I found myself older than Professor Tovar!

My designer sunglasses couldn't correct my... what was

this, myopia? I could still see the Moon, well in the distance... but not the eternally young face of my platonic sweetheart. I realized she wore glasses to read her notes, so perhaps she was farsighted too... Now I would never be able to finish reading Tovar's second tome of Traversal stories.

Young Eva has lost some of her allure, too. Nowadays, I just close my eyes and listen to her cadenced voice, as if her intelligent words formed the musical notes of a nostalgic song.

December drew to a close and the last day of 11799 stretched on. Had Lisbeth lied to me? Could I trust the words of an illusionist? Old demons lurked. I saw little purpose in continuing to live here alone. I remembered the gun, the Luger. Where had I put it?

Dark thoughts clouded my mind again. I trudged through the desolate halls, feeling empty.

Then Grimley materialized at my side, matching my languid pace. Traversers could no longer surprise me. We walked in silence for a while before he spoke.

"Vision is being key."

I nodded, contemplating the challenges of finding a good oculist in the future.

He swung an arm in a generous arc. "You are seeing The Castle here, being my creation. What else are you seeing?"

"What do you mean?"

"Is there being more potential for this timeless space?" He went on to suggest that my organizational skills and diligence might be better utilized at some other era of The Castle.

I could contribute according to my newfound interests. Establishing a psychiatric facility to address mental disorders of Traversers, while detaining the occasional Rogue. Creating entertainment venues for purposes of therapy. And so on. All within the grand confines of The Castle.

"Are you meaning I would also be warden of a prison? Would it be humane?"

"That is being your decision."

His offer left me feeling grateful and inspired. But did I dare believe him?

Someone would come to transport me, along with any artifacts I held to be meaningful.

"Soon," he added.

How I dreaded that word.

Before I could inquire further, Grimley ended our conversation and stated his intention to depart for Las Vegas. I cautioned him to be vigilant, aware of the troublemakers and perils one could find around the Strip.

I pushed aside negative thoughts, choosing instead to focus on my own psychological health. I resolved to spend my time reading about depression and mental illness – a final attempt to save myself. And maybe... prepare for a future life. And endure as long as possible.

*   *   *

"Mrs. Winnie! I know where and when is Royce!"

The noisy Ford Model T screeched to a halt near the cliff's edge. Director McGready hopped out, brimming with energy. "I've already informed Alexander and sent him on his way, with my full blessings. The hell with Arp. I'm an Eternalist! I have power and authority." His smile twisted into a smirk. "It is being time I be exercising them."

He waited for her response, squinting to make out her form in the moonlit grass. "I would be honored to serve as your chauffeur this evening, Madame Evangeline, if you'll permit me. It will be my pleasure to personally transport you back to La Casa Grande."

Malcolm McGready experienced another sudden wash of déjà vu. He had stood here before, on this very cliff, watching the Aurora Borealis... The songs of the drunk Traversers slapped him back to the present with renewed urgency.

"Mrs. Winnie? I trust you will find sufficient comfort in my modest motorcar?"

Should auld acquaintance be forgot,
And never brought to mind?
Should auld acquaintance be forgot,
And auld lang syne!

"Eva!"

*   *   *

The end was near, I knew it. A sense of doom overcame me. I looked down at my empty hands protruding from the arms of my parka, checking them, turning them over. The beginnings of wrinkles and spots, but they looked as capable as ever. I ran my fingers through my hair and found it to be less full. I rubbed my chin. Lately I had kept clean-shaven.

I squinted into an insipid setting sun, looking southwest. An unadorned beach downslope, bereft even of tufts of grass. The ocean, featureless gray and white.

Behind, gigantic cliffs of ruddy ice crept over the land behind The Castle.

Grimley appeared. To visit me one last time, probably to say goodbye. I looked into his eyes but found nothing there.

"It's been a long time, Morgan. I never had a chance to ask you. What did you think of Sin City?"

My words were shrouded in clouds of water vapor as I spoke. The temperature inside some parts of The Castle had dropped below minus fifty Fahrenheit.

The architect looked at me blankly.

Back to taciturn, I guess.

I pointed to the frozen ocean, extending to the horizon. "If I'm not mistaken, the sea ice doesn't melt here anymore."

Grimley said nothing. Not a problem. I really didn't want to know.

"Morgan, I acknowledge the gift of seeing the far future. Even more, I acknowledge the greater gift of expanded horizons, the glimpse of an astoundingly larger and wondrous world. But there is nothing more for me here."

Morgan Grimley looked at me impassively. "What is being your final wish, then, Malcolm McGready?"

I spoke my final words, loud and clear, without regret, without second thoughts: "I wish to go back. With the perspective I've gained, I sense the work in my own era is far from complete."

Grimley gestured to a... chair. More the outline of a chair.

I sat, gingerly. The seat took my weight. I looked around. There was The Castle, unchanged, softened with draperies of thick ice. Nearby, sad lonely stones, occasionally lining up with others, irregularly. The gardens, long gone. The air was beyond frigid.

"Your wish is being granted," he said, his words obscured by his own puffy clouds of breath. "But remember, it is always being December for you... Eternalist."

I heard no irony in his words.

I removed my parka. Underneath, I was already suited for the return trip.

The architect reached for his wrist.

*   *   *

Still shrouded in darkness, Malcolm heard the audience outside erupting in laughter and enthusiastic applause. Brightness returned.

He emerged from the magic cabinet wearing coat and tails. Teetering, he planted his feet and stood firmly at center stage.

An elegant, mature lady stood in the front row, hand over mouth. Director Malcolm McGready searched for something to say. Somehow, he remembered his line.

"Ladies and gentlemen, remain calm, and please accept our sincerest apologies."

PART IV

At the end of Tuesday, December 31st, 1799, just minutes before midnight struck, the partying Traversers sang, cried, and hugged their goodbyes in La Casa Grande. They prepared to depart the eighteenth century onboard their vintage Race Machines, journeying to diverse destinations in the near and distant future.

After somberly assisting and verifying their departures, Malcolm McGready knew he needed to confront his fears and embrace his fate – without gambling.

He hurried back to the Control Room, feeling a pressing need to watch over Aidan, especially as the Rest Stop for Weary Travelers began to empty. It was more than the typical end-of-year melancholy this time. Fear of death took him.

He ran through the labyrinthine corridors, clinging to a faint hope of escaping his fate, getting away from an elusive painful memory etched into nightmarish visions of a frozen beach.

Perhaps it was due to the rushing or his nervous distraction, but for the first time since becoming Director, he got lost in the passages of his own Castle. Where was the Control Room now? He had taken a wrong turn somewhere. He found himself at a dead end.

A large tapestry covered the wall in front of him, hiding something – what? A forgotten alcove! Another secret room! He pushed aside the heavy fabric and opened the vault-like door.

Entering the chamber, he felt a suffocating sense of confinement, as if the walls were closing in. He waved his flashlight around. The paintings came alive: colors danced, and shadows whispered tales. The veil of his memory lifted, revealing forgotten beauty.

The painting of mixed blooms! Something odd caught his attention amid the juxtaposition of summer-blooming poppies and lilies with winter roses, daffodils and tulips.

All set against the fiery foliage of deciduous trees in an autumn landscape.

He noticed a feature he didn't remember seeing before: against a cerulean sky, the gibbous Moon appeared to show signs of habitation, with lights twinkling within one of its craters. Adjusting his glasses, McGready could swear those elements were not there in the painting before!

At the bottom of the image, on a stone table beside the base of a large bronze vase, he noticed a familiar silver bracelet. The painter must have been a Traverser!

He turned off his flashlight to leave *L'Atelier*, and the stained-glass triptych panels revealed his beloved Control Room behind. He smiled. There, at arm's length, his safe sanctuary...

A shadow slowly entered the frame!

A figure in a black knitted cap broke into the Director's private space, moving stealthily like a burglar! Carrying a stainless steel, full-size Luger in his left hand!

As the figure turned, face contorted in a wild frenzy, Malcolm's heart skipped a beat. His worst fears were confirmed. He recognized the gun – and the intruder.

His assassin was absolutely relentless in pursuing his mission.

Malcolm McGready would never escape his fate. He took a deep breath and prepared to move to the adjacent room, determined to confront his nemesis, making one last attempt to reason.

*   *   *

The panel of The Armoire swung inward, violently.

McGready was beckoned, goaded inside at gunpoint, by his persistent killer-for-hire. The stocky man stood defiantly, scanning.

"So, this is your little escape room," Aidan Carynx remarked coolly, pointing his silver, red-stained handgun at the Director. "Well, you know how this works, Greedy Mack – I win. You will send me out of this primitive era, back to Las Vegas in my present time. Or you will still catch the hollow-point bullet that was meant for you."

McGready nodded solemnly. "Very well, Mr. Carynx. I accept defeat. My mistake, to divulge this place to you. I took a gamble, believing you had reformed, even more than your sister, but... alas, my trust was misplaced. Please, take a seat."

Aidan glanced at the two throne-like chairs adorned with brass fittings. He settled into one, his eyes darting to his mechanical hand.

The assassin realized he couldn't move.

Panic flickered in Aidan's eyes as his prosthetic hand lost grip on the weapon. The handgun landed at his feet with a loud thud, causing the pin to strike and fire a bullet that blasted a hole through the wall, into The Armoire.

The shot reverberated through the halls as all clocks chimed the midnight hour simultaneously, signaling the start of the New Year's fireworks celebration for the cheering Traversers in The Castle.

"You said I'd be treated humanely," the thug stammered.

"And so I did," agreed the Director. He calmly examined the hovering displays, studying them briefly before approaching the prominent brass column at the room's center. With practiced hands, he manipulated the controls, triggering a sequence that generated a blinding flash of light.

A second, younger Malcolm McGready rose from the other chair, his expression cold and unwavering.

"But *he* might not agree," said the older Malcolm McGready, stepping aside. "He thinks you should be placed in solitary confinement."

"Oh, yeah?" Aidan sneered. "For how long?"

"Your sentence should last into endless future times," the younger Malcolm replied, leaning forward.

Aidan hissed back to him. "You know I'll make you pay your debts in the end, Greedy Mack!"

Young Malcolm's expression softened as he pulled the rolled-up knitted cap down over Aidan's face. "Better protect your nose and ears from frostbite," he said, adjusting the snug fit of a ski mask.

He proceeded to the brass column and uttered the magic words.

"*Hasta mañana*, motherfucker!"

*　　　*　　　*

January 1st, 1800. Another New Year cycle begins.

Malcolm McGready – erstwhile manager of the Hi-Hat club; past, present, and future Director of The Castle, and A Rest Stop for Weary Travelers, and more – adjusts his prescription spectacles and examines his multi-purpose monitoring console at leisure, noting the approach of the special event's VIP guests.

He smiles, semi-consciously practicing his lines, knowing that soon, he would be turning on the charm.

He has reached the top of Maslow's Pyramid: Self-actualization.

He is an Eternalist who loves his job.

And his younger version is learning that job by remotely viewing the Control Room.

But soon, and there, the two must rewind their clock back to the past, to keep a date.

*　　　*　　　*

What a special tour of the present, indeed!

The portal dilated, and Mrs. Winnie emerged elegantly, with young Malcolm holding her left arm and older McGready holding her right. They were followed by other recipients of the special invitation. The VIP visitors nonchalantly avoided the giddy group of local tourists exploring Hearst Castle and followed instead their own designated docent for the occasion.

With an aura of mystique and ancient wisdom surrounding her, adorned in flowing, colorful garments – and an incongruous black and green armband, Cara Carynx spoke with the melodious cadence of a seasoned oracle.

"Greetings, seekers of knowledge and wonder," she proclaimed, her eyes tracing the pages of the brochure in her hands. "I am Madame Zelda, keeper of the Veil, consort of Traversers.

"Today, our threaded journey is dedicated to unraveling the enigma known as Julia Morgan, illustrious, whom I had the honor of meeting in a past existence. But fear not, we shall not merely scratch the surface; we shall embark on a clandestine quest into the hidden realms of Hearst Castle, where the echoes of Julia's brilliance always resonate!

"Allow me to regale you of that Northern and Central California trailblazer, the pioneer who shattered barriers with the force of her unparalleled talent! Julia Morgan wasn't just an architect; she was an enchantress who wove spells of architectural marvels through private estates, academic sanctuaries, sacred grounds, and this esteemed Castle. She dazzled with creativity long before society embraced such female grace and power!

"Julia's legacy isn't confined to mere structures. It is a tapestry of dreams woven into reality. Join me, mighty Traversers, on this extraordinary odyssey, where we'll witness her masterpieces firsthand, glimpse her hidden spaces, and experience her genius – witnessing secrets so profound, even her patron, Mr. Randolph Hearst, remained unaware! We are holding the keys to her personal vault, where each design element holds a story waiting to be told – and remembered.

"Follow me, brave souls, and let us unlock the mysteries of Julia Morgan's unprecedented realm, together!

"Repeat after me, lasses and lads: '*Perpetuis Futuris Temporibus Duraturam.*'"

*   *   *

Hours later, all tours converged in the Ballroom of Hearst Castle – at the event Madame Zelda insisted on calling, whimsically, 'The Conflux.' Local actors from nearby

Cambria listened to classical music of Johann Strauss, stylishly attired in period costumes.

The Guest of Honor and birthday girl, Mrs. Evangeline Wilhelmina Fontanarrosa, stepped out into the first dance, an interwoven three-part interpretation – accompanied by both Halliday brothers. With a radiant smile, she then gracefully segued to the 'Traverser Waltz,' with her twin McGready suitors, thereby fulfilling the Director's promise and privilege – twice over.

Afterword

There is No Conflux

Eva W. Fontana
Published posthumously

I am lying on my back, gazing at Polaris in the night sky, thinking about love and limerence, while an old song 'Possession' plays in my head. I am recording these words, thankful for my journey through life, most of which I hadn't seen coming. Which is ironic, given my unique abilities to *anticipate*.

I lay claim to being a scientist. I dedicated my body to science! I have the training and the mindset to seek after truth through careful experimentation and interpretation. But science does not give me final joy. Let me restate. Having done science gives me great satisfaction and feelings of reward, and I am happy to have made my humble contributions. But what gives me joy, truly, is *fast, extreme movement*. Not speed – there's a difference. Speed measures how quickly you reach a destination, while I speak of... the excitement and thrill of the experience itself.

I am genuinely fortunate. My adventures in movement allowed me to tap fully into my personal energy, and to lean into life exuberantly. My experiences include not just simply embarking on many instances of Spacetime Traversal, but... I have traversed and seen farther than – I humbly submit – well, anyone else in history.

I should point out that I am trained in *physics*. But I am at heart a hopeless, romantic *racer*, and I have been privileged to redefine the concept, reshape its boundaries, and show what can be achieved. I am also a doer, more than a thinker. I offer that self-observation as an important caveat in what I am about to say, which may stray into *philosophy*.

Spacetime Traversal creates the seeming potential for paradoxes, which swirl around scenarios when a Traverser encounters their own world-line. These paradoxes are resolved in a formulation of time travel I call the *Knowscape*. In this model, when a Traverser loops their world-line, the revisiting action may result in *new* events being layered over *known* events. As long as the new knowledge does not contradict what is already recorded in the collective memory-line. Here we note that *world-lines* and *memory-lines* are different constructs. A world-line may twist and loop arbitrarily, while a memory-line is a repository for strictly accumulating knowledge. In a universe without time travel, they are indeed the same. But that is less fun!

You might object, memories do not collect so cleanly. Memories can be inconsistent, and narrators may be unreliable. You would be correct. But memories are what remains of any of us.

One way to visualize the *Knowscape* is to invert the metaphor of mice eating a block of cheese. As Traversers proceed along their worldlines, they deposit traces of events, recorded in memory-lines, gradually *building up* the block of cheese. Each subsequent passage encounters more "debris" from previous passages, making return visits less fruitful, or more to the point, less *meaningful*. Thus the cumulative process of layering is one of *ossification*.

The fate of the universe may be bound to an end-state in which all possible outcomes *have occurred and been recorded*, leaving no untouched time or space which can manifest new outcomes – either physically or logically. After we collectively journey more than one million times – much more! – we become *stuck*. The proverbial last three miles only avail to arrive at The Conflux – the ineluctable end of our cosmos. When and where all movement, and all meaning, cease.

I simply refuse to accept such an outcome. A meaningless end-state for our universe. Cosmic semioticide.

There may be a clue in the Traversers' ostensible preference for our era. Although this may be an illusion – a matter of *our* perspective.

Why are they coming here? The end of the universe

need not be in the far future. Perhaps the end is in *our* era. And Traversers are coming here… to mourn, to rest, to understand, or to… fight back. To resolve the problem. We already know that Traversers are not one monolithic group. Professor Tovar's records identify many Waves, call them what you will: Technologists, Anthropologists, Psychologists, Enforcers, Geneticists… perhaps they are all coming to rewrite The Conflux.

I choose to believe that *we* – the collective we – are up to the challenge. Even if the *Knowscape* is a correct picture, it is, after all, only a model. And models do not account for everything. This one does not account for our having *imagination*. We are not only and simply about memory, reasoning and computing. We are capable of seeking truth – and sometimes finding it – through imagination. We are *storytellers*. If we get stuck, we invent around and through the obstacle.

I have shaped my own life through storytelling.

And to the extent that I seem to possess power over others, I lovingly shape their lives too. Being aware of limerence, if I sense a tryst may land at infatuation, I steer us a different course.

Even Tovar – and I say this with respect and affection – is more of a storyteller than a scientist.

Our strength is in both.

Along my exhilarating and fortunate path, I have learned that we all need to lean into the continuing adventure together – and now here I use the term unconventionally – revealing, shaping, and building *our future*.

Acknowledgements

Rogelio wishes to thank Jorge Quaroni, Eduardo Cisneros, Michael Roth, and Katie Barber – for unwavering friendship, visionary ideas, and for safeguarding the early blueprints of this project. Also, Mike Appel, Rudy Sugueti, Harry Scott, Miguel Delgadillo, and Pepe Casillas – your belief in us and your resources powered our first working prototype. And Chris Baker, Alejandro Burdisio, Elle Kelly, and Ariel Iglesias – your maps, landscapes, and songs defined horizons for this ship to explore. Keith Jefferies – your creation of the space-time logo gave 1M*t* its identity, a shining beacon for all traversers. Pat Scott, Fernando Sorrentino, and RC Matheson – your encouragement, wise counsel, and steadfast support ensured every gear turned smoothly. Carol Goodwin of NovaCon, Esther MacCallum-Stewart of WorldCon, and Samantha Davidson Green of JAM – you tested and refined our device through transformative events. And last, but certainly not least, Nina Allan – for gifting the magic spark that brought it all to life.

Richard wishes to thank his multi-talented family members for their ongoing support, making space and time for him as the late-arriving author: Joanne, who enlivens characters with a marvelous range of voices; Ryan and Brennan, who impressively balance the technical and the creative. Also, Caltech's creative writing club TechLit for valuable critique, from Rachael Kuintzle, Yinzi Xin, Rumi Khan, Tatyana Dobreva, Ashish Mahabal, Christine Chen, Hoppy Price, and others. And the Caltech Playreaders and campus theatre company TACIT led by Brian Brophy, for performing an early table read of our material. David Brin for weighing in on our world concept and sharing experience. Colleagues Vahe Peroomian, Jason Bernstein, and Jody Kuby-Thaw for advice, inputs, and insights. Super-fan Tori Carillo for undying enthusiasm. And many others.

Finally, together, we deeply wish to thank Adriana Ocampo, who recognized our common thematic interests and introduced us, birthing our collaboration.

Any lapse of detail or message is on us.

Thank you all, one million times over, for helping us build this time machine and launch it irrevocably into the future.

Elsewhen Press

delivering outstanding new talents in speculative fiction

Visit the Elsewhen Press website at elsewhen.press for the latest information on all of our titles, authors and events; to read our blog; find out where to buy our books and ebooks; or to place an order.

Sign up for the Elsewhen Press InFlight Newsletter at elsewhen.press/newsletter

You might also enjoy the following

TOMORROW WAS BEAUTIFUL ONCE

AMY ORRELL

Jack can only choose one future…

2150 – time travel has accelerated climate change and set humanity on the brink of destruction. As a Person of Mixed Era Origin with the ability to recall parallel versions of time, British historian, Jack Elliot, seems the perfect candidate to travel to the past and prevent the advent of time travel.

The catch? Success means Jack will cease to exist.

Critically injured when he arrives in the past, Jack's life is saved by Maddie, a second-generation immigrant and resistance fighter, who mistakenly believes he's connected to the disappearance of her sister, Suraya.

Jack's denial soon unravels with the discovery that Suraya can lead him to his father – the man who robbed him of his mother – and that they are all searching for the inventor of time technology.

What begins as a fragile alliance soon puts their feelings and their missions to the test. Jack's won't be the only life affected by his sacrifice, but does he have the right to decide who should live and who should die – and will it be worth it for the futures he and Maddie hope to create?

ISBN: 9781915304759 (epub, kindle) / 9781915304650 (396pp paperback)

Visit bit.ly/TomorrowWasBeautifulOnce

Overstrike

Fixpoint: Volume 1

C.M. Angus

When Matt Howard's grandfather told him he must alter history to protect his newborn son, Matt thought the old man was crazy…

…Then he realised it was true.

Overstrike spans 4 generations of a family haunted by the prospect of an approaching alternate reality where their child has been erased from history.

It touches on themes of retro-causality, ethics and free will, explores ideas of cause, effect and retribution and follows the path of Matt Howard, whose child, Ethan, is at risk, as he, his father and grandfather attempt to use their own abilities to manipulate reality in order to discover and prevent whoever is threatening Ethan.

Overstrike is the first volume of *Fixpoint*, a speculative fiction trilogy with a strong narrative spanning four generations of a family who discover their inherited ability to manipulate reality. It enables them to effect changes in order to safeguard themselves and all that they hold dear. But even seemingly small changes in a timeline can have unforeseen and far-reaching consequences. As we follow the stories of the Howards, the three books take us on a journey that goes around and comes around, exploring reality, time and our own sense of self.

ISBN: 9781911409700 (epub, kindle) / 9781911409601 (paperback)

Visit bit.ly/Overstrike

About the authors

R. James Doyle

R. James Doyle (aka Richard J. Doyle) held technical and managerial roles in Information and Data Science at NASA's Jet Propulsion Laboratory (JPL) over a career arc spanning forty years. He worked primarily at the exciting interface of space exploration and computer science, with a focus on autonomous space systems. He remains an active technical consultant.

Richard holds a Ph.D. in Computer Science specializing in Artificial Intelligence from the Massachusetts Institute of Technology (MIT). He was a member of a JPL team that consulted on the Babylon 5 sci-fi TV Series in the 1990s. He had the pleasure of visiting Sir Arthur C. Clarke in Sri Lanka, in the year 2001.

Richard wrote the story *Disentanglement* in the recently published speculative fiction anthology *INNER SPACE AND OUTER THOUGHTS* by Caltech and JPL authors.

Rogelio Fojo

After a successful career as an award-winning journalist and science writer from Uruguay, Rogelio Fojo transitioned to filmmaking. He studied in Los Angeles, gaining hands-on experience with various film crews. With a Kodak grant, he created his debut film, *Chimera*, which won the Best Film Award at the Pasadena Film Festival. Following Kodak's recommendation, Rogelio joined the IFP/West Project:Involve mentoring program and worked on the Hollywood movie *Buying The Cow*, starring Ryan Reynolds.

Rogelio followed *Chimera* with two more award-winning shorts, *Mary* and *The Movie Pitch*. In 2018, he directed the film *The Stooge*, written by acclaimed science fiction author Christopher Priest *(The Prestige)* and featuring Pat Scott and Robert Picardo *(Star Trek: Voyager)*.

David Gerrold

David Gerrold is the author of over 50 books, hundreds of articles and columns, and over a dozen television episodes. He is a classic

About the authors

sci-fi writer that will go down in history as having created some of the most popular and redefining scripts, books, and short stories in the genre. TV credits include episodes from Star Trek,Star Trek Animated, Babylon 5, Twilight Zone, Land Of The Lost, Tales From The Darkside, Logan's Run, and others.

Novels include many sci-fi classics. The autobiographical tale of his son's adoption, *The Martian Child*, won the Hugo and Nebula awards for Best Novelette of the Year and was the basis for the 2007 movie, Martian Child, starring John Cusack, Amanda Peet, and Joan Cusack.

Paul Kincaid

Paul Kincaid is an award-winning science fiction critic. He is the author of THE UNSTABLE REALITIES OF CHRISTOPHER PRIEST, along with other works on writers including Brian Aldiss, Iain M. Banks, Robert Holdstock, and Keith Roberts.

RC Matheson

R.C. Matheson is a #1 bestselling author/screenwriter/ producer praised by The New York Times as "a great horror writer". He has worked with Steven Spielberg, Tobe Hooper, Joe Dante, Aaron Spelling, Mel Brooks, Dean Koontz, Roger Corman, Stephen J. Cannell, Stephen King, and written/created/executive produced feature films, pilots, and drama and comedy series. He has also adapted novels for film and limited series by Roger Zelazny, H.G. Wells, Stephen King, Whitley Strieber, Dean Koontz and George R. R. Martin. Spielberg has praised Matheson for having the "greatest story and idea mind I've worked with in a decade". His short stories have appeared in over 125 major anthologies.

Christopher Priest

Christopher Priest (14 July 1943 – 2 February 2024) was a celebrated British novelist and science fiction writer known for his intricate and imaginative storytelling. His acclaimed works include *Fugue for a Darkening Island (1972), The Inverted World (1974), The Affirmation (1981), The Glamour (1984), The Prestige (1995),* and *The Separation (2002). The Prestige*, which explores the

About the authors

intense rivalry between two magicians, was adapted into a successful film by Christopher Nolan. Priest's talent extended to screenwriting, including his work on Rogelio Fojo's *The Stooge*. Influenced by H.G. Wells, Priest was vice-president of the international H.G. Wells Society. He received numerous accolades, including the BSFA award, the James Tait Black Memorial Prize, and the World Fantasy Award. He lived in various parts of the UK, most recently on the Isle of Bute, and was married to speculative fiction writer Nina Allan until his passing.

Teika Marija Smits

Teika Marija Smits is a UK-based freelance editor and the author of the short story collections *Umbilical* (NewCon Press) and *Waterlore* (Black Shuck Books), as well as the poetry pamphlet *Russian Doll* (Indigo Dreams Publishing). A fan of all things fae, she is delighted by the fact that Teika means fairy tale in Latvian.

Fernando Sorrentino

Fernando Sorrentino, born in Buenos Aires on November 8, 1942, is a renowned professor of Language and Literature. His stories seamlessly blend reality with fantasy, often leaving readers unable to distinguish between the two. Starting from everyday situations, his narratives gradually become bizarre and unsettling, all while maintaining a surprising sense of humor. Since 1969, he has published around ninety books, including short stories, novels, essays, interviews, and anthologies, with many translated into various European and Asian languages. Notable works include *El crimen de san Alberto*, *El forajido sentimental* (essays on Borges), and interviews compiled in *Siete conversaciones con Jorge Luis Borges* and *Siete conversaciones con Adolfo Bioy Casares*, published by Editorial Losada in Buenos Aires.

About the artists

Chris Baker "Fangorn"

Chris is a renowned conceptual and storyboard artist who has significantly influenced the film industry. Born in Birmingham, England, he gained recognition through his work on the *Redwall* book covers and caught the eye of Stanley Kubrick with his art for David Gemmell's Legend. This led to his involvement in designing concepts for Kubrick's *A.I.: Artificial Intelligence*, a project he continued with Steven Spielberg after Kubrick's passing.

Chris has since collaborated with filmmakers like Tim Burton and Sam Mendes, contributing to iconic films such as Road to Perdition, War of the Worlds, Charlie and the Chocolate Factory, Alice in Wonderland, Skyfall, Star Wars: The Force Awakens, Ready Player One and the TV sequel to The Man Who Fell to Earth. He is a member of the Royal Birmingham Society of Artists.

Alejandro Burdisio

Alejandro Miguel Burdisio, known artistically as Burda, was born in Córdoba, Argentina, on May 9, 1966. He is a self-taught artist, dedicated to drawing, painting, and illustration professionally since the age of 19. His academic background includes an incomplete stint at the Córdoba School of Architecture, which was pivotal in shaping his career as an illustrator and designer. With over 30 years of experience as an illustrator, he now runs his own graphic studio (which bears his name), working for both local and international clients.

He has long been dedicated to fantasy art, which currently allows him to participate in animation productions, short films, video games, and movies as a concept artist for various production companies worldwide. He travels, giving training lectures and presentations at universities throughout the country and Latin America. He is also known as a concept artist for the Netflix anthology series *Love, Death + Robots*.

Ryan Doyle

Ryan Farrar Doyle is a freelance artist. He graduated from the Rhode Island School of Design in 2017 with a B.F.A. in illustration. He favors black-and-white media utilizing pen and ink as well as scratchboards. Ryan works days as an instructor, coder, math and science consultant, and artist at a private STEM tutoring firm specializing in robotics-themed design and development team projects for kids ages 6-18. He plays bass guitar in a variety of genres and settings and is an accomplished Dungeon Master for the game *Dungeons & Dragons*.

Daniela Giraudin

Daniela Giraudin is a self-taught Uruguayan artist who has been passionate about drawing since the age of nine. Specializing in realism and hyperrealism, she works with graphite pencils, charcoal, and pen to create highly detailed portraits of people and animals.

Her artwork in *Paula's Exclusion Syndrome* showcases her exceptional precision and her ability to capture the essence and expression of each subject.

Emma Howitt

Emma Howitt is a UK-based artist known for her captivating illustrations in speculative fiction and fantasy. She has contributed to works such as The Forgotten and the Fantastical 3 (2017) and Witch Hunt (2022), with more recent projects like Nine Dioptres and Lanterns in 2023. Emma's distinctive ability to bring intricate details to life is showcased in her illustration of Teika Marija Smits' story "The Art of Time Travel".

Keith Jefferies

Keith Jefferies is an accomplished graphic designer and filmmaker who has shot several award-winning films, directed on BBC World, and founded a successful regional TV station for British cable company NTL.

As deputy arts editor at the *Watford Observer Group*, he designed arts and entertainment pages for this major newspaper group, earning a nomination for a UK Press Gazette design award. He also won the Marque Design competition at the prestigious Type 90 international typography conference, and his artwork is now part of the permanent collection at the Design Museum, London.

As a cinematographer, Keith has shot several multi-award-winning films, including *The Stooge*, written by Christopher Priest and directed by Rogelio Fojo. His TV credits include work for Paramount+ (*Picard*), NBC (*Timeless*), and HBO Max (*Made for Love*).

Elle Kelly

Elle Viane Kelly was born in Seattle, Washington and graduated from Bellevue College with a degree in Film Production. She is a Producer and Actress with professional experience in illustration and computer graphics.

Alex Storer

Alex Storer is an illustrator and graphic designer with a deep passion for science fiction, an influence which has shaped both his visual art and music. He is the creative force behind 'The Light Dreams', a conceptual instrumental music project blending electronic and ambient styles to create immersive, otherworldly soundscapes.

Alex's artistic journey began in his childhood, inspired by classic science fiction such as Doctor Who, Star Wars and Tron alongside the work of the SF art masters of the 1970s and 80s. Alex has developed a distinctive style that merges retro-futuristic aesthetics with modern techniques. His illustrations often feature vivid, dream-like depictions of futuristic landscapes and environments.

In addition to working with numerous authors and publishers, Alex's work is frequently exhibited within the UK science fiction convention scene and has previously appeared in Doctor Who Magazine, ImagineFX Magazine, Computer Arts, Writing and Illustrating the Graphic Novel (Mike Chinn) and How to Draw and Sell Comics (Alan McKenzie).